THE GOLDEN POMANDER

Hilda Petrie- Coutts

Chapter One

It was May 1660. The village street quiet, orderly, workmen carrying out their regular tasks and women modestly dressed in black or grey, hair drawn back beneath white caps, busy at their washing, baking and other household chores, whilst in the houses of the more affluent, maids turned rushes in dining halls, scrubbed, cleaned, polished silver, carried in heavy buckets of coal and went unsmiling about their labour. Although the Lord Protector, Oliver Cromwell was dead this two years and Richard, his feckless son who had followed him thankfully out of office, the country now ruled by the Rump Parliament, the Puritan atmosphere that had dominated England in all this time had not abated.

But there were rumours—exciting rumours, that the eldest surviving son of the late Monarch Charles 1st beheaded in 1649—and also Charles by name, currently living in France, was about to return to the country— England once more to be a Monarchy! None dared to discuss this amazing possibility, for the authorities and clerics still ruled the land with a rod of iron. But people longed for a return to their ancient freedoms, for jollity, celebrations of Christmas and New Year—even the simple pleasure of watching the village maidens dancing about the maypole, flowers in their unbound hair, a smile on their lips for any likely lad who took their fancy.

At the end of the main street in Langley Morton, where it was bordered by Cuckmere Copse, next to the old Longstaff Inn, stood a well proportioned, red brick house, behind high neatly clipped yew hedges. Within the neat parlour sat a young girl, head bent over the sampler she was painstakingly stitching.

'Look at me when I speak to you, girl!' The man who so addressed her in hard, angry tones, stood in front of the fireplace, legs astride, one hand on hip, the other on his walking cane, narrow, ice blue stare beneath shaggy grey brows fixed imperiously on this daughter, who was so daring to defy him.

The girl raised her head.

'Father?' her tones were soft, musical, the expression in her deep blue eyes, serene even thoughtful.

'I require an answer from you girl—also an apology for your outrageous behaviour! Will you now consent to be wife to my esteemed friend and esteemed Elder, Jack Masters?'

'No, Father—I will not wed a man, who despite her ill health fathered a score of children upon his unfortunate late wife, at least a half of them dying shortly after birth. This is my answer and the reason for it!'

She stared at him analytically, this aggressive man who was her father and for whom she had never experienced any of the deeper feelings supposedly expected of a child. To her he was an alien being, who from her youngest childhood for what reason she could not fathom, had treated her with coldness laced with an underlying contempt.

'What was that you said, girl?' His face darkened with anger, as scandalised at her reply he strode across the room and caught her by the arm, fingers biting cruelly into her flesh. The sampler dropped to the floor, as he wrenched her up to her feet and raised his cane. He slashed it down across her shoulders in what was an oft repeated scene of violence which today jarred her into open rebellion. The fine wool gown gave little protection to the violence of his blows, the pain making her lose all control as suddenly she seized his upraised arm and caught at the cane, snatching it from his grasp. With unexpected strength she broke it across her knee and threw the pieces on the floor.

'You will never raise your hand to me again—do you hear me?' She jerked out the words through shaking lips, but her blue eyes stared at him imperiously, with a hardness of expression such as he had never seen before. For a full minute they stared wordlessly at each other. Then with a roar, he leapt on her, his fingers about her neck, his apoplectic face contorted with rage. She tried to scream, to struggle but his hands were on her windpipe. Almost automatically she brought up her knee and thrust it into his groin. With a cry of anguish he loosed his hold, clutching at himself as he retched at the unexpected pain.

It was then that he turned his head away from the girl and saw the woman who was holding onto the doorpost, eyes wide with shock.

'Husband—what is happening here?' Martha started forward, not to comfort her husband but to place protective arm about the girl, who trembling in aftershock, stood looking contemptuously at her assailant. Her eyes dropped to the broken cane almost disbelievingly. She had done it—fought back after all the long years of his abuse—but what now?

'I am going to get the constable and have this little bitch arrested for common assault,' he managed to splutter, as he straightened up. 'I will have her put in the stocks—whipped! Stand away from her wife! You girl—go to your room until I return! Thank the good Lord you are no seed

4

of mine, but a strumpet's droppings!' The door banged heavily, as Rachel turned bewildered eyes on her mother.

'What did he mean—his words?'

'Not now child, let us go to your room. Make haste! We must pack a few of your belongings. You dare not stay here longer, he is capable of anything. Come quickly—quickly now!' And Martha pulled at the girl's arm. Rachel needed no further prompting, but followed the woman she knew as her mother up the solid oak stairway into the meagrely furnished bedroom, that had been hers since her babyhood. She watched as Martha Haversham lifted a leather travelling bag down from a shelf in the wardrobe and commenced to throw the girl's few gowns into it.

'Quickly child—your blouses, personal bits—scarves, hairbrush and comb.....!' Now Rachel sprang into action, hastily snatching at all she could cram into the bag. She snapped its fastenings and straightened, staring at her mother from questioning eyes.

'Now tell me—what did father mean by those horrible words of his—that I am no child of his?' Could it be true, she wondered as she waited with baited breath for the older woman's reply.

'You are not his daughter, Rachel. Nor alas, are you mine! Would that you were, for I love you dearly, always have! You are my late sister Lucy's child, born out of wedlock. Your father, Lord James Hawksley, a friend of the late King, fled the country to France after one of the many bloody battles between the Charles Stuart and Cromwell's army!' She put her hand on Rachel's arm.

'But—why have you never told me of this before?'

'There is more! Your true name is Sophie Louise—and should have been Hawksley. Your mother so named you after Hawksley's French mother. My name before marriage was Wheatley, my father Dr John Wheatley, a respected physician, retired and living in the village of Stokely. Go to him now.'

'But—he—may hurt you if he finds me gone!' She would not again name him father, this bully who had made her life and his wife's such a misery, 'Come with me, Mama?'

'Child, I dare not. I will try to pretend not to have been aware of your departure. After that awful scene, he will probably believe me!' Martha spoke firmly. 'One thing more—something you must take with you.' Standing on her toes, she lifted her hand to a loose panel in the back of the wardrobe and withdrew a large envelope with a wax seal also a black velvet purse. She pressed these into the girl's hands, the expression in her hazel eyes urgent.

'But what is....'

'No time to talk now. Here is your cloak—put these items in your pocket. Do not open them until you are safe in your grandfather's house—now go, my darling child. Let me make sure he has not returned yet,' and she crept to the top of the stairs, then beckoned to Rachel, who was her niece and not her daughter, whom she must now call by her rightful name of Sophie Louise Wheatley—perhaps Hawksley if her true father could ever be made to acknowledge her.

The door creaked as Martha opened it and pushed the girl away with trembling hands. 'Your grandfather's house is called The Willows! He is well known and any will point the house out to you. You have a five mile walk—take the country path through the Copse and then over the style, not the road, for your father may send men out looking for you.' She caught Sophie in her arms and kissed her.

'But how can I leave you, Mama?'

'You have no option. May God be with you, my darling girl—hurry— please hurry...!' And Martha stood watching for a brief minute as she saw Sophie's brown cloak fluttering in the light spring breeze. Then she quietly closed the back door and went through to the parlour. First she picked up the broken ends of the cane and threw them into the fire, then bent and picked up the sampler the girl had dropped, folded it and placed it behind a cushion. She dropped into a chair and started to weep, partly in reaction, but also to give credence to the story that she had not been aware of Sophie's departure, having collapsed in shock at the scene she had witnessed.

She heard him arrive back, as the front door slammed and seconds later he thrust into the parlour and glared at her. To her relief she saw he was not accompanied by an officer of the peace, but his face still carried that dangerously high colour, preceding another angry scene.

'Where is she, woman?'

'You told Rachel to go to her room,' she faltered. 'I suppose she is waiting up there. Roger, will you not sit down? Shall I fetch you a glass of ginger wine?' She rose to her feet.

He stared at her. 'A drink, yes—not your noxious ginger wine—brandy!' He almost snatched the glass from her hand, noisily gulping the fiery liquid. 'Would you believe it—the sergeant refused to come and arrest her! Said it was up to a father to discipline his daughter! Not to put such duty at the expense of the Commonwealth!' and he snorted his disgust. 'When I have finished with her, she will never dare offer disobedience to me again!'

'Oh but Roger—she is only a young girl still, and surely expecting of our love and protection!' She had to delay the moment when he discovered that Rachel—Sophie, had fled. 'Please be calm, husband!'

'Calm—be calm after what she dared to do to me? Are you crazed, wife?' He started towards the hallway and she heard his feet upon the stairs, then his blows upon the girl's bedroom door.

'Rachel—Come out here!' There was a pause during which he violently pushed the bedroom door open. He saw the wardrobe open—empty, the dressing table bare of Rachel's toilet articles and stared in stupefaction. She—had gone? Gone—but where? His heavy feet thundered down the stairs as he confronted his terrified wife.

'She has gone—and you knew it all along, didn't you?' But Martha merely lifted a wondering face.

'Gone—our daughter has gone?'

'Don't play the innocent with me, Martha. You must have seen her go, helped her I've no doubt!' She stared back at him steadily, despite the pounding of her heart in her breast.

'Are you sure she is not hiding somewhere? She certainly did not pass through here that I can swear!' And it was true she thought, as she remembered gleefully how Sophie had left by the back door. Perhaps her satisfaction showed in her eyes, for he lashed out at her, felling her with a heavy blow to the head. She collapsed on the floor, just as Bessie the cook returned from market, her basket laden, and her knock remaining unanswered, opened the parlour door to see her mistress fall fainting on the floor, the master with his bunched fist standing above her.

'Did the mistress fall over then sir? Here—let me help her up. I will take her to her room and bring her a glass of cordial!' Bessie was a big woman, full of breasts and massive of belly and hips and arms like those of a boxer. She placed these arms on her hips now, as she surveyed Roger Haversham challengingly.

'Yes! Take her to her room and tend to her, Bessie. And I must tell you, that our daughter has left home, will never be returning to this house—one less mouth to feed!' and he subsided into his favourite chair, chagrined to have been seen showing violence to his wife in front of a witness. So uncomfortable did he feel over this, that he negated his first instinct to have Rachel found and brought back to the house in disgrace, to receive a severe beating. She had gone? So much the better—her name never to be mentioned in his presence again! He reached for the brandy bottle.

Sophie had left the fresh green leafiness of Cuckmere copse, with its fans of pale primroses and budding bluebells far behind and was taking the path bordering the fields that she knew would lead her to Stokely, the village where an unknown grandfather lived. As she walked she sang from sheer happiness and relief at having left her childhood home far behind. Never again would Roger Haversham raise his cane to beat her—but her voice faltered as she thought with a sinking heart of how her mother—who was really her aunt, would now fare at his hands.

'Somehow I will make a new home, a good future and perhaps bring Mama to live with me,' she whispered and thus resolved began to sing again.

The winding path through fields and woodland was longer than the five miles Martha had suggested to her and her feet were weary and the sun sinking low in the heavens, as Stokely's church spire came into view. The bag she was carrying although not heavy, had made her arm ache and the pain of the welts Roger's cane had raised on her shoulders, now throbbing badly.

She saw a young lad bending low over a ditch beneath the hedge bordering the lane she now took. He was clearing the debris of last autumn's dead leaves. He looked up as she called to him

'Boy—can you direct me to the house of Dr Wheatley—it's called The Willows!' She smiled at him and he nodded, rubbing his muddy hands on his breeches.

'Of course I know it! I'll take you there if you are so minded, lady!'

'Why, that is very kind of you. I will give you a penny for your time.' He put out his hand, not for the coin, but to take the bag from her.

'I'll carry that for you,' he said firmly. 'My name is Richard. My father owns this farm. The old doctor was always very good to my family!' And with that he started to stride out in front of her. Without the weight of the bag, Sophie found her own feet treading lightly. Ten minutes later they reached the outskirts of the village. Sophie noticed a large imposing house on a low hill to the west, and a cluster of small cottages around the church which stood on one side of the village square, which was bordered on its north side by the village green. A few more substantial houses were set further back amongst shady trees. Perhaps fifty or more dwellings she guessed.

It was to one of those larger houses that the boy led her. The Willows was set slightly back from the winding lane that led into the heart of the village, a sturdy stone built house with thatched roof and its leaded diamond window panes reflecting the scarlet brilliance of the sinking sun. The gate creaked as the boy pushed it open and proceeded up the pathway, with a backwards glance to ensure the lovely young woman with chestnut hair and those amazing blue eyes, was following him.

He rang the bell and stepped back shyly, as Sophie joined him on the door step. The door was opened by an elderly woman, white apron covering the front of her grey gown. She fixed an inquiring glance at Sophie, whilst apportioning a nod to the boy at the girl's side.

'Good Evening to you, mistress—if you have come to see the doctor, then I have to tell you that he is retired, does not see patients these days.' She turned to the boy. 'You should have told the lady so, Richard!'

'I have come to see Dr Wheatley on a personal matter—not medical one,' replied Sophie with a smile, 'Would you kindly inform the doctor that Sophie is here to speak with him—Sophie Wheatley!' The woman looked at her uncertainly. She had been housekeeper here for the last fourteen years, had never heard of a family member of this name. But even as she stared into the girl's eyes, she realised that she seemed almost familiar, that the direct stare reminded her of the doctor's own penetrating glance and....

'I am Beth Giles, his housekeeper. Well—you'd better come in then I suppose,' she said slowly. She opened the door further and Richard darted forward and placed the bag inside. He flashed a smile at Sophie. He bowed jerkily and made to go, but Sophie placed a hand on his arm.

'Wait Richard—your penny!'

'No Mistress—it was a pleasure to help you,' he said and walked off as she stared after him in surprise, then followed the housekeeper into the hallway.

'What is going on out there, Beth,' called a deep voice. Sophie's eyes searched the dim passageway as a door opened, and a tall, silver haired, white bearded man wearing a suit of dark green breeches and long doublet appeared and stood staring towards her curiously.

'We have a visitor, Beth?'

'That we have sir. The young mistress says her name is Sophie Wheatley!' replied Mrs Giles. 'She wishes to speak with you on a private matter,' she added. She looked in surprise as the doctor uttered a sudden gasp, reached out a hand to the doorframe to steady himself, then quickly recovering his composure gestured that his housekeeper should return to the kitchen, and regretfully she retreated, casting a curious backwards glance at their visitor.

'You are Sophie? I take it you mean—my grandchild?' He straightened and came slowly along the passageway until he was within a foot of the girl. 'Let me see your face!'

He placed his hands on her shoulders, noting the way in which she flinched at his touch, as one questioning hand lifted her chin and looked into eyes as deep a blue as his own. And he knew—knew without a shadow of a doubt that this girl was the tiny girl child born to his beloved daughter Lucy who had died a few weeks after giving birth to her babe.

In appearance the girl was a complete replica of Lucy, same eyes, finely arched brows and dimpled chin—and yet he realised there was a subtle difference. Lucy had been all gentleness, this girl who stood before him,

9

held her head with a slight hauteur, in similar fashion he remembered to that of Lord Hawksley, at their one and only meeting.

'I take it that my daughter Martha has sent you to me?' He questioned gently, as taking her arm, he led her to a comfortable study, lined with books, anatomy charts on the walls and where his leather topped desk bore many illustrated papers, a fire burning in the grate. He took her cloak from her shoulders and gestured towards one of the two fireside chairs. She sank down, face betraying tiredness, as she realised that she felt safe for the first time since she had made her hurried journey away from the home where she had endured so much heartache.

'Are you truly my grandfather,' she asked urgently?

'So it would seem, child.' He saw her take a deep quivering breath of relief. 'I will explain all to you, Sophie, but first tell me—something happened to you today, my child,' he asked quietly?

'I was beaten by the man I had always understood to be my father— beaten as I have been on innumerable occasions on any slightest pretext. Today I refused to marry a man of his choice—and I fought back. I brought my knee up—well where I knew it would hurt!' She thought her words would shock him, but instead she saw his eyes crinkle in amusement.

'Serve the damn fellow right! Someone should have done it long ago. I have heard rumours that he treats my daughter Martha with scant respect, but you at least I imagined would receive consideration at his hands! When Martha told me she wished to marry him—eighteen years back, I could have refused permission and regretted that I did not do so ever since! He had inherited the Longstaff Inn on his father's death, and made much of the fact that my daughter would lack for nothing! She seemed so much in love with this man whom I considered nothing but a good looking scoundrel!'

She bent forward in her chair and reached out a sympathetic hand to him and he took it between both of his, feeling the fine bones, the underlying strength in it. 'Mama has led a miserable life I fear,' she said quietly. 'He drinks too much—is rough with her! He pretends to be a good living member of his church, but I have heard tales of other women—and smuggled brandy, brought by pony to the inn in the hours of night.'

'I can't say I'm surprised! Martha should leave him, come here and live with me! Surely she knows my door is always open to her. But I've not received a word in all these long years, not since a few months after your true mother Lucy gave birth to you and sadly died a mere four weeks later. As a busy physician, a widower, it would have been hard to care for a young child.' He paused and shook his head, his eyes under his shaggy grey brows sad.

'Go on, grandfather!'

'Martha begged to bring you up as her own which had been Lucy's dying wish. Haversham reluctantly agreed, but demanded a settlement for his pains. I gave him a goodly sum, to be spent on your upbringing and education. It was thought best that you should be known as the daughter of their marriage.' He shrugged. 'I imagined I was acting for the best. Who better to care for her dear sister's child than Martha?' He gave a deep sigh. Sophie's face betrayed sympathy for him, but a need to discover the true circumstances of her birth made her pursue the matter relentlessly.

'Grandfather—I know my mother's name was Lucy. I have also learned that my father is a Lord Hawksley—that they were not wed when she gave birth to me. Is this true?'

He responded to her directness with an inclination of his head and rose to his feet. 'Child, I will give you a detailed account of these events later. Now Sophie—I was about to eat. Perhaps you would like to join me, for I think I hear Mrs Giles calling!' And certainly at that moment there was a knock at the study door.

'Ah Beth—would you please set two plates. From now on, my granddaughter Sophie is to be a member of my household. You will prepare a room for her, the back bedroom overlooking the garden, take her bag and cloak up there please.' That room most suitable he reflected, as it had been her mother's many years ago. As he held a chair for Sophie to sit at table in the pleasant oak panelled dining room he felt slightly troubled. He wanted time to consider how best to lay events of seventeen years ago before the young girl, but also knew that nothing but complete honesty would serve.

The juicy spring lamb and fresh vegetables tasted good and Sophie set to with a quick appetite. He watched her eat with a smile as he poured her a glass of wine. The housekeeper returned with a steamed fruit pudding. It was delicious. Sophie sighed in satisfaction as she ate the last spoonful.

'Mrs Giles is a good cook, grandfather,' she exclaimed as she lifted the linen napkin to her lips.

'She looks after me very well, has done so for over ten years now. She is dependable and discreet, the last of importance when patients came to my consulting room. Now I am retired she continues to give me excellent service.' He smiled and rose to his feet. 'Sophie, I will do what I should have done earlier, show you your room. Follow me, my dear—Mrs Giles will have prepared it by now.' He walked slowly, carefully up the steep creaking stairs of the old house and Sophie realised that his knees pained him. One of the bedroom doors on the red carpeted landing stood ajar.

She followed him in and exclaimed in delight at the room, where faded rose coloured velvet curtains had been closed against the night and a bed with an embroidered spread, covers pulled back invited and an oil lamp gave soft glow to two crystal vases on the mantle-piece and an enamelled clock, above which hung a portrait of a young girl in her late teens.

'Why—it could be me,' she exclaimed in wonder.

'Yes, truly—and this is why I recognised you as soon as I saw you. You are so like your dear mother, my beloved Lucy whose memory still lingers in this room.' He paused and pointed to a marble topped table in a recess, bearing a large jug and basin. 'Mrs Giles will bring up warm water for you to bathe. For now, I bid you goodnight child.'

'But you were to tell me of my mother—my birth?' She looked at him anxiously. She could not sleep without knowing the truth.

'Tomorrow morning I will tell you all, after you have slept. I have placed a jar of salve on the small table there, by your bed. Apply it to the hurts that bully Haversham caused you. Sleep well and God bless you, my child,' He raised her hand to his lips and kissed it gently. He closed the door after him.

Sophie sank down on the bed. Her cape had been brought up and placed across the bed, a bulge in one of its large inside pockets reminding her of the packet and purse thrust upon her by Mama—she would always think of her so, not as aunt. She pulled both out of the pocket and with a deep breath, broke the seal on the envelope—opened it.

It contained a letter and a document, both slightly yellowed with time. The letter was addressed to her as Sophie Louise—Hawksley! But surely if she had been born of wedlock, the name was not hers to use? She unfolded the letter, written in a fine, slightly wobbly flowing hand.
'My Dearest Sophie,

I write this to be given to you when you reach years of discretion. What I have to tell you is of importance. I know that my death is near and I will not have the joy of watching you grow from tiny babe to the fine young woman I am sure you will be.

You will be told by others that I was not wed to your father at the time of your birth. But you are no bastard my child, but the daughter of my true marriage to Lord James Hawksley. He is a Catholic, the ceremony secretly performed by a priest just over a year ago. The document with this letter is proof of what I say.

The feeling against Catholics in England at this time is very strong. I have kept knowledge of my marriage to Lord Hawksley from my father and my sister in case of any problems it might cause them with the harsh servants of the Commonwealth.

Your father was part of the King's army when it suffered a heavy defeat in a bloody battle. James was wounded but managed eventually to escape to France with many other royalists. His mother after whom you are named came to this country in the train of Queen Henrietta Maria but later returned to Paris.

Your father left the country before knowing of my pregnancy—is not aware that he has a dear little daughter. Perhaps I shall recover from the fever that is burning me up—but I fear I came too late to my father's house for his physic to bring healing. If you receive this letter it will be because I am no longer on this earth to watch over you. But my love is with you always. God bless you my child

Lucy Hawksley.

Lucy read that letter over several times, tears flowing unchecked down her cheeks. A knock at the door made her raise her head.

'I've brought your hot water, Mistress Sophie,' and the housekeeper poured water into the china bowl from a large copper ewer. 'Is there anything else that you need?' Her curious brown eyes sped from the letter Sophie held on her lap, to the painting above the fireplace.

'My mother,' said the girl quietly glancing at the painting in turn. 'No—there is nothing else, but thank you, Mrs Giles.'

'Call me Beth, my dear. The doctor does most times,' said the woman with a smile. 'I bid you goodnight then.' Sophie stared after her. She liked the big boned, fresh faced, middle aged housekeeper. Her eyes returned to the precious letter once more—and then to the folded document. She opened and smoothed it. It was a document of marriage between Lord James Hawksley and Lucy Wheatley witnessed by a John Digby and Michael Dereham, the name of the officiating priest, a Father Benedict. She placed the papers safely back in the envelope where they had been for the last almost sixteen years and sat thinking. What did the future hold? Then almost absently, her fingers touched the velvet purse. She unsnapped its ornate clasp and exclaimed in surprise.

A heap of gold coins fell into her lap—and a ring. The ruby glowed in the lamplight with a rich lustre in its intricate gold setting. Sophie slid it onto a finger and looked down on it wonderingly. Her mother must have worn this—a gift possibly of her father. There was also a fine gold chain with a heart shaped locket. Sophie prised it open with her finger nail. Two miniatures stared up at her. One she recognised at once as her mother Lucy—the other must be her unknown father, James Hawksley. She moved closer to the lamp and peered curiously at the handsome, slightly haughty face surrounded by long, dark waving hair, eyes almost black. There was a slight smile about the lips. 'Father,' she murmured, and again her eyes were damp with tears.

At last she rose to her feet, and started to remove from her hastily packed leather bag those few possessions she had carried from the violent home she would never see again. She opened the wardrobe and paused as she

13

saw it already contained some garments—and as she touched the skirts and blouses hanging there, realised wonderingly that these must have been her mother Lucy's, left hanging here by the father who grieved her.

She hung her own few clothes beside them, then undressed, stripped off her shift and washed herself with the warm water, now rapidly cooling that Beth had brought. As she dried herself, she glanced into a mirror above the dressing chest, and brushed her long chestnut hair and drawing it back from her forehead, making a thick plait. The action of brushing brought pain to the angry welts across her shoulders. She thought of the salve her grandfather had left for her. As she smoothed it into her throbbing flesh, she found the pain abating.

Before getting into bed, she fell to her knees, head on clasped hands and whispered a prayer of gratitude to God who had so graciously rescued her from the cruelty of Roger Haversham. She prayed also for Martha, that she should not receive violence at her bullying husband's hands. Then with a last prayer for the grandfather who had received her with such kindness she clambered into bed and fell asleep almost at once.

She was awakened by birdsong as a blackbird trilled a greeting to the dawn, song joined by a sudden chorus, inviting Sophie to slip out of bed, run to the window, pull the curtains aside and stare out. Below her stretched a garden bright with beds of spring flowers, bordered by a hawthorn hedge densely white with clustered blossom, while close to the house, she noticed a small pond fed by a tiny stream overhung by willows, where a bench and table were set. A small orchard stretched beyond, whilst to the extreme right she could just glimpse a stable.

A knock at the door announced Beth Giles, who bid her a cheery good morning and poured fresh water into the tall, china jug, emptying the bowl used for last night's ablutions into a bucket.

'Breakfast will be ready in half an hour, Mistress Sophie. Did you sleep well,' she inquired?

'Very well, I thank you, Beth! I was just looking out at the garden—it's beautiful!'

'So it is, mistress. The doctor has much joy in his garden.' With an inclination of her head beneath its starched white cap, the woman retired.

Sophie washed, towelled herself dry, taking care with her bruises, but they seemed considerably less painful this morning, then slipped into a fresh shift and pulled on her best, fine wool, grey skirt, and full sleeved white blouse, topped with a deep white collar, a grey shawl about her shoulders. She let her hair fall in shining brown waves to her waist, delighting in being able to wear it so and not under a restrictive cap such as both she and Martha had been required to wear by Roger Haversham,

'Sophie my dear—what a delight you are to an old man's eyes,' greeted Dr Wheatley approvingly, peering at her over his long, thin nose, as he held a chair aside for her to be seated. 'You bloom like a wild rose this morning!' She certainly looked much better than the tired, bewildered girl who had crossed his threshold last night. Her blue eyes were still faintly shadowed though, a legacy no doubt of the unkindness which had surrounded her until now. Those dark shadows like the bruises he knew marred her shoulders, would soon fade in an atmosphere of love and security.

They ate a simple breakfast of newly baked bread and eggs and drank a beverage unknown to Sophie—coffee. Then the doctor rose from the table.

'Sophie—how would you like to take a turn about the garden, where we may walk and talk in peace,' he suggested and led her along the passageway to the back door. She drew the shawl closer about her, for although the May sunshine was bright, it still lacked summer's warmth. He talked quietly, putting her at her ease, knowing that the one overriding question in her mind was the mystery of her birth. She tried to concentrate as he pointed with his walking cane at various herbs, used he explained in healing potions and salves. But when they approached the wooden seat by the gardens small pond, she sank down on it and looked up at him pleadingly.

'Grandfather—we must talk. Last night, when I retired to my room, it was to open a sealed package Mama—Martha that is, had hurriedly pressed on me, as I prepared to escape from Roger Haversham's violence. From reading the contents, I now already know somewhat of the circumstances surrounding my birth—that I am not a bastard, but the true daughter of my parents' marriage!'

'What is that you say, child?' He sank down beside her and glanced at her in astonishment. Without further explanation, she withdrew the envelope from the pocket of her skirt and pushed it into his hands. 'You want me to read the contents of this, Sophie?'

'Yes.' She watched his face, as his eyes betrayed his emotion at beginning to read his late daughter's words. His expression changed to bewilderment as he perused the letter and then opened the document attesting to the wedding that had taken place seventeen years ago. A wedding of which he had been totally unaware and his face expressed hurt and shock, followed by a growing delight.

'Why ever did Lucy not sufficiently trust me to take me into her confidence regarding her marriage? Did she really think it would have caused me any great concern that she had wed a Catholic?' He snorted in disbelief. 'To me, a beings relationship with our God, the way in which it seems right to worship, is a very personal and private matter. In my humble opinion, no one branch of the Christian church holds all the answers to man's quest for the sublime truth. Each of us embarks on our own personal journey!' He jerked out the words with heartfelt emotion as he reached for her hands.

'I feel exactly the same way, grandfather! The Bible says that God created man in His own image—but I suspect that man is trying to fit God into the harsh, unyielding image he has created in his own imagination. Where I wonder is the God of love?' She found herself speaking of matters that had never passed her lips before, but had much exercised her mind. And the old man stared at her in astonishment, that a girl should harbour such thoughts.

'You read then—have studied the Bible, Sophie?'

'I have.'

'So you have had some schooling? Haversham provided you with a teacher,' he said in satisfaction. A derisive smile touched her lips.

'No grandfather! It was my mother, who taught me all I know! Roger Haversham would never have spent good money on teaching a girl!'

'I saw to it that both of my daughters were well versed in the classics, fluent in Latin and Greek, spoke some French,' he said slowly. 'Are you telling me that Martha personally gave you such an education?' She nodded and he smiled his content. 'Well, well my dear, this is excellent news. But let us return to the details of your birth. So we now know that Lord Hawksley married your mother! That she did not reveal this vital fact fearing that a Catholic ceremony might bring opprobrium on Martha and on me.' He shook his head in bewilderment. 'As if I would have cared what others said! I am no Papist myself but follow the teachings of the Episcopal Church, which is also despised by the Puritan majority who have held power in this land for the last eleven years.'

'Surely a man's conscience should be his own,' she breathed.

'As you say! But when politics intrude into man's basic inalienable right to follow his heart in matters of faith, then nothing but disaster comes upon a people!'

'Producing bigotry,' she said feelingly, thinking of the unctuous church elder she couldn't bear, whom Roger Haversham had tried to force her to marry.

The doctor smiled. 'We talk of deep matters, my child. Thank you for showing me your letter and the other document. Keep both safe, you may need them in the future, the more especially because it is widely rumoured that the young King Charles, the eldest son of our late martyred King, is to return to England, our land once more to become a monarchy! You had not heard this, Sophie?'

'Why—no!' she exclaimed in surprise. 'Mama and I heard little of what was happening in the country. It suited Haversham to keep us close—no visitors!' her eyes were bright with excitement.

'Well I assure you that from what I have heard, it is most like to happen before the month is out! Charles Stuart will be on his father's throne and I have no doubt his friend Lord James Hawksley will attend him! Your future is about to change out of all recognition, young Sophie Hawksley!'

Chapter Two

Two weeks had passed, a time of growing happiness for Sophie, as she came to love and respect the elderly grandfather with whom she had become very close. For his part, Dr John Wheatley was delighted to discover she had a quick mind and was showing an unusual interest in medical matters such being unusual in a woman. He started to explain the anatomy of the human body, demonstrating its structure from a wired skeleton kept discreetly concealed behind a small curtained alcove in his study—his housekeeper disliking the doctor's unpleasant trophy. Sophie showed no such unease.

'Doctor's have always held that the human body is served by four humours—fluids that is,' he explained with an amused smile. 'They are of course, blood, phlegm and then yellow bile and black bile!'

'The way you said that suggests you do not agree with this opinion, Grandfather?' Sophie looked at him curiously as she leaned forward, staring down at the book that lay open on his desk, pushing a lock of hair back from blue eyes intent in concentration.

'I believe that for many centuries men have studied those laws of medicine passed down from the Greeks, without really pondering on whether these ancient treatises are indeed accurate. I fully expect that by the end of this present century, physicians will have a more accurate, complete understanding of the many functions of the human body, the most complex creation of the Almighty!' He smiled. 'Enough of these matters, Sophie child...' he paused as they heard a heavy knock at the front door. Minutes later, Beth Giles voice could be heard speaking firmly to the visitor.

'We'd better see what is happening,' said John Wheatley rising to his feet. He walked down the passageway and stared in surprise to see his housekeeper confronting a large, determined looking woman, who had obviously arrived in the horse and cart stationed on the road outside his garden gate, a young lad holding the reins.

'I will see if Dr Wheatley will speak with you, mistress,' said Beth then turned as she heard the doctor's step behind her. He stared curiously at the large, unknown female, who showing a somewhat belligerent attitude, was attempting to push past his housekeeper.

'You are Dr Wheatley? Father of Martha Haversham,' she demanded?

'Indeed I am—and who are you may I inquire?'

'Bessie Pawson, her cook and housekeeper! You need to do something to help the poor mistress sir, or he will surely kill her!'

'Who will? You had better come in,' he exclaimed, wondering if perhaps she was slightly deranged. But as he looked into her honest brown eyes was reassured. He ushered her into the parlour and indicated that she should seat herself.

'Now then—er Mistress Pawson—what is all this about?'

'Haversham will kill your daughter sir, if she is not brought safe out of that house! He almost did for her three weeks ago, when their young daughter escaped after a beating! I carried the mistress up to her room that day, a huge bruise on her head. She kept to her bed for days afterwards.' She had his full attention now as he heard this account in horror.

'How is Martha now, Mrs Pawson? Was a doctor called?'

'No!'

'Why not?

'I wanted to call one—but he wouldn't have it. Ashamed that any should see how he treats his women folk I suppose. Said if I troubled him more on the matter, he would dismiss me! Not that that would have worried me too much, but I am very fond of the Mistress! I dare not stay talking too long. I had my son Jacob drive me over here when that devil Haversham went out this morning and must return before he arrives back. Will you do something to help, sir?'

'Yes. You have my word that I will. Go quickly now...!' he paused as Sophie appeared at the doorway, for she had recognised Bessie's strident voice.

'Bessie!'

'Oh, Miss Rachel! Is it really you then and looking so fine?'

'My real name is Sophie now!'

'Is it my dear? Well, at least you are safe then, the Lord be praised!' She gave a relieved smile. 'Now I must get back to your mother. It's urgent, the doctor will explain.' She bustled out before Sophie could question her and settled her large frame next to her son's in the cart, as he flicked the horse lightly with his whip and the couple disappeared.

'I can hardly credit what I have just heard!' The doctor's eyes were hard with anger, as he faced Sophie who was white faced with shock.

'It's my fault,' she whispered. 'I should never have left Mama, when she bade me, for then he might not have treated her so. But what Bessie said is true. He has always been free with his fists and his cane!'

19

'If I had but known,' he ground out. 'She wrote me years back that it would be better if we enjoyed no further contact. Fool that I was to accept it!' His face was grim. 'Time now to remove my poor child from that brute's clutches.' He called for Mrs Giles who had been hovering near the door, concerned that her master was so upset.

'Beth—Have Jack Dawlish prepare my carriage. I am going in to Langley Morton. Prepare another bedroom for my daughter Martha. Have all in readiness.'

'Yes, doctor.' She hurried round to the back of the house and crossed the small courtyard separating it from the stables. 'Dawlish—the Doctor is wishful for you to drive him into Langley Morton. He is in great haste, so hurry—hurry!'

As John Wheatley allowed his stableman Dawlish to assist him up the steep step into his small functional carriage with its faded paintwork, he found Sophie attempting to clamber in after him.

'No child—you remain at home—safer so!'

'No grandfather. I'm coming with you,' she exclaimed and staring into her determined face, reluctantly allowed her to seat herself next to him. Then they were off along the narrow, unmade country lane, as the horse trotted at a good speed, between hedges bright with May blossom and elderflowers, snorting in pleasure, glad of this sudden activity in its now quiet life, as the carriage swayed over stones, ruts and potholes.

They overtook the cart containing Bessie Pawson and the woman gave a smile of relief as the carriage swept past. Now Martha Haversham should have some relief at last, poor woman.

Sophie's heart started to pound uncomfortably as they proceeded up the main street of Langley Norton and then the house she had hoped never to see again came into view behind its yew hedges.

'I must say this street—whole area seems strangely empty—apart from that group of children shouting and dancing in that disorderly manner,' exclaimed John Wheatley as his driver pulled back on the reins and the carriage rolled to a halt. Certainly there was none of the usual activity seen in a village high street. He helped Sophie down. 'Now you stay at my side, but run back to Dawlish if I so instruct you.' She nodded, also looking around curiously as she wondered why the place seemed somewhat deserted today. She turned as an elderly woman came along, bending over her stick, back crippled with arthritis.

'Where is everyone,' asked Sophie, recognising old Mary Honeyset.

'Bless you—why, haven't you heard, mistress? They say the new King has landed at Dover—on his way to Canterbury now, Rochester and so on to London. The whole village has gone off to get a sight of him as he passes by—where our road meets the main London road!' And with a smile she walked slowly on.

'So that is why Haversham left the house this morning,' cried Wheatley. 'Come along child.' She followed him up the pathway to the house. He rang the bell and also thumped on the door. It was some minutes before a pasty faced girl of about fourteen opened to them and stood staring doubtfully at the doctor.

'I am Dr Wheatley and I have come to attend your mistress, girl,' he informed her.

'But the master said I wasn't to let anyone in while he was away and I dare not disobey him. You should come back later sir—when Mr Haversham has returned home.' For answer, he pushed her impatiently aside and it was then that the girl saw Sophie for the first time.

'Oh—you are back, Mistress. Mrs Haversham will be that glad to see you—or would if she could tell you so!' she burst out.

'Is Mama in her bedroom, Nan?' asked Sophie.

'She has been there since that awful day when you left!' But by now no one seemed to be listening to her words, for the doctor and Sophie now pushed in past her and made for the stairs. Sophie flung the bedroom door open. She uttered a cry of dismay, as she saw Martha lying back against her pillows, hair dishevelled about her white, strained face—bruises starkly dark against her throat.

'Mama---Oh, Mama, what has he done to you?'

'Rachel—is that really you child?' The words came weakly, forced between cut, swollen lips. 'I feared it was my husband returning.' She attempted to sit up and saw her father for the first time. She gasped.

'Father—tell me I am not dreaming.' Her puffy, contused face flooded with a joy it was painful to see.

'Do you think you can walk down the stairs if we hold you one on each side, my dearest?' he asked gently raising her in his arms. 'Sophie—hurry, she needs her cloak about her—shoes!' Then somehow and with great difficulty, they assisted the badly hurt woman down the stairs, where the frightened maid, Nan stood watching.

'You can't take the mistress, sir! Mr Haversham will kill me, if he finds her gone!' she blurted this out, eyes wide in with fear.

'Tell him that her father has removed her from his brutality—and that he will pay dearly for his treatment of her! Do not fear for yourself—Mrs Pawson will be here soon and will protect you from him!' With that he managed with Sophie's help, to get Martha into the carriage, called a quick word to Dawlish who flicked his whip and the carriage left that house of bitter memories and the deserted street far behind.

Martha was near swooning as they helped her into the security of Dr Wheatley's house, where Beth Giles had the bedroom prepared in readiness.

'Allow me sir,' she said, quickly recognising Martha's inability to mount the stairs and Dr Wheatley's arthritic knees making it difficult for him to take his daughter's weight. 'If Mistress Sophie will help, we will soon have this poor lady comfortably in bed!' and with a sigh of relief, the doctor allowed them to lift the daughter he had not seen for so many years up to the haven of the room she had occupied during her girlhood.

An hour later, John Wheatley sank into the fireside chair in his study and reached for a diluted infusion of foxglove. The shock of discovering his daughter in such condition—having now examined her and found her obviously the recipient of many beatings, with the complication of two broken ribs, this shock then had caused him a painful spasm in his chest. One such as he had been experiencing over the last six months. The spasm passed, but the doctor knew what these pains about the heart portended. Now above all times he needed to be resolute, to help both his daughter and grand-daughter.

He lowered his head on his breast and murmured a few words of prayer.

'Almighty Father—In the name of the Blessed Jesus, my Lord and Saviour, I pray for strength to protect those dear ones whom I love. Keep them I beg, safe from all harm!' He lifted his head, his eyes serene and smiled as Sophie came quietly into the study.

'She is still asleep, Grandfather!'

'The potion I gave her will allow her to sleep for many hours—and the sleep will bring healing,' he said quietly. 'Sit beside me Sophie, for there is much we must speak of.' She smiled and sat down on the chair opposite him, hands folded serenely on her lap.

'Yes, grandfather?'

'Sophie, tomorrow I am going to ask my lawyer to draw up my will. It is something I should have attended to long ago. Now that you have come into my life I intend to rectify this.' He noted the instant anxiety on her face and held up a restraining hand. 'It is just a formality, child,' he said.

'Are you ill, Grandfather? I have noticed the way in which you sometimes raise a hand to your side. I know you say it is merely a twinge of indigestion. Is it more than this?' Her blue eyes met his and he knew he could not lie to her.

'I have a condition of the heart that gives me small warnings that I must take life at an easier pace. It was for this reason that almost a year ago, I decided to retire from my work as a physician.' He leaned forward and put a hand under her chin, seeing the worry in her eyes, the strain about her mouth.

'Grandfather, I couldn't bear it if anything happened to you!' she whispered. The very idea that the grandfather she had come to love so dearly in the short time they had known each other, might soon die, was a thought too dreadful to contemplate. She lifted her hands to the one that touched her face, withdrew it and held it close in hers in mute appeal.

'Nay child, death comes to each one of us sooner or later. Hopefully I may have several good years yet to spend with you my dear. There is much I still have to teach you about medicine, for who knows, it may stand you in good stead in the future.' His tones were firm and she nodded, knowing that he needed her to be calm.

'I will attend to all you teach me most diligently sir. I confess that at times I wish I were a man rather than a girl, that I might become a physician in my turn. Why is it that women, are treated as of less account than men in such matters?' She burst out with those last words which had troubled her since her childhood. Why indeed had the man she had been taught was her father, that bully Haversham, treated her with such coldness and contempt—also treating his wife with discourtesy and of recent years with unbridled cruelty?

'Do not wish to be other than you are, my dear—a beautiful young woman of a quick intelligence. Yet just as I believe that the intricate workings of the human body may one day be made clear to us—as will the right of every human being to worship Almighty God in their own way be established—so also do I believe that in the long years ahead, man may give woman the respect that is her due, women take their place of equal status beside men.' He rose to his feet. 'But I fear all this lies many years ahead—perhaps even centuries. But it will come—it will come!'

There was a cautious knock at the door and the housekeeper stood there, her face bright with excitement.

'Is it true, sir? That the King arrived in England to take up his father's throne? Twas Dawlish told me so—such wonderful news!' She stared at the doctor waiting for corroboration of this most amazing event. He smiled at her excitement.

'Yes, Beth—it is indeed wonderful news! If I had not been so concerned for my poor daughter's health, I would have suggested long before this, that we all lift a glass in celebration. Call Dawlish here—and that boy who helps in the garden, young Richard Appleby!' Minutes later, John Wheatley reverently poured five glasses of that prized brandy kept for special, rare occasions such as this.

'A health to our new King Charles 2nd, by the Grace of God—may he long rule over us, his reign be blessed by peace and prosperity!' he said solemnly. 'I pray it be a new beginning for these islands, where men may cease to speak hatred against each other and all conflict cease.'

'What will happen now, Grandfather,' asked Sophie, as the staff left the study. 'Will the new King take revenge against those who executed his father?'

'Who can say,' he replied musingly. 'What happened under Cromwell and the Commonwealth was shocking in my opinion. Perhaps the late King was not wise in all his ways, but I truly believe that he was a good man, often badly advised. To have sent him to the block like a common criminal was an atrocity. But I could never speak out like this to any in the past. To have done so would have been to court arrest and death.'

'How the prince his son must have suffered after he had sought refuge in France, when he learned what they had done to his father,' replied Sophie feelingly. 'But his mother was kept safe was she not?'

'That is so. Queen Henrietta Maria made her escape across the water in good time, some years before her husband's execution, but from what I have heard received only poor succour from her French relatives.' He smiled at Sophie. 'I imagine that your true father, Lord Hawksley will have accompanied the new king back to England, in his train. Many other Royalists who made their home in France and the Netherlands will no doubt be returning to these shores. We live in an exciting time, young Sophie—an exciting time indeed!'

They continued to talk together for another two hours, as he began to tell Sophie of his own family history. She learned that he was the younger of his father's two sons. Sir George Wheatley had lived and died a quiet country gentleman, his elder son Morris inheriting the small estate on his father's death, while the younger, more studious John Wheatley struck out on his own in his chosen profession of physician. He was about to explain to Sophie how he had come to settle in the pretty village of Stokely, when he was rudely interrupted.

'Listen to that shouting, sir and there's guns being let off!' cried Beth Giles, rushing into the room without knocking. The doctor turned his head listening.'

'Come then—let us step outside. See for ourselves what is happening!' He strode down the passage leaning on his stick and opening the heavy front door stood watching in amazement, as he beckoned Sophie to his side.

It was evident reports of the King having landed at Dover had spread across the village, for there seemed to be huge excitement, a huge bonfire lit on the village green, with youths and maidens dancing about it, their Puritan elders looking on, some with disapproval, others plainly bewildered, whilst others yet were throwing their caps into the air with joy.

John Wheatley drew Sophie's hand under his arm, as he opened the garden gate and started along the street towards the square. Now the church bells were ringing, chaotic peals deafening the ear. They walked slowly along, crossed the square, bordered on one side by the village green, until they were on the fringes of the crowd of excited villagers.

'We want no king back in this land,' Sophie heard one disgruntled, black robed church elder muttering. 'How do we know that he is no papist—having lived for years amongst them?'

'Think of all those honest Englishmen who died in battle, to bring down this man's corrupt father,' spluttered another at his side.

'Quiet there—you croaking ravens—you dismal seers of doom!' cried a tall, broad shouldered man with red hair. 'This is a day of joy for our country! Now men may start to live again, enjoy life, nor fear a night time knocking at the door, as neighbour informs some small venal sin against neighbour and grudges are cunningly settled in this way—men thrown into prison for a careless word!'

'You mind your words, Thomas Appleby!' ground out the pinch faced elder, but his face evinced his uneasiness. 'This village always was and has remained whole heartedly for the Commonwealth and Protector Cromwell! We want no king—no corruption of morals!'

'Are you telling me that you can honestly say that our country has been a happier place for the last decade and more? When men raise their hands against their rightful king, only evil follows!' Another man, the village blacksmith took up cause of the new king as contention raged amongst the villagers—but now more and more seemed to be crying out the new monarch's name in evident approval.

It was at this point, that a party of riders descended on the crowd, horses snorting as they were pulled sharply to a halt. Their leader was a self important, sour faced man wearing a black, velvet lined riding cloak, strong leather boots spurred, a sword at his side.

'Who is that, Grandfather,' asked Sophie? 'I don't like the look of him!' They were near enough for her to see the dark, narrow eyes holding harsh expression, thin compressed lips with bitter down turned lines, square aggressive chin and short cropped black hair greying at the temples.

'His name is Sir Mark Harrison—he lives in that fine mansion on top of the hill. He was a friend of Cromwell—the house once owned by your own father—Lord Hawksley!'

'What! But how did he come to be in possession of my father's home,' cried Sophie, eyes smouldering as she glanced across at Harrison, who was in turn staring contemptuously at the noisy crowd as now he restrained his nervous stallion.

'You there—yes, you man!' shouted Harrison, having to raise his voice in order to be heard and pointing at the blacksmith. 'What in the name of all that's holy is all this commotion about? Where is the constable? He should be keeping these people in order!' His eyes swept over the excited mass of people, moving on until he noticed the doctor with Sophie at his side. And he stared at the girl from eyes suddenly fearful. Harrison had once loved the doctor's daughter, Lucy—had offered marriage, but faced unexpected and painful rejection. Soon afterwards, the lovely young woman had disappeared with Lord Hawksley. News of her death on return to her father's house—that a child had been born, had caused him little grief, for his love had withered and turned to hatred of both Lucy and Hawksley.

Now this young girl, who was the image of her late mother—for it must be Lucy's child, the resemblance too close to be accidental, shook him badly. He had thought the child had died at birth! But even as he stared at Sophie, his mind returned to more pressing matters.

'What's that you say, smith? Charles Stuart has returned to this land—proclaimed King? Not just a rumour then?'

The blacksmith turned a scornful face up at Harrison. 'Yes! Our land to be ruled by its rightful king, son of a Royal father murdered by you and your damnable mob! How long do you think you will be allowed to remain in your fine house now? Not long I expect!' He spat on the ground and turned his back on Harrison, as the sparks of the roaring bonfire rose and glittered against the evening sky. 'Hurrah! Hurrah for good King Charles. Long may he reign over us!'

'Amen,' murmured Dr Wheatley. 'Come child, let us return home, for I must see how my poor daughter fares!' They left the villagers behind, as they began their return to the house. Sophie turned once and saw Harrison staring after them, his face a malevolent mask. Then with a curt word to his attendants, he turned his horse and beckoned them after him as he returned to Hawksley Manor and an uncertain future.

In the days ahead, Martha Haversham made slow and painful progress towards good health, her face now lit by an inner joy that she was at last free of the cruelties of her bullying husband. Eventually her broken ribs began to heal. Dr Wheatley listened in horror as he heard of how she came to sustain the injury—sharp ends of those broken ribs could have pierced her lungs.

'I don't want to speak of it—but if you insist, will tell you all, Father,' she said in a low voice. She was trembling as she began.

'I was in bed, following my husband's savage treatment of me when he discovered Sophie had escaped. I remained there, was experiencing severe headaches.' She paused, finding it difficult to relate what had followed.

'Go on, Martha—you must,' he said gently, taking her hand in his.

'For two weeks he avoided me—I heard he stayed at the inn, was drinking heavily. I continued upstairs. Then one dreadful day—he burst into the bedroom, pulled me from the bed by my hair! He tried to force me to divulge Sophie's whereabouts. I refused to speak. In a fury of exasperation, he had set his hands about my throat and came near to throttling me. He dropped me at his feet—crossed to the side of the room and stood staring down at me lying helpless on the floor—then with a roar—I'll never forget it—arms spread wide, he rushed at me and kicked my body with all his might!'

John Wheatley bit back a curse. 'Go on if you can daughter.'

'I heard my ribs break—but thought it was my back. I lay there for many hours completely helpless, until Bessie courageously mounted the stairs, found me groaning in pain. She managed to get me back into bed. I asked for her help.'

'I will see that Bessie Pawson is rewarded! There is no doubt that she saved your life, when she came to me. As for Haversham, he deserves to hang for his vile treatment of you!' cried her father, stroking her hair soothingly. 'Have no further fear my dearest, you are safe now!'

The practice was to bind the chest of a patient with such injury—but the doctor had long believed this could cause adhesions, Martha was allowed to heal in nature's way. Sophie had been present when Martha who had always cared for her so tenderly, despite fear of her husband and whom she would always call her Mama, revealed those happenings after Sophie had escaped from Haversham.

'I will be revenged on the brute,' she said to her grandfather, blue eyes hot with anger. 'Why is it men are allowed to beat the women and children of their household? '

He shook his head. 'It is looked on as an ancient law—not in statute, but men do ever quote it when their violence to those whom they should love and protect is brought into question. Sadly no judge will apportion blame to such a husband—unless he takes the woman's life.'

Sophie stared at him in outrage. 'But it is wrong—barbarous!'

'I agree, Sophie. In all our day together, I never lifted my hand to my dear wife. Yet many of my patients told me they suffered such distress in their marriage. Men even quote a certain rumoured judgement, that a man may beat his wife providing the stick be not thicker than his thumb!'

'The laws of our country need changing,' stated Sophie wrathfully!

'Have patience, my child! Such change will come—although perhaps not in our lifetime.' He smiled. 'Now come into the garden with me. There are certain healing herbs I wish you to recognise readily.'

It was the last day of May and news was brought to the village of the ecstatic welcome London had accorded its new King on the 29th. Now the villagers began to speak out boldly for King Charles, even those who opposed the reintroduction of a monarchy, biting back their adverse comments and beginning to feel a growing unease that Charles might punish those who had stood against that first Charles, his royal father! How would he deal with those parliamentarians who had signed the late king's death warrant? And how also would those fare who had earlier taken up arms against their king?

One of those suffering a certain fear and frustration at the turn of events was the man who had been given the sequestered house and lands of Lord Hawksley! Those fears were to be justified.

In his spacious Whitehall apartments, their refurbishment ongoing in the months ahead, the King had his head bent over the intricate workings of the tiny, exquisitely enamelled French clock, a gift from his beloved sister, Henrietta Anne, married to Philippe d'Orleans, brother of Charles fellow Monarch, Louis X1V of France.

'It's typical of Minette's kindness to send this! She knows my fondness for clocks!' He turned his dark, saturnine face towards the small group of courtiers who surrounded him, some of them faithful royalists who had followed him into exile, giving up all for his sake. Others though, part of the regime that had ruled the country since his father's execution. He stared at them now, his heavy lidded, dark sparkling eyes giving no indication of his real thoughts.

'Sire, there are many matters of state which require your immediate attention,' said a portly figure robed in gold slashed black velvet gown, his shrewd gaze bent respectfully on the king, whose guardian he had once been.

'Then they can wait until the morrow,' replied Charles with a courteous smile. 'We have other pressing matters to attend to!' He whispered to a young page boy, who bowed and silently withdrew. 'Gentlemen, we wish to retire—are somewhat weary. I will send for you again in the morning!' The small group of men, who would form his council, with the supreme responsibility together with parliament in helping the new monarch to rule the country, exchanged glances and made to withdraw.

'No—wait! Hawksley, you remain for now!' He addressed this remark to a man who bore a slight resemblance to him, of similar height and in that his eyes were black as also was his long, waving hair. But there the likeness stopped, for whereas the King wore an almost inscrutable expression, softened at times by a smile that charmed and delighted the observer, the other presented a handsome visage that betrayed his emotions without pretence.

'Majesty,' he inquired?

'James—now we are alone, as in the past I have somewhat to discuss with you in private. As you know, I am constrained by those documents of state I have had perforce to sign, as part of the agreement made for my return as monarch. Properties belonging to the Crown and to the Church and forfeited during the commonwealth, are to be reclaimed! It is a more difficult matter with houses and estates sequestered from private individuals, the countless loyalists who lost all in my service. It is thought that many difficulties may arise in the country, if these properties are directly returned to their rightful owners!' He spoke quietly, his eyes scrutinising the features of the man who stood listening so intently, slight disillusionment causing him to lower his head.

'Sire—are you telling me that I am not to receive my estate back? It is a heavy blow, I admit. But my service and loyalty remain always true to my king and friend.' Hawksley forced a smile. 'After all—the most important part of this is that you are safely back on the throne of your fathers.' He met Charles gaze levelly and saw a smile soften the lips of the thirty year old king, the lines on whose face evidenced the suffering endured since his earliest youth.

'Well said, James. In fact, I was about to say, that in your case and a few others, I am going to override the wishes of my advisors!'

'Sire—do you mean...?' whispered Lord Hawksley

'It is true that I have to abide by the Declaration of Breda—but your house and lands shall be restored by the House of Lords. It will take a few weeks. But it will be done!' He held out his be-ringed hand as James Hawksley fell to one knee and held that hand to his lips. 'Would that I could so reward all those who gave up so much for my cause,' he added.

'Accept my heartfelt gratitude, Sire!' said Hawksley softly rising to his feet.

'You are not married, James?'

'I was once—a secret marriage, to a fair and beautiful bride. When I escaped to France like so many others after Worcester, word eventually reached me that Lucy was dead.' He shook his head. 'There has been no other woman in my life since—apart from those—well!'

'Which reminds me—the beautiful Barbara awaits me!' said Charles his eyes darkening as he thought of the voluptuous Barbara Villiers, daughter of the Duke of Buckingham and married to Roger Palmer. 'Take my advice James. Find yourself another wife, one who will give you children—and keep your Catholic faith a private matter.' This very personal interview was at an end and Hawksley bowed as he took his leave. But his heart was pounding with joy and relief, that his estates were to be restored. To wait a few weeks would be nothing after the long years of exile, experiencing penury, humiliation, often like his Royal master, having little to eat. But his heart bled, for those hundreds of friends who had fought alongside him, suffered like exile and according to the King's word were to receive little or no compensation, in order not to provoke unrest in the country, where so much property had changed hands. But he also knew that Charles would try to help as best he could, by offering paid positions at court.

Chapter Three

John Wheatley leaned on his grand-daughter's arm as they walked together through nearby Epilson woods. Early June had carpeted the forest floor with bluebells and anemones, whilst wild roses starred the undergrowth and the wind gently stirred the whispering, verdant green loveliness about them. They paused to watch as a squirrel leapt and looped its way along the branches above their heads. Then Sophie sighed from sheer delight as they stopped by a tiny brook gurgling its way between low banks guarded by fronds of young bracken—for even as they stood there quietly side by side, a tiny fawn appeared between the trees, stared at them and took fright, disappearing in a flash.

'This is a magical place, Grandfather!'

'Indeed it is. I used to wander here often in the past, to seek those herbs and even mosses, berries and bark, whose use in physic is so vital.' He paused as they heard the noise of angry shouting and a woman's screams! It jarred their senses and made Sophie hold her grandfather's arm in sudden alarm.

'What can be happening over there?'

'I can guess,' he replied grimly. 'Old Jessie Thorne lives in the small cottage you can just about glimpse in the clearing over there. She is a poor, elderly woman, to whom people turn for help in certain medical problems best referred to a physician. Some call such a person a wise woman—others with evil intent call poor Jessie a witch!'

'Whatever she is, she obviously needs help, Grandfather!' Sophie ran forward as the woman's screams became ever more piercing.

'Wait, child. We'll attend to this together. Those annoying Jessie would show scant respect for a young woman on her own!' He set forward as fast as his arthritic limbs would permit, Sophie at his side. Within minutes they reached the clearing where a small thatched cottage stood, door wide open, its owner in the hands of two ruffianly looking fellows, who were leering at her, as a third man was preparing to throw a lighted torch into the dwelling. Jessie had a cut at the side of her mouth, her cap hung about her neck by its ribbons, grey hair hanging loose and dishevelled on her shoulders, the top of her gown torn.

'Quiet there, you foul, wicked besom! It's the fire for you—and your house. That's how we deal with witches!' cried the man with the flaming torch, staring malevolently at Jessie, as he whirled it above his head.

'Stop! Release that woman at once or I will have you haled before the magistrates! I know your names—and your condition. One word from me and you will all end up in prison—or sent as slaves to America!' John Wheatley spoke crisply and with authority. The men swung about and stared at him uneasily and at the young woman at his side. The man with the torch lowered it.

'And who might you be, sir? We are here on the instructions of the owner of these woods, Sir Mark Harrison himself!'

'Indeed? Well, Harrison is mistaken if he believes these woods are part of his land. This is common land as inspection of the plans in the Sheriff's office will clearly show. Even apart from this irregularity, this elderly dame is deserving of courtesy and respect to enjoy her home in peace!

'She be a witch! A witch!' cried one of the men who still held Jessie in a cruel grip. 'The law has a way with dealing with such!'

'And also with those who make false accusation—Edward Jackson. Yes, I know you—and you Catesby—and you too Warren! I will vouch for the honesty and good character of Mistress Thorne. Now loose her at once and be on your way. As for Sir Mark Harrison, now the King is returned to his country, perhaps the manor and lands may not remain your master's for much longer!'

'I recognise you now—Dr Wheatley, retired physician who lives at The Willows,' ground out Jackson and swung round to his companions. 'Let's leave the old bitch alone and return to Harrison for further orders. After all, we don't want any complications, eh lads?' Minutes later they were gone, the noise of their feet crashing through the undergrowth, voices raised angrily, swearing loudly at being denied their sport, fast fading away.

With Sophie's help, John Wheatley raised the old woman to her feet, for she had collapsed, near fainting, when those holding her had thrown her contemptuously to the ground.

'I regret the distress those ruffians have caused you, Mistress,' he said gently. 'Let me help you back into your cottage, my arm about you—so.'

'Bless your kind heart, doctor,' she replied shakily, 'and you also, young mistress. Without your help, they would have had me hanged or thrown in the river. Once a person has been accused of witchcraft, there is no redress in law. Suppose those men come back? What can I do?' Her face was still taut with fear.

He led her into the cottage where Sophie pulled a chair forward for her to seat herself. 'Calm yourself, Jessie, all will be well now,' and he smiled at her encouragingly, as he pulled a small phial from his pocket, one he regularly carried with him to combat the symptoms of his heart condition. A drop of this on your tongue now—time to trust my medication!' A few minutes later, the colour returned to her face and with it her usual indomitable spirit.

'I recognise it—foxglove, doctor?' she smiled up at him, as one hand stole to restore modesty to the torn bodice of her poor gown. 'Strange indeed is it not, that the leaves of the second year of this most poisonous of plants can bring healing to the heart when used in the right proportions.'

'I have learned much from you of herbs such as I had not previously thought to use. Of this we will discuss further on another occasion, when you are feeling more yourself again.' He reached out and took her wrist in his hand, feeling the pulse. He shook his head. 'You must take life easily now, Jessie!'

'Do you think that cruel bastard at the manor will allow me to do so? I fear his minions will return!' The fear was back again in her dark eyes, but she thrust her chin forward, turning her gaze now on the young girl, who was studying her so earnestly. 'What is your name then, young mistress?'

'Sophie Hawksley,' replied the girl.

'You be Lucy's daughter—the doctors grandchild then? Your face should have told me this, for you resemble your mother greatly. Give me your hand child,' she demanded reaching across for it

Sophie stooped and extended it with a slight reluctance, for she sensed a strange power in the elderly woman who was regarding her with those piercing black eyes.

'I am not sure it is right to attempt to look into the future,' she said uneasily. 'The present has enough difficulties of its own.' Her blue eyes were apprehensive, as she glanced at her grandfather for support.

'That's as maybe, young mistress! Yet here in your hand I see a life filled with rare opportunities—danger too from allowing your heart to rule your head. Beware a man with a scarred forehead and a viper's tongue.' She loosed the girl's hand and shook her head. 'You have suffered much already through fault not of your own. Take care you do not bring further hurt upon yourself.'

'What do you mean, Jessie,' she asked curiously? But Jessie merely shook her head and refused to elucidate, but lifted her eyes to Dr Wheatley. 'You said the King is returned. Does that mean that the manor will be returned to its rightful owner, this girl's father?'

'I sincerely hope so. It is said the King signed a certain document at Breda, which may make returning their lands to his loyal supporters, matter of difficulty. But Hawksley fought bravely for Charles at Worcester. I have the feeling that he will remember this.'

'So Harrison's days as lord of the manor may be limited. I pray this be true, doctor—and that this child's father may return to the village soon!'

'Amen to that,' put in Sophie feelingly, 'I long to meet my father!'

'And so you shall in the near future.' said her grandfather encouragingly. 'Well now, we must go, Jessie. My daughter Martha lies at home far from well. Roger Haversham came near to killing her.'

'Bad cess to him! His own end will not be pretty,' said Jessie, a strange look in her eyes. She rose to her feet and walked over to a drawer in her oak cabinet. She ran her fingers through the many packets there and paused. 'Give this powder to Martha. Tell her to mix it with wine, the merest pinch though. It will cloud memory of all she has endured, until she is strong enough to face it.' And John Wheatley took the small packet without hesitation.

'Thank you Jessie. I will have my gardener, young Richard Appleby pass by your cottage each day, to ensure that all is well with you. But I think my warning to your tormenters will have had salutary effect.'

The birds were still singing sweetly as they traversed the forest floor on their walk back to the village, but the joys of the day had been sullied by the cruel little incident back in the clearing.

'She is not a truly witch, is she, grandfather?' asked Sophie in a low voice, as they reached the outskirts of the village.

'Bless you child—no! Perhaps Jessie has a rare gift, that of seeing into the future and a profound knowledge of herbs of all kinds—but a witch— no, definitely not!' He smiled. 'She is a woman who has undergone much persecution because she chooses to live alone, has a strange way with wild animals and birds and is able to affect cures through the herbs she prepares. People are always suspicious of what they do not understand!'

Sir Mark Harrison walked through the gardens of Hawksley Manor, slashing at the budding roses with his gold tipped cane. His face was dark with anger—and apprehension. The news that he had been thwarted in his attempt to have the old witch Jessie Thorne brought to justice—for surely killing a witch was honourable course for any man to bring about, had infuriated him. But the news that Dr Wheatley, father of the woman he would once have married, and on whom he would have been revenged for her rejection had she not died following childbirth of Hawksley's bastard—that it was this man who had gainsaid his orders and suggested that he might soon have to vacate the manor and lands he so highly prized, this had thrown him into a blind fury.

'Surely it could not happen—that he would lose all he held dear? But looking on the matter logically, he had to admit that it would be in keeping with the family tradition of this latest of the autocratic Stuart Kings to reward his friends. That in actual fact that he had had no legal right to

Hawksley Manor, beyond the gift of Oliver Cromwell was inconsequential in his mind.

He thought back to the day when he had last seen Dr Wheatley—and the girl at the elderly physician's side, whom he had instantly guessed to be the child of the woman he had loved and then hated with all his heart—Hawksley's bastard daughter! So she had been with Wheatley when he had disputed Harrison's orders to deal with the old witch—a curse on all three of them. And venomously he slashed at a border of gillyflowers.

He returned to the great hall with its ancient rafters, in the imposing manor house and shouted for his attendants. They came and stood before him nervously. He ran his eyes over them and selected a man he could always rely on.

'You there, Warren—I have a mission for you. You are to go into the village and find out all you can about the girl living with the old physician. I wish to know how long she had resided in his house—where she was living before this! Make sure that the information is correct—or it will be the worse for you!' He tossed a purse with few coins to the man. 'There will be more if the facts you bring are correct—and useful!'

Warren nodded and pocketed the purse. 'I will discover all for you, Sir! Stuck up looking young piece she is—pretty though!' A look from Harrison's eyes quelled further comment from him and he turned to go. But even as Warren started to ride his horse down the hill to the village, his thoughts were confused. Suppose his employer was indeed about to lose his lands and power—and to the father of the young girl he was to report on—was it politic to make an enemy of a young woman who might be in a place of authority in the near future? He pursed his lips in thought. A man had to be careful at this time of change in England.

Jack Warren paused as the doctor's handsome stone built house came into view, and tethered his animal to a tree, wondering how to proceed. He couldn't risk Dr Wheatley catching sight of him for he feared the consequences should the respected physician indeed report him to the magistrate for attempting to harm Jessie Thorne, despite the fact it had been on the orders of Harrison. But even as he stood there stroking his brindle bearded chin, shifty grey eyes narrowed in thought, he saw a woman approaching the garden gate, a heavy basket of provisions on her arm and recognised her as the doctor's housekeeper, Beth Giles.

'Why Mistress—allow me to help you with that basket. It looks heavy!'
'No thank you. I need no help from such as you!' she retorted acidly, for she had heard evil reports of this man.

'The doctor seems to have a goodly appetite these days, judging by the appearance of that basket,' he continued, as though he had not heard her scathing comment.

35

'We have more mouths to feed these days—Doctor's daughter Martha and grand-daughter Sophie. Now, out of my way fellow!' she snapped. 'Or should I have the doctor come out and have words with you?' And glaring she watched as he turned away on his heel and remounted his horse.

So—his daughter living there as well as the haughty looking young lass, he thought. But the girl's mother was dead—lying in the churchyard sixteen years or thereabouts. So this must be the doctor's other daughter, married as he'd heard to an innkeeper in the next village—Langley Morton. Suddenly a light dawned in his mind. That must be where Hawksley's child had been reared and kept a close secret these many years. The answer to his curiosity lay in Langley Morton.

He dug his heels into the horse's flanks and set off at a good speed. The inn was not busy at this time of day, but that was to be expected, most men still at work. He ordered a flagon of ale and stood eyeing the dour looking individual who had served him.

'Nice inn,' he said affably. 'Yours is it, friend?'

'I ask you--do I look like a wealthy man? No—I just work here, landlord!'

'So where is the owner then? Does he not work here too?' asked Warren casually.

'Mr Haversham? No—he doesn't work here—maybe a bit of special work at midnight!' ground out the other caustically.

'Smuggling then,' grinned Warren?

'Hush, you fool! Want to get me thrown out of a job?' The man turned away nervously. 'Foul temper he is in these days too,' he jerked over his shoulder at Warren.

'Any more news about the King—when he is to be crowned,' asked Warren still attempting to hold conversation with the landlord.

'How should I know? Think he sends messages to me,' growled the other and moved away. Warren seated himself on an oak settle where two elderly men were exchanging views on possible changes to the country's laws, now it was once more a monarchy.

'At least Luke, it may no longer be considered a sin to smile at a pretty woman,' said one greybeard reflectively.

'Perhaps dancing may be allowed once more,' replied the other hopefully. 'Not that I would be able to dance these days with my stiff knees, Jake—but it would be good to watch the young ones enjoying themselves again.'

'Who knows? Certain it is that change will come and those who came against this king's late father should look to themselves!' The man Jake raised his drink. 'To good King Charles,' he toasted, then laid a restraining hand on his companions knee, as he noticed the stranger who was edging nearer to them, listening intently and who had raised his tankard with theirs. 'Who might you be then,' he inquired?

'Name of Warren—I'm from the village of Stokely. You know of it perhaps?' said Warren affably.

'Of course—be strange if I didn't seeing it's only two hours walk away!'

'This is a fine inn, as I told the landlord just now. Said he doesn't own it though—but a man called Haversham. You know him friends?' He was rewarded by a nervous, suspicious glance from both the greybeards. 'Your tankards are empty. Allow me to recharge them!' and Warren called across to the landlord. 'We need more ale, landlord!' he held out a couple of coins and waited until the sour faced attendant had filled their tankards to the brim. The ale seemed to loosen their tongues and Warren probed again.

'You were about to tell me of the fortunate man—er Haversham was it—who owns this place. Does he live above the inn?'

'Haversham? Nay—not fine enough for the likes of him. He lives in that big house across the way—behind the yew hedges. Pretends to be pious—but there are tales you know!' said Luke meaningfully.

'Tales, friend?'

'Wild drinking parties above stairs here in the inn—in the early hours when most decent folks are asleep. Women too—fornication I've no doubt!! Yes and Haversham pretending to such great piety! Face like a patient saint in the church of a Sunday—hypocrite, that's what he is! Luke's tongue once started seemed unable to slow down.

'Then there are the masked riders of the night!' put in Jake. 'We've all heard of the boats arriving in at the sandy cove two miles away, when the moon is at the dark side, those barrels of brandy—ponies trotting over the cobbles—disappearing behind the inn yard.'

'A lucrative trade if I mistake not! So this Haversham is a rich man then—has a fine wife I suppose and well fed children?' At this sally both his elderly companions broke into sneering laughter.

'His wife has up and left him. Can't say I blame her, for his cook, Bessie tells me that he brutalised her in private. As for children—his only daughter, a pretty lass called Rachel disappeared two months ago and no one knows where she is now. A fine temper he has been in ever since!' snorted Jake

'Young Rachel was beautiful and modest, but always with a smile on her lips. Heard Haversham was minded to wed her to church elder Jack Masters, who buried his wife last year.' nodded Luke. 'I rarely saw either woman abroad though—he kept them close in his house!'

'Of what appearance was the daughter—golden hair and rosy cheeks is my guess,' asked Warren casually.

'No! Brown hair with glints of red—what do you want to know that for?' Luke demanded. 'She wouldn't be for the likes of you!'

'I meant nothing—idle curiosity! Well, I've business to attend to.' He made to rise.

'Well, Mr Warren—that's Haversham coming in through the door now, since you are so interested in his affairs.' Jake eyed the stranger who had asked so many questions. Would the man now make himself known to Haversham? But Warren slipped quietly away, without giving Haversham a second glance. He had discovered all he needed to know—and had also garnered some interesting information about Haversham's smuggling activities which might always prove useful in the future.

As he rode back to Stokely, Warren wondered why those at the inn had referred to the girl as Rachel, while the doctor's housekeeper had named her as Sophie—another mystery surrounding her! But certainly she appeared to be the same person and thought to be Haversham's daughter. Perhaps the intended marriage to the church elder had not been to her liking. Couldn't blame her for that he thought, no life for a spirited wench!

He presented himself before Harrison on his return to the manor house.

'Well—what have you discovered about the girl?'

'She's been brought up as the daughter of Haversham and his wife Martha. Seems she fled their home two months ago followed soon afterwards by Martha Haversham, the woman she looked on as her mother!'

'So that was the way of it!' Harrison took a pinch of snuff. 'And now you say both women are living with Dr Wheatley. 'Why did they leave Haversham?'

'From what I heard, he used to beat his wife—and probably the girl too! Seemingly, he tried to force the girl into marriage not to her taste.' He looked expectantly at Harrison. 'I got the information you wanted.' he held his hand out. 'You promised me something for my trouble.' The poor coin he received made him curse silently as he turned away. It barely covered the expense of buying drinks for those yokels at the inn.

Harrison sat long in his study that night, drinking a potent brandy, glancing with unseeing eyes at the marvellous collection of books garnered by Hawksley ancestors and now his, like all other furniture and belongings of the previous owner of the manor. How he joyed in his present position, the respect with which he was held by all in the village and more particularly by his servants, who jumped to his every command. The thought that all this might have to be forgone in the near future, was a bitter chalice from which to sip.

If Hawksley prevailed on the king, for whose sake he had given up all he held dear—fighting at his side, severely wounded by all accounts, going into exile with other passionate royalists, living in penury in France and the Netherlands—if then Charles decided to ignore certain of the regulations laid down in the charter made at Breda and reward his friend with a restoration of his property—where would that leave Harrison?

He gave a sudden savage curse and threw the brandy glass into the fire, where it splintered the final drops of brandy flaring up in sudden puff of flames. He would not give up the manor and its fine lands without a fight. He needed a bargaining tool of some sort to use against Hawksley, the man who had forestalled him in the affections of young Lucy Wheatley. Served the bitch right, that she had died soon after giving birth to Hawksley's bastard!

As he sat there, staring into the fire, thought of Lucy's daughter came into his mind. He considered what little Warren had been able to glean about her upbringing. Cared for by her aunt, Lucy's sister Martha and her boorish husband Haversham, the girl was probably untutored—would find it hard to secure a husband of distinguished background, the stain of bastardy outweighing the delights of her person. She was very fair he remembered, same exquisite features, flowing chestnut hair and bright blue eyes as Lucy had portrayed, same shapeliness of person.

A sudden thought came into his head. At first he almost dismissed it then examined it more closely. Suppose—just suppose he were to make an offer for the girl's hand? Poetic justice that would be, having in his power the daughter of the woman who had trodden on his affections and run away with a papist! Just think what a weapon he would possess to taunt Hawksley with! His brain was too sodden with brandy now to think further at present. He staggered off to his bedroom, flinging himself down on the fine four poster bed, managing to kick off his boots before pulling the covers over him. He fell into a deep and snoring sleep, the picture of Sophie, her subjugation materialising in fretful dreams.

He woke with a sore head and sour taste and rinsed his mouth with ale. The impulsive plan of the previous night gradually began to take shape in his mind again as he descended to the dining hall, where his servants had laid out a meal of new baked bread and a fine ham. The food helped to restore his usual bombastic spirits, the headache receded. He decided to make a call on Dr John Wheatley to explore the possibility of marriage to the man's bastard granddaughter—a notion that would surely delight the man.

John Wheatley frowned in surprise as both he and Sophie raised their heads from the box of finely detailed notes on most major diseases he had written over the last many years. For there was a determined knocking at the front door and the firm tones of Beth Giles heard remonstrating with the caller. Minutes later she knocked at the library door and opened it with apologetic expression.

'There is a visitor asking to see you, Doctor. He's most insistent. Should I admit him?' Beth's face held an uncertain look.

'Why who is it, Beth?'

'It be that Sir Mark Harrison, sir!'

'Harrison—what does he want here?'

The doctor stared in shocked surprise. Seventeen years ago, this man had come seeking his daughter Lucy's hand in marriage It was a father's prerogative to choose his daughter's husband. Nevertheless, although holding a low opinion of Harrison even in those days, he had informed his daughter of the offer and was not surprised in fact delighted when Lucy had given her blunt refusal to the unwelcome suitor. But Harrison had not accepted her rejection easily, but tried to waylay Lucy whenever she walked in the village, always pressing his suit despite her continual refusal to comply with his wishes.

The doctor had originally thought her refusal was merely on the grounds of personal dislike of Harrison, a dislike in which he concurred, had not known at first of her love for the handsome young landowner, Lord Hawksley who lived in his imposing manor house on the hill. When he did hear it rumoured that Lucy had been seen walking with Hawksley in the woods, their arms entwined, he had questioned her sternly as to the truth of it. For Lord Hawksley, who had recently inherited the estate on his father's death was a Catholic. He remembered what was said.

'No Lucy, I forbid this association. Firstly this man may not have marriage in mind, but even if he does, a conflict of religions would not make for a happy marriage. There again, with so much unrest in the country—this young royalist may even lose his life in conflict with the forces of the Commonwealth—this is no time to get embroiled in such a relationship!' How well he remembered his words—and her answer.

'I love James with all my heart, father! Will be his and no others! This I swear!' And she had rushed off to her room. She had not come down for breakfast the following morning. Inspection of her room showed she had fled, taking merely a change of clothes with her.

A year later she had returned to her sorrowing father, heavily pregnant now and hours later gave birth to the squalling, red faced infant who had become the lovely young woman at his side—an almost replica of her mother in appearance. He had tried to use all of his medical skill to save the life of this beloved daughter and she had dwindled on for another three weeks, yet despite his devoted care, had died shortly after a private visit from his elder married daughter, Martha. It had been her dying wish that Martha should bring up the tiny babe. He had respected those wishes.

Harrison had been darkly furious at the news that Lucy had spurned his advances for a papist. After the battle of Naseby, a badly wounded, James Hawksley had managed to escape over to France, leaving the woman he loved behind and his house and estates prey to the officers of the Commonwealth. Harrison had then prevailed upon his friend Oliver Cromwell to hand the Hawksley estate over to him and had promptly moved into the manor house and sacked the few remaining retainers. Later he was to hear that Lucy had returned to her father's house and given birth. By this time he both detested and despised the young woman—and hated Hawksley.

Two years after the Charles 1st had been executed on a cold January morning in 1649, Wheatley heard that Hawksley returned to England at the side of the late King's son, in an abortive attempt to overcome the forces of Cromwell, had fought bravely at the disastrous battle of Worcester and once more escaped to mainland Europe. No doubt he would have heard the news that Harrison was now was in possession of his house and estate.

Now this man Harrison, who had a deservedly evil reputation, had come knocking at his door, despite knowing the doctor's opinion of him—so why? He got slowly to his feet and even as he did so, the housekeeper, Beth Giles uttered a cry of outrage, as Harrison pushed her firmly out of the way and entered the study.

'Forgive my impatience to see you doctor,' he began in his usual hectoring tones. 'I have something of importance to discuss with you regarding the young lady at your side—your granddaughter I believe?' His eyes swept critically over Sophie, grudgingly admiring her fresh youthful beauty, as her bright blue eyes stared at him disdainfully, bringing sharp memory of her mother. Yes, she was very like to Lucy. But there was a subtle difference here—and with his acute sense of perception, he realised that she held herself with that certain hauteur, reminiscent of her father, James Hawksley.

'You are not welcome in this house, sir! Past events make any communication between us abhorrent. I ask you to leave!' Wheatley stared at Harrison, his eyes hard as iron.

'I would we could leave the past in the past, doctor! Seventeen years ago, I asked your daughter Lucy's hand in honourable marriage—and as you well know she rejected my offer and ran off with Hawksley and later as I understand it, died following childbirth, no doubt the shame in bearing an illegitimate child contributing to her death!' His eyes strayed lazily over Sophie, whose eyes were now blazing in outrage. Before her grandfather could reply, she addressed Harrison for the first time, her voice deep with suppressed anger.

'My parents were married sir! Though what possible business my affairs are to you I fail to understand!' She watched the incredulous expression of dismay spread over his features, to be replaced with disbelief.

'I fully comprehend your attempt to believe the best of your parents, young lady—but no degree of female fantasy can camouflage the truth! It is because of the stain of bastardy, that with feelings of pity for your situation I have come here today, to ask your grandfather's permission to wed you girl!' he came out with the words with a slight bow to John Wheatley, who almost spluttered in indignation.

'You come to this house—attempt to humiliate Lucy's daughter and then make this outrageous offer? I can only believe that you are suffering some disturbance of the mind sir!' Wheatley pointed to the study door, where his interested and astonished housekeeper still hovered. 'Mrs Giles—this person is leaving! Please ensure that he is not admitted in the future!'

'You will regret this—both of you,' sneered Harrison. 'When details of this girl's birth are made public, I doubt if any suitors will come knocking on this door, anymore than I will!'

'My daughter Lucy was the legal wife of Lord James Hawksley—the necessary documents attesting to their marriage exist and can be examined. Be careful that you are not brought before the courts on a charge of slander. Now get out!' Harrison stared at the doctor in sudden shock. He knew enough about the man to realise that he would never lie about such a matter. What at first had just seemed the young girl's attempt to defend her mother's reputation, now appeared to be the unpalatable truth.

He swung about and left the study without a further word, and the sound of Mrs Giles slamming the front door after his departure, brought a faint smile to Sophie's lips.

'Why did he propose to me, grandfather? I know it was obviously from no spirit of kindliness towards me?' She turned a questioning glance at her grandfather, then gave a cry of distress, as she saw him clutch at his chest in obvious pain. He sank onto his chair.

'Quickly, Sophie—my drops! The bottle in my coat pocket—give it to me.' The words were spoken faintly, his face devoid of colour. She acted immediately. Minutes later he seemed to rally.

'Oh, Grandfather—please won't you lie down on the couch. I could kill that man for upsetting you so!' Her face betrayed her agitation, for she knew his condition, that he had to be kept calm at all times and nor should he take those long walks which he so enjoyed. But even as she helped him over to the couch his colour returned, and he bent a smiling face up at her

'Thank you, child, I will rest for a short while. As for you, take great care not to leave this house without escort in the future. I do not trust that man Harrison. He obviously knows that now King Charles is on his rightful throne, the possibility exists in the fullness of time, that your father may have his estates returned. In this I feel is the reason that he desires to make you his wife—that he might hold you as a card against your father.'

'He seemed shocked to learn that I was legitimate.' She smiled as she remembered Harrison's look of discomfiture when the doctor had reaffirmed her own disclosure of her parent's marriage. Was this because it left her less vulnerable to his plans? But now was not the time to speak of the matter. She pulled a soft woollen shawl over the elderly man who had come to mean so much to her and bent her lips over his forehead.

'Now just you sleep, grandfather. And don't worry about me. I would rather die than marry that repulsive creature whom my mother so wisely rejected! The very cheek of him—to make advances to me!' He smiled at her words and closed his eyes and Sophie crept quietly out of the room.

She found Martha sitting in the garden on the seat overlooking the pool, enjoying the sunshine, a book in her hands. She had become a different woman since her arrival at her father's house, carrying herself with a new confidence, yet still she flinched at any unexpected noise, a surface gaiety masking nervousness born of the cruelty she had suffered at Haversham's hands throughout their marriage.

'Mama!'

'Sophie, child—what is wrong? You look upset?' Martha reached a hand up to the girl. 'Here, come sit beside me.' She patted the cushioned bench.

'We just had a visitor, Mama—the man who lives at Hawksley Manor—Sir Mark Harrison!' Her cheeks were still flushed with annoyance. 'He came for the most extraordinary reason, to make a proposal of marriage to me!'

'What did you say? You are not joking, Sophie?' Martha's face whitened in shock. 'You know of course that he made an offer of marriage to your true mother, my dear sister Lucy?'

'Yes—I know it, and that she rejected him, and that he managed to persuade Cromwell to hand over Lord Hawksley's house and lands to him in pure hatred of my father!' She dropped on the bench beside Martha and took one of her hands in hers. 'Grandfather asked him to leave! You should have seen the way he faced up to Harrison! He had been taunting me by calling me a bastard, offering marriage as a great favour! His face when I told him of my parents' marriage was a picture! He didn't believe me at first, until grandfather spoke of the certificates proving it.'

'My father never could abide the man. We heard scurrilous rumours circulating after my sister's death—spread by Harrison. None knew that you had survived and that I raised you as my own daughter. Neighbours were told that you were the orphaned child of a distant cousin. My husband had not wanted the responsibility for your care, but your grandfather paid him a substantial sum of money. Haversham was tempted by that money and made promise to treat you as his daughter. We never knew that Lucy and James were married!' Martha's face was troubled as she mentioned her husband's name, for it brought back disturbing memories.

'You went through so much to help me, Mama! Had you been my own real mother, I could not love and respect you more.' She bent forward and kissed Martha. 'But I am worried about grandfather. He had one of those frightening episodes when he clutches his heart and loses all colour. He is resting now which is why I've left him to come and speak with you.' Martha's face registered alarm.

'I must go to him!'

'No, Mama—it is better that he sleeps now,' she said reassuringly. Martha nodded, but her worry persisted. Her thoughts returned to the girl.

'I cannot understand why Harrison should make offer of marriage to you! He spoke most viciously of Lucy after her rejection of him. So why wish to marry her daughter?' Martha's face was puzzled.

'Grandfather thinks it a possible ploy to put pressure on Lord Hawksley, should he attempt to regain his house and estate. But I suppose my father does not even know of my existence. Was he ever told of me, Mama?'

'I think not. From the battle of Naseby onwards, which was when Lucy last saw him, until he finally escaped to France from the West country, we had no way of contacting him. The Royalists were always on the move. We heard of his astonishing bravery though. He returned first to Scotland and then England at the young King's side when Charles attempted to regain his father's throne. Then following the disastrous battle of Worcester managed to escape to France once more. You may be sure that the new King will reward him for his loyalty—hopefully by restoring his estate!' Martha's face was animated as she explained all this to the girl she had brought up as her daughter, yet until now, had been unable to speak of, keeping the promise made to her dying sister, who had sought to protect her child so.

'Why was it that Lucy did not trust grandfather or you with her marriage?' Sophie asked. Bending and picking a daisy from the grasses around the bench and plucking its petals.

'Because I imagine, news that she had undergone a Catholic ceremony would have brought trouble on her family—and no doubt the officiating priest would have been sought. Death would have been his portion, child.' Martha sighed. 'I have no great love of Catholics, yet believe they should be free to practice their faith in peace. The harsh laws of the Commonwealth from which I hope the country will soon begin to disengage itself, these I fear will linger on for many years regarding the treatment of Catholics. You child have been brought up as a protestant.

The church at Langley Morton was severely so. The Episcopal Church which I attended as a child, banned. All condemned as popery.' She shook her head.

'How can anyone really believe in religion that causes so much pain and division in peoples' lives? I want none of it,' cried Sophie passionately. 'I cannot make sense of the way people behave to each other! There is only one God and surely He must wonder at the cruelty folk show to each other in His name!' Sophie rose to her feet. 'What should bind people together, their faith in Jesus, seems only to provoke controversy in the way they worship!'

'I agree, Sophie. But let us go into the house now and see that my father is recovered. I worry about his health.'

'So do I, Mama—but he is strong,' replied Sophie, more to comfort Martha than because she believed it so. What would the future hold should John Wheatley succumb to pain that afflicted his heart?

Chapter Four

Charles yawned and turned his head away from his brother James, Duke of York. He had listened for over half an hour in the privacy of his closet to complaints against Anne Hyde, daughter of his foremost politician, whom it appeared that James had made pregnant.

'She is demanding marriage I tell you! How can I marry a woman who has neither grace nor beauty? After all, my future wife is of importance to the nation, for whereas I am sure you will provide many heirs upon the body of the fortunate woman you select as queen—until this time, I am your heir brother!' So exploded James, smarting from the loss of support he was receiving from an amused Charles.

'Now look you James—the lady obviously suited you well enough when you sought her bed and it would appear that her interesting state is due to your own attentions and no others—er when is the event deemed to take place?' He rose to his feet and stood staring down at James with his slightly cynical smile. Although he acknowledged that James would have done better to have sought a female from one of the royal houses of Europe, it would cause great rift between Chancellor Hyde and himself should that man's daughter be slighted.

'She thinks possibly in October. I mean—but the child may not be mine!' said James, his heart sinking as he came to the reluctant conclusion that he was to receive no support from Charles.

'But you have already told me that she had no other lovers!'

'Not that I know of—but that means nothing, as you are aware!' He looked up at Charles pleadingly. But his royal brother merely chuckled.

'Well James, seems we are both to become fathers, for the lovely Barbara is also with child! Of course, it may well be her husband Roger Palmers—can be said to be so! Ah me, what problems we poor men have. But as for Anne, I consider that you owe her a duty of marriage.' He withdrew his snuff box and inhaled a satisfying pinch. 'I think we have said all that is necessary on this subject!'

James nodded miserably and got up. 'I think it will be a different matter when it comes to choosing your own bride!'

'How wrong you are. My marriage will be merely matter of State, the appearance and attributes of a future wife dependant on her ability to fill my empty coffers! The Infanta of Portugal is suggested among others by my ministers. We need money, James!'

'What do you mean? Surely as King you have no such worries?' James stared at him in surprise and realised from Charles expression that he was not joking.

'The government have supplied a sum inadequate for my needs. Have you any idea how many men and women who supported our father, now come to me, quite reasonably I suppose, for recompense of some sort or other. Many can be given minor official positions about court. But such have to be funded. Already I have to borrow heavily, which is thing I detest doing. No James, if my future wife brings beauty as well as wealth then that will be a bonus. There we have it!' His dark eyes surveyed James calmly as his brother regarded him analytically in his turn, perhaps recognising the bruised spirit of an elder brother whom he had always taken for granted.

'I suppose we should not complain,' said James slowly. 'Surely it is miracle that you are now safe on our father's throne. Perhaps marriage is not of the most importance now, whereas security for the future is!'

'James, I remember as a youth, the anguish with which I heard the shocking news of our father's beheading, the despair of years living in penury, treated with contempt by our relatives abroad. False hopes all too often dashed—so now I take nothing for granted. Hopefully the inhabitants of these Isles, will never again raise hands against their King, commit that most dastardly of crimes, regicide!' The lines that ran from long nose to chin, encircling his sensual lips, seemed to deepen as he spoke, his eyes to sadden. 'Come brother—I fancy a game of chess!'

'I fear I could not concentrate!' said a dejected James.

'Why then, let us rejoin the ladies!'

Officials bowed before the two royal brothers, as they made their way along the carpeted passageways to the large reception room. As he was announced, Charles stood for a moment, nose registering the mixture of heavy perfumes and stale perspiration, and stared about him where men doffed their hats and bent their bewigged heads while women curtsied like so many flowers bending before the wind and his favourite hound sprang from a corner to greet him. He caressed its shaggy head affectionately then strolled to his chair set on a small dais.

He signed to a group of musicians who had been playing as he entered, their music submerged in the babble of voices, to continue. This time their music was heard. Charles considered the faces of the surrounding courtiers, who were watching him closely, all with plans of future possible preferment on their minds. What were their true thoughts as they smiled politely upon him? Did any feel slightest true affection for him as a man, rather than one who could fulfil their small ambitions?

He sighed, then his eyes lighted upon one man whom he knew he could trust, had done so with his life on more than one occasion, James Hawksley. Recollection that he now had the necessary strictures lifted on Hawksley's house and lands made him smile slightly, as he gestured that Hawksley should approach him.

'Your Majesty?' greeted Hawksley sweeping a polite bow, as his eyes lit across the features of one who was his good friend as well as king.

'Come closer, James, I have news for you—excellent news!' Charles looked affectionately at this man who closely resembled him in appearance, save that although five years his senior, had not the same lines upon his face.

'News, Sire?' Hawksley dared not believe what those words might possibly mean.

'Your house and lands—all your possessions are now officially restored to you! If you wait upon me tomorrow, I will see that the relevant documents as ordered by parliament at my request are given into your hands!' At these words, Hawksley fell to one knee before the king, who had kept this promise, although so many other despoiled Royalists had been disappointed.

'Well—are you happy now, my friend?' demanded Charles, placing his hand on Hawksley's head.

'Incredibly happy, my king,' replied Lord James Hawksley, eyes bright with unshed tears.

'I wish I had it in my power to grant money to you as well as your estate, but am hard pressed myself at this time! Now listen, in case you experience any problems in removing the present incumbent from your home and lands, then you may call upon the local constabulary there to aid you.' Charles nodded that the conversation was at an end. At least he had been able to help one who had proved wonderfully loyal to both his father and himself. People stared curiously at Hawksley as he withdrew from the king's side. Perhaps he was one whom they should mark for the future.

The late summer sunshine streamed in through the small paned windows of John Wheatley's study, as he checked the contents of various jars and small linen bags of the varied dried herbs he had found of great use as physic over the years. The doctor tut-ted under his breath as he realised that some had run low. Not that he really had need of them now in his retirement, but occasionally old patients still came to his door, braving flagellation by Beth Giles tongue, as she protected his privacy.

He made a list and set aside his quill as Sophie knocked and came in to bend and kiss him on his forehead. He reached up and squeezed her hand affectionately noting with satisfaction the difference three months had made to her appearance. Gone was the slightly tense look in her eyes, while her graceful young figure had blossomed into womanhood, now seeming even more like to his dear Lucy.

'What are you doing grandfather?'

'Why, making list of a few herbs that I am hopeful old Mistress Jessie Thorne may be able to supply me with. I thought we would take a walk over to her cottage today—perhaps you would like to accompany?' and he smiled up the lovely inquiring face above him as he leaned back in his chair, 'Well?'

'I do not think you should take such long walk any more, grandfather. A stroll around the garden or as far as the village green beyond the square—that is more than enough for you!' she said firmly. Then she looked down at the list he had prepared. 'Are these the items you need from Jessie?'

'Yes. They are not of any urgency, but I like to keep them by me, an old man's duty of care to patients I no longer have, I suppose. No, we will forget them child! You are probably right. I should not venture so far these days.' And he sighed regretfully

'I will get these for you, grandfather! I know the way to Jessie Thorne's cottage well.'

'Oh no—you are not to venture that far without me, Sophie. I do not trust that man Harrison or those ruffians he employs.' His eyes betrayed his concern. But she merely smiled.

'I do not intend to spend the rest of my days worrying about Harrison! He had my answer when he made that outrageous offer to marry me! As though I would have any dealings with the man who took my father's lands and spoke as he did about my mother!' She bent and picked up the list, in the doctor's fine handwriting and before he could prevent her and placed it in the pocket of her sapphire blue skirt. It was one of Lucy's she had found in the wardrobe and which needed no alteration. She joyed in wearing her mother's clothes and blessed her grandfather for keeping them over the years. They made her feel a special bond with Lucy, who had died so tragically soon after giving her birth.

'I forbid it, Sophie!'

'No you don't! You know you want these herbs. Suppose I were to take Dawlish with me?' She looked at him from determined blue eyes. A walk through the woods would be sheer joy—to hear the birds singing—perhaps if she were lucky to see one of the elusive deer.

'Dawlish?' His eyes cleared. 'Yes, that should serve. He will be in the stables no doubt. You should be safe with him!' He smiled as she ran off to get her shawl and heard the front door bang. He returned to his notes.

But Dawlish could not be found in the stables. Sophie called his name, then checked he wasn't in the loft—then realised that the horse was not in its stall. She saw the young lad who helped in the garden and called to him'

'Richard! Richard—where is Daniel Dawlish?' The boy lifted his head from the flower bed he was weeding and came across to Sophie.

'He has taken the horse to the blacksmith to get shoed! Can I help you Mistress Sophie?' He looked at her eagerly always glad to do her bidding.

'No, you see I promised grandfather that I would ask Dawlish to walk through the woods with me to Mistress Thorne's cottage. I cannot go alone, he is worried for my safety, there was trouble there once before!' her blue eyes held disappointment.

'No need for you to change your plans, Mistress Sophie. I'm a man. I'll go with you and bring a stout stick to lay into any who show less than respect for you! After all, I walk past Mistress Thorne's cottage every day at the doctor's bidding—to see she has come to no harm.' He grinned. 'I'm tired of these weeds. Please say I may come?' She looked at him. Richard Appleby son of a neighbouring farmer, who divided his time between helping his father on the land together with his older brothers and earning a few coins by working on the doctor's garden, was now nearing fourteen years of age—hardly a man, but already tall for his years and with strong shoulders

'Go wash your hands and get that staff of yours! Don't tell Mrs Giles where you are going. I'll slip out of the gate at the end of the garden, meet me there.' She knew she should not break her word to her grandfather, but the woods beckoned with their rich, dense, spicy, damp world of growing things, delight of dappled shade and feeling of mystery, an enchanted place for Sophie.

Richard walked proudly beside her, staff in hand. They were entering Epilson woods now, the golden sunshine suddenly extinguished as the trees closed about them and Richard slashed with his stick at brambles that had spread across the faint pathway they followed. Soon they came to the bridge across the small stream that gurgled its way through the forest floor, wild flowers and bracken caressing its banks as a cloud of small insects rose at their advance and a dragonfly hovered, bright green in a gleam of sunlight.

'How I love this place,' sighed Sophie. She paused and looked around. No deer made their illusive presence apparent today and strangely no birds sang sweetly as before. But the sound of the stream was music and blended with the faint soughing of the summer breeze in the trees.

'It's alright here I suppose,' replied the boy. 'Good blackberries to be had soon—and hazel nuts later!' he added practically. 'Shall we go on, Mistress Sophie?' Although Richard did not believe the tales that old Jessie Thorne was a witch, nevertheless he felt slightly uneasy as he always did when he approached her cottage—wanted the business over and done with.

Another few minutes brought sight of the cottage in its small clearing. Sophie looked towards it and saw the door stood open. They walked closer when Richard held back. Sophie recognised his reluctance and guessed the cause.

'You wait here, Richard. I will not be long inside and then we will make our way home!' She knocked at the open door and called out.

'Jessie—Jessie, may I come in? It's Sophie Wheatley,' and she stepped inside.

'Come in and welcome,' said a harsh voice, and before she could even attempt to struggle, a sack was thrown over her head and shoulders and secured with a rope, her scream instantly muffled. But even before she was plunged into a world of fear and darkness, she had made glimpse of the figure lying horribly dead on the floor. Jessie Thorne's throat had been cut!

In those first minutes her mind was full of terror as she struggled ineffectually to rid herself of the sack, only to be thrown roughly to the ground. Understanding the futility of further attempt she lay still, pretending to a swoon, as she forced herself to be calm, to think clearly, as the suffocating sacking filled her nostrils.

She realised she could hear their voices, harsh, gloating at the success of their mission.

'Paid off, the days we watched around the cottage for the wench to come! Harrison should reward us well for today's work! The old witch dead and the girl to be delivered safe into his hands!' She thought she recognised the man's voice, as that of Jack Warren, one of those who weeks back had attempted to kill and abuse poor old Jessie. Now that she had seen the old woman's body, Sophie realised her own fate was in perilous state

'Where did you say he wants her brought?' asked another.

'He said to leave her in the old hay barn near the big house.' replied Warren.

'Better look outside to see that none accompanied the girl. Could be the doctor is not far away! Harrison said no harm was to come to him—might cause repercussions, eh!' said another.

'You go then, Catesby! Give a shout if you want help!' Warren grinned as he gave the order. Should the elderly doctor be around then he would be easily dealt with, doddering old fool!

Will Catesby sidled softly to the open door and peered out. He pulled back inside. 'There's someone out there, Warren! A young lad—can't see anyone else.'

'Then damned well deal with him, what are you waiting for?' came the impatient reply. Catesby nodded, made sudden rush outside, his momentum bringing him face to face with the surprised youth, who attempted to raise his staff a little too late. Now he lay bleeding of a knife wound below his shoulder from a blow that had narrowly missed his heart. Catesby looked down on him with no slight sign of pity, merely kicked the body with his booted foot.

'He won't be telling anyone what happened here today,' he said shortly as he rejoined the other two.

'Then we had best be off,' said the third man, Edward Jackson.

'You bring the horses to the door. None here to see us now,' instructed Warren and Jackson disappeared into the trees and returned with their three beasts. Warren mounted swiftly

'Right—now help get the girl up beside me here,' instructed Warren, leaning from his horse. He felt a moment's unease as they manhandled the girl's inert figure. Surely she could not have expired? There would be the devil to pay should they deliver her dead, for she lay apparently lifeless beneath the sack. With a curse, his fingers loosened the knots securing it about her shoulders. Her face as he exposed it was deathly white and he feared the worst—but a pulse in her neck reassured him.

'Let's be off. The sooner we get her to Harrison the better for us all!' He dug his heels into his horse's sides, it sprang forward. Soon all three men disappeared amongst the trees, in the direction of Hawksley Manor, Sophie still feigning unconsciousness.

'Two hours later John Wheatley, who had dozed off in his chair, heard the sound of his housekeeper's voice.

'Lunch, doctor—is Mistress Sophie in there with you?'

'Sophie?' He opened the door, eyes suddenly alert. 'Sophie went with Dawlish into the woods to Jessie Thorne's cottage. But that was three hours ago. She should have been back well before now!'

'But Dawlish was at the blacksmith's all morning. Barnaby needed re-shoeing,' exclaimed Beth Giles. 'I've seen no sign of Sophie since breakfast, when she joined you in here, sir!'

'The garden—go check in the garden!' cried Wheatley, a sudden dread constricting his heart. Surely Sophie would not have gone on her own after his warning to her?

'There's no sign of her out there, doctor! I would have asked Richard if he had seen her, but he has gone too. Come to think of it, I did notice him cross the lawn two hours back, carrying his staff—and thought he had arranged to help his father on the farm!' Beth's face was full of worry.

'I have it, she is probably in Martha's room, helping her with that tapestry they are both working on,' said Wheatley. 'That will be it.' But Martha also had seen no sign of Sophie and turned a frightened countenance on her father. 'What can have happened to her,' she asked? He did not reply, not wanting to upset her at this stage.

'Get Dawlish to come with me! We will go into the woods and search for her!' Nor could either of the women dissuade him from this course of action. But it was Dawlish who laid a steadying hand on the doctor's shoulder.

'Look you sir, I am going to get Big Paul Masters, the blacksmith and any others I can round up. If as you fear some of Harrison's lads have taken the girl, then we'll need some determined fellows to bring her safe home again. You can leave it to me, sir!' The doctor looked at him uncertainly, and then nodded, as common sense took over. What good would he be to Sophie, should he have an attack of the heart far from home, so causing delay.

'Hurry then—God be with you. Bring her safe back,' he instructed.

The blacksmith raised his head from his anvil at the sound of Daniel Dawlish voice.

'Master Dawlish—back so soon,' he exclaimed, staring in surprise at Dr Wheatley's stableman.

'Paul Masters—I need your urgent help!'

'In what way, my friend,' asked Masters rubbing his hands on his leather apron and straightening up? He saw from the expression on Dawlish face, that something was badly amiss.

'Doctor sent me. Mistress Sophie has disappeared. We think she went into the woods on her own—to visit old Jessie to buy some of the herbs she collects.'

'The lass would be safe enough with Jessie. She's no witch you know, just a lonely woman with a goodly knowledge of healing,' declared the blacksmith with a smile.

'It's not Jessie the doctor is concerned about. He fears Sir Mark Harrison has designs on the young lady. The man made her a recent offer of marriage which she refused, and according to Beth Giles he was furious, even threatening. Weeks before this, the doctor caught Harrison's thugs attacking Mistress Thorne at her cottage, until he saw them off. All may be well with Miss Sophie—but doctor is desperately worried for her safety!'

'Say no more, my friend! I have no time for Harrison—or those he employs! I'll come with you.' He pulled off his apron, closed the furnace and seized a heavy metal bar.

'And so will I,' came a deep voice. Dawlish turned around.

'Thomas Appleby—will you come along with us then?' Dawlish nodded at the tall, muscular farmer, father of the lad who helped in the doctor's garden 'The matter could be urgent,' he added seriously.

'My son Harry will come too,' said the farmer calling to a young fellow who topped his father's six feet by two inches and was standing just outside the smithy. 'We go to help young Sophie Wheatley! It might mean a fight with Harrison's men—which will please you!' His son grimaced wryly and nodded.

'Let's go then, father!'

The four men plunged in to the woods, taking the path that led towards Jessie Thorne's cottage. Harry Appleby paused as they reached the bridge and pointed down to two sets of footprints in the soft soil bordering the stream.

'These must be Mistress Sophie's footprints, and there are those of another with her—see!' His father bent and looked carefully.

'If I didn't know better, I'd say the other prints be those of young Richard. See—like to those new round toed boots he's so proud of!'

'That's it then! Richard disappeared from the garden early and they thought he must have returned to help you on the farm, sir,' said Dawlish. It explained why Sophie had ventured here, feeling safe with the youngster at her side. They walked on, moving faster now, until Jessie's cottage came into view. They saw the open door, then as they stepped free of the trees. Appleby stumbled over something in a tangle of foxglove and bracken. He stared down and uttered an anguished cry.

'It's my son—it's Richard! Dear God, I think he's dead.'

He stooped down over the youth, whose shirt was dark with sticky congealed blood. Almost trembling in fear and emotion, he laid his head across Richard's breast and gave sigh of relief as he thought he heard a faint murmur. The boy's heart was still beating—there was hope for him. He pulled the shirt apart and exposed the knife wound that had almost killed him. Ripping off his own shirt, he made a pad, and tied it firmly in position to stop further bleeding. Only then did he raise his head and see that his three companions had entered the cottage and were strangely silent. It was Dawlish who came out to the distraught father. His face was grave.

'Richard?' he asked.

'He lives—just. But I must get him to the doctor quickly if he is to survive!'

'Thank the Lord. Then you go back, friend Appleby! We have other grave matters here, sickening to behold. Old Jessie lies within, her throat cut—and signs of a struggle. And I found the blue ribbon which Mistress Sophie wears in her hair, trampled on the floor. No sign of her though! Damn them to hell—if they have harmed her!' choked Dawlish.

'Father, let me carry Richard to Doctor Wheatley,' said Harry Appleby. 'He'll be safe with me. You go on with the others and I will send extra help, as soon as I can!' His face was grim as he lifted his youngest brother gently from his father's arms.

'Look here, leading away from the cottage—marks of horses hooves! And I can identify one beast. It belongs to Harrison's man Warren. See how the shoe is slightly short on one side. His horse had an odd shaped, front right hoof.' said the blacksmith. 'There's our proof as to who did this deed!'

'May they swing for it,' cried Dawlish! 'Try not to worry the doctor too much, Harry. He has been unwell recently—his heart!' But he knew his words were useless. As soon as he heard what had happened at the cottage, Dr Wheatley would need all his mental strength to remain calm. He muttered a prayer under his breath for Sophie and her grandfather. Then together with Appleby and Paul Masters he plunged on into the woods, trying to follow the trail of horses' hooves on the damp forest floor.

Sophie lay on her back on the pile of hay where the men had carelessly tossed her, after first tying her wrists and ankles with strong twine. She pretended continuing unconsciousness until she heard their voices recede and they left her, laughing and making course comments about her appearance, for her skirts were high above her knees.

She lay still trying to subdue the panic that brought choke to the back of her throat. What now? Would Richard run back and tell her grandfather what had happened? But suppose they had killed him too—as they had poor old Jessie. Memory of that brief horrifying sight of the woman lying throat cut, in a pool of blood was one that she knew would haunt her dreams forever.

She heard voices again. The men were coming back. She opened her eyes and looked desperately around—a barn, but where? And what was their purpose with her? Had they intended rape, they would have done it before now. She thought she recognised one of those voices, knew it to be that of Harrison! She had worried that sooner or later Harrison would come and now a chill of fear shuddered through her.

Suddenly he was standing above her, staring down, a cold insolence in his almost unwinking eyes. His gaze sped from her dishevelled hair and torn blouse, to the skirt above her knees.

'So—we meet again, my dear Mistress Sophie! I must tell you how very like you now appear, to that whore your mother! Yet even such as you, may be tamed through marriage! Later, this very evening in fact when the preacher I have summoned arrives, we will hold a ceremony—our wedding! But be under no illusion that it is your body that attracts me. Until then—rest well my bride to be!'

'I will never marry you sir! You delude yourself if you think so. I will tell the preacher of my kidnap, and of Jessie's murder! And if your men have harmed Richard Appleby, believe me all of you will pay for it!' Her eyes flashed outrage at him. He stared down at her in surprise.

'Richard Appleby—one of the farmer's sons you mean?' and he turned to Warren who stood smirking at his side. 'Come with me. You have some explaining to do,' he snapped, a slight look of apprehension crossing his face.

They disappeared and she was alone again. The thought of what lay ahead, a marriage with this man she both detested and despised shocked her into action.

She must try to escape. Her fingers writhed against the cords that bound her, but the knots held good and her wrists soon felt raw. It was then that she remembered the small clasp knife she carried in her skirt pocket, to cut specimens of hawthorn for her grandfather. She wriggled down in the hay, so that her skirt rose higher and then with a frantic effort, managed to withdraw the knife. She gave a triumphant smile.

Now she had opened the knife, but could not fathom how to use it with her hands tightly bound. Then on inspiration, drew up her knees and clamped the knife firmly between them. It took several attempts and she cut her wrists in the process, but at last she was free. Now for her ankles! Minutes later she rose stiffly to her feet and thrust the knife back in her pocket. She found she was up on a shelf high in the hayloft and the ladder beneath had been moved away. There was nothing for it. She would have to jump. On inspiration she threw down a thick heap of hay—and leapt down into it. It broke her fall, but she had twisted her ankle.

Outside in yard, the late afternoon sunlight stroked red gold onto the ancient timbers of the barn and other outbuildings. She looked around anxiously. Which way should she go? A massive stone built mansion reared up atop the hill on which the farm buildings stood and she knew this must be Hawksley Manor—where Harrison lived, but which belonged to her father! She turned in the opposite direction, along a dusty lane furrowed with cart tracks. This surely must lead to the road that led back into the village, for to the left she could see the dark outline of Epilson woods.

She hesitated. Should she make for the safety but rough going of the woods, but with an ankle that was increasingly painful, or press on along the lane knowing that she might be pursued at any moment? She decided for the lane and the quicker progress she could make. If she heard noise of pursuit, she would dive into the thick hedge bordering the lane, with its snarl of honeysuckle and un-ripened nuts and berries, above banks of tall, pink bay willow herb, rust red sorrel and nettles.

She did not hear or see the horseman until he was almost upon her, for the man in wine velvet suit and soft leather boots, a feathered hat upon his long dark hair suddenly exploded over a low gate set in the hedge from the neighbouring field, pulled back on his reins and drew his horse to snorting up reared halt.

'Now by all the Saints!' the man swore. 'Mistress, I could have killed you!' Then as he leant from his horse to regard the girl, his face froze in sudden shock. It wasn't—couldn't be. She was dead, he had found her grave in the churchyard. But it was—Lucy!

He dismounted. 'Lucy—wife,' he murmured. Surely this was some strange hallucination. The same face, gown, eyes as blue as hyacinths— and he stared at her distractedly

As for Sophie, at first she stared at the stranger in incomprehension, then as his features registered, memory stirred of the face in her mother's locket, and she knew!

'I am not Lucy, sir, but her daughter. And I think—yours also?'

'I don't understand,' he said dismounting and still observing her with distracted look. 'My wife is dead, our child did not live. And yet you, so very like to Lucy? Who are you—the truth now!' and he pulled her close to him and tilted her face up to his. And as he looked he realised that although so similar in appearance to Lucy, this was no miracle of his dear wife having survived, nor yet an elusive ghost come upon his path in the twilight.

'My name is Sophie Louise—Hawksley!' There, she had proclaimed it for the first time. 'I was brought up by my mother's elder sister, Martha and her husband. None knew who I was except these two, and my grandfather!'

'Sophie Louise, why, my mother's name!' he exclaimed. 'So Lucy named you for her.' He drew her to him and planted a kiss on her forehead. 'After the long years of exile and loneliness what wondrous blessing the Lord has now given me? My estates restored to me—and a daughter of whose existence I had no knowledge!'

'Please, may we get away from this place—father,' she interjected as reality of her situation arose in her mind. 'I was kidnapped by men employed by Sir Mark Harrison! Only short time since I managed to escape the barn where he held me. He was to force me into marriage this very night!' The words poured out almost incoherently and she saw an incredulous expression cross Hawksley's face at what he heard.

'He dared do that to you? To my daughter! I'll have his life for this!' He lifted her up onto his horse and sprang up in front of her. Even as he did so, there was a loud shout as three men clambered over the gate in quick succession.

'Put her down, you bastard!' cried one, rushing up to the horse and attempting to pull Sophie down. Hawksley dealt him a blow to the head, as the other two made to attack him.

'Dawlish—stop! Stop! This is my father, Lord James Hawksley!' At the girl's cry the men pulled back and stared dumbfounded at the mounted stranger. Was it possible? Lord Hawksley whom none had reported sight of since the battle of Worcester so many years ago—he had returned?

'Be that truly you, my Lord,' asked Dawlish, nursing his bruised head. 'We thought you to be one of Harrison's ruffians who had kidnapped the young mistress and murdered old Jessie Thorne.' As he looked, he realised from the stranger's garments that this was no member of Harrison's roughnecks, and further inspection brought back memory of a younger Hawksley

'They almost killed my youngest son,' cried Appleby! 'Even now I do not know for certain that he lives, a knife wound meant for the heart!'

'Why, I remember you. It is Master Appleby is it not, your farm bordering my land—and you my friend, Paul Masters, blacksmith?' He reached down and took their hands in turn. He looked regretfully at Dawlish. 'Forgive me that blow, friend!'

'It is forgotten sir.' Dawlish attempted a smile, despite his aching head. Then the men looked at each other in excitement. Did this indeed mean that Hawksley was going to reclaim his property—to dispossess Harrison?

'If there is anything we can do to help your Lordship in any way, then but say the word,' cried Paul Masters heartily. 'I think that for now though we had best get this young lady back to her grandfather, whom Dawlish says is deeply distressed on her account. He's not that well these days you know.' He added quietly.

'Oh—grandfather! Please, I must go to him,' cried Sophie. But even as she said this, Hawksley stiffened in the saddle, for he had noticed a band of men riding hard towards them from the direction of the Manor.

'Sophie, get down—over that gate with you. Hide until I call you!' With a frightened glance towards the oncoming men, she obeyed his terse command without question. Her ankle shrieked message of pain as she put her weight on it once more, but she barely noticed it in apprehension of what was to follow. She noticed a slight gap in the hedge and crept close to it to observe what would follow.

Lord Hawksley sat his horse in the centre of the lane, behind him the three village men, shoulders drawn back, legs astride, the blacksmith tightening his grasp on the iron bar he had brought.

'Who are you trespassing on my land!' cried Harrison in a strident voice, having satisfied himself that Sophie was nowhere to be seen. His eyes narrowed as he saw the quality of the mounted man before him, wearing a sword at his side—pistol butts glinting in the dying sun. He stared more closely and his jaw dropped. Even though there had been a gap of many years, he recognised the handsome, autocratic features of Lord James Hawksley. So he was back and likely to prove a danger to his continuing possession of the Hawksley lands.

'I see you recognise me, Harrison! I am here to tell you that the King has seen fit to reinstate me in my home and estates. I carry the necessary papers approved by parliament!' His voice was ice as he stared at the man who had taken his house and all he possessed and further more had attempted to force his daughter into unwanted marriage.

'Forgeries I have no doubt,' blustered Harrison. 'We want no papists here! At him men—and those who support him! I will pay a goodly sum to have him bound at my mercy!' As he said this, he spurred his horse into sudden leap forward as he drew his sword and thrust towards Hawksley's breast. But the seasoned soldier easily deflected the blow and minutes later Harrison's weapon lay in the dust, his face suddenly fearful.

At that moment, Warren assessed the situation and yelled at his comrades to turn back. If Hawksley was here with the King's authority to resume ownership of his house and lands, then to remain hereabouts in danger of arrest for the murder of Jessie Thorne and the Appleby lad and the abduction of the rightful landowner's daughter made no sense whatsoever.

After a minute's hesitation, they turned their horses about and to the chagrin of the three villagers who had been anticipating opportunity of a fight to wreak retribution for the dastardly actions of the murderers—fled the scene, leaving Harrison sitting on his horse in shock at their disobedience to his orders.

'Bloody cowards,' raged Appleby, face mottled with rage and shaking his fist at the retreating forms, as the blacksmith swore a violent oath and regretfully lowered his iron bar. There was no way in which they could catch up with mounted men on foot! Dawlish however looked slightly relieved. His immediate concern was for the doctor waiting anxiously for news of his young granddaughter. Hawksley held up his hand for silence and then addressed his chagrined adversary.

'So Harrison, you would give much to see me bound at your feet! Well, the scum who work for you obviously saw the futility of that hope! I could kill you now for the dishonour you sought to bring on my daughter. But I prefer to have you dealt with by the law!' and Hawksley eyed him contemptuously.

'The law treats papists like you most severely, Hawksley! As for me, I am well respected. I have no fear of the law!' But he had. His face registered his growing unease—the realisation that this man had it in his power to have him arrested and thrown into prison at the least.

'Listen to me, Harrison! You will vacate my house before mid day tomorrow, at which time I will return with officers of the law who will deal with you—should you be so foolish as to remain!' And Harrison paled before the anger in the other's eyes. It was at that moment that Sophie who had heard and seen all, from the other side of the hedge, left her refuge and stepped down into the lane and proudly placed one hand on her father's horse.

'I told you that I would never marry you, Mark Harrison!'

'I was fool to contemplate union with a whore's droppings,' spat Harrison, then, before Hawksley could call him to account for this insult to Sophie, turned his horse and spurred back towards the Manor.

'Ignore him, father! He has no power over either of us now. He is an evil man and like his men a coward!' Hawksley's face softened as he leaned down and caught her up on the horse. His reckoning with Harrison could wait his first priority had to be his newly discovered and very courageous young daughter.

'I will take Sophie directly to Dr Wheatley's house. Meet me there, when I will reward you for your kindness to my daughter!' He smiled at these men who had been prepared to fight Harrison's bullies in her defence. But the blacksmith shook his head reprovingly.

'We want no reward for trying to rescue the young mistress from those blackguards! Any decent Englishman would have done the same!' Minutes later, they had taken the path through the field and into the woods, the shortest cut home for them, while Hawksley gave his horse rein along the easier going of the lane. The horse bore its double load with ease.

The three village men had progressed about a hundred yards and were approaching the woods, when Paul Masters called to his companions to stop. They did so and stared at him inquiringly.

'You two carry on back to the village. I'm going up to the manor house. Want to keep an eye on any unusual goings on there! Perhaps Harrison has it in mind to employ a few good for nothings to attack Lord Hawksley when he arrives there tomorrow—and forewarned is forearmed!'

'Be careful then Paul my friend,' said Appleby. 'I'd come with you, but I must see how my son fares—and Dawlish needs to return to the doctor's house!' But the blacksmith merely grinned and brandished his iron bar, then set off at a swinging stride, as the others raised their hands in farewell.

John Wheatley bent an anxious head over the pale face of the youth whom his elder brother had carried to the doctor's door, with a plea to do what he could for him. He had cleansed and dressed the wound It was a miracle Richard Appleby had survived. The knife had struck perilously close to the heart. For long hours, Wheatley had fought to keep death at bay and now thought he saw slight touch of colour returning to the lad's cheeks. Perhaps the doctor's efforts had helped to distract his fears, as he worried that the worst may have happened to Sophie.

'That should suffice I think, Beth,' he said to Beth Giles who had quietly assisted him in his ministrations. 'He is in the Lord's hands now.'

'See, he is opening his eyes, sir!' Mrs Giles tiredly pushed a strand of hair that had escaped her cap out of her eyes, as she pointed down triumphantly at Richard.

'So he is. Richard—can you hear me?'

'Where—where am I?' the lad glanced about him in confusion. Then memory came rushing back, the sight of a man rushing towards him before he could defend himself, sudden terrible pain, before all had gone blank. He drew a deep breath which caused increased pain in his chest, as his thoughts crystallised He had been supposed to keep watch over Mistress Sophie! Where was she—what had happened?

'Now praise the Lord,' whispered Wheatley. 'How are you feeling, Richard? Nay boy, do not attempt to move!'

'Doctor, how came I here? Where is the young Mistress? If those fiends have hurt her, I'll....!' He attempted to rise, but the doctor firmly pushed his shoulders back on the pillow.

'To move at the present time, may cause the bleeding to start again. You cannot afford to lose any more blood. As for my granddaughter, whom I imagine you were trying to protect, your father and others have gone to her rescue. We can only wait!' The doctor's own face was pale with anguish, as he considered what might have happened to the young girl he loved so deeply.

'Do you know who struck you down, Richard?' asked another voice and Richard turned his head, to see Harry smiling gravely down at him.

'Yes brother—I do! It was Catesby, one of Sir Mark Harrison's men. Mistress Sophie had bid me wait outside the cottage while she went in to speak with old Jessie. The door was wide open, nothing to suggest danger. She went inside. I heard no sound of anything wrong, I swear it. Then suddenly this man was rushing at me before ever I could think of raising my staff. I saw his knife flash in the sunlight—then—well I cannot remember more.' The effort of relating this had caused him to close his eyes in exhaustion and Dr Wheatley signed that Harry should not question him further.

It was then that they heard a heavy, insistent knocking at the door.

'I'll go, sir,' said Beth Giles, suddenly worried that evil news of Mistress Sophie might have arrived and feared the affect it might have on the doctor. As it was, her face broke into a huge smile of relief as she opened the door and saw the doctor's granddaughter standing before her, a man's strong arm clasped about her waist.

'Oh—Miss Sophie, thank God you are safe!' Her eyes sped over the girl's attire, noticed the torn bodice and skirt covered in dust, her hair stuck about with fragments of hay, the tiredness on her face. Then she looked up at the man who was supporting Sophie's drooping figure. A gentleman he looked, fine clothes and a sword, long hair like one of those cavaliers, and suddenly she guessed who this might be. 'My dear, have you found your father?' she blurted.

'She has indeed. I am James Hawksley. May I speak with the doctor? Sophie also needs to lie down, has a badly sprained ankle.' Hearing the authority in the man's voice, Beth hastily stepped aside and let him help Sophie in.

'In here, sir! In the parlour—I'll just call her grandfather! He will be that relieved!' She watched, as with utmost tenderness the man helped the girl onto the couch and placed a cushion beneath her head. Then Beth Giles turned to the door, calling aloud in her excitement as she ran along the passage, almost colliding with Dr Wheatley who had heard the sound of voices. 'Doctor, doctor, come quickly! Sophie's home—safe home!'

'Calm down, Beth!' he said in a voice he tried to keep steady, as he pushed past her into the parlour as he almost gasped with joy as he caught sight of the lovely girl he had feared he might not see again, reclining smiling on the couch.

'Grandfather!' cried Sophie, as she saw him. 'I'm so sorry I went into the forest without Dawlish. I should have heeded your warning!' Her face implored forgiveness.

'Sophie, my darling, you are safe, that is all that matters. Are you hurt, did that swine Harrison.....?' he paused as he noticed there was another in the room. He stared at this stranger in lace cravat and wine coloured velvet, standing negligently close to Sophie. He moved protectively in front of her.

'And who are you, may I ask,' he demanded brusquely. Then as he looked more closely at the man, he knew him, older perhaps, but surely?

'Why—can it be you, James Hawksley? You are come at last!' His face registered both astonishment and delight.

Hawksley gave a bow and came to greet the father of the woman he had married and who had so tragically died in his absence. He glanced down fondly at Sophie as he did so.

'Sophie is unharmed apart from natural shock at the rough handling she received, and has a sprained ankle! And yes, Doctor, I ask your pardon for my tardy appearance.' He held out his hand which John Wheatley took wonderingly, hardly able to believe the Royalist cavalier was actually back. 'It is matter of regret that I have lived abroad for the last many years, totally unaware of my daughter's existence.' He gave the doctor a level stare.

'Perhaps I should have got word to you,' said Wheatley slowly. 'But you must remember that the country was in turmoil then and the easiest solution was to have the child brought up by Lucy's sister Martha, in the neighbouring village! None knew she was Lucy's child—and remember, at that time I was unaware of your marriage!' He knit his thick grey brows together, face troubled. But James Hawksley reached a soothing hand on the other's arm, realising as he did so, just how frail John Wheatley had become.

'I was at fault for not asking your permission before wedding your daughter, sir. But Lucy and I were deeply in love, the ceremony performed by a priest who risked his life in so doing.'

'You gave her the protection of your name—and for that I thank you.' The doctor turned to look down on his grandchild, noticing the disarray of her costume, her smudged face and his lips tightened. 'Would that you had arrived here sooner,' he said. James Hawksley nodded soberly.

'Thank God, that at least I was in good time to save her from the man who dared to kidnap her, with the intent of forcing her into an unwanted marriage! She was running from him along the lane, when I came upon her!'

'You confronted him—the man Harrison?' Wheatley's face broke into a slow smile of satisfaction. It was more than he could have dared to hope for.

'I most surely did. Disarmed him of his sword—his men fled! He is to leave Hawksley Manor by noon tomorrow. The King has graciously restored my sequestered lands and house, all legally approved by parliament, which took time. I will make the old manor into a good home again, where Sophie may spend her time but also accompany me to the court at Westminster!'

'Why, that would be wonderful,' cried Sophie, sitting bolt upright on the cushioned sofa, eyes shining. Then she glanced in dismay at John

Wheatley's face. It was as though his joy at her return had been extinguished like a snuffed candle. 'And of course I will visit you often, dearest grandfather!'

'It's a big enough house. Why not consider making your home there too, doctor?' suggested Hawksley, but he shook his head.

'I have officially retired as a physician, but people still come here in emergency and how can I turn them away---even though my housekeeper defends my privacy like a man at arms! I have a patient here at the moment. Young Richard Appleby, who almost lost his life in Sophie's service!'

'Richard? I had almost forgotten to ask after him! What happened to him, grandfather?' Sophie's face betrayed her worry at the news, as she rose from the couch and leaning on her father's arm followed the doctor through to his study, where the patient raised his head as he saw her.

'I'm that sorry, Mistress Sophie, that I let those men take you, but...' She bent over and kissed him lightly on his forehead.

'Not a word, Richard! You have been gravely wounded in my service, which I shall never forget, nor I am sure will my father, Lord Hawksley,' and she drew back to allow the youth sight of the royalist of whom he had heard much over the years, but never met before.

'I shall see you are well rewarded, Richard. For now know this, that you and your father and others who have assisted in the recovery of my daughter will never be forgotten by me.' And he pressed Richards shoulder gently.

'We should allow him to sleep now,' said Dr Wheatley. 'Come, you must greet my daughter Martha, whom Mrs Giles has gone to fetch her from her room. Soon we will dine, until then, let us take some wine and toast a wonderful reunion, son-in-law!'

Hawksley looked searchingly at Martha. She had changed greatly from the girl he had previously known, this elder sister of his beloved Lucy. Her face still held a certain grace, but thin lines of suffering were apparent, her soft blue eyes betraying nervousness. The doctor had mentioned earlier in few words, that Martha's husband had treated her with cruelty. The man had also mistreated Sophie. One day he should pay for that, thought Hawksley grimly. But for now, he bowed to Martha and kissed her hand.

'I have much to thank you for, lady,' he said. 'Sophie has told me of your kindness and care of her, that she regards you as her mother.'

'It was so that she'd been told I was. It seemed the best way forward, the state of the country so uncertain—and it was Lucy's dying wish that I should look after her baby. I love her as though she were truly my own child, my lord!'

Later over a delicious dinner prepared by an excited Beth Giles, determined to excel herself in the kitchen, Martha relaxed somewhat which pleased her father He worried that she still suffered nightmares wrought of Roger Haversham's previous violence. Now that James Hawksley had returned, perhaps all their lives were to undergo change!

Paul Masters was feeling stiff and more than a little cold, and hungry. He had managed to enter the grounds of manor unseen and positioned himself behind concealment of thick flowering shrubs growing against the west facing wall. From here he could dart back and forth to watch any who came and went from either the imposing main door of the old Tudor building, or from the back door used by the servants.

The first to leave in the late afternoon was a black gowned clergyman, with a sour expression. Not a local preacher, mused Masters, studying his face. He watched as a stable lad brought the man's mule and assisted him to mount, skinny legs appearing like two sticks under his flapping black gown as he rode disconsolately away, for he had arrived there to conduct a wedding service, the ceremony cancelled as was his officiating fee.

Then suddenly the place became a hive of activity, wagons drawn up before the house and to be loaded with an assortment of the departing residents possessions. There was laughing and some cursing, as men bruised arms and legs in manhandling furniture and wooden crates. Then the wagons were driven away along the lane leading to the main road.

For a further hour, nothing happened of note, then a crowd of Harrison's employees poured out of the back door, some going across to the stables and mounting and riding away ahead of those workmen whose own sturdy limbs would take them into the village and beyond.

It was night now and Harrison still within. Above, the stars were a glittering cape of light against the night sky. Paul Masters altered his position to ease his aching limbs. Then some instinct made him slide quietly round to the front of the house and he blinked as he saw the brilliant light from the windows of the dining hall. This was no normal illumination of lamp and candlelight—but leaping flames! As he stared in stupefaction, the door swung open and Harrison rushed out and running to the stables, untied his stallion waiting there saddled and ready for his swift departure.

Masters stared. Should he confront Harrison—tell him that he was witness of what was undoubtedly arson? Better rather to see what could be done to douse the flames. If only he had others to help him! Harrison galloped past him, not noticing in the darkness the smith who was hurrying towards the still open door.

Inside the thick acrid smoke attacked his throat, as he hurried into the large, high vaulted the dining hall. The source of the flames was immediately apparent a bale of straw, some books and beautifully carved dining chairs, the flames reaching outwards and upwards. Tying his neckerchief over his nose and mouth, Paul Masters rushed to the undrawn, heavy, velvet curtains at the windows and ripped them down and attempted to beat out the conflagration. Again and again his arms flailed, until the flames were all but extinguished. Then as he paused for painful breath, he heard a crashing sound from the room above.

He ran upstairs in great leaping bounds. A bedroom door was open, inside the curtains of the four poster bed wreathed wildly on fire causing the frame to collapse, pillows and bed covers now a seething mass of flames! He looked desperately around—saw the jug and basin of water on a marble topped table and threw the contents onto the flames, before ripping down the window curtains and beating at the flames as he had in the fire below in the hall.

'Sir—sir, can I help you?' Masters turned at the sound of the young voice and saw a young lad in the still leaping fire light. 'I saw the flames from the window, came in to see if anyone was still within!' He thought recognised the stable lad, had spoken with him on previous occasions when the boy brought Harrison's horses to be shoed.

'Ben—is that you?'

'Yes, sir, they've all gone—left me here alone!'

'Help me to beat out these flames—but mind you don't burn yourself boy!' He tossed a curtain to Ben, who set to with darting enthusiasm. At last the flames were out, just a smouldering, smoking, stinking wreckage remaining in the middle of the room.

'Well done, lad. Now we must check all other rooms to ensure Harrison has not done further mischief!' Together the boy and weary, smoke blackened man hurried from room to room, but saw no further trace of fire. But much had been vandalised and Paul Masters shook his head appalled.

'Lord Hawksley will be much aggrieved to see what destruction has been wrought on his home! Now look Ben lad, will you be afeared to run down to the village in the dark? We have to get word to His Lordship of what has happened here.'

'There is a lantern kept in the shed by the stables. I'll take that. I will go as fast as I can sir!' And the youngster stared at him from red rimmed eyes. 'I can hardly believe that a gentleman like Sir Mark Harrison would have behaved like this!' Masters clamped a hand on his shoulders.

'Once this is all over, Ben, I've no doubt you will be needing a new job. I could do with a steady youngster to train up at the smithy. But go now, and make haste!'

Daniel Dawson was finding sleep difficult. The blow Hawksley had dealt him had left him with a headache. He left his sleeping quarters above the doctor's stables and went outside to see if the cool night air would bring relief. As he stared around him, his eyes swept up to the large house on the hill, the windows of Hawksley Manor were bright orange in the dark night. Someone was up late there, but hold, this was not normal light—but fire!' Across the courtyard dividing stables from the house he sped and thundered on the doctor's door.

'Wake up in there! Fire! There's a fire at the Manor!' he shouted. John Wheatley opened his window and peered down.

'Is that you, Dawson?' he called, indignant at having his sleep disturbed.

'The manor be on fire, sir! We'll need to get help up there! I'll go along and wake the fire officers,' and he hurried off. Fire in the Manor, the doctor stared up at the distant building crowning the hill, and he saw that leaping, unnatural orange light. He must wake Hawksley, but as he turned saw his son-in-law at his side.

'My house—I must go there at once! That fiend Harrison, this is surely his work!' There was anguish on his face. His beloved home yearned for over the many years and now at last his once more, was all to be destroyed?

A horse drawn fire carriage with pump and hose accompanied by many men from the village proceeded swiftly up the lane towards the manor, but in front of them went a man hastily dressed in shirt and breeches, long hair flying behind him as he rode. Hawksley drew in his reins as he saw a dancing light, a boy running desperately towards him, clutching a lantern.

Hawksley dismounted and caught the lad to him, saw the smoke blackened face, read the trauma in those scared, reddened eyes.

'The blacksmith sent me for help, sir! The manor was afire—but we put out the flames! There is much damage, but...' and he clutched onto the stranger in delayed shock.

'Steady, boy—steady! Come now, up on the horse behind me. I go to see what has become of my house!'

The last of the glowing embers had succumbed to the efforts of the firemen, but they had to admit that their work had been almost completed by the man who now sat exhausted on the steps outside the house, slowly breathing clean air into smoke inflamed lungs.

'Paul Masters—I have much to thank you for!' exclaimed a voice above him, as he glanced up to see the handsome face of Lord James Hawksley smiling down at him. 'I know what you have done for me, at risk of your life! Are you much burned, friend?'

Masters shook his head. He looked up gravely at the man bending solicitously over him. 'Some burns to my hands, and my lungs be sore, my Lord. But I'm well used to working with fire in my work as smith. It is a good servant but a bad master!'

'How did you come to be here—I thought I saw you leave earlier with Dawson and Appleby for the village?' Hawksley asked curiously.

'I told them I would return and keep an eye on the house. I thought Harrison might have some mischief planned for the morrow. There were wagons loaded up, and I saw many of his men leaving as the evening passed. It became quiet and I risked walking round to the front of the house. I saw flames at the window! I realised the place was afire—and saw Harrison come running out and off on his horse like the wind!' It hurt to speak and he put his hand to his mouth protectively.

'So—definitely arson!' breathed Hawksley. 'I suspected as much, damn him to hell!'

'The stable-boy Ben, he helped me when I was fighting the flames in the bedroom. He's a good lad, my Lord!' Then he shook his head and motioned to his chest. 'I cannot speak more!'

'We must get Dr Wheatley to look at you, Masters.' He called to the firemen who satisfied that no spark remained to reignite the fires, were preparing to leave.' 'Take this man with you. The doctor must examine him. Be careful with him, for he saved my house this night!'

Then James Hawksley mounted the stairs once more and stood staring down at the blackened wreckage of what had once been his marriage bed. It was obvious to him why Harrison had chosen this room in revenge for Lucy's rejection of him long years ago. How great must be the man's hatred of him, that he had behaved so—first causing the kidnap of his daughter Sophie, the plot to force her into unwanted marriage, and now the attempted destruction of his house! Well surely the worst was over now. A bright future beckoning ahead nor did he guess what fresh dangers would beset him.

Chapter Five

The following day officers of the law were sent in search of Sir Mark Harrison on charges of kidnap and arson. It had been thought the man might have returned to his original home, a long sprawling building set amongst rich farmland, some ten miles west of the village. Here he had lived before Cromwell had rewarded his efforts for the Commonwealth, both in raising his men against the royalists and in battle, by awarding him the manor and lands of Lord James Hawksley, whose military exploits were legendary and who had successfully evaded capture on many occasions.

But there was no sign of Harrison in his earlier home. But according to the couple who now lived there and farmed the land and sending Harrison almost extortionate rents, he had called there in the early hours in a violent temper. He had been seen digging in the garden, had retrieved a metal bound box and ridden away! In spite of the officers' threats, the couple seemed unable to furnish any idea of where their master had gone. So the officers rode disconsolately for home. It would have delighted them to have arrested Harrison, whose officious behaviour had made him abhorred by most in the village.

Today Sophie rode beside her father, as they took the path through the woods. She loved the pony he had bought her and had taken to riding with ease and enthusiasm. But today's outing was one that filled her with some concern and foreboding. They were to visit the late Jessie Thorne's cottage. Leaves were beginning to change to autumn's early gold and the September sun made a pool of light as they left the mystery of the forest and came into the clearing. She pointed to the cottage where old Jessie had lived.

'That was Jessie's home, father! I shall never be able to get the terrible picture out of my mind, seeing her lying there in her blood, throat cut!' They dismounted and stood staring at the cottage. 'Can you just imagine, I went in there to speak to her—found her dead on the floor, and then to my horror those men threw a sack over my head.' She had already admitted to having nightmares over the happening, which was why Hawksley had insisted on their coming here today. It was important that she revisit the scene, to be able to let it go.

'Come,' he said and lent her his hand. She hesitated. Then taking a deep breath followed him inside. She glanced down apprehensively at the wooden floor. Nothing remained of the blood. Someone had scrubbed it clean. Jessie's belongings remained in their usual place—the bundles of herbs hanging drying in a corner, jars of powders, bottles of physic—and books. Sophie had never really thought about the strangeness of finding books in the house of a woman thought by many to be illiterate, and by others to have been a witch.

Hawksley opened a drawer in the old woman's work table. It held a folder of papers, some yellowed by time, contents handwritten in almost copperplate writing.

'Look at this, Sophie! Here are details of plants, leaves, roots, bark and berries and other strange ingredients, even urine, to be used as cure for many diseases! See—the exact dosage given, how extraordinary!' He shook his head. 'You say your grandfather used to visit with Jessie and that she supplied him with items for his own use as physician?'

'I heard him speak with her of foxglove leaves—a cure for heart disease, but to be used with extreme caution! He knew that Jessie was no witch, but a wise woman who had studied ancient wisdom passed down in her family.'

'Why, look here, Sophie! There is a document marked WILL! He broke the wax seal and stared at the document in surprise.

'What does it say,' she asked curiously, realising as she did so, that her memory of the hideous events in the cottage, had been strangely assuaged from her mind.

'You will hardly believe this, child. She bequeaths all that she owns to you—this cottage, and in particular her medicines and notes made over the years. See, she says here that she senses in you the wisdom and courage to use this knowledge when the time comes!' Sophie took the will from his hands scanning it herself in utter bewilderment.

'But—why to me? I hardly knew her!' she stared at him in bewilderment. 'It's true that grandfather has been instructing me in medical matters, but she couldn't have known that. As it happens had I been a man instead of a girl, I would have loved to become a doctor. Surely there is no greater path for an individual to take, than to bring care and healing to their fellow human beings!' She blurted this out, revealing to him for the first time her secret ambition. Hawksley looked at her in astonishment.

'But Sophie—it is thing unheard of for a woman to become a physician! For one thing, no college of medicine would be prepared to open their doors to a woman!' He sat on the edge of Jessie's table, swinging his booted leg as he spoke, his glance serious. 'A woman may become a midwife and yes, it is acceptable a wife may treat the simple ailments of her household, but to become a doctor? No, it's quite impossible!'

'There has to be a first time in all things!' she replied firmly.

'Maybe in years to come it may be acceptable. Who knows! But at the present time even to attempt such daring innovation would bring opprobrium on your head and irretrievably damage your reputation.'

'But why, father?' Her blue eyes scanned his face in outrage.

'Well—one bone of contention might be that a woman would be called to look upon the naked form of a male patient!' He retrained a smile as he put this forward.

'And does not a male physician look upon a woman in like state, when a state of sickness requires it?' she riposted.

'But the man in such position is an accredited doctor, the situation I suppose one that has prevailed throughout all ages!' He rose to his feet. 'Look you Sophie child, to show interest in a few herbs that may possibly help to reduce fever, well that is one thing. And even in this you would have to show care that none miscall you a witch, even as Jessie was.'

'I suppose you are right, father. But in the meanwhile, I shall learn all that I may of means of bringing relief of sickness and suffering.' She lifted up the thick wad of hand written papers bequeathed to her by Jessie and glancing around saw a bag hanging from a nail on the door. This she took and started to fill it with those precious notes and books which she intended to study in the privacy of her room. She decided she would return here at a later time to bring Jessie's remedies back to her grandfather's house, all those jars of ointment, powders and potions. No need to speak of this now to her father, who looked impatient to be away from the cottage.

They remounted their horses.

'Poor Jessie, I will never forget her!' murmured Sophie, as she took her reins. Hawksley merely glanced at her impatiently.

'Come, let us speak of happier subjects, and I must get you home to your grandfather.' He mounted in his turn.

'When shall I come to live with you, father?' she asked wistfully

'Soon I hope! At a time when I have prepared a special room for you, my darling girl. Then I will bring you to live with me as we planned. There is still a smell of smoke lingering about the place, even after all has been scrubbed and windows thrown open for weeks. I want to get the hall and the upper room repainted. The trouble is that although I now have my home and lands once more in my possession, I lack the money to proceed with any haste.' It was the first time that he had mentioned the question of money to Sophie and she looked across at him in surprise!

'But surely the King will have rewarded you for your devotion to his cause?' she asked.

'Charles would have done so gladly—but strange though it may seem, he is strapped for cash himself! True parliament has awarded him a goodly sum, but not nearly the amount he really needs to pay for the state in which he is expected to live! The vast number of servants of all degrees he employs, the trappings of royalty, all this costs an inordinate amount of money, Sophie!' He sighed, and urged his horse forward.

'I may be able to help a little, father?' He turned his head and looked back at her where she sat her pony, blue eyes smiling.

'What mean you?'

'Why, that mother left a bag of gold to me. My Aunt Martha had kept it safe from her husband's eyes, in a secret place in a wardrobe, together with my mother's letter and the locket I wear about my neck!'

He looked at her in astonishment. Then he remembered the sum he had left with Lucy on that last poignant night they had been together, telling her to use what she needed of it and to keep the rest safe for his return. Neither of them had thought it would be their last meeting in this world, that she would bear him a child and not live to see her baby grow into the lovely girl who now rode at his side.

'My darling, if Lucy left that gold to you, then you must keep it as your dowry for a future marriage!' he said quietly.

'But I do not want to marry! I will not be instructed what to do by a husband,' she said firmly. 'As for the gold, I will show you how much I have, and some of it at least will be used to refurbish our home!' Then the subject closed as far as she was concerned, she tugged at her reins and let the pony have his head and laughing he followed her.

There was still no sign of Sir Mark Harrison although still diligently sought. The man had disappeared as though the earth had swallowed him up. His former servants had also dispersed apart from the stable lad Ben, who had accepted the blacksmith's offer of work at the smithy. The three men involved in the murder of Jessie Thorne and Sophie's kidnap had also fled the area. There was a warrant out for their arrest and a reward should any come across them.

Lord Hawksley had found quite a few of the villagers willing to help him put the manor house back in order, despite suspicion that he was a Catholic. He paid them with a little of the money Sophie insisted he use and which he was determined he would replace one day. So now with the house scrubbed, inner walls repainted, fine paintings hidden away for safety during the civil war in a secret chamber—the priest's hole, now back once more in their accustomed place, as woodwork was waxed and silver polished, his books such as remained of the once fine library after Harrisons depredations, tidied on their shelves, the house was at last ready for his daughter Sophie, as was the garden. October was cold but dry and bright that year, allowing work to take place in attempt to restore the grounds to their former glory. But it would take at least a year or two to make good the unkempt flower beds and once fine lawns. At least a good start had been made.

Hawksley had found his father's carriage in the stables, but badly damaged, paintwork peeling. It was Dawson who lovingly made it fit to be used once more, and so it was that Sophie, accompanied by Martha and John Wheatley, took their places in the carriage, on the long awaited trip to Hawksley Manor, so soon to be Sophie's new home. If she froze slightly as the massive house came into view, she quickly disposed of the slight fear it engendered with memories of her incarceration there, by Harrison in his attempt at a forced marriage.

It looked different she thought as the carriage rolled to a halt outside the steps leading to the massive oak door, now open wide as a smiling James Hawksley prepared to welcome this girl so like to her mother to the home she should have grown up in.

'Why father—all looks absolutely beautiful,' she breathed, as he led them from the hall which has so nearly succumbed to the flames, to all other rooms downstairs and the up to the bedrooms. Some of the bedrooms were empty of furniture still. Hawksley had ordered all bedding used by the former occupants destroyed and replaced as soon as this was possible. At last he opened the room that was to be Sophie's and stood back glancing at her face to judge her reaction.

'This is for me? Oh father, thank you! Those wine velvet curtains, quilted bedcover—all as I would have chosen myself.' she breathed, tears spilling into her eyes as she stared up at a portrait of her mother, surely the one her grandfather had treasured and had given it to her father to hang here. Martha and the doctor crowded in behind her and exchanged smiles at her enthusiasm, for indeed her long lost father had prepared all so very perfectly for Sophie. The work in the house and grounds and this chamber, all must have taken much time and effort and explained why it had taken him so long to invite them here.

'It pleases you then Sophie? Then all has been worthwhile!'

'Oh, it's wonderful, father! But you should have let me help you,' she reproved gently.

'I wanted to. But I thought it better that I remove all traces of Harrison from the place, before you made it your home.' He turned to John Wheatley. 'My offer to you still stands, doctor—that you should make your home here and Martha too!' But the old doctor shook his head.

'The offer is extremely tempting, but the answer remains the same. My own house retains special memories, which mean a lot when you reach my age, James. But I shall enjoy visiting you on frequent occasions and I've no doubt that Sophie will be very happy here!'

It was two days later and John Wheatley's eyes were sad, as he watched the last of his grand-daughter's possessions being stowed in the carriage which now bore its former red and gold and black crest of a swooping hawk on its doors. Although he would have many opportunities of seeing her in the future, he would miss their meals together, their talks in his study, as he gradually imparted precious medical knowledge that it had taken so many years for him to accumulate, as together they examined anatomy charts, or studied books on the healing properties of plants, the correct dosages of infusions for child or adult.

He forced a smile onto his face as he embraced her and watched as she mounted her pony and sped ahead of the carriage, turning once to wave to him and to Martha, who had tears in her eyes. What lay ahead for Sophie, he wondered? But at least he had the companionship of his daughter. He took Martha's hand.

'Like a bird loosed from a cage, she needs freedom to soar,' he said. 'James Hawksley will have a good care of her!' He gave a sudden shiver. 'There is a chill in the wind,' he said. 'Let us go inside, Martha dear.'

The first week in the manor was full of interest and excitement to Sophie as she explored the many rooms and passage-ways, staring at the portraits of her ancestors frowning down in the great hall. But in especial she took great joy in the company of her handsome father, noting that when not in animated conversation, his dark eyes held a deep sadness. She pressed him now for further details of the mother she never knew.

'What was she really like, my mother Lucy?' she asked, as she lovingly handled the old, leather bound books in the library. James Hawksley turned from the volume in his hands to glance whimsically at his daughter.

'Why Sophie—just look into your mirror and see the answer there! You are her exact image, same deep blue eyes, chestnut hair and even to the dimpled chin. Wearing those gowns of hers you seem her double!'

'That makes me happy,' she cried.

Yet there was a difference, he mused for he had sensed in Sophie strength of purpose to match his own. True Lucy had possessed a bright courage, whilst always displaying a yielding tenderness towards him. But she would never have held to unswerving purpose to study medicine as did their extraordinary daughter! Even now she was holding an ancient Greek treatise in Latin translation. It had belonged to his grandfather, Anthony Hawksley who had been reputed to have a great interest in medical matters, the book a gift from a physician who had treated James 1st. It must be from his grandsire that Lucy had inherited her own passion for matters unseemly in a woman and he smiled at the thought.

'Do we truly go soon to the Court, father?'

'The Court—why yes, child!' the question jerked him out of his reverie.

'Then these gowns of mothers—are they still fashionable for such a visit?' she queried.

She glanced down at the faded blue velvet skirt she wore. Why the thought had occurred to her she was not sure, for Sophie who had led all but the last few months of her life most plainly dressed and had accepted the fact as normal. It had been the fashion before the King's return for all women to dress simply in dark colours, with white collars, hair drawn modestly back under caps. Lord Protector Cromwell's England had carried a puritanical stamp, which extended to the whole of society. Pleasure was thought to be of the devil, men and women expected to be of a sober appearance and church attendance strictly observed.

'My darling, you shall have two new gowns before being presented to his Majesty that I promise!' He smiled. It was good to see her mind set on normal feminine affairs, he thought. 'We will have them made up in London. Here in the village I doubt if any would have the expertise.'

'But do we have enough money for new clothes? She looked at him in sudden dismay, suddenly remembering that her father was far from rich, for it was the gold entrusted to her mother and carefully guarded for Sophie by Martha that had provided the means to bring the old Elizabethan manor house back to some slight semblance of its former dignity.

'Most people supply their wants on credit, Sophie!'

'But is that fair to the trades people?'

'Probably not—but it is the way of the world. But if it makes you happier, we will pay our way in town.' He glanced at her with amusement. 'You really do care about others, don't you, sweetheart?'

'What was it like—spending all those long years in exile on the continent?'

'Grim is the correct answer to that question!' He paused and cast back into recent memory. 'There were quite a few of us, Royalists that is over there, moving from one country to another with Charles, often hungry, clothes in sad disrepair, but always hopeful that one day he would receive help from France or Spain or Belgium—or German Princelings to enable him to win back his father's crown.'

'But what relief you did not have to face another battle for his restoration, the enormity of fresh civil war!' She had put her book down and studied her father's face curiously, reflecting how different their present situation might have been, had the King tried to regain his throne by force.

'No Sophie. I believe it was God's hand that prompted General Monk to insist that England was best ruled by a monarch! So many hopes had been dashed in the past, but Charles never gave up the intent of regaining the throne. He has a wonderful courage, Sophie, even went hungry like the rest of us at times. But now he is back where he should be and hopefully this land may never again become a republic.'

'What about those cruel men who sentenced his father to death! It seems to me that it was an unspeakable crime—to behead a king!' She stared at him. 'Will they be arrested, dealt with?'

'Of that I have no doubt. But the King seeks no vengeance on other citizens apart from the regicides. It is his contention that men need to live tolerantly of each other now, for the good of the country.'

'But what of other Royalists like you father, who were despoiled of their estates by Cromwell and the Commonwealth? '

'Sadly only a few of them will be reinstated in their former lands and homes. I was most fortunate that in my case the King showed a particular gratitude for my services to him and applied to parliament to restore my manor and lands. He would I am sure prefer to act with equal kindness to all others who gave up so much for his cause and shared his exile. But the treaty he signed at Breda constrains his good intentions.'

'So you don't think we will ever suffer civil war in this country again father?' she probed anxiously. He shook his head as he crossed to the huge fireplace and threw another two logs upon the fire. November had brought cold and heavy mist and the blazing log fires did little to heat the high ceilinged rooms in the manor house. She joined Hawksley in front of the fire, spreading her hands out to its welcome warmth, as they stared down into its dancing, fiery depths.

'No man can answer that for certain, Sophie, but my feeling is that the people crave for peace and a relaxation of the harsh laws introduced by Cromwell. Did you know that he was offered the crown? That he almost accepted it! King Oliver—it sounds laughable now, but it could have happened!' He snorted his contempt.

'They say he was a most religious man, all that he did was according to his knowledge of the Bible.' She was frowning as she puzzled over this conundrum.

'In the Bible, Jesus told us to love one another—to forgive our enemies! What Cromwell ordered done in Ireland and elsewhere will be a stain on our history for generations to come.' He shook his head. 'I believe it possible that Cromwell was originally a good living country gentleman. But power corrupts, child. Men seek to justify their deeds by quoting only those words from the Bible that condones their own practices.'

Sophie stretched out her hand and slipped it into his. There was another question to which she required an answer and did not want to cause offence by asking it.

'Father, you are a Catholic are you not,' she began. He bowed his head in assent.

'My family have always been so.'

'What will happen now? The Catholic religion is banned in this country is it not? Priests arrested if discovered and thrown into prison—the Mass forbidden by law.'

'Sophie, I know that the King would prefer that all men should have freedom of worship! But those around him will not allow him to have his way in this. Charles himself conforms to the Anglican Church like his late father, yet it is thought that he has a kindness for Catholics for his mother's sake. Whether he has any deep beliefs of his own, I am not sure, for in some ways he is a very private person.'

'Then how will you manage to practice your Catholic faith, father?' the question had been nagging at the back of her mind ever since she came to the manor. She was fearful that having found her father, she might perhaps lose him again over the vexed problem of religion. He did not give a direct answer at first, but then withdrew a small silver crucifix from under his shirt and lifting it to his lips, kissed it.

'Sophie, I may not be able to practice my faith openly. Perhaps I may even have to attend the Episcopal Church on occasion to conform to England's unfair laws. No doubt I will have to confess this to whatsoever brave priest may visit this house in the future!' He pulled at her hand. 'Come with me, Sophie. There is a place I must show you, a secret place!'

'A secret place—but where?' she asked in surprise. He took her hand and led her across the far corner of the room.

'Here in this very library. See you this last section of books in the Latin?'

'Yes.'

'The forth shelf down—put your hand along the panelled wood wall beside it.'

'But there is nothing there!'

'Not to the careless eye. But look more carefully, Sophie. See that small carving of a hawk—put your hand upon it, turn and push!' He watched with a smile as she obeyed. He saw her gasp as a panel of the apparently solid wall gave way, revealing a dark, unlit space, where stairs led downwards. She turned her face back to him.

'What is this used for, father?'

'It leads down to a small chamber where any in danger may hide. Wait while I get a lamp and we will go down.' First of all, he turned the key in the library door, so that none might disturb them unawares.

'Now Sophie, I will go before you.'

'It smells damp—and there are cobwebs!' But she followed him down the steep stairs trustingly. He held the lamp high illuminating the small chamber they now entered. There was a simple table altar above which hung a plain wooden cross. It was obviously a tiny chapel. Her eyes travelled on and saw a low couch against the wall and a locker.

'It was here that your mother and I were wed by a courageous old priest known as Father Anselm.'

'Oh father! What a strange place for a wedding!'

'But safe from prying eyes. It has been used for generations by those visiting priests who risk death or imprisonment at all times if discovered. The man Harrison never learned this secret. It is known to none but family and a few trustworthy friends. I require your word Sophie, that you will never disclose knowledge of the place to anyone.' His voice was unaccustomedly stern.

'You have my word, father!' Then as she watched fascinated, he genuflected before the simple altar with its dusty embroidered, once white covering and made the sign of the cross. He remained some few minutes on his knees, then rose with a quick smile and took her hand.

'Let us go up again. But always remember this place, should you personally ever need refuge!' He smiled. 'Hopefully such a day will never dawn.' She followed him back up to the top of the musty stairs. 'See this small wheel upon the inside of the door?' he said. When you wish to find your way back into the library, you turn it so. The Hawk opens it from the library—the wheel opens or closes it from this side of the secret place.' She tried the mechanism for herself—stiff but it worked.

'None would ever suspect that little chamber to exist!' They closed the door behind them and Sophie shook the dust and spider webs from the bottom of her gown, resolving that one day she would sweep and clean Hawksley Manor's secret chamber.

'You do know that I am not a Catholic,' she queried? 'I was brought up strictly attending a non conformist church with Martha, who had to obey her husband's wishes in this as in all else. Roger Haversham attended only as a matter of form. No true Christian could have behaved with such cruelty shown to Martha—and to me! Now I feel at home in grandfather's Anglican Church. It was banned under Cromwell, symbol of a simple cross and candles called idolatry.'

As he listened to her words, James Hawksley felt sudden wave of anger sweep over him, as he considered how the lovely young girl had been treated by a man with whom he would one day settle a score!

'You have never spoken much of your life with Haversham and Martha. Tell me of it now,' he probed gently. He held a chair out for her, by the wide, open fireplace and sat facing her. At first she said nothing, wondering if it were better to leave such events in the past. But then as she thought of that cane raised cruelly over her shoulders, as he beat her, as he had on numerous occasions, sometimes catching her by the hair and twisting her neck so that she feared it would snap.

Her words came out jerkily, blue eyes damp with tears, as the full revelation of her previous life became known to the father, who now rose and took her into his arms.

'Hush now, child! You are safe from that brute. None shall ever hurt you under my care!' She forced a smile and dashed the tears of emotion from her eyes with the back of her hand.

'He almost killed Mama. I still call Martha by this name, for she is the only mother I have ever known. He attacked her after she helped me to escape! His cook Bessie came to grandfather's house to ask his help, as she feared her mistress might die!' She told him more and watched his lip become a grim line.

'He deserves to be horsewhipped—hung on a gibbet in front of his own inn!' he muttered, clenching his teeth.

'He pretends to a piety that is a sham. Tried to force me into marriage with a local minister whose previous wife died of repeated child bearing. It was when I flatly refused to comply that he began to beat me. Somehow I had the strength to tear that cane from his hand and break it. He gave a roar, leapt on me and held me by the throat. I was choking. I couldn't breathe. I thought he would kill me, so I brought my knee up into his groin!'

'Well done—go on, child!' he breathed, dark eyes anguished at what he heard.

'Mama came into the room, saw what was happening. Her face was horrified! He was holding himself in pain and ran out to get a constable to arrest me for assault.' Sophie's cheeks flushed as she remembered her last sight of Haversham storming towards the door. 'Mama the mother I knew helped me to pack a few clothes—then gave me the packet left to me by the mother I never knew and that bag of gold. She revealed the fact that I was not Haversham's child, nor her own. That she was my aunt. She told me to take the path through the fields to the next village, this one, where her father, Physician Wheatley lived.'

'So that was the kind of household in which you were raised. If only I had known of your existence Sophie, I would have risked arrest, come back to England to get you. Yet how would I have brought up a child, wandering penniless as I was around the courts of Europe!'

Father, there would have been nothing either of us could have done at that time. Now, with the King come back into his own, life will be good!'

'Most certainly it will,' he replied and lifted her hand tenderly to his lips.

James Hawksley began to employ a few men from the village. Some still heavily influenced by the extreme views and laws of the Commonwealth and Cromwell, were at first reluctant to take employment with a papist. But the Hawksley family had been lords of the manor for many centuries, had a reputation for being good to tenants and workers alike. It was yeoman farmer Thomas Appleby's agreement to accept the position of farm manager, leaving his own small farm in the capable hands of his elder son Harry that helped others to make decision to work for Lord James Hawksley.

Now he engaged a shepherd for the small flock of sheep and men skilled in hedging and ditching, two ploughmen for under Harrison's stewardship the land had remained untended, and a housekeeper, maid and a cook. He worried about payment of wages for his new staff. Sophie's small supply of gold was rapidly decreasing, yet it was only by making the farmland productive that would ensure future prosperity. He made a quick visit to the secret place. There in an alcove in the wall, there was a loose stone. He eased it up, revealing a small cavity. He felt inside with his hand and withdrew a velvet pouch.

In the library once more, seated before the fire, he opened the pouch and poured its contents onto his lap. The emerald pendant in its simple gold setting glowed with mysterious green fire. There were other jewels too of lesser value—and another object which he stared at considerately. It was an intricately carved golden pomander! It had been received as a gift by his ancestress Lady Jane Hawksley from Henry Tudor's first wife, Spanish Princess Catherine of Aragon. Like the family jewels, it appeared in several of the paintings adorning the walls. It was a heritage passed down to successive generations.

'I'm glad I had the foresight to hide these treasures,' he muttered. 'I think the present dire financial situation calls for some at least to be sold that the house and estate be improved. He raised his head as the library door opened and Sophie stood there smiling across at him.

'I was looking for you, father, I thought we might go riding! It's a beautiful day, despite the frost!' She walked across to him and stared wonderingly at the glittering heap on his lap. 'Where did this come from?'

'These are the family jewels worn by successive Hawksley women since the last century. I hid them when the Roundheads were advancing on the manor. Now I think the time is ripe to turn some of these baubles into gold!' He smiled at her astonishment. 'I suppose I should allow you to wear them though,' he said uncomfortably. But she merely laughed.

'Father, our few gold coins are disappearing fast. The jewels are beautiful, especially that emerald! However, I cannot see myself wearing such things—too fine for me! But may I look at that golden pomander?' He handed it to her and she walked over to the window to examine it more closely.

'It's exquisite!'

'You have good taste. It was the gift of a queen.' he said quietly, coming to stand beside her. 'The enamel work is particularly fine. I had meant that your mother should have it. You may keep it, Sophie. I ask only that one day you pass it on to your own daughter, should you have one!'

She stared at him dumbfounded then attempted to hand it back to him, but he withdrew his hand and the pomander fell to the floor. The jolt released an unseen spring in the golden sphere and one of the tiny chambers designed to hold the usual spices to ward of sickness, flew open. Hawksley gave an exclamation of surprise and bent to pick it up, fearing that it had suffered damage.

'I'm sorry! Oh, I'm sorry! It was so clumsy of me, father! Is it broken?'

'No—but look, Sophie, this small compartment has opened. I will try to close it.'

'Something fell out of it, see father, sparkling down there on the floor!' Sophie bent and retrieved the tiny object, wrought of a flawless diamond set in gold.' She handed it to him. 'What is it?'

'Why, it's meant to represent a pomegranate, which was part of the royal crest of Spain!' He shook his head in wonder. 'I had no idea this even existed! See, it has the Queen's initial carved into it, which I imagine must make it quite valuable.' He was about to hand it back to Sophie.

'No! I will keep the pomander, but this beautiful little jewel may sell for enough money to help at a time when we need funds!' He nodded thoughtfully and came to a decision.

'Sophie, I suggest then that we ride into London and sell some of these jewels and the pomegranate. We will celebrate Christmas there. You shall have your new gowns and be presented at Court! Will that please you, daughter?'

She threw herself into his arms, for the notion pleased Sophie very much indeed!

The next day the Hawksley carriage stopped outside John Wheatley's house where an excited Sophie told her grandfather that she would not be able to spend Christmas with him, was going to London with her father and would bring back gifts for Martha and for him. They had left the manor in the capable hands of Thomas Appleby.

'Take great care in the city. Not a healthy place,' he advised in concern.

'Father will have a care of me, never fear!' The doctor looked across at James Hawksley's smiling face and nodded satisfied—but as the carriage drove off, he experienced a sense of unease. He turned to Martha whose eyes were damp on seeing the girl she looked on as a daughter disappearing on the long road to London.

A few days later Sophie was standing impatiently in the centre of one of the two small rooms they had rented in a property close to Whitehall, as the dressmaker her father had engaged, chatted about people whose names meant nothing to the girl while she busily pinned the expensive fabric about the girl's slim figure. Sophie sighed as the woman decided to re-pin the skirt and stared broodingly around at the room's old and very basic furniture and the dingy windows curtained in moth eaten brown curtains, for like many other impecunious returning royalists, James Hawksley had chosen the cheapest lodgings within easy access of the palace.

'When will the gowns be finished, Mistress Fox?' she asked plaintively as the woman gathered up materials, carefully folding them and placing them in her voluminous bag together with measure, scissors and pins.

'Why lady, if I work hard, then in a week's time. Don't forget there are also your new shifts, bodices and blouses, the velvet mantle and.......'

Sophie cut off the list before the woman could proceed further. 'Perhaps if you work especially hard, dear mistress, then my new clothes may be ready in two days time? I have urgent need of them! You will be well paid!' The dressmaker smiled and nodded. Perhaps this youthful client had more money than was suggested by her present poor apparel. Certainly she was startlingly beautiful and should do well at court.

'I will do my best for you. Do not forget that you will also need to purchase silk stockings, shoes and gloves to complete your wardrobe!'

Sophie breathed a sigh of relief as the woman took her departure. She opened the stiff casement and stared down into the street below, and as she did so, unpleasant smells from the open sewer into which all manner of refuse was thrown, assaulted her nostrils as the vociferous cries of street vendors filled the air spiced with curses, when a carriage clattered over the cobbles too close to their stalls. So many people hurrying along the pavement! She made out a chimney sweep with brushes held high, two gaudily dressed girls in their early teens flaunting their half exposed breasts to gentlemen sauntering on their way to the nearest coffee house, a sailor man with a monkey grimacing on his shoulder and so the flow of people continued in never ceasing stream.

Did she really like this city, with its noise and smells and tension experienced as soon as one left the security of these rooms? But once they were suitably apparelled, then she would then be able to accompany her father to Whitehall and actually see the king! Surely his palace must smell sweeter than this narrow street, where wooden houses leaned towards each other and in early mornings housewives tipped the contents of their night jars out of the windows with a warning cry to passers-by.

She sighed and closed the casement.

'Sophie—Sophie?' her father came into the room. 'How did your dressmaker get on? It is to be hoped that she will work speedily, for I am anxious to arrive soon at court!' He smiled at her and Sophie regarded him thoughtfully. In some way which she could not fathom, he seemed changed from the quietly assured figure which had given orders and made plans for the restoration of Hawksley Manor. Now he seemed full of a feverish excitement, an impatience to be part of the great beating heart of London.

'She will have all ready in two days time, but I had to promise to pay her well! I hope we will be able to manage her bill?' She looked at her father anxiously, but he merely smiled and walking over to the room's rickety table, poured a mass of gold coins from a bulging purse. She gasped in surprise and ran her fingers exploringly over this newly acquired wealth.

'How on earth—you sold the jewels then father?'

'Some of them only, I am not convinced that I received a fair price, yet must not grumble. I have retained one of the finer pieces—and the diamond pomegranate!' He sighed. 'I wish that I was able to present you with the pomegranate as a gift my darling, but we must be practical. I have a royal purchaser in mind for Queen Catherine's pomegranate!' And they both knew he referred to the King.

Chapter Six

Sophie stepped gingerly down from the hackney carriage, velvet skirt held high to keep it safe from the muddy pavement, pulling her cloak closer about her. A fine rain was falling, as she hurried at her father's side up many steps until they were within the palace itself, and on along countless corridors.

She experienced a moment of panic as doors were opened by uniformed footmen. Her father touched her arm reassuringly and taking a deep breath she glanced around curiously at the fashionably dressed men and women in the long, narrow, ornate reception room they entered, where the combined odour of heavy perfumes did little to disguise that of perspiration. There was a constant buzz of conversation, almost drowning out the sound of lute and viols played in the gallery above.

After years of experiencing nothing but the sober apparel of those long puritan years, it was a shock to the senses to see the richness of dress displayed here equally by men and women, silks, satins, velvets, jewels and lace, rich embroidery, hair of both sexes dressed in curls, ringlets, complexions enhanced by cosmetics, women wearing tiny black patches, gowns dipping low and displaying most of their breasts. She stared about her then in utter fascination.

Nor was the curiosity solely on her side. Many had noticed the entrance of Hawksley, known to be a close friend of the monarch, an associate of his years in exile, who had fought at his side against Cromwell. Men came forward, bowed in greeting, questions about his lovely companion on their lips, as the door at the far end of the reception room opened and a tall, regal figure stood there, eyes sweeping inquiringly over the assemblage, as men bowed deeply before him and women sank in curtsies in sudden rustling of skirts.

Charles gestured that they should rise, noticed Hawksley and beckoned him forward. The crowd parted to allow him through.

'Come child,' whispered her father and Sophie realised that she was being led into the presence of the King.

'James! It delights my heart to see you back at court once more!' His dark sardonic eyes turned lazily from Hawksley to the girl at his friend's side and smiled his approval. 'It would seem that you found more than your estates in the country? Pray introduce me to your beautiful companion?'

'Sire, this is my daughter Sophie Louise Hawksley.'

'But I thought you were childless, James!' The King stared at Sophie in astonishment.

'So I believed until just recently. As you know years back I received word that my wife Lucy had died shortly after childbirth, her babe with her. It was not so. She lingered on a few weeks, leaving our child to the care of her sister and her husband, a foul brute of a man. Sophie escaped their household and has recently been living with her grandfather, a respected physician and has lately joined me at Hawksley Manor.' He smiled and added, 'She is the exact image of my dear Lucy!'

'Well, here is an extraordinary tale indeed,' breathed Charles, as his eyes slid appraisingly over the young girl before him, admiring her graceful young figure in her gown of delphinium blue, her only jewellery a gold locket at her throat, as he noted in amusement the way her blue eyes were openly examining him, 'You are welcome, Sophie! How did you come to meet with your father again?'

'Well, his horse almost knocked me to the ground, when I was escaping the man who had kidnapped me and was trying to force me into unwanted marriage—Sir Mark Harrison! When father realised who I was—his daughter and not a ghost, then we became properly acquainted!'

'Harrison, the man who was in possession of your house and lands, James?' asked the King in astonishment. 'I must hear more of this. We will retire to a place more private.' He beckoned them to follow him as a slight hum of disappointment sounded from the attendant courtiers.

The room into which he led them was obviously his private chamber, hung with tapestries and fine portraits, one in particular of a lovely woman taking Sophie's eye,

'Who is she,' she demanded, as she stared up at the portrait?

'Sophie, hush,' reproved Hawksley uneasy at her familiarity with the King.

'My sister Mary of Orange, the Princess Royal,' replied Charles with a smile, 'the portrait next to hers that of her son William. She is visiting with us at this time, as is my mother the Queen and my younger sister Minette.'

'Minette, a pretty name,' said Sophie.

'A pet name—it slipped out. Her real name is Henrietta Ann, wife of Phillipe Duc d'Orleans, brother of the King of France.' He sank into what was obviously his favourite chair, crossing his long shapely, white stockinged legs before him on a footstool, indicating that they should seat themselves on the sofa as he watched Sophie, her lack of sophistry strangely appealing.

'It must be good to have sisters,' said Sophie musingly. 'Do you have brothers as well?' In vain did her father try to signal to her to desist.

'Sadly one died of the smallpox last September,' said Charles shortly. 'Harry is sorely missed.' His eyes betrayed his emotion.

'Oh, I'm sorry,' she blurted, remembering now that she had heard of the Duke of Gloucester's death, but had not realised that this was the King's brother.

'Sophie has led a very private life in the country and knows nothing of the court, only that she is loyal subject of your majesty and takes great joy in the return of her King.' So spoke Hawksley, hoping that Sophie would choose her words more carefully, as he laid a restraining hand over hers.

'My grandfather says that smallpox is a most virulent disease and suspects that it is transmitted both by inhaling the breath of the sufferer and handling the pustules.' Sophie's blue eyes were fixed on the King's dark stare. 'He is a very fine physician,' she explained, 'As I would aspire to be, were I a man instead of woman!'

He surveyed her now with deepening curiosity. She looked so young, flower like in her unspoiled young beauty, innocent of the usual feminine wiles and subterfuge. 'You—would like to be a physician, mistress,' he probed, 'Such a course is not open to females as you must surely know, and yet,' he continued musingly, 'The world is changing fast! New wonders of the new philosophy science discovered every day as we find from the Royal Society formed last month.' He leaned forward. 'But let us take things in due order. I would hear your history—and how you came to be kidnapped by Harrison!'

Charles listened to the tale that unfolded, as father and daughter explained the strange sequence of events that had led them here today, his face darkening as he heard details of old Jessie's murder and Sophie's kidnap as Harrison schemed to force her into marriage. That he had also made abortive attempt to set fire to Hawksley Manor

'Harrison shall suffer for his crimes, never fear,' said Charles firmly. 'I am delighted James my friend, that you have discovered this delightful daughter of yours and are managing to restore your house to order. It is my fervent wish that one day you will marry again, find new happiness.'

'Sire, I wish that you too may find a loving wife,' replied James.

'Many princesses are being proposed for political reasons. A king may not marry for love, Hawksley! It seems like that ultimately the choice may be the daughter of the King of Portugal, the Infanta Catherine! Our fathers discussed it many years past in our childhood!' He spoke tonelessly. 'I needs must be wed and provide sons to succeed me.'

'Charles,' said Hawksley now, slipping his hand into the pocket of his embroidered jacket. 'Is it possible that your future bride might like this as a token of your affection?' The diamond pomegranate that had once belonged to another royal personage sparkled on his palm. 'I would I could make it a gift, but I have been forced into selling the family jewels in order to survive financially. They should have been passed to my daughter, but needs must and I took them to a certain Jew in the city who gave me a reasonable price—but I did not part with this.'

The King took the jewel from Hawksley and stared at it curiously. He bent forward to a small table on which lay manuscripts and maps and reached for a magnifying glass with which he examined the pomegranate. His lifted his eyes and stared at Hawksley.

'Is this what I take it to be—a pomegranate bearing the crest of Spain?'

'It was given to my ancestress Lady Mary Hawksley by Queen Katherine of Aragon, the first wife of Henry V111 for services she did her.'

'Indeed it would make a wonderful gift for this other Catherine, the more so as Portugal and Spain are at odds! She would no doubt enjoy possession of this!' He stared at Hawksley. 'Look you James, money is tight even for a king, but I will pay you well for this trifle, if you wish to dispose of it that is—and if you also are willing to forego it,' he said watching Sophie's face. 'It is sad that your father has had to let go jewellery that should have graced your form.'

'I have no need of jewels,' she replied casually. 'I prefer books dealing with the efficacy of herbs used in healing, the history of medicine. My grandfather has taught me much, but there is more I would learn.' She was rewarded by a chuckle from the King, who had listened to her almost incredulously.

'So you have a liking for books, Mistress Sophie? Well, I may boast of a not indifferent library. I tell you what we will do. You shall both have chambers here in the palace, where you may wile away as many hours as you wish with your head lowered over hundreds of books. As for you my friend Hawksley, I will find a post about my person which will bring you in an income!' He rose to his feet. 'I must go. There are many waiting to petition me. Came back here tomorrow and your rooms will be made ready, even if I have to dispossess some other courtier to make room!'

As they made their way back to their lodgings, Sophie and her father were deep in thought. It was still raining as they stepped out of the hackney carriage, paid the driver and mounted the many stairs to their apartment.

'I am not sure that I desire to be part of the court and live at Whitehall with all its petty rivalries,' said Hawksley heavily. 'There is so much I would achieve at the manor.'

'But father—others will look after the house and estate for you! I am just so excited to think I will have access to the King's library!' Sophie's face was flushed with excitement and seeing her so obvious delight her father smiled.

'Daughter, you will never cease to amaze me,' he said now and kissed her forehead. 'Now off to your bed. Tomorrow will be a busy day.' As he threw himself onto the unyielding mattress of his bed, James Hawksley found sleep hard to come. Had it been wise to introduce his beautiful but unsophisticated young daughter to the vanities, temptations and pitfalls of court society? As for Sophie, she quickly fell asleep dreaming of those books to which she would have free access in the palace of a king.

Two footmen had helped to carry their few possessions along the maze of corridors to their new home. The two bedroom apartment boasted a small sparsely furnished reception room, but now at least they were actually living in Whitehall and despite his reservations about the move, James Hawksley was touched that Charles should have ordered it so.

Sophie had finished bestowing their clothes in the carved wardrobe and examined their new home critically. It was certainly not as comfortable as either her grandfather's home or the manor house, however grand the King's own chambers in this palace of Whitehall were. They had a good outlook however as Sophie realised as she opened the casement and looked out curiously on what she knew was the Privy garden, where a few people were sauntering well wrapped in their cloaks against the December frost.

'Father, surely that is the King below down there surrounded by all those courtiers, see he has three spaniels with him and is bending over a sundial!' Hawksley joined Sophie at the window

'The sundial—they say he likes to set his watch by it each day,' he replied. 'Tell me, did you note the variety of clocks in evidence in his chamber yesterday? He collects them and has a great interest in all things mechanical and boasts a fine telescope for examining the heavens, embraces all new learning.'

'Who is that fine lady upon whom he smiles so fondly?' she inquired, leaning further out of the window. 'See the one in the furred velvet mantle and a large, feathered hat upon her head.'

'Ah, Mistress Barbara Palmer, a great favourite of Charles to the chagrin of her husband Roger.' And he chuckled then noting his daughter's look of surprise gave a quick sigh. She knew so little of the ways of the court, but she must learn and quickly if she were to survive here.

'Do you mean...?' She looked at him in consternation.

'That she is his mistress—yes I do.'

'But you said she is married!' Sophie stared at her father in surprise, the more so as he apparently was not shocked by the situation. 'Moreover she looks as though she is with child,' she added.

'Yes, of the King's making! The night of his return last May, well it is thought that Charles spent the night with Barbara.'

'Will the baby be acknowledged as the King's?'

'No doubt Roger Palmer will be content to allow it as his own. I imagine we will know the answer in February. However the King already has children you know. Lucy Walters gave him a fine son, young James of whom he is very fond and Catherine Pegge bore him a son and a daughter, and there are rumoured to be others.' He paused and shook his head. 'Your face registers surprise sweetheart, but I fear the way of the court is not that of the quiet village where you grew up. Many of the nobility, both men and women have scant respect for their marriage vows.'

'It all sounds very strange.' She stared at Hawksley in sudden concern. 'Father, have you any other children.' His dark eyes crinkled in amusement at her question but he shook his head soberly.

'I will not pretend that I behaved altogether as a monk when I was living in exile. But no, Sophie, I have no children but you!' He placed a kiss on her forehead. 'Come, let us join those about the King.'

By the time they made their way along the honeycomb of corridors and out into the crisp December sunshine, they found the King in animated conversation with an elderly portly man of grave demeanour that her father softly informed Sophie was Chancellor Edward Hyde.

'He looks like an elderly bearded cherub,' she whispered back.

'His daughter Anne is married to the King's brother, James Duke of York. They married just last September, their baby son sadly died at birth in October. James would have liked to escape the marriage, but Charles insisted that it was legal and showed his support for Anne.' Hawksley's tones expressed his approval.

'Her father must be well pleased that his daughter occupies such high position,' guessed Sophie?

'On the contrary, he was much angered for he had thought James would have made a good political marriage. Such is the way of the world!' he added. Sophie did not reply but shook her head deep in thought. It was then that a small group of women approached the King, one of whom seemed familiar. The woman seemed to feel Sophie's gaze, for she turned her face full upon Sophie who realised that this was the Princess Royal, Mary of Orange, the elder of the King's two sisters whose portrait hung in the King's chamber..

The widow of William Prince of Orange spoke a few words to her brother who nodded and beckoned Hawksley and Sophie. The surrounding bevy of courtiers, holding their cloaks tightly about them against the chill December wind, fell back to allow them through.

'This is the young girl I spoke to you of, who delights in studying medicine!' He introduced Sophie, adding, 'Her father of course you already know James Hawksley who fought so bravely at my side and shared my exile.'

'James, you never mentioned that you had a daughter, and such a lovely one,' said Mary curiously. 'She is quite delightful, is she not mama?' But she spoke the words mechanically, as though forcing herself to follow the conversation. The elderly lady to whom she turned fixed Sophie with an examining stare, as the girl suddenly understood that this plain, slightly built woman with her French accent was Queen Henrietta Maria, the widow of King Charles 1st.

For a moment Sophie stared, mesmerised.

'Majesty,' she murmured, as she curtsied first to the Queen Mother and then to Mary, as yet another lady caught her attention. If Mary of Orange was beautiful, then the young girl with bright blue eyes, a delicate complexion and carefully coifed chestnut hair was charm exemplified. This as she was to learn as another introduction followed, was Charles younger and favourite sister, Henrietta-Anne.

'Your name is Sophie Louise I understand,' said the Queen Mother suddenly. 'You remind me strongly of one of my much loved ladies, a Sophie Louise de Chantignon, a delightful and loyal friend. Alas she is dead now,' and she sighed.

'Majesty, you speak of my mother, who became Sophie Louise Hawksley and after whom my daughter was named,' said James quietly, with a bow. Henrietta Maria gave an exclamation of approval, as did the King who had been listening to the exchange.

'So, this is the grand-daughter of Sophie Louise!' said the Queen. 'It explains the similarity.'

'Mama—I feel a little unwell.' The words quietly spoken caused Sophie to glance at Charles elder sister. The young woman looked flushed, not the healthy colour induced by the kiss of the winter wind, but a look that Sophie had sometimes noted on her grandfather's patients. Without thinking of protocol, she reached out for Mary's wrist, the pulse was racing, the skin hot to the touch. Her blue eyes too were unusually brilliant, feverish.

'Lady—you are ill,' said Sophie. 'You should be abed!'

'Yes. I feel I must retire to my room,' replied Mary. 'I fell strangely tired. My brother says you have knowledge of medicine. Will you accompany me, Sophie Hawksley?'

'My knowledge is slight, but of course I will do anything I can to help,' replied Sophie, suddenly feeling slightly nervous. Most of her learning so far had been acquired through studying her grandfather's books and listening to his teaching. Suppose she were asked to make diagnosis of what afflicted Mary of Orange—but of course there would be the King's own physicians to call upon, wise and learned men, although from what she had heard, most physicians resorted to severe bleeding and purging, often with disastrous results.

Mary was lying in the large, imposing state bed, looking small and forlorn against the silken sheets. She was in high fever and turned her head restlessly from side to side.

'My throat hurts,' she whispered to Sophie. 'I fear it is probably influenza.' Her two attendants glanced at each other and then to Sophie. They had already followed her suggestion that Mary should be bathed and a cold compress placed on her forehead. What now? At that moment came a knocking upon the chamber door and a man of self important appearance, clad in black, white hair worn long and making stark contrast to his black brows, paused on the threshold, bowed and approached the bed.

'Your Royal Highness,' he began. 'I hear that you are unwell.'

'She has a high fever,' said Sophie quietly, her eyes locking with the man's brown gaze. 'I fear it is more than just flu.'

'And who are you, Mistress that you take it upon yourself to pass medical opinion here?' he demanded brusquely.

'My name is Sophie Louise Hawksley, daughter of Lord James Hawksley and here at the request of the patient.' She spoke calmly, not allowing herself to be intimidated by his impatient demeanour.

'Stand back, girl,' he said authoritatively, stooping over the feverish form of Mary of Orange, who was beginning to murmur irrationally to herself.

'She calls for her late husband,' said one of her attendants, face worried. 'What ails her, doctor?'

'This I will attempt to discover, if you gaggle of women will be good enough to give me space!' He checked Mary's pulse and persuaded her to open her mouth. 'There is much inflammation,' he explained. 'Has she been coughing?'

'No,' replied Sophie.

'It is certainly influenza. She will need careful nursing. I will leave medication to be administered to her, a few drops in a glass of water mixed with wine. But first I will bleed her, to reduce her fever.' Sophie watched as he applied leeches to the patient's body, then catching the blood in a small metal bowl. Then he held a glass with the physic to her lips and smiled approval as Mary swallowed the draught down.

'See she is already quieter,' he said with casual satisfaction.

'Thank you, Sir Physician,' whispered Mary, trying to concentrate on his face

'Perhaps you will keep her under observation during the next few hours, Mistress Sophie,' he said the doctor in soft aside. 'Send one of these ladies to summon me, should you note any adverse change in her condition.'

For four days Sophie kept watch by Mary's bedside, as the fever showed no sign of abating. She retched violently and vomited, her temperature continuing to rise. Her two attendants were keeping well back from the sick woman now, leaving all nursing tasks to Sophie, who mindful of advice given her by her grandfather as to the nursing of those with infectious disease, now wore linen gloves when bathing the patient a muslin kerchief over mouth and nose.

Worried messages were sent by the King, his mother Queen Henrietta Maria and the lovely Princess Henrietta Anne. The physician advised them not to visit. He had revised his earlier diagnosis and having examined her mouth and throat and detecting lesions, now approached his patient with caution, allowing Sophie to tend her under his instruction. When that first pustule appeared on Mary's brow, Sophie looked at it in shock, as her brows knit together questioningly. She had never seen a case of smallpox, but read of the disease in John Wheatley's medical tomes, seen graphic illustrations. She also was aware that this disease was often fatal and could be passed to those in close contact with the sufferer. There was no known cure, only palliative care.

'Is this smallpox, Sir Physician,' she asked quietly, not fearing that Mary would overhear, for she was in high fever, tossing and turning and muttering incoherently.

'It might of course be cowpox—but no, the degree of fever lends credence to your suggestion, mistress! We lost her brother to this cruel disease only last September.' He looked at Sophie with slight compassion in his dark analytical gaze. It was probable that this young girl would also succumb to what was such hideously disfiguring disease, those few who survived it, often masking their deeply pitted faces from their fellow human beings.

Over the next few hours pustules began to appear not only on the sufferers face but on her trunk and more noticeably on her extremities, the blisters even found on the palms of her hands and soles of her feet. There was no doubting the diagnosis now and the physician shook his head. He had listened to Mary's laboured breathing. She was suffering from pneumonia which often developed as the smallpox infection ran its course. Days passed.

'At first these pustules seemed filled with fluid and leaked—now they are firm to the touch—like tiny lumps,' exclaimed Sophie.

'Eventually they dry up and flake off and some fortunate patients recover.' He shook his head as he looked down at Mary, who detached from reality, was moaning in her pain. 'Alas, she is dying and I must send word to the King. Can I rely on you to remain here, Mistress Sophie?'

'Yes,' replied Sophie calmly. He smiled slightly, considering the girl as she sat on a chair at the bedside. She looked so very weary but a stubborn determination had helped keep her awake during the night hours, as she had tended Mary during the last week. He felt he owed it to her to express his gratitude.

'No real way for one as young as you to spend Christmas Eve,' he said. 'I should tell you, that your father has expressed grave concerns regarding your own safety in all this, was wishful that you should leave the sickroom. Also I must mention that the King is most grateful for your services to his sister.'

Tell my father not to worry,' was all she sighed, as she rose to speak words of comfort to Mary, to which her patient was deaf, yet seemed to sense a loving presence as she turned her head. How long she waited for the physician to return she was not sure as anxiously she watched Mary's breathing become shallower. Suddenly Sophie became aware of a change. Mary lifted her head from the pillows and held her arms out in front of her, a strange look of joy suffusing her ravaged features.

'Father—I come,' she whispered and then Sophie who had never heard the death rattle before, knew it as Princess Mary of Orange fell back and expired. Sophie looked about her almost fearfully. Had Mary seen a vision of her late father, or was it her Heavenly Father whom she had so addressed? She fell to her knees by the side of the bed and commenced to pray, tears falling down her face as she did so.

'Lord, please have mercy on her soul,' she whispered. 'But why should one so fair, so good have to die in such manner? You are a God of love, so why should your children have to suffer so? Why so many face pain and early death?' She was not aware that the door had opened and that the physician had returned, with a cleric clad in rich robes at his side. The bishop walked softly over and placed a hand on Sophie's head as she knelt there in prayer.

'My child, the One whose own dear Son died on cruel cross is aware of our human suffering, but through it we are refined so it is thought. I take it that the Princess is dead? I am summoned too late to give her extreme unction. Let us therefore pray for her together, child.' Sophie lifted her head and saw the very real sympathy and kindness on the man's face. But the words he spoke, although wonderful and full of comfort, floated past her ears discarded.

The Princess Royal was buried at Westminster Abbey amongst deep court mourning. On the physician's advice, Sophie kept herself apart from others until two weeks had passed. She had not succumbed to smallpox. Sophie sat staring out of the window from the small room they had allocated to her, trying to make sense of recent weeks. Of one thing she was now very sure, her path in life to be that of medicine. She must try to understand the way in which infection passed from one individual to another and the over pressing need to find cure for all obnoxious diseases.

'For every hurt, there must be a cure,' she muttered as she paced to and fro about the chamber. 'For instance, where nettles thrive and sting, dock leaves also grow close by to cool the hurt. Nature has provided help for most of our ills, of that I am sure. Look at Grandfather's use of concoction of deadly foxglove in right proportion to alleviate angina.' And so she pondered, wondering how she would be able to find correct answer to her speculation.

When Sophie found herself folded into her father's arms once more, he sensed a change in her. At first he told himself this was the result of the trauma experienced in tending the sick bed of Mary of Orange.

'I am so sorry that I was unable to visit you when you were closeted with the Princess,' he said regretfully, his dark eyes sad. 'The fear of smallpox was so grave, that court officials allowed none but the physician to pass along the corridor to her rooms. The King has asked that you attend him soon, that he may express his own gratitude for your devotion to his sister.'

'She was very brave,' whispered Sophie. 'I think she knew that she was to die. She once bid me to leave her—to look to myself. Her attendants kept to the dressing chamber without. I was the only one permitted to tend her.'

'Did you know that both of her Dutch attendants are now themselves showing signs of illness? Yet you who were constantly at her side escaped the pox! It is a miracle!' He pressed a kiss on her forehead. She stared up at him. He was very handsome, her royalist cavalier father who bore a definite resemblance to the King. Yet his skin was not as swarthy as Charles, eyes not so heavy lidded—and yet?

'You stare at me very earnestly sweetheart?'

'I was merely considering that you are very like to the King!' she said frankly and was surprised that he drew her back from others in the room.

'Never say that again in public,' he reproved, iron in his tones.

'Why ever not?' she demanded, hurt.

'There were some who suggested that my mother had been very close with this King's father!' There was indignation in his eyes. Sophie drew in her breath in surprise. Could he mean that her grandmother, the Sophie Louise after whom she was named, and the late king had been lovers?

Surely not! Certainly it seemed her father wished no such possibility to be bruited.

'People who have nothing better to occupy their minds, will ever spread ugly rumours,' she said gently. 'Yet should the rumour be true, would this be such tragedy, father?' Her blue eyes stared up into his earnestly.

'We speak of my late mother's honour,' he replied stiffly. 'You will never raise this subject again!' Then he slipped his hand about her waist. 'The King has ordered new gowns be made for you, the first of course will be black,' he said. Previously she would have shown delight at this prospect, but now since the death of the Princess Mary, the girl merely smiled slightly.

'It is very kind of the King! I would prefer instead that he gave me access to any books he has on medical matters, as he promised,' she exclaimed. He shook his head. Still it appeared she retained this unseemly obsession with medicine. Perhaps it would be wiser to move Sophie back to Hawksley Manor, where she could meet with her grandfather John Wheatley and her leanings towards the masculine domain of healing would cause less comment than here at Westminster. He wondered uneasily what the future held for his headstrong daughter.

Chapter Seven

Charles was frowning as the Duke of York came towards him. He still was offended by James lack of respect towards Anne, who even though not of noble blood and certainly no beauty, nevertheless was his brother's legally married wife and daughter to Counsellor Hyde, his esteemed premier minister. He felt sorry for the girl who had been his sister Mary's Maid of Honour when earlier she had been seduced by James. This feeling was now mixed with the sorrow for Mary's so recent death, the wound so inflicted, making him acutely aware of his own mortality.

Life was short, he reflected and one should do one's utmost to treat fairly those to whom one owed a duty of care. He smoothed back the frothing lace on his black velvet coat, for he was still wearing mourning as were his courtiers.

'You look glum, brother,' said James, bowing before him and studying his face.

'Is it any wonder, with a second death in the family, first our young brother and then Mary this last Christmas Eve! I must say that I also miss mother and Minette now they have returned home.' His dark eyes held trace of his pain.

'Don't pretend that you have any tender feelings towards mother, she was ever a thorn in your flesh!' said James lightly. 'As for Henrietta Anne, with her engagement soon to be announced to the Duc d'Orleans, brother to Louis, King of France, surely this is matter for jubilation. She will make a much more advantageous marriage then mine.' His face bore a sour expression.

'My dear James, you have none to blame but yourself for your choice of wife! It was you and no other who made Ann Hyde pregnant,' said Charles evenly.

'What relief then for you not to have been required to marry one of the mothers of your many bastards?' The words were spitefully spoken, but then James lowered his head in sudden shame. 'Forgive me brother. I should not have spoken so.' He noted the flush of sudden anger that crossed Charles face.

'Indeed you should watch your tongue, James,' replied Charles, his voice dangerously quiet. 'Now what was it that you wanted?'

'To speak of naval matters—that new yacht you desire? It would seem that most of those landowners wealthy enough are wishful of owning one too! We will have a miniature fleet of them! But there again, we need to discuss our ships of war—although we are at peace, you never know when hostilities may start of a sudden.' James face became animated, his eyes shone as they discussed the topic nearest to his heart, for was he not Lord High Admiral of the fleet and never happier than when he had the deck of a fine ship below him.

Charles also had an abiding love of the sea and for once the brothers were at one. At last their conversation lagged.

'So brother—are you decided on the Portuguese Infanta to be your wife?'

'It makes sense! She brings a good dowry—including Tangiers and Bombay,' said Charles philosophically, 'And of course two million crowns, a tidy sum and one much needed by the treasury!'

'What like is she to look upon?' inquired James?

'Not so as to be called exactly beautiful, but I am assured that there is nothing in her visage to offend—good eyes, dark hair and properly designed in her female shape. I consider we will get along together, for our ambassador is convinced she is of a docile nature—is convent bred.' Charles spoke with less enthusiasm than he had shown over matters regarding his new yacht. Royal marriage was an alliance between countries, rather than to pleasure the participants.

'I would that Anne had brought me such a dowry! Nay, I meant not to mention it again,' and James grimaced. 'Have official overtures been made to Catherine?'

'Yes and will probably continue for an unconscionable time. Yet I have that which I hope will appeal to the Infanta's own heart and which Sir Richard takes with him on his return to Portugal—this!' And Charles pulled a small object from his pocket and proffered it to his brother, as it lay sparkling on his palm. James took it curiously.

'A pretty jewel—and worthy for a queen I would judge!'

'And probably will prove of greater worth to my future Queen! This, my dear James, is not only meant to represent a pomegranate but part of the Spanish coat of arms and belonged to Katherine of Aragon, first queen of Henry V111. She gave it as a gift to one of James Hawksley's female ancestors so he tells me. He is hard set like most of those who spent years in exile at our side and recently needed to sell certain of his family jewels. He knew this would interest me. I have bought it for Catherine!'

'But of course! With the constant friction between Portugal and Spain, it will please the young Infanta to own a jewel that once belonged to the royal Spanish house. Well thought on, Sire!' and he bowed slightly mockingly, as he returned the glittering pomegranate to Charles. 'Fortune ever seems to smile on you, these days!'

'Do you grudge me my position, brother? I assure you that it has many burdens as well as advantages. Now I will summon Sir Richard to take this jewel with him, as he brings my official offer of marriage to Catherine to Lisbon.' He smiled. 'This should have belonged to Hawksley's young daughter, Sophie. I owe her much, not least for her devoted care to Mary in her last days. She is an extraordinary girl, James—desires to be a physician!' and he smiled whimsically.

'Pshaw! That is quite ridiculous of course! It is said by many knowledgeable physicians, that the learning of medicine would be too much for the female brain, would upset their monthly cycle and cause them to be barren!' He fingered his foaming lace cravat as he spoke in scornful dismissal. Charles merely lifted an eyebrow.

'I am sure you do not believe such nonsense, James! You really should attend some of the meetings of our newly formed Royal Society where matters of extreme interest are discussed.'

At last the conversation waned and James took his departure. Charles sat reflecting now on the girl with those amazing blue eyes—Sophie Louise Hawksley. Perhaps he could find a good husband for her. Yes, that should suffice to show his appreciation!

Sophie smoothed the skirts of her black velvet gown, the bodice discreetly filled with white lace at the bosom. As the weeks passed since Mary's death, she had waited hopefully for a summons from the King, so that she could remind him of his promise to allow her access to his library. Now today, at long last a uniformed flunkey knocked on the door to inform her that the King desired her presence. She was to follow him.

'You must wait until I am prepared then,' she said firmly and perforce he nodded. Sophie stared into the ornate framed mirror. Her glossy chestnut hair was tied back severely in a bow at the nape of her neck, her only ornament being her mother's gold locket. She splashed her face at the china basin, towelled it dry. Not for her the cosmetics and artfully placed black patches worn by the ladies of the court. But at least she decided, she would look as good waking in the morning as when she retired!

Why had her father decided to go riding on this of all days? She would have liked his reassuring presence. Realising she could delay no longer, she joined the official who was waiting impatiently for one who was no great court lady, merely a young women from the country so it was said.

'Follow me, Lady!' As they traversed the many passageways where noisily chatting groups of courtiers watched her pass speculatively and then crossed a courtyard, Sophie was aware of a gathering excitement. If any had told her a year ago that she would be at Westminster and summoned to the King, she would not have believed it.

He received her in the familiar lavishly furnished antechamber to his bedroom, where portrait of Mary, the late Princes Royal hung. His dark eyes examined the girl approvingly. Even the black of mourning and the fact that she wore no jewels, no paint on her serene young face, could not detract from her loveliness, he thought. She would make some man a very fine wife or perhaps a mistress—a royal mistress? He dismissed the thought. Hawksley was a good and esteemed friend.

'So Mistress Sophie, and how are you finding life at court? I have not seen you at any of the normal gatherings and functions, why not?'

'Perhaps because I do not find watching a great many artificial people all trying to outdo each other in their salacious remarks, vying for attention in finery possibly not yet paid for—especially edifying!' she said smoothly. The King's jaw dropped and then he burst in to a great gale of laughter.

'Why sweetheart, I never heard the like,' he choked. 'Do we so offend your sensibilities that you must deny us your company?' He held a stool out for her and she sat and stared at him as he lolled back in his own throne like chair.

'I will gladly speak with you, Sire,' she replied. 'You have a fine mind, this I know and my father speaks of you very highly. But all these vacuous hangers-on at court, noble or otherwise are I find extremely boring!' She came out with the words without due thought and now blushed as she heard her own words. How foolish he must think her. But he did not.

'Sophie, among some of the titled creatures of the court you will find those of integrity to advise me and help me to rule this country. It is not an easy task you know child!' He sighed. 'Well, after disposing of these pleasantries, I now come to my reason for inviting you here. I have never really thanked you for our selfless care and devotion to my sister Mary.'

'I will never forget her—her extraordinary courage,' replied Sophie quietly.

'I have heard how you would allow none other to attend her apart from the physician, depriving yourself of sleep and facing grave risk of smallpox yourself. Indeed, it is a miracle that you survived infection!'

'My grandfather holds it, that by covering the face with muslin, we do not inhale the infectious breath of the patient,' said Sophie. 'I also used gloves when touching the pustules and ordered those gloves burnt afterwards. I am not sure why such precaution seems to help—but it does!'

'Yet our esteemed physicians hold it that infection is caused by an imbalance of the four humours—blood, phlegm...!'

'And yellow bile and black bile,' interrupted Sophie. 'But consider Sire, just because it was thought so two thousand years ago by the ancient

Greeks, does not mean to say that they were right! I also believe that disease spreads the more readily in poor overcrowded conditions such as you find in a city. People living in the country are on the whole healthier I would say!'

'Well, we can hardly tear down whole cities and rebuild to test your theory,' he said broodingly. 'Yet I see the sense in it.'

'Why did you send for me? Was it that you remembered your promise to allow me access to your library?' Her face was glowing with excitement as she at last broached the question.

'Is that all you truly want of your King, Sophie—to glance through his books, dusty tomes no doubt quite unsuited for the average female mind!' He watched her face mischievously as he spoke.

'If women were allowed the same education as men, then they would demonstrate the same intellect! Perhaps it is that men are affrighted at the prospect!'

'I had thought to suggest a possible husband for you, Sophie, to ensure you a good and comfortable future. Young Viscount Lansdale comes to mind. He is brave, good looking and will inherit a fortune when his father dies.'

'No thank you. I do not desire to marry!' she said impatiently. 'I want no man telling me what I may or may not do!' He stared at her and seemed to lose patience.

'Sobeit, Mistress Sophie! If you return tomorrow, I will see that you are conducted to my library. I wish you joy of it.' If his tones were brusque, he was nevertheless touched by the look of gratitude that suffused her lovely face and the joy in her blue eyes, as she bowed her head before him.

'Oh—thank you a thousand times!' They both rose to their feet.

'Well—off with you, Sophie! Perhaps I should appoint you as helper to my own physician, yet this notion might not please him I fear!' Suddenly and without thought, Sophie rose up on tiptoe and kissed him on the cheek as she would her father. In almost automatic reaction to her unexpected close proximity, he placed his hand in the small of her back and pressed her against him and forced a kiss on her mouth. It was like no kiss Sophie had ever experienced before and she attempted to tear herself away in shock and outrage. Then another, stronger emotion than annoyance caused her to relax and she found herself returning his kiss with one of her own, soft, lingering as she began to tremble and hid her face against his breast in confusion..

'Why sweetheart—forgive me!' he said in contrition. Then looking down at her realised that Sophie for all her love of medicine was possessed of other unexplored passions.

'I had always wondered what it felt like to be kissed by a man,' she said huskily, at last daring to raise her eyes to his face.

'Now you do,' he said gently, still holding her close. 'But not by a man, child—by a king!'

'I must go.'

'Must you? Why not stay awhile, take a glass of wine with me?' He knew it was wrong to envisage the seduction of his friend's daughter, but she was unlike any girl he had ever met before, honest, challenging and although she did not yet realise it, possessing a power to set men's blood afire. He watched her face. Saw the refusal rise to her lips, while her eyes told another tale. He took decision. He released her and reached for a brandy decanter on a nearby table and poured two glasses.

'Come—join me in a toast to our better acquaintance, Sophie!'

She accepted the crystal goblet and lifted the amber fluid to her lips. The smoothness of the fine old brandy slid down her throat, burning like fire, and taut muscles gradually relaxed. It could do no harm—to drink just one glass with him. To refuse would seem churlish. When he seated himself once more on his gold framed cushioned chair and beckoned her, she drew cautiously nearer. Then she was sitting on his lap. His lips sought hers again and this time she did not resist, although every deep instinct told her that she should. His hand went down under the white lace at her bodice and his fingers gently kneaded her nipples. Then his lips caressed them and she could no longer think logically nor desired to.

Later—much later, as she lay between the rumpled, silken sheets of his splendid bed, she felt his hand lightly brushing the hair back from her forehead as he pressed a last lingering kiss on her bruised lips.

'Thank you for the gift you so wonderfully, so innocently gave me—the delight of your body, for it was the first time for you, was it not Sophie sweetheart?' he asked in almost contrition. Yet he had known all along that it would be so. 'Time now for you to dress, for we have been closeted here for quite awhile, it will have been noticed,' he added. And reality flooded back. She sat up and stared at him, her lips swollen from his kisses, her cheeks burning, skin flushed.

'I suppose, I am now what is commonly referred to as a fallen woman,' said Sophie shakily.

'Say rather one who is held in high esteem by her King,' he replied. 'I fear you must leave soon, sweetheart. Here let me assist you with that bodice, your skirt and shoes so.' And he knelt and slipped her shoes on her stockinged feet.

'I know you do not love me,' she said uncertainly.

'What is—love? Does anyone really know? We have shared our bodies' passion, my dear. But we also have a very special friendship flowering between us. It will last longer than lust and make for a greater closeness in the years to come, for I know that you will always be my very special friend and I have never said that to woman before!' He watched as she washed her face and tidied her hair, adjusted her clothing. He handed her a black, jewel encrusted fan. 'Hold that before your face until you are away from my suite,' he instructed.

Sophie did not know how many curious faces were turned on her as she paced serenely along the corridors abuzz with those seeking audience with the king in the state chamber that evening. She held her head erectly and paced along with a certain hauteur, nor did she shield her face with his fan.

'Another favourite, perhaps,' suggested an elegantly attired man leaning on his gold knobbed cane. 'Cousin Barbara will not be pleased!'

'Oh, they come and go, Buckingham—but Barbara is a royal fixture!' Sophie heard their words and turned and stared at both men scornfully.

'I never realised that men could be such interfering busybodies,' she snapped and stalked on. When she arrived back at her apartment, she found her father waiting for her.

'Where have you been, Sophie,' he asked in concern. Then he noticed her bruised lips. The look of feverish excitement still apparent in her eyes and he knew.

'Who was it, child,' he demanded, placing his hands down forcefully on her shoulders, furious that any should have abused his child.

'Father—it was the King,' she replied. 'There will never be another!'

'Do you tell me that—Charles?' He went white to his lips. Never would he have expected such perfidy from one who was his friend as well as monarch.

'Did he—did you...?'

'Yes. He is a lonely man for all his wealth and high prestige father, and beneath the cynicism one who seeks honesty yet denies the existence of love.' She spoke quietly and he was astonished at her insight. 'We will always be friends,' she said, adding-'Tomorrow I will have access to his library!'

He opened his mouth to reply, to express his outrage at what had transpired, this deflowering of his child, but knew it would be pointless. Sophie had taken her own decision in this as in all else she did. Instead he put his arms gently around her. He did not kiss her mouth bruised by the King's embrace, instead lifted one of her hands to his lips.

'Sophie, as your father I will always be ready to support you. Unlike Charles, I do know what love is, love for the brave and beautiful woman who was your mother and that of a parent for a child. We all need love, Sophie. To deny it is to demean ourselves intellectually and physically. But never seek to replace love with the tawdry swift enjoyment of bodies need!' His dark eyes, so like those of the King looked at her tenderly.

'I know what you are saying, father, and have no fear. I will always protect my honour in the future.' She released her hand and stepped back. 'I think I will go to my room now.' Her black velvet skirt disappeared through the door. She had left the jewelled fan behind her on the table. He picked it up thoughtfully. He had last seen this in the hands of Charles beloved sister, Henrietta Anne. To have given such a gift to Sophie must be mark of an especial esteem.

Three months sped by, months during which Sophie spent long hours poring over books and manuscripts such as she would never have ordinarily had access. And she studied the huge subject of medicine, looking with particular concentration at drawings of anatomy detailed in a way that made her realise that they had been made from actual exploration of the human body. For any person found actually cutting up the dead, would invite the punishment of death—yet it had been done. And how else would man ever learn?

She had brought paper with her and studiously copied these charts for future reference. There were books on ancient philosophy, as ancient man tried to understand the meaning of life. She was glad of her knowledge of Latin and Greek. Some there in Hebrew, and these she regretfully put aside.

Today she found it difficult to concentrate and went to the window. She had been feeling squeamish, almost faint at times and had an inkling of what this might mean. It was early May. Outside in the palace gardens the birds were singing. She knew great preparations were underway for the King's coronation. It was to be a prestigious event, to impress on the nation the fact that the country was no longer a republic, but once more a monarchy! Nor would this King be party to civil war as was his father. The country would be ruled wisely by a man who knew how fortunate he was that fate had restored him to the throne of his fathers.

Charles would always be spoken of as a merry monarch—yet merry he was not, as Sophie well knew, but always watchful, surrounding himself where possible by those he ould trust. Although she had decided never to enter again into that initial intimate relationship yet she did so, knowing that what they shared was more a bonding of spirit than mere bodily satisfaction. Afterwards they would lie together as he discussed matters of State with her, letting his guard down, as he opened hidden hurts of the long years of exile, to her inspection. And Sophie in her turn told him of her earlier life—the aridity of her existence in the house of Roger Haversham, his beatings, her joy to discover he was not her father and bewilderment to learn that the kindly woman she loved as mother, was indeed her aunt.

Charles let himself quietly into the library today and his dark eyes examined the work she had been studying.

'I would that my grandfather could read this,' she said.

'You must bring your grandfather to court one day soon, sweetheart,' he said now. 'He sounds a most interesting man, Perhaps he could become a member of the Royal Society.'

'I think that I will soon be returning to him in the country—not my grandfather to Westminster. I am with child, Charles!' There, she had come out with it, this secret knowledge of which even her father was unaware of. But in a few weeks her state would be obvious and ever practical she knew arrangements must be made. He stared at her. Although he had obviously been aware of the possibility of this happening, yet it surprised him. For Sophie was so unlike all other women in his life. The only woman he equally esteemed was his young sister Henrietta Anne.

He took her in his arms and gently questioned her.

'How long do you think, Sophie?'

'I think perhaps three months!' She turned an anxious face up to him. 'I am fearful of what people will say when I return unwed but with child to my village.' He placed a comforting arm about her shoulders.

'The child you bear will be member of my family, always under my protection—as will his mother! Perhaps the better course is to get you wed, Sophie.' He started to cast about in his mind for a suitable prospect. 'How say you to an older man, one who would not overburden you with his attentions, but glad of companionship in his failing years. I am thinking of Sir Gareth Mereton, a fine old friend of my father's. He is childless. His two sons died at Naseby. Your child would inherit his estate!'

She stared at him, about to dismiss his suggestion out of hand then tried to think logically. Yes, she could bring up her child on her own, with the help of her father, grandfather and Aunt. But although this felt the right, the independent way, would it not be better for the child to have the protection of a father's name?

'But it would be totally wrong, dishonest to make this Sir Gareth imagine he was the father!' she turned her blue eyes on him searchingly.

'I will speak with him, explain the situation. Your father also needs to be made aware of the situation, Sophie.' He bit his lip. He knew he must speak to Hawksley personally and it would not be easy. A definite coldness now existed between them following on Hawksley's realisation that his daughter now shared an intimate relationship with him. It was regrettable for Hawksley had ever been a most loyal friend.

Her father had been shocked but not surprised when she had given him her news. It had seemed inevitable owing to Charles proclivity for paternity. His interview with Charles had been frosty, but he had seen the sense in the proposed marriage between Sophie and the elderly royalist, whose estate was adjacent to his own.

Now Sophie waited for introduction to one who might be her future husband. Wearing her favourite blue gown, already finding it tight about her waist, she sat in the small parlour to which she had been led, hands folded modestly on her lap, her head bowed in reverie, her thoughts troubled.

'Lady?' she heard the deep voice and looked up startled, had not been aware of his quiet entrance and wondered how long he had been standing thus leaning on his cane, quietly observing her.

'Sir Gareth Mereton,' he said with a courteous bow, 'And you I believe are Mistress Sophie Louise Hawksley?' She rose to her feet, inclined her head and curtsied. He saw how young she was and obviously embarrassed. 'I understood from his Majesty that he considered it expeditious that we meet. He has spoken very highly of you.'

'Did he tell you of my circumstances, Sir Gareth,' she asked directly?

'He did, my dear. I understand the situation perfectly. But please, will you not be seated again—and I will seat myself next to you if you permit.' He lowered himself stiffly onto an adjacent chair. 'I have spoken with your father, a man I much esteem and depending on your wishes in the matter, now ask whether you will consider accepting my hand in marriage?'

She stared at him. She had expected a long preamble before they even discussed marriage—and yet it was a relief to speak of it openly. He had a kind face, with shrewd grey eyes and deep lines of pain about his mouth. His hair was silver, thick still despite his obvious years. At first sight before he seated himself she had judged him to be about six foot, possibly even taller, for he stooped somewhat over his cane.

'You would seem to be of an age with my grandfather,' she said, coming out with the statement without thinking.

'And you my dear in the tender springtime of your years! You are wondering if such age gap makes marriage between us—difficult.'

She nodded. 'A natural thought perhaps.' she said warily.

'I can see that for you, such may be the case. Youth ever responds to youth, not to age. Yet I dare to suggest that based on what I have heard about you from the King, nor I do not refer to the child you carry, that you would make me an excellent wife, have an exceptional mind and a deep interest in medicine. I am also aware of the care with which you tended the late Princess Royal, at risk to your own health.'

'I will never forget her,' said Sophie softly. And then continued, 'And yes, I have a real interest in medicine. If I were a man, then I would be a physician—find it difficult that my gender makes this prohibitive.' She spoke with passion in her voice.

'I imagine that once your child is born, then a desire for the more usual feminine pursuits may come about.' He smiled. 'I like you, Sophie! I had never thought to marry again after my late wife's death. I loved Norah with all my heart, mourned her deeply. Our sons died fighting for the late king of blessed memory. Since then, I have managed my estates and buried myself in my books!' He watched her expression as he spoke.

'You have many books, sir?' She looked at him with new interest.

'An extensive library luckily not despoiled by those ruffians of the commonwealth who once occupied my house! I live but a few miles away from Hawksley Manor, my dear. The house is old—but comfortable. I would engage a nurse to help you with your babe when born and see that you enjoy every comfort. In return, I hope to enjoy your company, but not in any intimate sense, to put your mind at rest!' He nodded understandingly at the look of relief that spread across her face.

'I think we might become good friends,' she said shyly. 'You know of course that the King is father of my child.'

'So he told me. But the child will be known as child of mine and legitimate heir, to safeguard his or her future.' She stared at him for a long moment. Then Sophie reached forward and stretched her hands out to him.

'Are you sure about what you are proposing?' she asked quietly. For answer he raised one of her hands to his lips.

'Very sure,' he replied!

'Then I accept your offer, Sir Gareth, and will try to make you a good wife!' She rose to her feet and went to stand next to him. He attempted to rise with her, but arthritic knees made the movement difficult and she slipped an arm under his. He looked at her with a flash of humour.

'It would seem that your wifely duties have already started! Painful joints, my dear.'

'I have an ointment that may help that,' she said practically and he burst into self mocking laughter.

'Was ever a marriage so planned?' And now she joined in his laughter. 'Came, let us go to your father, that all may be done correctly!'

James Hawksley glanced from one to the other in the long gallery, as his daughter accompanied by Sir Gareth looked at him expectantly. Sophie saw by the look on her father's face that he did not seem happy. Nor was he! He had hoped for a good marriage for Sophie, but one where she would experience love in the full meaning of the word. Perhaps this intended marriage with his old friend Gareth was the best she could hope for now that she was enceinte, but oh how he wished it had been otherwise. And of course it was kind of Gareth to agree to the King's suggestion that he should wed the young girl, despite the difference in their ages.

Gareth was not a Catholic, but this did not matter as Sophie had been brought up in the reformed church and now attended Anglican services. The wedding would have to be a quiet one, so as not to lead to unpleasant gossip and conjecture, for all knew of her friendship with the King. At the present moment, Sophie showed no sign of her pregnancy, apart from a loss of appetite in the mornings.

And so it was arranged. Sophie had a fine new gown of white silk sewn with tiny blue bows caught up over a turquoise underskirt for the ceremony which was conducted in a sumptuous private chamber set aside for the purpose by the King, who was present for the occasion. Indeed he stood at Sir Miles side, as they waited by the improvised table altar, for the bride to appear on her father's arm. How beautiful she looked, thought James Hawksley fondly, so like her late mother and he stifled a sigh as led her to her elderly bridegroom.

The priest who officiated smiled at the couple whose nuptials were being overseen by the King himself. Nor did he find it unusual that they presented such contrast in age and appearance. It was common practice for marriage to be used to form bond between wealthy landowners. This young girl would have a secure future with the groom, a man high in the royal favour for his devotion to the late King's cause, in which his two sons had given their lifeblood. A few members of the court were present, two to act as witnesses. If any of them wondered at the marriage, they said nothing although some looked thoughtfully at the bride's waistline, but it betrayed nothing.

At last it was over and Sophie felt numb. She could hardly accept the fact that she was a married woman and subject to this man whom she hardly knew. What now of all her dreams of studying medicine? Two carriages rolled out of the narrow congested streets of London. One bore the Hawksley coat of arms and contained her father, the other the crest of Sir Gareth Mereton and it was in the latter that Sophie sat on the cushioned seat opposite her husband, as the wooden wheels jolted over the cobbles and Sir Gareth tried not to flinch as his painful joints shrieked protest.

The journey was long. They stopped overnight at a country inn, where to her relief Sophie was given her own chamber. When she rose she realised that she felt slightly nauseous and tried to conceal the fact at table, where the heavy smell of ale and food and stale perspiration of the serving maid, the clatter coming from the kitchen, and the noise of other vociferous guests shouting at the land lord for their breakfast all combined to make her feel faint.

Her father saw her turn pale. He touched Sir Gareth's arm.

'Sophie is unwell! I will take her outside for a breath of fresh air.' Sophie's husband nodded and rose from his seat. He patted the girl's shoulder reassuringly.

'I will be glad to be out of this place myself. Let us go---Landlord! The bill if you please!' and he settled the reckoning. They left the noise and bustle behind and took breath of the clean soft wind blowing scent of May blossom towards them. How very fair the countryside looked, thought Sophie. She had almost forgotten how much she loved it, when back there in the artificial confines of Westminster. Here the banks were spangled with wind tossed wild flowers in gold, white and pink and in the hedgerows red tipped buds of dog rose were opening, pink and gold honeysuckle sweetened the air and little lambs gambolled in the pastures. England was looking at her loveliest.

It was dark when the two carriages rolled up the driveway of Hawksley Manor, for James had invited Sir Gareth and Sophie to stay overnight. It made sense, for they were all weary, especially Sophie.

The house looked welcoming and well cared for as they entered the great hall and the housekeeper Mrs Sarah Thompson whom Hawksley had engaged to care for the house shortly before he left for London, hurried towards them in amazement.

'Why my Lord, I had no idea we were to expect you,' she said. 'Welcome home, sir! I will prepare a meal for you and Mistress Sophie— and your guest?

'Mrs Thompson, this gentleman is Sir Gareth Mereton, my daughter Sophie's newly married husband. Perhaps we could have some wine—cold meats. Something of the sort, and then we will retire.'

'Where shall I sleep, father,' asked Sophie awkwardly, as the housekeeper bustled away, calling for the maid Sally to help her.

'You are obviously exhausted my dear. In your own chamber if Sir Gareth has no objection,' replied Hawksley. He locked glances with the older man, who bowed his consent. 'I will have the guest room next to mine prepared for you Gareth.'

'Sophie shall have her own chamber in my house also.' He saw the look of relief in her eyes and knew how concerned she had been at the prospect of his taking his marital rights with her. 'It is under the circumstances best for both of us. Because of my stiff and painful joints I am a light sleeper and often get up in the night to ease them. So tonight we will start in the way we will continue!' His grey eyes held the slightest touch of amusement.

Sophie bent forward and placed a light kiss on his cheek. 'Thank you, Gareth—for being so understanding,' she said quietly and he lifted her hand to his lips.

'I look forward to our life together my dear, to your companionship! Tomorrow, you shall see your new home and must always feel free to visit back here with your father whenever you so wish.'

Hawksley breathed a sigh of satisfaction, 'A glass of wine, Gareth? Let us drink a toast to new beginnings!' His dark eyes swept over his daughter. 'Yes—and to the new little life to come!'

It was dawn, and in the garden birds filled the air with the sweetness of their morning song. Sophie rose, pulled back the curtains and looked out. How good it was to be back. Over there she could see the woods where she had so often wandered with her grandfather—and where old Jessie Thorne had lived. Poor Jessie, she had almost forgotten the old woman who had been so brutally murdered, and amazingly left her cottage and possessions to Sophie.

Grandfather! She had meant to write to him many a time, but there had always been yet another visit to the king's library, where the call of those rare and treasured volumes obsessed most of her waking days. Now as she bathed in the water brought to her by a shy young waiting girl, she made decision to visit John Wheatley before proceeding to Sir Gareth's house, her new home.

Her father and Sir Gareth rose to their feet as she entered the dining room, looking they observed much refreshed after yesterday's journey. At first she felt somewhat shy as the man who was still a stranger, but now her husband, asked solicitously about her health.

'I am well, Sir! I hope that you also slept well?'

'Reasonably so, I thank you my dear.' His grey eyes smiled at her. 'Your father has asked whether we would like to spend a few days here at the manor, before leaving for Oaklands—my house that is. Well?'

Sophie eyes lit up. To spend a precious few days back here at the manor was more than she had dared to hope for. 'Thank you, I am most grateful. I wonder whether I may further ask visit to my aunt and Grandfather who live in the village. And if you have no objections, I would like to stay with them for two or three days. I have missed them so!' He nodded assent.

'I will have the carriage brought out for you later Sophie,' put in James Hawksley, but she shook her head. 'I want to ride my mare, the one you gave me, father!

'But in your condition?' He stared in concern.

'Pregnancy is not an illness, father! I am perfectly healthy!' The men looked at each other, about to remonstrate, but she quelled them with a look. And now dressed in her green riding habit, she made her way to the stables where the groom had already saddled the mare. Thomas Appleby, who had been running the estate in her father's absence and doing so very efficiently, came to help her mount..

'I will ride along with you, Mistress—Lady Mereton, that is,' he said with a twinkle in his eye, then as she attempted to protest, 'No, it is better so, for they have not yet captured that villain Harrison. When I see you safe at Doctor Wheatley's house I will stay in the village until you are ready to return! Your father insists on it!' he added.

'Very well, Tom! You can bring me up to date with happenings in the village as we ride.'

But they rode along the lane in silence at first, as Thomas Appleby tried to frame the question that was bothering him. At last he drew his horse in as Sophie stopped to snap a spray of golden honeysuckle from the hedge, and held it to her nostrils.

'Such sweet fragrance, Thomas!' she sighed.

'Yes indeed, lady.' He glanced at her. 'We were all much surprised that you are now married, Mistress Sophie? They say that Sir Gareth is a good man, but somewhat on in years to be a husband to one as young as you?'

She knew she must face the question head on. She had planned what she would say. 'It is not a love match, Thomas, but Sir Gareth is a good friend of my fathers and his land is next to the manor. Should we be blessed with a family, then our heir would inherit both properties.' There, she had said it and thankfully he nodded. It was not unusual for the landed gentry to manage matters so. But a shame that one as lovely and vivacious as this young girl should be wed to an elderly man who might not be capable of providing the hoped for heir!

They were taking the path through the woods, fresh and green with the tender leaves of spring, the forest floor lushly carpeted with bluebells and primroses and wood anemones. It looked and felt idyllic. Then she saw it. Sophie reigned in her horse sudden shock as they arrived at the familiar clearing where old Jessie's cottage stood—only now it was gone, only a blackened ruin remained amidst scorched earth.

'What happened here, Thomas—and why?' she asked bewildered.

'It was not done by any in the village, Mistress Sophie. It is suspected that Harrison's villains were responsible, one of his men involved in Jessie's murder was reported seen recently!' His face was grim as he spoke. 'If ever I get my hands on any of them,' and his eyes spoke volumes!

'Thomas, you must leave it to the officers of the law. They already have warrants out for the arrest of Harrison and all others of his loathsome crew!'

They rode on without further conversation, for the sight of that ruined cottage had brought back all too forcibly Sophie's memory of her abduction. But as they approached The Willows her grandfather's familiar house she brightened. Even more than the manor house it felt like home to her and she dismounted and left Thomas to take the horses round to the stable as she proceeded lightly up the path to the front door. She knocked and waited. It seemed a long while before the door was finally opened by Beth Giles.

'Beth—I'm back,' cried Sophie happily. She paused, wondering why the woman was looking at her so oddly.

'And just in time, I would say,' replied the housekeeper bleakly. 'Your grandfather is sinking fast. He has been asking for you, Mistress Sophie!'

'Grandfather is ill? Why wasn't I told? No word of it arrived at Westminster,' she cried in dismay. She pushed past the housekeeper's ample form and hurried through to the doctor's study and found it empty, of course, he must be in his bedroom if ill, and she raced upstairs.

She pushed the door open and froze. Sunlight from the window streamed across the patchwork quilt outlining the still figure on the bed. He lay there on the pillows, face pale and emaciated, white hair brushed back from his forehead, as Martha bent over him sponging his hands and face. She looked up as Sophie burst in with a cry of relief.

'Sophie, my child, thank God you've come! Your grandfather is.....'

'Dying, I fear,' whispered a faint voice, as John Wheatley endeavoured to sit up. 'Help me, Martha! Put these pillows behind my shoulders, that I may see my granddaughter properly.' With a cry of concern, Sophie ran forward and helped Martha raise him.

'Grandfather, why did you not send word, that you were ill? I would have come to you at once!' He looked at her worried young face and nodded.

'I know it, Sophie. But there was nothing you could have done.' He forced a slow smile. 'This old heart of mine is tired—like the rest of me. Why burden you with the inevitable? Besides, word came that you nursed Mary of Orange through her fatal attack of smallpox. I knew that you would have been much distressed at the outcome and didn't wish to place further worries on those young shoulders.' He was studying her face as he spoke. He saw the dark shadows around her eyes that bespoke concerns other than this final reunion. Her face also held new look of maturity.

'Grandfather, I was studying books in the King's library—he gave permission as reward for my care of his sister.'

'Why, this was great honour, Sophie!' he said softly.

'Perhaps, but I have something that I must tell both you and Mama.' She bit her lip. How could she actually bring herself to speak of it? It was Martha who noticed the gold wedding band on the girl's finger.

'Sophie, you are married,' she cried, 'See father—her ring?'

'Is this true, Sophie?'

'I am married to Sir Gareth Mereton. And I am with child, grandfather!' She flushed a bright red as she came out with the shameful secret. 'The child is not my husband's—but the King's!'

'Sophie,' poured the combined cries of distress from Martha and John Wheatley.

'It is true. The marriage one of convenience, that the child may be born in wedlock and so become Sir Gareth's heir. The King wished it so.' She sat down wearily on the side of the bed and took her grandfather's hand. It felt rigid to her touch, unyielding. She realised the shock her words had caused. Martha too was standing with her mouth slightly open, eyes bewildered, 'No—no,' she whispered.

'You have become the King's mistress, Sophie?' he asked stiffly at last.

'Oh, how could you be so foolish my dear,' whispered Martha. 'Did he force you?' It seemed the only logical answer to the situation, knowing Sophie as she did and Martha was filled with fierce anger against the King who had so abused her child.

'No. He did not force me, Mama. He—I—well, it just happened. I knew what I was doing, but had not the strength or the desire to draw back. But I am not his mistress rather we have become good friends, who discuss many matters together. He said he would like you to come to court, grandfather to become a member of the Royal Society where many subjects of scientific interest are explored.'

A tremor passed over John Wheatley's face. How wonderful such an invitation might have been had things been otherwise. As his tired brain tried to focus on the fact that it was not merely passion that had drawn his beloved grandchild and the promiscuous monarch together, but a love of learning which bound them, his face relaxed.

'You discuss such matters with the King, child?'

'He has a great interest in medicine, the curiosities of nature and all things mechanical, clocks for instance his special delight and he studies the night sky through his telescope.'

'Unusual all this in a monarch,' mused Wheatley, listening to her intently.

'He is surrounded by courtiers who are self seeking, among them many he does not trust. True he has his mistresses, but I doubt whether he actually loves them, foremost of them Barbara Palmer, now Lady

Cleveland, a bold and beautiful woman who behaves outrageously.' She paused seeking to be fair in her assessment of Barbara.

'She has shown a certain friendship towards me,' she continued, 'for she knows I am no rival. She calls me Charles little bookworm!' The words poured tumbling from of her lips, as she tried to make them understand the situation.

'And what does your father say to all this, Sophie? Surely he does not condone the King's usage of you?' The doctor tried to recall Hawksley's face to memory, the slight hauteur with which he carried himself, how did such a man respond to this wrong done to his daughter? 'Well?'

'His indignation was great! But now he has accepted the situation. The King wished me to marry and Sir Gareth is a friend of father's. He seems kind. We were wed three days past and the King attended the ceremony.' Now that she had lain all bare before aunt and grandfather, she drew a deep breath. 'I am home now, well at least I will not be living far from here and can visit often.'

'I am glad you are back from the sophistries of the court, child! For myself, I will not be here much longer. It is therefore good that you have arrived in time for me to discuss certain matters with you.' He started to cough and the effort left him breathless and shaken.

'Father—take a sip of this cordial,' urged Martha anxiously.

'Very well.' and his lips barely touched the cup. 'Now what I have to discuss is what will become of The Willows after my death. No don't interrupt me either of you. This is important. You Martha are still legally married to that scoundrel Haversham. If I leave the house and all my possessions to you, then your husband may claim them in law. He has not dared to show his face here while I am still alive to protect you, but when I am no longer around—it may be different!'

'Oh, I had not even thought of Roger,' breathed Martha in shock. 'But surely as many are now aware of his treatment of me, that he nearly killed me, surely he would not risk coming here?' But even as she spoke, Martha acknowledged secretly that Haversham might and the thought brought panic to her breast.

'To prevent any possible future villainy on his behalf, I am leaving all I possess to Sophie!' his eyes regarded the girl solemnly. 'I lay it on your heart Sophie to look after your aunt who has been such good and caring parent to you and that you will call upon your father Lord Hawksley and your husband to have a care of her.' He sank back on the pillows.

'Oh, grandfather! Of course I will look after mama! She may come and stay with me at Oakhams. She will be safe there from Haversham and I know Sir Gareth will welcome her for my sake. Do not worry for her future.' As he heard her words, John Wheatley relaxed.

'My lawyer has my will, all drawn up correctly and signed before witnesses. What will you do with this place Sophie, sell it perhaps?'

'Sell it—never! Whatever happens in life, this house will remain a haven to return to for both Mama and for me. You have my promise as to that, dear grandfather.' Her voice almost broke on a sob. For Sophie realised that the sick man had not many moments left, that he had spent his last strength in making his wishes known to them. He spoke again.

'Then there is Mrs Giles—Beth. She has ever been good friend as well as housekeeper. I have provided for her in my will, but....?'

'We will look after Beth! Now try to sleep,' she whispered, holding his hand to her lips. He shook his head.

Soon I commence my last deep sleep. Before this I would make my peace with my Saviour. Martha dear, please send for the Reverend Markham.' He closed his eyes, exhausted. Martha called for Beth Giles.

'Beth—he's asking for the minister!'

'I'll get him directly Maam.' And the housekeeper threw a shawl about her shoulders and hurried along the street to the rectory. David Markham was a close friend of Wheatley's of many years. Despite the difficulties endured by Anglicans during the years of Commonwealth persecution, he had courageously performed his pastoral care of his flock and now rejoiced that the king had restored the Anglican Church as the national church of the land.

'What's that you say—the Doctor is dying? Why did you not send for me sooner, Beth?' He picked up the carved wooden box in which he kept the sacred communion bread, goblet and small flask of wine. 'Let us make all speed,' he said.

Chapter Eight

Sophie's blue eyes were reddened with weeping, her nose swollen, as she stood with Martha's arm about her, watching as the coffin was lowered into the cold chasm in the dark waiting earth. She listened to David Markham's comforting words about the resurrection, but her mind screamed protest that she had been bereft of the one person whom she so deeply loved and respected. She would always feel guilt for not returning sooner to the home where she had been received with such love and kindness by the wonderful man who had opened her mind to knowledge. Now he was gone, would never speak to her again.

She threw a handful of earth onto the oak coffin, as did Martha. Now it was over and they stood alone, the mourners making their way back along the church pathway. David Markham smiled gently before also taking leave. He knew they needed time to make their private farewells.

'Come—let us go home,' whispered Martha at last. 'There will be many who will call to pay their respects, friends and patients he cared for over the years.' She was right. They were kept busy during the late afternoon and evening as people came to the door and offered their condolences to the doctor's daughter and lovely granddaughter, and drank a glass of wine to his memory.

She slept that night exhausted, too tired for tears, or to think of her future. She woke early the following morning. Outside in the garden a blackbird sang his ear sweet, distinctive song, to be joined by the rhapsodic morning chorus. Sophie drew the curtains and stared out. The sun was shining, casting shafts of gold between the whispering trees bordering the garden, striking crystal brilliance onto the small pool, next to which was situated the wooden bench where she had so often sat with her grandfather in the recent past. It was hard to believe they would never sit and talk there again.

She joined Martha at breakfast, served by a subdued Beth Giles, her own face bearing trace of her grief. Neither of them felt hungry and rose leaving their plates barely touched. They withdrew into the doctor's comfortable parlour, as Beth Giles bent and laid a match to the fire. It was then they heard a knock at the front door. The housekeeper rose, excused herself and rubbing her hands on her white starched apron, hurried to open it.

'It's your father, Mistress Sophie and another gentleman!' she whispered then stood aside to let the visitors pass.

'We only heard this morning, my dear—or we would have come sooner,' cried James Hawksley. Sophie gave a cry of relief as her father folded her in his arms, and stroked her hair soothingly. Then he released her and Sophie acknowledged the elderly man who stood beside him, with a curtsey.

'Sophie,' Sir Gareth bore her hand to his lips and saluted it gravely. 'I am chagrined that you have had to cope with the hurt of your grandfather's death on your own,' he said quietly.

'Not on my own. Allow me to introduce my Aunt Martha. From my infancy, she took the place of my mother who died weeks after giving birth to me, and now is grieving death of her father, as I am of a deeply loved grandfather!'

She stood back slightly, as Martha stepped forward and inclined her head to both Hawksley and this stranger who was married to Sophie. She noticed the lines of pain etched on his face but that his eyes were kind and she relaxed He smiled encouragingly, took her hand and bowed over it.

'But of course, James mentioned you to me, Mistress!'

'Would it be possible for my aunt to live with us, Sir Gareth?' asked Sophie, thinking that she had better get the question out of the way at once.

'Would this make you happy, Sophie?' he questioned.

'Oh yes! The more especially as she is in fear of her estranged violent husband, whose cruelties were such that grandfather rescued her when she was lying near to death in their house.' She blurted out the story and saw Mereton's eyes narrow in outrage. 'He never dared come near her while grandfather was alive, but may come now thinking she will have inherited this house!'

Now Martha spoke for the first time, watching Sir Gareth's face as she further explained the situation..

'In fact my father left The Willows to Sophie for this very reason, so Roger Haversham should have no legal claim to the house or any other of my father's possessions! I certainly do fear him, sir—in the past he showed violence to Sophie as well as to me and possesses a vile temper! But I would not wish to be a burden to you!' Her embarrassment plainly showed.

'Lady, you will be most welcome. My old house has much need of the feminine touch and I will be glad of the company. Sophie will no doubt find your presence comforting as she takes up her new duties.' He spoke decisively and so it was settled.

'As for Haversham,' spoke up James Hawksley, dark eyes smouldering, 'Let him attempt to come near either of you and he will have me to deal with! I should have dealt with the bounder months ago for his treatment of you both!'

'Perhaps I might have a seat,' suggested Sir Gareth, glancing around. 'These knees of mine...!' Beth Giles hurriedly pulled a chair forward for the elderly visitor, whom she now realised was Sophie's new wed husband. So much was happening and her face showed her distraction.

'Beth—a glass of wine for the gentlemen and refreshments,' said Martha, taking charge of the situation. 'We expect father's lawyer this morning, coming to discuss the details of the will! I am glad that you will both be present at the reading.'

At last the long morning was over, all legalities observed and now Sophie and Martha sat opposite Sir Gareth in his carriage, as they set off for their new home, James Hawksley following behind on his stallion. They discovered that Oaklands was only a bare three miles past Hawksley Manor and despite her tiredness and grief, Sophie looked around with interest, as the carriage proceeded down the long tree lined avenue of gracious mature oaks and the fine old house of cherry brick, crowned with tall slender chimneys came into view.

'Why—it's beautiful,' exclaimed Sophie, as the carriage drew up outside the main entrance and the driver helped them out. Sir Gareth mounted the front steps to the balustraded porch with care, leaning lightly on his young wife's arm, his cane giving further support, as Hawksley joined them, after giving orders to the groom for the careful stabling of his horse.

'I remember this place so well,' cried Hawksley, as a white haired footman bowed them in as they stood in the high vaulted hall and Sophie exclaimed at the pine clad walls, where portraits of Mereton ancestors stared down at them, seemingly frozen in time.

'You have preserved more of your pictures than I have been able to,' cried Hawksley. 'I managed to store some away from Cromwell's predatory bastards and the library is relatively unspoiled.'

'I heard that Harrison's men tried to set your house on fire,' said Sir Gareth, turning to face the younger man inquiringly. Hawksley nodded, his eyes blazing with sudden anger.

'It would have burned to the ground, had not the blacksmith Paul Masters and a young lad, Ben doused the flames! I am eternally grateful to them. The damage has been repaired, burnt items replaced as best I've been able—but if ever I get my hands on the perpetrators!' He scowled, then relaxed, for now they stood staring up at a painting of three young boys, one of whom Sophie realised was her father as a child.

'Remember when this was painted, James? None of you wanted to remain still for the artist, a Frenchman who was in despair—until my wife produced some sweetmeats. Had they not died at Naseby, my two sons would have been almost of an age with you now and likewise rejoicing in the Restoration!'

'The coronation is to take place this month,' said Hawksley. 'I plan to return to London. It promises to be an outstanding occasion with much pomp and ceremony. I would have liked Sophie to have seen it—but perhaps she should take life quietly for the next few months.'

'I agree,' replied Mereton firmly. 'Sophie will find plenty to engage her here in her new home,' he added and her father nodded reluctant agreement.

They are discussing me as though I have no say in the matter, thought Sophie. I suppose this is how it will be now I am married! Oh how I wish that I had refused to take a step that limits my personal freedom. Just let this baby be born and then I'll start to reassert my independence. But even as the thoughts chased through her mind, she felt Mereton's eyes upon her and saw the rigidity behind the undoubted kindness glimpsed there.

Three weeks had passed, weeks in which Sophie began to settle into her new routine as mistress of Oaklands. She soon realised that the beautiful old house had been let go somewhat of recent years, not surprising considering that it had been occupied by the troops of the Commonwealth and Sir Gareth had only regained control of his house and estate by paying an exorbitant fine to the government. Little money remained to put repairs into effect. The fact that his beloved wife Norah had also died following the deaths of both his sons left him with little desire to do more than restore a pale semblance of Oakland's former glory.

The servants who had led a relatively easy life until recently, had a shock as Martha took them in hand. Now all was polished and clean, meals served in a way that delighted Sir Gareth, who was satisfied that his decision in inviting his wife's aunt to stay with them had borne such excellent fruit. As for Sophie, she spent much of her time in her husband's library avidly reading the dusty volumes that lined the shelves, tidying and cataloguing them. Sadly only a couple dealt with medicine.

'I want to visit The Willows today,' she said to Sir Gareth, as they walked in the gardens where roses and hollyhocks bloomed. 'I would like to bring some of grandfather's books here.' He smiled at her indulgently.

'Providing you take the carriage, Sophie, with two of my men to accompany you, for protection,' he said. 'I do not want to risk any harm befalling you. After what Harrison's men did to old Jessie's cottage and their attempt to burn down your father's house, we cannot be too careful!' His voice brooked no dispute and she nodded. Much as she would have delighted in a ride on her spirited mare, she knew this would only provoke a dispute. She turned a warm smile upon him.

'Well if I am to take the carriage, perhaps Mama may come too?'

'If Martha wishes to, but don't stay there long, this is your home now,' he said incisively. 'Yet I suppose it is only right that you check that the housekeeper Beth Giles is looking after the place properly!'

So they set out, Sophie and Martha in the carriage, driven by a young groom and two of Sir Gareth's men mounted on stout ponies following behind. There was a slight shower of rain, followed by a rainbow looping the sky behind the woods and a dazzle of bright sunlight stroked across the roof of The Willows as the carriage drew up and Sophie and Martha stepped down. They directed the groom and their attendants round to the stables, as they started up the pathway together for the first time since they had left the house in deep sorrow, three weeks before.

Sophie knocked. When Beth Giles saw who it as who stood at the door, she gave a cry of delight.

'Why, Mistress Sophie—come in, come in! And you Mistress Wheatley!' She always referred to Martha so, for the doctor had forbidden the name of Haversham to be uttered in the house.

'Beth, it's so good to see you,' cried Sophie. 'Listen, our driver and two of Sir Gareth's men came with us. Perhaps they could have refreshments in the kitchen?'

'I'll call to Dawlish to tend them!' and she did so. 'How well you are both looking!' She glanced discreetly at Sophie's waistline, which had thickened as she approached the fifth month of her pregnancy. They followed Beth through to the small parlour and smiled as she fussed about them, offering wine and some of her new baked cake.

'It hardly seems to have changed' said Sophie at last. Yet that was not true, for the house lacked the vital presence of the kindly physician who had spent his life in the care of others. 'If only grandfather was still here!' she sighed.

'I gave you my word that I would keep the house the way it always was and I aim to keep that promise, Mistress Sophie. 'The garden he loved is still being well tended.'

'I miss that garden,' said Sophie.

'But surely you have a much larger and more beautiful garden at that Oaklands? It is said that the house is magnificent!' she probed.

'I would give it all up in a trice if I could only return here to live!'

Looking at her sharply, Beth Giles knew that the girl was not happy. 'That old Sir Gareth Mereton will not live forever, my dear. Eventually you will be able to choose to live wheresoever you wish!'

'Beth,' said Martha reprovingly.

'It's true, Mistress! May and December are not well matched together! There, I have said enough. As I told you, the house is being well looked after as you can see. I feel a bit lonesome at times, but there is always Daniel Dawlish to have a word with and young Richard Appleby calls by to see if I need anything from the village.'

'How is young Richard? I remember how grandfather saved his life, when he was gravely injured trying to save me from Harrison's villains!' Sophie smiled as she thought of the youth.

'He is fine, Mistress—shooting up still. Will be as tall as his father I shouldn't wonder.' She paused. 'I am not sure whether to mention it, for it may just be my imagination.'

'What is it, Beth,' asked Martha, leaning forward, and brushing the cake crumbs from her lips. The housekeeper frowned. She stared at the window.

'Well, it's just that I have seen a strange man watching the house recently. He disappears as soon as I walk to the garden gate. I have the feeling that he is up to no good!' She glanced back to the window and they saw from her expression that she was deeply uneasy.

'Have you told Dawlish?' She knew the doctor's stableman and gardener would always keep a watchful eye on Beth.

'Daniel just laughed and said I must have an admirer! But I thought I saw the man again, as I opened the door to you both just now!' She shrugged. 'Probably just some stranger come to live in the village.'

'I will have a word with Dawlish before I leave today,' said Sophie firmly. 'Now Beth, I want to go through some of grandfather's books and will take a few back with me to Oaklands. I know Mama wishes to go upstairs to her old room.'

Some hours had passed, before Sophie rose from her grandfather's desk, where she had been exploring some of concise medical notes written in his distinctive fine script. She would take these with her, together with a pile of books she had selected. She had also collected a few jars of dried herbs. She was just packing all into the canvas bag she had brought for the purpose, when she heard a loud knocking at the front door, voices.

'You can't come in here, do you hear me!' she heard Mrs Giles shout. 'Get out! You have no business here!'

'Woman—my name is Haversham. I'm sure you must have heard the name. I have come for my wife!' Sophie went pale, listened incredulously to the harsh, pompous tones of the man who had brutalised Martha and beaten her also, so unmercifully in the past. He was here? But how had he known to come on just this particular day—unless the stranger Beth had reported as watching the house, had been an informer for Haversham?

'I must remain calm,' she whispered. 'He probably doesn't know that I have three of Gareth's men in the kitchen and Dawlish must be nearby!' Then she heard Martha's voice raised in fear.

'Get out of this house! I will call for help!'

'And who will prevent a man taking his runaway wife home, eh? I heard the old doctor has died, and likely left this place to you—and that you had disappeared no-one knew where!' By now Sophie had hurried down the passageway and reached the hall, where Martha was struggling to free herself from Haversham's grip as Beth rushed past calling for Dawlish.

'Unhand her at once, you bully! How dare you come to this house?' cried Sophie in sharp authoritative tones. Roger Haversham raised his eyes from Martha and stared in fiendish delight as he saw Sophie standing there.

'So, the ungrateful wench I looked after with such care all her life and who dared to raise her hand to me? Well now, I will take two back for the price of one!' he snarled. Then his eyes slid down to her waist and he stared at her knowingly. 'No doubting what you have been up to, girl, whoring like your late mother!' he sneered.

'You had better not let Sir Gareth Mereton hear you speak to me so,' snapped Sophie furiously.

'Mereton—Sir Gareth Mereton of Oaklands?' he looked at her uncertainly. 'What's he to you then? '

'My husband, sir,' and he saw the truth flash in her eyes.

'You are married?' He noticed the gold band on her finger, the quality of her clothes. 'Well I wish the old dotard joy of you!' he blustered. 'But this one is coming with me. I have a legal right to take my wife home. Yes and as her husband, this house now belongs to me!'

'You are wrong on both counts, Roger,' said Martha between shaking lips. 'My father left this house and all his possessions to his granddaughter, in order to protect me from just such a plan as this! I now live at Oaklands with Sir Gareth and Sophie—that's her real name as you know not Rachel! So your journey here avails you nothing!' His face went a dark red as he heard her words and the chords of his neck stiffened in his rage.

'You will come with me if I order you to,' he screamed, cheeks turning puce. It was at this moment that he found himself surrounded by four men, one of whom he recognised as Dawlish.

'This fellow annoying you, Lady Mereton,' asked one of those who had accompanied the women here.

'He is! Please make him go,' cried Sophie.

'You—get out of here, unless you want a broken jaw,' growled Dawlish dangerously, as the others gleefully manhandled him to the doorway. He broke free and uttered a series of curses. He turned back and shook his fist at Martha.

'Don't think you have got away with it,' he shouted. 'I will drag you home one day woman, and will beat you within an inch of your miserable life!' He staggered away down the pathway, still shouting and raving, then of a sudden stood stock still. They saw him raise his hands to his head and he swayed, and then he fell as though poleaxed to the ground.

All watched in shocked bewilderment. Then Sophie walked slowly down the pathway and bent over the man who had caused such misery in her life. She placed her fingers to his throat—no pulse. His eyes now held a glassy stare. It needed no physician, to diagnose his death from stroke.

None truly mourned the pompous, outwardly pious, but corrupt late owner of the Longstaff Inn at Langley Morton. He was buried in the churchyard, with no family member to witness the dark clods of earth falling on his coffin, for none existed apart from his widow, who had not been present at the funeral. Was Martha Haversham now the owner of the popular coaching inn? It would seem so. But for now its doors were closed, waiting the new owner's instructions and men went thirsty at the end of their day.

Martha sat with the lawyer, still hardly able to comprehend that the bestial husband who had terrorised her for so many years would do so no more, slept beneath a gravestone at Langley Morton. Mr Colton cleared his throat.

'Well, Mistress Haversham, under the law, since your late husband left no will and had no children of his begetting, then the house and the Longstaff Inn are yours to dispose of as you will. I suppose you could put in a manager for the Inn, indeed the man who has held this post of recent years, might seem a good choice—the continuity of service smoothly carried on.'

'I think I will sell both properties. Can you attend to this on my behalf, Mr Colton? I never wish to set foot in either again!' Martha's eyes were hard.

'If that is what you wish, mistress! I will get the best price I can. You may depend on my best efforts.' He shuffled his papers, rose to his feet and bowed. He departed, walking confidently down the pathway of The Willows considering that Martha Haversham—Wheatley as she preferred to be called, would probably receive many future offers of marriage. She had retained her looks and would bring a goodly dowry to a new husband. It never occurred to him that this was one woman who would never willingly embrace the bonds of matrimony again!

Martha returned to Oaklands in the late afternoon, a week after she had left there. Sophie ran forward to the door embraced her aunt, demanding to know all that had been happening over the last few days.

'I should have stayed with you after Haversham's death,' she said softly, seeing the lines of strain on Martha's forehead and noting that she wore black. But there was a new note of decision in her voice when she spoke.

'Child, you did exactly the right thing in returning here. Sir Gareth would have been terribly put out had you remained after the horror of what happened that day!' She shuddered as she remembered it.

'I only left reluctantly and at your insistence, Mama!'

'There was nothing you could have done,' said Martha incisively. 'Now at last, neither of us need fear Roger Haversham again! Today I instructed the lawyer to sell the house and the inn. The money will give me the independence I crave. Never again will I have to fear a man's cruelties!' And Martha smiled.

'I am so glad he is dead!' declared Sophie. 'But I know not all men behave towards women as he did!' But even as she said the words, Sophie experienced her ongoing sense of resentment that a man could in law use a wife or daughter as he chose. 'I wish I was not married,' she said vehemently.

'But child, it is better so for the babe you carry to be born legitimate and Sir Gareth is a good husband to you.'

'October cannot come quickly enough,' frowned Sophie crossly. 'I missed the King's coronation last month because of this pregnancy and I feel so restless shut up in the house every day. Gareth refuses to let me ride my mare and where can I go in the carriage? Father is away at the court. I do so long to walk in the woods again as I used with grandfather.' She ran her hands over the small mound that was her unborn child and tried not to think that before long she would look huge and probably waddle around like a duck! Why should women have to bear children—why not men?

'My Lady, Sir Gareth is asking for you,' said a respectful footman. Martha smiled, squeezed Sophie's hand and started up the wide staircase to her room. Sophie sighed rebelliously. She returned to the spacious drawing room, where her elderly husband sat before a blazing fire despite the warm summer sunshine outside, his legs resting on a cushioned stool.

'I'm sorry, Gareth. Mama has just returned from the village, her affairs now in order after Haversham's death.' He glanced up at her with a twinkle in his eyes. How very young she looked he thought, despite her advancing pregnancy.

'I'm glad she is back, Sophie, for she has a wonderful way of controlling the household, for you are much taken up with your books.' It was not a rebuke exactly, but she coloured, as it was true she had little interest in the running of the house, for she did not look on it as her own.

'Mama is better at these matters! After all, once the baby is born, I will probably not have much time for books!' She drew a chair up next to him.

'How are your knees today, Sir? She leaned forward and touched one of them lightly. He placed one of his hands over hers.

'The discomfort seems more bearable since I took that potion you made up for me! I think I shall have to call you my young physician!' He considered her from shrewd eyes and lifted a bushy eyebrow. 'Try to be patient, Sophie—we must both take great care of the King's future son or daughter!'

It was the first time since the day they had met that he had alluded to the true paternity of her future child, and Sophie wondered why he now spoke of it openly. It probably was not any easier for him than it was for her, this situation!

'Why did you agree to marry me,' she asked?

'Because my King asked it of me,' he replied. 'But I must say when I saw your winsome face child, the decision was easy.'

'I am not being a very good wife to you, I suppose!' she bit her lip guiltily.

'You give me the joy of your companionship and at my age, what better could I ask? You have brought new life into this old house, my dear.' He squeezed he hand gently. 'And yes, I know it irks you not to be able to go riding, but safer so for your child's sake.'

The long summer days were long gone, the harvest gathered in and late September's mists drifted along the tree lined avenue to Oaklands, where leaves were beginning to colour in suggestion of their deeper vibrant autumn shades. The mist dampened Sophie's cheeks as she walked heavily around the formal garden, her hand resting lightly on Martha's arm.

'Just a few more weeks, child,' said Martha encouragingly.

'Yes! And then I will be free of this monstrous stomach!' said Sophie petulantly then smiled, 'Will it be a boy of a girl do you suppose? Somehow it still doesn't seem quite real, that I am to be a mother!'

'When you hold the little one in your arms, it will give you great joy! How I wish that I had been able to bear a child. It's something every woman takes for granted—but what sorrow when it does not happen.' They walked on, Sophie considering Martha's words and the hidden pain she had never mentioned before.

'Why did you marry Roger Haversham?'

'I thought I loved him, the marriage promised security. He was handsome then, flattered me with his attentions. My father was against the match and I fool that I was, would not listen to his good advice.' Martha sighed. 'We cannot go back in life, Sophie, only forwards and if wise to learn from our mistakes.' She shook her head sadly.

'I can barely imagine how difficult conditions must have been at that time, with the country in the upheaval of a civil war, neighbour turning against neighbour.' But it was of her own mother Sophie was thinking as she spoke, of the girl who had thrown away her good name to courageously run away with a Catholic royalist—for none had known of Lucy Wheatley's secret marriage to Lord James Hawksley. She could not have been much older than Sophie was now, when she died a few weeks after childbirth. For the first time Sophie wondered if this might be her fate also? Many women died in childbirth. It was a fact. Others became old before their time, worn out with constant pregnancies to satisfy their husband's passions.

Her silver buckled shoes kicked the light scattering of acorns and fallen leaves from the oak tree beneath which she paused. It would be November before it was bare of its gold and bronze and winter commenced to hold the land in its freezing grip. Her babe moved suddenly and instinctively she placed protective hands over her stomach. Another two or three weeks!

A warm fire roared in the grate in Sophie's bedroom, the casement firmly closed and curtains drawn that the mother to be should not suffer any ill effect from evil humours from the outside world. She had been in labour for a full twenty-four hours and now set her teeth into her kerchief as another contraction wracked her. The urge to bear down was almost impossible to ignore, but the elderly midwife Gareth had called to deliver his wife shook her head after examining her yet again.

'Not yet, my young mistress, hold back lest you tear.' She wiped Sophie's forehead with a wet cloth and set a glass of cordial to her lips. 'Just a sip now—cry out if want when the pain comes.' But Sophie grimly set her kerchief back between her teeth, trying to subdue a moan. How much longer must she endure this outrage of pain that reduced logical thought to an animal endurance? She looked up as Martha came back into the room bearing a glass of wine and water.

'Perhaps you could take a little to sustain you?' she said softly, but Sophie shook her head and groaned as another contraction tore through her. She attempted a smile at Martha, then closed her eyes and gave way to the forces within her body. Dimly she heard the midwife's voice as she felt a splitting sensation between her open thighs—heard a thin cry as the realisation smote her that her child was born.

'A girl, a fine girl,' cried the woman. 'Look Lady Mereton, you have a beautiful little daughter!'

Sophie sat propped up on her pillows holding the baby in her arms. It had been washed and wore one of the tiny lace trimmed gowns Martha had painstakingly sewn for it. A girl—and she felt strangely glad, as she stared at the little one's face, a mass of dark hair and eyes blue as forget-me-nots and determined small chin. Her daughter's mouth was making little searching movements as she held her close—of course—and she put her gently to the breast, the sensation strange, yet enjoyable as the babe gave suck.

She looked up as there was a knock at the door and her husband stood there smiling.

'I hear I have a daughter, my dear,' he said quietly as he walked over to the bed and peered at the tiny human being in Sophie's arms. 'She is delightful. What shall we call her?' He reached out an exploring finger to the baby's cheek.

'Her name is Minette,' replied Sophie serenely. 'Minette, Mary Mereton.'

'Why, that is very pretty,' he replied softly. He realised at once, why she had so named the child. Minette was the King's pet name for his dearly loved sister Henrietta Anne—Mary no doubt for the late Princess of Orange. Sophie was making statement of the child's true father. And he sighed.

He should have felt offended, but did not. After all, this marriage made to please the king, was one in name only, where they performed the courtesies as man and wife and if any members of staff wondered at the precise nature of their feelings for one another, none dared publicly to express their thoughts.

Most of those employed in different capacities at Oaklands, had served there over many years as had their forebears and were glad to work for Sir Gareth Mereton who had a reputation for being firm but just. Small wages were paid, but then as Sir Gareth had suffered a hefty fine during the Commonwealth for his allegiance to the royalist cause, all knew and understood that he struggled financially to maintain the large old mansion house, which still bore traces of careless usage by the occupying forces who had once moved in

It had been hoped that his new young bride might have brought a good dowry. Well, if she had none had seen trace of it. But Sophie was well liked for her charming manner—and for the gift of healing which seemed to come naturally to her.

'The mistress has given birth to a daughter!' The news spread about the house and was confirmed by Martha who asked cook for some chicken soup to revive the strength of the new mother. As for Sophie, she lay back against the pillows, enjoying the strange feeling of her infant's mouth at her breast, as a close bonding took place between them. At last the tiny girl child loosed her mother's nipple and Sophie stared down thoughtfully into her daughter's face. With her wisps of dark hair and startlingly blue eyes, Minette was a winsome little thing. What did the future hold for her?

A week later, Sophie was nursing her baby, when Martha came to her, face strangely uneasy.

'Sophie, my darling—your father is here!'

'Father, why but that's wonderful. Let him come up here to me. I long for him to see his grand-daughter!' She replaced the baby in the cradle and straightened her bodice. But Martha just stood there. 'Mama—what is it?' At last the woman blurted out that which she knew would disturb Sophie.

'He is not alone, my dearest. He has a lady with him and he shows a fondness in his speech towards her.' Sophie rose to her feet and gently placed her baby in the wooden rocker cradle that had been in her husband's family for many years.

'What exactly do you mean, Mama?' Then the door opened and she heard her father's familiar, much loved voice.

'What Martha is trying to tell you, is that I am married, Sophie!'

'Married,' she murmured stupidly, staring at him in consternation.

'Yes, married and have brought my wife to meet you,' he continued. Then in a rush of enthusiasm he crossed the room took a bewildered Sophie in his arms and kissed her. He turned to the tall, slender, black haired, dark eyed woman who had entered behind him. 'Madeleine, may I present my dear daughter Sophie to you.' He smiled encouragingly at his daughter.

'I must explain that Madeleine and I were acquainted in France many years past and where lately, she was lady in waiting to Henrietta Anne. We were married but a week ago and I couldn't wait to bring her to see her new home at Hawksley Manor—and also to meet you!'

Sophie allowed the strange woman embrace her, breathed in her alien perfume of rose and musk, while she tried to control the shock she felt. It would never be the same again, her relationship with her father. Now another had taken her position both in his heart and what she thought of as her own home at Hawksley Manor. Perhaps she had dreamed that eventually she would leave Oaklands and its elderly owner, had been biding time until the birth of the child, who was official heir to Sir Gareth to make decision. This house Oaklands would one day belong to her daughter Minette Mereton. But she wanted nothing of the place herself, knew that she felt stifled here.

Then she noticed her husband standing quietly behind the newlywed couple, his eyes fixed on her analytically. She forced a dutiful smile at him. But what now—thoughts shot through her mind at lightning speed. She remembered her first ever meeting with her father, then the sheer delight of getting to know him. She recalled her bedroom at Hawksley Manor, prepared with such care for his daughter by James Hawksley and for the way in London that she had tossed aside her filial relationship with him, in exchange for the fascination of the King's library—her attraction to Charles person. She it was who had caused the separation through her own actions. She could hardly blame him now for seeking companionship of a wife after the long years of mourning her mother.

'My Lady Hawksley, I am delighted to meet you,' she said in a firm grave voice. 'I wish much joy to both you and my father!'

'You are as beautiful as James told me,' said Madeleine, in her charming, accented English. 'But I thought he said that you were enceinte—expecting a child?' Then her eyes strayed curiously to the cradle and she gave a cry. 'Do but look, James! I believe Sophie has made you a grandfather!'

'Correct, Lady Hawksley, our daughter, Minette. She is one week old and thriving!' put in Sir Gareth firmly taking command of the situation. He walked to stand beside Sophie, taking her hand supportively, for he had seen the barely concealed shock on her face.

'A grandchild,' said James shakily. 'I had not realised the birth to be so near. May I....' and he lifted the infant from the cradle and at that moment Minette opened cornflower blue eyes and looking down at the child, his own filled with tears. 'Is she not delightful, Madeleine?'

'She has her mother's eyes—and perhaps your dark hair and brows, husband,' said Madeleine reflectively, thinking that there was also a marked resemblance to the King.

'I like to think that she favours me as well,' said Sir Gareth incisively. 'My late wife and I had always longed for a daughter, but it was not to be. We had two fine sons—you knew them well, James. They died in battle in the late King's service. Now with this young lady to keep us all busy, this old house will come to life again!'

Martha touched Sophie's arm sympathetically, guessing at the turmoil the girl was experiencing.

'Should we go downstairs, Sophie? You might wish to alert cook to prepare a special meal for such a joyful occasion! Also, Lady Hawksley will wish to refresh herself after her journey?' And she beckoned Madeleine to follow her, whilst the others made their way down the steep, oak staircase into the magnificent old hall, where portraits of Gareth's Tudor ancestors brooded down on them, as they then turned left and proceeded into the drawing room with its comfortable worn couches and where a blazing log fire blazed a crackling welcome in the huge grate.

Sophie had her features well under control by the time Madeleine and Martha joined them. An elderly footman poured wine in crystal goblets and glasses were raised first to Hawksley's new bride and then to the baby sleeping peacefully above them, watched over by a nursemaid as her future was toasted. Later cook excelled herself, the dinner delicious. Then Hawksley took his daughter in his arms again, regret in his eyes, until Madeleine took his arm and his own slipped about her waist.

Sophie with Sir Gareth at her side watched them drive off on the short journey back to Hawksley Manor. Her thoughts were rebellious, as with a sigh she turned away and the footman banged the heavy door shut.

'She seems a fine woman, your step mother,' said Sir Gareth thoughtfully as he walked at Sophie's side, back into the drawing room where the fire was dying down in the grate. 'Beautiful too,' he added.

'I suppose so,' said Sophie shortly, tossing another log on to the fire.

'Are you perhaps disturbed that your father has taken a wife?' he asked gently. 'He is still a handsome man in the prime of his life and that house of his a lonely place with but a few servants to run it. I know all too well what it feels like—to be alone!' There was no self pity in his voice, merely a statement of fact. But as she heard him, Sophie suddenly realised that any nebulous plans she had for leaving him, could not go ahead. It would be too cruel. No, she had made her bed and now must lie on it.

'But oh, I feel so trapped,' she whispered into her pillow that night.

Chapter Nine

It was Christmas Eve and the wind howled about Oaklands, booming down its slender chimney's, making cook uneasy with its disturbing keening as she laboured over the mince pies for tomorrows festivities. But it was good that Lady Mereton had persuaded her husband that the house should be garlanded with fir boughs, holly and ivy all caught up in scarlet bows, bringing back treasured memories of how life had been before Cromwell and the Commonwealth—killjoys that they had been and cook snorted at the recollection.

She looked up as Martha came in glad the kitchen was a hive of activity, her two maids scurrying about at their tasks under her demanding eyes.

'Mistress Wheatley?' She rubbed floury hands on her apron.'

'Sir Gareth is taken with a nasty cough, Joan! Lady Mereton wishes him to have a glass of brandy with a spoonful of honey stirred in it.'

'At once, ma'am,' and Joan Pyke reached for her jar of honey. 'A spoonful of butter and honey is good for a cough too and some say lemon,' she suggested. 'It is to be hoped the master's cough improves before Christmas morning!'

Sophie looked down at Sir Gareth, her face worried as he fought to get his breath, veins in his neck straining in the effort. This cough had developed after a heavy cold last month, and showed no sign of improving and she feared it might be a congestion of the lungs, or the wasting sickness. He took the glass from Martha's hand and sipped the sweetened brandy.

'Thank you, Martha,' and took another sip. Then he turned his head to his young wife, his face slightly grey with the effort of trying to control his hacking cough.

'I know the physic you give me is more efficacious, Sophie my dear, but brandy certainly tastes better on the palette!' And he attempted a smile before glancing up approvingly at the evergreens above the fireplace. The sight reminded him of a time when his sons had been small children and loved to see the house decorated to celebrate birth of the little Christ child.

Life had been good in those days, before the sour faced Oliver decreed that England should never again celebrate Christmas or Easter, that churches should be stripped of all ornamentation, such being of the devil. Had they never read of how Solomon had decorated the Temple? His eyes closed, as he dozed off in his chair and Sophie bent down and pulled the shawl closer about him, then threw another log on the fire. Soon his snores announced he was deeply asleep.

She walked over to the window and stared out at the oak trees tossing and struggling in the gale and drew a deep sigh. It was as though the trees fought to be free of the ground they were rooted in, but for all their thrashing limbs struggled in vain. Martha came to stand beside her and placed a sympathetic hand on the girl's arm.

'You are remembering last Christmas Eve are you not, when Mary of Orange died?'

'Yes. And how I hoped after that happening, future Christmases would be happier ones.' She sighed again.

'Well my darling, you have the joy of motherhood now! Minette is such a little treasure, a lovely child. I have sewn a pretty lace cap for her Christmas gift!' and Martha smiled fondly. But still she saw Sophie's face remained pensive, as though she brooded over some deep hurt.

'What is really wrong, Sophie?'

'I just want life to be different! To feel a man's arms about me, to feel that I am truly a woman and not merely nurse to an old man!' She regretted the words as soon as they had left her lips, knew them to be ungrateful of the kindness of an elderly husband who had offered her his name and protection, that her child should have future security.

'Sophie!' there was quiet reproach in Martha's voice.

'It's not only that! I want to be free to pursue my own path in life. I want to return to the real world—to London where there is excitement, challenge!'

'And the King,' challenged Martha?

'Yes! I want to see him again. Not for any emotional reason Mama, but because he has a fine mind—and yes, I know he has his women, but they mean nothing to him, beyond passing pleasure!' she declared.

'Passing pleasure such as you obviously presented to him? Admit it, that he despoiled you merely to while away a careless hour?' Martha spoke hotly, the words regretted as they fell from her lips.

'It was more than that, Mama! I think we both recognised the inner loneliness of the other, and I could have denied him—and chose not to!' Sophie's eyes revealed something about the girl that Martha had not recognised before. She had developed a mental strength and an analytical thought process such as was more normally found in men. But was that because women were continually repressed? Martha suddenly realised that such was the case. She herself had lived firstly under the kindly dominance of her father, and then the cruel control and repression of Roger Haversham.

'Have you considered how your child would fare should you seek to return to London? The air there is supposedly noxious to infants!' said Martha anxiously, suddenly fearful that she would lose contact with Sophie and little Minette

'Then I wonder how it is that so many thousands manage to rear families there?' She saw Martha's worried face and realised the cause. 'You could always come with me, Mama! As for the fear of sickness, I believe that you are right to a degree, people living in overcrowded conditions are more prone to disease, but should I ever return to London then I would hope to occupy an apartment in Westminster, as previously with my father!'

'But while you have an ailing husband you cannot in any conscience desert him,' said Martha firmly. 'Yes, he is considerably older than you, but has treated you with every kindness and Minette bears his name. No Sophie, you must just accept the situation with a good grace!' then she added 'And after all, this is a most beautiful old house!'

'Yes! Yes, you are right! But that doesn't mean that I cannot dream of my freedom. One day I will have it!'

But as she fed her tiny daughter that night and stared down into the baby's questioning blue gaze, she felt the strong bond of motherhood, an invisible net of love. She stroked the soft, fine dark curls and touched the delicate arched brows, traced the small nose and determined chin. 'I will never be parted from you, my little Minette,' she promised gently, kissing the child's petal soft cheek and laughed as a tiny hand reached up and caught a strand of her mother's hair.

Christmas morning dawned coldly. The wind had dropped. Sophie stared from the bedroom window and saw the courtyard littered with debris from the storm and realised the temperature had dropped, for puddles had iced over and dark clouds overhead promised more rain—or snow.

She pulled her robe tightly about her and shivered slightly, for the fire had died down in the grate. Then the door opened and a maid appeared, carrying a bucket of hot water, which she poured into Sophie's white and blue china washing bowl.

'Thank you, Ellen.'

'I'll just attend to the fire, Lady Mereton. It's a rare cold day outside. Looks like it might snow!' The red cheeked maid knelt by the grate, raddled the ashes with a poker and soon flames were licking up the chimney again. She looked up as she rose to her feet. 'Mistress Wheatley is already below, my lady.'

'And my husband—is he up yet, Ellen?'

'Yes, my Lady. His man Calder says the master had a bad night's sleep, but seems more himself this morning!' The maid curtsied and picking up her bucket withdrew. And so starts another day, thought Sophie, as she hurriedly washed and brushed the shining, waving mass of her long, chestnut hair. It was after all Christmas day and she decided to wear one of her court gowns for the occasion. After all, there was no other occasion to keep them for!

She went in to the nursery and attended to little Minette, who had already been washed and changed by the nursemaid, Jenny.

'She's wearing the pretty lace cap Mistress Wheatley made for her Christmas gift,' explained the girl. 'She is such a beautiful baby!'

'She is, Jenny. Well, I will just feed her before I go down to my own breakfast!' The girl smiled and ventured a tentative suggestion.

'Perhaps you might like a warm drink before you start. My mother does say it helps to bring the milk in,' said the practical maid. 'Better put this towel over your lap so that your fine gown does not stain. Babies are always busy at both ends!' Sophie smiled. Young Jenny at fifteen was full of ancient wisdom passed down through her family. She looked at the girl thoughtfully. If ever she managed to return to London, she would bring Jenny with her.

'I think I would like to attend morning service in the village church,' announced Sir Gareth, as he rose from the breakfast table.

'The roads may not be good this morning, no doubt littered with fallen branches after the storm,' advised Martha solicitously, 'And it is very cold!'

''It's Christmas morning and I am determined to go. After all, now that the old ways are once more established in the church after Cromwell's depredations, it behoves us to attend! It is only three miles or so!' He smiled across at Sophie, eyeing her blue gown, with its delicate lace across her young breasts and observing approvingly her waist was now trim again, as she rose to join him at the window. He would enjoy showing off his attractive wife to the congregation.

'Perhaps my father will be there,' surmised Sophie.

'And your step mother, Madeleine!' he noted how her face fell at his words. It was obvious that Sophie did not enjoy the prospect of meeting the French woman again.

They seated themselves in the coach, Sophie next to her husband, Martha sitting opposite and noting with relief that Sir Gareth was coughing less this morning. Perhaps he was on the mend. But she still felt it was unwise to make this outing in the present cold weather. How lovely Sophie looked, she thought—and how gaunt the face of her elderly husband. The carriage stopped several times for the driver to clear the road of sizeable branches torn from the trees by last night's wind and once the wheels almost caught in a deep rut, but at last they arrived safely.

Many there were who stared curiously at Sophie as she sat beside her husband in the pew private to the Mereton family. Before the service started, whispers were heard from village matrons surprised that old Sir Gareth had it in him still, to father a child on his new young wife. How long had they been married? Did any know details of where and when the marriage had taken place? But their faces were kindly, for the young wife's grandfather had been highly esteemed as a wonderful doctor and his granddaughter regarded as a charming young woman. She had done well for herself in this marriage!

The vicar appeared and genuflected before the altar and the congregation quietened. It was at this moment that latecomers opened the door. Lord James Hawksley with his new French wife at his side walked up the aisle to sit in the pew behind Sophie and Gareth. He reached forward and lightly touched his daughter's shoulder.

'Sophie child—what delight to see you here, and you too Gareth!' At the sound of his voice, she swung around and a smile lit up her face, which faded as she saw Madeleine. But how could it be otherwise. He was married now and she must accept the situation. She forced a polite greeting to Madeleine, who inclined her head in return. The vicar started to speak, the lovely old words he used about the love of God who had made wondrous gift of his son to man, bringing all in the church to realisation of the special occasion they were here to celebrate. The familiar hymns and carols rose from a hundred throats and Sophie felt unfamiliar tears pricking at the back of her eyes, an unaccustomed feeling of inner peace stealing into her rebellious heart.

'Will you break your return journey at Hawksley Manor,' asked her father, as they all filed out of the church. But Sophie shook her head.

'Gareth has been unwell and needs to be back in the warm as soon as possible—and my baby awaits me!' She couched the refusal politely but saw her father's face fall.

'Another time, perhaps James,' approved Sir Gareth, who had started to cough as they left the warmth of the church and walked towards the carriage. 'I think we should all get home before it starts to snow. There's a feel of it in the air. Look at those clouds'

In fact it started to snow quite heavily even as their driver Ned flicked the horse with his whip. Thick swirling flakes quickly coated his face intruding into eyes and nostrils. He swore and drew an arm up rubbing his sleeve down from his forehead to clear his vision. He drove on, as the wind that had raged in last night's storm arose once more in relentless fury as his whip encouraged the horse to greater speed on the slippery road that he might get Sir Gareth and the ladies to Oaklands the sooner. They were a mile from home when it happened. A sheep that had escaped its pasture, leapt down the bank directly in the path of the oncoming carriage, the horse reared in fright and the carriage swayed and overturned, far wheels still spinning. As it did so the door flew open and Sir Gareth was thrown onto the road twisting his neck. He lay there very still.

Sophie struck her head as she was tossed against the side of the carriage. Blood streamed down her face from a cut at her temple. Only Martha was unhurt although badly shaken. The driver was trying to quiet the horse, releasing it from the carriage that it might not hurt the stricken owner in its panic. It moved forward a few yards where it stamped and snorted its unease.

'Are you much hurt sir,' asked Ned anxiously as he bent over Sir Gareth, gently lifting the elderly knight's head and shoulders, then as he looked into the lined face, saw the pallor and staring eyes, knew there was nothing more to be done for him in this world. He swallowed. Would this be held against him for his driving? He turned his attentions to the carriage which was on its side and in which the two women were trapped. The only way to release them was to persuade them out of the far door of the carriage, helping them to clamber out and jump to the ground.

Sophie stood there dizzily in the snow, her head throbbing from her injury. 'Where is my husband, Ned?' she asked shakily, for it was difficult to focus with the snow stinging her face as it cascaded down, driven almost horizontally by the power of the wind. She tried to look around her.

'Oh Sophie—look,' exclaimed Martha as she saw the dark mound in the snow.

'Gareth!' and Sophie ran to his side and knelt down in the snow beside him. There was no need of a shamefaced, confirming nod from Ned that Sir Gareth Mereton was dead and most probably of a broken neck.

'My lady—I'm so sorry! It was that damned sheep that leapt in front of us,' he blurted. 'So sudden you know, no time to control the horse. See, the sheep lies dead in the ditch. The poor master. I have served him many years, many years!'

Martha pulled Sophie into her arms, for the girl was sobbing in reaction to the shock. 'Hush child, there is nothing we can do for him now. But you are hurt. Your head is bleeding.' She pulled a kerchief from her pocket and dabbed at the blood trickling down Sophie's face.

'Ladies, I will go forward on foot and bring back help from the house,' cried Ned. He reached inside the unstable carriage and pulled out a blanket which Sir Gareth normally kept over his knees. He covered the dead man with this.

'We will come with you, Ned,' said Martha shakily. 'The snow is getting thicker and Lady Mereton needs attention for that cut.' She looked at Sophie, who nodded agreement. Both women pulled their cloaks tightly about them and followed in Ned's footsteps, their eyes partly closed against the driving snow, their light footwear giving little protection and their feet soon felt like frozen blocks, as they shuffled onwards in Ned's wake.

Sophie's mind was coming to grips with this new situation. Her thoughts were chaotic as they walked. Was this her fault? She had wished to be away from Oaklands, yet knew this was not honourably possible during Sir Gareth's lifetime—and now he was dead—and she was free. But were her selfish thoughts in any way to blame for his death? Logic told her no, but she was burdened with a sense of guilt. She swayed.

'Sophie, just you hold onto my arm. That's better. It cannot be far now,' encouraged Martha. The girl did so, drawing courage from Martha's strength as she had since her childhood. They raised their heads as they heard a shout from Ned.

'There it is—the house!' and he lumbered forward leaving them to struggle behind as best they could. Sophie could never remember the last hundred yards, or being carried upstairs by Paul the footman. She lay back on her pillows exhausted. Martha brought a bowl of water and bathed the cut, which was not deep but a large bruise was appearing around it.

'Does it hurt very much, my dearest?'

'I have a headache—that powder in the blue box, sprinkle a pinch into a glass of water. Grandfather gave it me as a painkiller. Martha, I need a clear head. So much to be attended to! Have men been sent to bring my husband's body home?' She forced the question out, knowing that she had to face the grim fact.

'They have. Now try to relax. I have asked that the minister be called. Sir Gareth would have wanted a prayer said over him I think, but with the snow coming down so thickly, he may find it difficult to come.' She held the glass to Sophie's lips and watched as the girl sipped it and slowly seemed to calm herself. Three deaths within six months, first John Wheatley, then Roger Haversham—and now Sophie's husband, it was a lot to contend with.

'My baby—I want Minette. She should have been fed two hours ago. Martha, ask Jenny to bring her!' With her tiny daughter's blue eyes fixed solemnly on her, as she drank at her mother's breast, Sophie realised that there was another more important person involved in the immediate future than herself. She must establish her daughter's rights to this house and lands. She remembered that Sir Gareth had mentioned a new will he had made, making Minette his heir instead of a distant cousin, a Rupert Mereton.

'Where would Gareth have kept his will?' she asked Martha suddenly, as Jenny bore the baby back to the nursery.

'Why, in the desk in his study! He kept it locked I noticed, the key probably with all those others on a hook in his bedroom,' stated Martha. 'Shall I get the key?'

'Yes, do so. I think I must act quickly now to protect my daughter's interests.' Martha stared at her, for Sophie was her resolute self once more.

'Perhaps you should come with me? They will have laid Gareth on his bed there you know. It would look strange were I to go in there on my own.' Sophie nodded and pulled blue wool robe about her, took Martha's arm and walked along the corridor to her husband's room.

He looked peaceful, she thought looking down at him dispassionately. She heaved a slight sigh. He had been kind if somewhat rigid in his treatment of her, but a gentleman in every sense of the word. She bent and placed a kiss on his cold forehead.

'Thank you, Gareth,' she whispered. The she straightened. At Martha's prompting she went to the small hook above his bed, below the portrait of his late wife and children, and from which a collection of keys were suspended. Which one? There were two smaller ones and she took both.

She cast one final look at the dead man, who had been her husband, but with whom she had never slept nor exchanged more than a courtesy kiss. Below stairs they found the maids hastily draping mirrors with black cloths and looks of sympathy were thrown towards Sophie. Less than a year married and now a widow. None noticed the two women enter the study. Sophie walked directly to the old Jacobean desk. The second of the two keys fitted. She glanced through the papers there—accounts, old maps of the estate—letters. Then she saw what she sought. The will was written on fine parchment. She examined it carefully. It was dated three months ago in the presence of his lawyer and witnesses.

In his will Gareth left small legacies to those of his staff who had served him well over the years and they were named. She read on. The main bequests were to his daughter Minette Mary Mereton and to his wife Lady Sophie Mereton, with a generous sum to his wife's aunt, Martha Wheatley. Matters had been couched in such a way, that the house and lands should belong to Sophie during her lifetime and pass on to her daughter at her death, but should Sophie remarry, then all should be transferred as from that time to the ownership of Minette Mereton under the guardianship of Sophie during her minority.

She handed the will to Martha, who read it thoughtfully.

'It is obvious Sir Gareth was hoping you would remain here at Oaklands. I know the old house meant a great deal to him, for sometimes he would tell me tales of his ancestors and worried that he had no male heir to succeed him—apart from a second cousin who had favoured the Commonwealth cause and had fought for Cromwell and whom he held in contempt for so doing. He knew Minette was the King's daughter and he loved Charles Stuart, his last loyalty very fine I think.' She spoke soberly. Sophie nodded.

'I will see that the house is well looked after, but cannot promise to stay here overlong. What about you, Martha? Would you be prepared to remain and look after the place, if I were to return to London?'

'Surely we must attend to your husband's funeral first, before making such plans,' reproved Martha quietly and Sophie nodded slightly shamefacedly.

'Of course—you are right.'

The snow continued to fall heavily. Somehow the Rev David Markham managed the journey to Oakhams on his sturdy cob. He took Sophie's hands in his and bowed regretfully at the young woman. A few months ago she had buried her beloved grandfather—and now this! To have widowhood thrust upon her so suddenly and violently called forth his deepest sympathy. He bowed also to Martha, noticing her where she stood near the window.

'Mistress Wheatley!' He turned his attention back on Sophie.

'Lady Mereton, I am sorrowful at your loss. But Gareth is in a happier kingdom. He had a good life and much happiness in this year with a lovely young wife and baby daughter to console him after his long years alone. He was a wonderful human being of whom none ever had a bad word to say!' He spoke the words, encouraging Sophie to seat herself, for she looked very pale.

'It just happened so quickly! One minute we were in the coach, the next he was lying in the snow—dead!'

'You have a hurt to your head I see?' He noticed the cut and contusion on her temple.

'It is nothing, Mr Markham. It is so kind of you to come to us through this weather. My husband lies in his chamber—we thought you might perhaps say a prayer over him?' she said awkwardly. He smiled at her.

'I know the way. We will talk later,' he said quietly.

The funeral was attended by many in the county. Lord James Hawksley and Madeleine stood close to Sophie, as the coffin was lowered into the cold earth, from which the snow had been cleared. 'Why do I feel nothing,' Sophie asked herself, her emotions numb, but she smiled gravely at those around her. Many came back to Oaklands to a repast prepared with much effort by the cook, laid out on trestle tables in the great hall, and many a toast was drunk in fine wine to Sir Gareth Mereton's memory. It was here as she was surrounded by neighbours commiserating on her loss, that she saw a stranger wearing suit of black velvet, with deep white collar, advancing on her, his face belligerent. He pushed his way amongst them and came swaggering forward.

'You I take it are Gareth's mistress,' he said in cold aggressive tones, facing her, feet astride, little eyes watching her narrowly from his florid face.

'I am Lady Mereton, Sir Gareth's widow. And who are you sir, who address me so discourteously?' Her blue eyes stared at him in disdain.

'Widow—you mean he actually married you? Well, no matter. No doubt I can settle a small sum on you for your welfare. I am Rupert Mereton, the new owner of this property, named so in his will!'

'Then I must disillusion you, sir! A new will made three months ago names me his heir, together with my daughter Minette!' She watched his jaw drop in shock and confusion. 'The will was drawn up by his lawyer and correctly witnessed as can be confirmed to you whenever you wish! Now, I feel you have place here today Rupert Mereton and will wish you good day!'

Those who had overheard the exchange looked at Sophie with sympathy and watched in amusement as the angry man took frustrated departure. James Hawksley followed him to the door.

'If you ever dare to enter this house again, or offend my daughter in any way you will have me to deal with!' His eyes were cold as he stared at the man, who after a minute recognised him and pointed a defamatory finger at Hawksley.

'Another of you bloody Catholic Royalists back here in the country again! Pity is that Cromwell didn't exterminate the lot of you. So Gareth married a daughter of yours, never heard you had one! No matter, I will challenge the legality of the will. The old man was probably senile, persuaded into it by....!' He never completed the sentence, for he found himself propelled out of the door to stumble clumsily down the steps. He turned and shook his fist back at Hawksley, who stood surveying him in contempt from the doorway.

'You'll regret that!' Minutes later a carriage bore him away.

Later that night, after the guests had all gone and Oaklands was quiet once more, James Hawksley sat speaking with Sophie. She looked exhausted he thought, but knew he must be sure of the will she had mentioned.

'Your husband's will—you have it safely, Sophie?'

'You wish to see it father? Mama, will you get it?' Martha rose from her chair, went through to the library and removed the will from one of the large dusty tomes on a high shelf where it was hidden. She returned with it and handed it to Hawksley. He ran his eyes over it keenly and nodded his satisfaction.

'It is absolutely concise. None can dispute the legality of this. Sophie, I suggest that once the weather improves and when Madeleine and I return to court, that you accompany us. It is important that the King should learn all that has happened from your lips.' He looked at her protectively.

'My husband is right,' put in Madeleine. 'I am sure the King would be delighted to meet your little daughter!' Sophie stared at her. Was this an illusion to the baby's paternity? But there was no guile on Madeleine's face, only kindness and she relaxed. The French woman smiled. 'I would like to be your friend, Sophie! You must not resent my having married your father—we love each other and I will do my best to love you too.' As she looked into Madeleine's eyes, Sophie nodded assent.

'Friends,' she said and submitted to the other's kiss and this time did not stiffen. 'Perhaps one day you will tell me of the King's sister, Henrietta Anne. I know that you served her?' The Frenchwoman inclined her head.

'Yes, I had the privilege of being waiting woman to 'Madame' as she is referred to now that she is married to the Dauphin. I fear it may be a sad marriage for her, because he is, how do you say it James? He likes men!' Sophie caught her meaning and sighed.

'You have been fortunate in having wed my father in a love match. Most women it seems are forced into a loveless marriage.'

'As you were,' put in her father. 'But consider Sophie, the King wished it so to protect your child. He chose an older bridegroom for you, knowing that the marriage would probably not endure too long for obvious reasons.' He looked at her kindly and placed an arm about her shoulders. 'You can now take your place again at court, with none to pass suggestive comments on the arrival of your baby.'

'I know you are right, and Gareth was always kind to me, more like an elderly friend than a husband. I never thought I would, but I shall miss him,' she added frankly. 'Can that man Rupert Mereton really do anything to overturn the will?'

Hawksley scowled and shook his head, 'No—impossible! He may try, but has no legal leg to stand on. Oakland's now belongs to you, Sophie and eventually to your daughter. Martha tells me that you have suggested that she should run the house and estate on your behalf. So I take it you have already had thoughts of returning to Westminster?'

'Yes! To the King's library,' she answered simply. He stared at her, had thought her obsession with medicine would have disappeared with her new duties as mother. Yes she had matured, had a new serenity, but as he stared into her determined blue eyes realised that Sophie was as dedicated as ever to the realm of healing. Where would it lead her? In the meanwhile, he would take it upon himself to meet with Gareth's lawyer who had drawn up the will and mention to him the threats of Rupert Mereton.

A few weeks later, Rupert Mereton did indeed try to overturn Gareth's will, demanding a hearing in court to establish that in his opinion, his cousin had been senile and had not understood what he was agreeing to when an unscrupulous young woman had persuaded him to change his earlier will in her favour and that of her child.

His lawyer had tried to dissuade him from the course, having spoken with the late Sir Gareth's own man of business, who had told him that his client had been in perfect control of his faculties and further that Lady Mereton had been unaware of the making of the will. The case was dismissed, it also having been mentioned to the judge that Lady Mereton was held in much favour by the King, as having cared for his late sister Mary of Orange, in her last illness.

Rupert Mereton was coldly angry. He knew he was helpless to take any other legal means to dislodge the attractive widow from what he had always looked on as his inheritance. He would not forget however. Nor would he forgive James Hawksley for look of amusement directed at him, as all filed out of the court.

He wondered what had happened to Sir Mark Harrison, who had been thrown out of Hawksley Manor by its original owner soon after the restoration of Charles Stuart. He was still sought for by the authorities it was said in connection with abduction and murder and attempted arson. Yet the man had been friend of his and esteemed by Cromwell who had awarded him the Hawksley property. Where was Harrison now?

April came at last, puddles dried up, flowers started to reappear in the hedgerows, bushes breaking into fine leaf and the roads became passable once more. It had been decided that Sophie, six month Minette and the nursemaid Jenny, should travel with her father and Madeleine to London. Martha had been asked to accompany them but steadfastly refused, saying that someone needed to oversee Oaklands.

Before leaving, Sophie paid a visit to The Willows. As Beth Giles opened the door to her, Sophie almost felt her grandfather's presence and glanced down the passage towards his study. Why she had come today she was not sure. Perhaps an inner longing for the love and security that she had so enjoyed here as he opened her mind to medicine and his own thoughts on theology. But he was gone now. She wandered out into the garden and sat on the bench she had so often shared with him, where the willows bent over the pool and watched as a tiny fish broke surface.

'You cannot hold onto people, or places,' she murmured wistfully. 'But there again, you never forget them.' It was then she almost felt a hand touch her shoulder and lifted one of hers towards it sighing his name aloud—'Grandfather?' Her hand fell back into her lap and a smile touched her lips. He had been there, she knew it.

She packed other of his notebooks into a leather bag, to study when she was in London. Now to say farewell to Beth Giles!

'I must go, Beth! I can see how well you are keeping the house.'

'It is what he would have wanted, Mistress Sophie—my Lady I should say!' The housekeeper glanced at her fondly. 'I wish you had brought your little one with you today.'

'I'm sorry Beth, but I wanted a quiet hour here in a place that still feels like home. We are off to London tomorrow and I may not be back for some time. I have written an address where you may reach me in case of need.'

She was tired and the baby fretful by the time they left the beauties of the waking countryside behind them and entered the narrow, odorous streets of London, where wooden houses reached anxiously towards each other over cobbles and the gutters were a foulness, and through the heart of the city the Thames wandered between mud banks bearing a multitude of barges on its waters, and church steeples pierced the sky, and still the carriage rattled on.

'She's been sick again, my lady,' murmured Jenny, wiping Minette's small mouth. 'Do we have much further to go? I think she needs changing!'

'We are almost there, Jenny,' put in Hawksley, smiling across at his tiny grand-daughter, 'Just a few more minutes!'

As they walked wearily along the honeycomb of passages, Sophie felt the old familiar excitement that they were now in the palace of Westminster again.

Her father's new apartments were much larger and better furnished than the original ones they had occupied on her first stay at Westminster—three bedrooms and a comfortable living room and kitchen. Madeleine showed Sophie into her room, the nursemaid Jenny to occupy a truckle bed in the neighbouring small bedroom, together with baby Minette, whose cradle they had brought from Oaklands. She left Sophie there and hurried off to oversee preparation for a meal for all of them.

For a few minutes, Sophie just sat on the end of the bed, her mind in turmoil. Had she taken the right course returning to the court and all its intrigues? But how else was she to continue with her studies in medicine, unless she had access to the finest books of knowledge such as those possessed by the King? She sighed and returned to the immediate present as Jenny knocked on the door, baby Minette in her arms.

'I've changed her my lady, but she's fretful, tired out from the journey no doubt.' The child gave an indignant cry as she saw her mother and stretched out her little arms.

'Yes, and as she is telling us—she is very hungry,' smiled Sophie, as she took Minette from the nursemaid, settling herself down as she put the baby to her breast. She stroked the little head gently as the baby gave suck. It released great waves of tenderness in her for this small girl child, who was the daughter of a king.

She sat there quietly, as Minette dropped contentedly off to sleep.

As she stared down at her small daughter, Sophie considered objectively for the first time what she had actually done with her life. She had entered into an adulterous relationship with the king—not for any great love of him, but because of a sexual urge which she could have resisted had she so wanted. But excitement and curiosity about the most intimate relationship between man and woman, reserved as she knew by God for marriage, had lightly overcome both common sense and all thoughts of morality.

What legacy had her reckless behaviour inflicted on her innocent daughter, little Minette Mereton? What indeed lay before Sophie herself in the years ahead? As she honestly viewed the outrage of her actions now, without recourse to protective veil of any false self justification, her heart sank. For now she accepted that her actions had deeply wounded her father, destroying that very special relationship between them, as well as causing shock and distress to her grandfather in his last days and to Martha who had always cared for her dearly as a mother.

What could she do now in expiation? Suddenly it seemed as though she had a vision—a terrifying glimpse into a scene from Hades. All around her men and women lay in a foulness of mortal sickness as she desperately endeavoured to bring relief and healing. The vision if such it was, faded. She sat there as though in a trance. At last she roused herself and kissed Minette's peach soft cheek, before handing her back to Jenny.

'She looks very contented now, my lady!' Jenny inclined her head respectfully and carried her small charge next door as Sophie rose to her feet and closed her bodice.

'But will I ever know content again,' she murmured to herself.

Her father, Lord James Hawksley and his wife Madeleine were invited to a reception by royal command—as was Sophie, who excused herself from attendance, pleading a monthly malaise. She was not yet ready to face Charles Stuart. She looked at Madeleine though with a slight pang, for her step mother was looking extremely beautiful in a gown of wine rich velvet, looped over a petticoat of cream silk, jewels her own before marriage, at throat and ears.

'I should be there at his side, not this French woman,' she thought, as she waved goodbye to them, then instantly dismissed the grudge. If Madeleine made her father happy, then surely he deserved such joy after the pain he had suffered over the years of civil war and exile.

She was sitting at ease in her chair, nursing Minette, when an excited Jenny burst into the room and rushed over to her.

'My lady, there's a fine gentleman called to see you, men outside attending him! I explained you were unwell, not receiving visitors, but......!' She looked round in dismay as the visitor she referred to followed her in.

'But unable to prevent her king calling on one of his loveliest subjects! Nor yet the delight of meeting a new precious member of his family!' he added softly as crossing the room he raised one of Sophie's hands to his lips and peered curiously at the child in her arms.

'Majesty!' cried Sophie in sudden confusion. She was acutely aware that she was wearing one of her plainest gowns, a protective apron across her lap as she nursed Minette. Then as she realised who this visitor was, Jenny dropped an awed curtsey and at a dismissive nod from her mistress betook herself out of the room.

'Greetings, Lady Mereton,' he said. 'I was disturbed and saddened to hear of your recent loss, but at least your husband enjoyed great happiness before his death. He was a good man and a friend!' His dark eyes registered genuine regret.

'He showed great kindness to me, and to our daughter,' she blurted, still in shock at his presence. Then, as she controlled her emotion on seeing the true father of her child once more, she stared at him interrogatively. 'I thought you were holding an important reception tonight Sire—my father and his wife invited!'

'As were you, Sophie! Are you truly unwell or this merely a device to avoid seeing me again?' His dark eyes raked her with amusement. She coloured under his gaze. He stooped and lifted Minette from her arms, and held her back from him, examining her small face with a whimsical smile. His daughter returned his stare with eyes as blue as forget-me-nots, but her face showing her royal heritage. He nodded and kissed her.

'She's beautiful,' he whispered softly. 'A mercy she has not inherited my ugliness but her mother's beauty.'

'You—ugly? You are no such thing,' she exclaimed, adding 'I think you all a king should be, except perhaps your eye roves too freely on the opposite sex!'

As the words came out, she wondered if she had offended him, but he merely put back his head and roared with laughter, causing Minette to screw up her little face in anticipatory roar, until this experienced father of

144

several children by different mothers, soothed her, stroking her dark curls so like his own with exploring fingers.

'Hush there, sweetheart! Wouldst scream at your father?' He turned his gaze back on Sophie who had risen to her feet, removed the offending apron and smoothed her skirt. 'Sophie, what have you named our daughter?' he inquired.'

'Her name is Minette Mereton,' said Sophie softly, reaching out for her child. A smile curved his lips

'So—for my sister then? This was well done!' He restored the baby to her arms. 'I must go, Sophie! I managed to slip away from the entertainment tonight, and must return.' He stood looking down at her. 'You have changed, haven't you?' he mused. 'Still as beautiful, but you've lost that childish innocence, replaced it perhaps with a new maturity if not an exact serenity!'

'Since we parted, I have stood by the graves of my beloved grandfather and latterly of the husband you had me wed, seen my father in a new marriage and given birth to a child. All this causes change, Sire.' She spoke quietly, dispassionately.

'I regret having been the cause of some of this upset,' he said broodingly, 'But not of the birth of this little treasure in your arms. I must go. I insist that you call on me tomorrow.'

'May I see your library again?'

'So you have not forgotten your interest in medicine?' he probed in surprise.

'It is stronger than ever—will even ensure that I do indeed come to you tomorrow.' She reddened as she realised her words less than politic.

'Good!' He turned on his heel with a harsh laugh and was gone. She heard the sound of his voice ordering his entourage, the sound of retreating feet. This visit to her, remain no secret then!

Many curious looks were trained on Lady Sophie Mereton, as she presented herself at Charles informal morning reception, marking her slim form encased in the formal black of widowhood, relieved only by a golden pomander that swung from her waist. She curtsied to Charles, who gave slightly mocking smile and gestured that she should join him at the window.

'You have come to see my library then—not to pay your respects to your Monarch!' His eyes betrayed slight hurt as he put the question.

'That I did last night, I believe,' she replied evenly. Then with look of concern, 'You haven't changed your mind, have you, Sire?'

.He glanced down at her quizzically. She was so different to all other women at his court. With her there was no careless badinage, no simpering looks, nor any self seeking, unless you could count her obsession with his library as such. And this request of hers one so easy to accede to, with no cost to his exchequer!

'Come,' he said, and taking her hand tucked it under his arm, as he signalled to the group of early hangers on that they should not accompany him. His steps were long and brisk and she seemed to take two to his every one, until he paused and opened a door leading off the main library, into a small room she had not seen before.

'I have had all medical tomes brought in here. It was done before your return, in the knowledge that one as persistent as you lady, would require it of me!' He smiled at the joy that spread over her features, her blue eyes dampening with unshed tears.

'You had this done –for me?'

'Could I do less, for one who has presented me with so fair a daughter and asked nothing for herself—save this?'

She rose up on her toes and kissed him on the cheek, then flushed with embarrassment at her action. His response was immediate. He took her in his arms, and pressed his own mouth down on hers. She found herself yielding then broke away.

'No! No—I didn't mean that I wanted....' She fought for the right words that would not offend. He nodded soberly.

'I think I understand. You do not want our friendship clouded by intimacy. Is that what you would say, little Sophie?' his dark eyes scanned her face thoughtfully.

'Why—yes,' she exclaimed in relief. 'The day when our little Minette was conceived will forever be a special memory. But what we did was morally wrong, Sire!' He snorted in surprise.

'We were both unwed, Sophie!'

'But you had no wish to marry me! Nor had I any intention of becoming your mistress. I would not wish to be one of those many eager, voluptuous women you take to your bed. It just—happened! But now, my life is to be given in the pursuit of medicine.' The words tumbled out as her face grew red with confusion, but her gaze was steady.

He placed an arm around her shoulders.

'Then Sophie, let us leave it this way. You are the mother of my child and as such will ever have a special place in my heart. But apart from this, we will remain dear friends and no more. Does this satisfy you?' She nodded.

'Thank you, Sire!'

Chapter Ten

In May, Sophie was invited to accompany Charles to Portsmouth, there to meet his future wife Catherine of Braganza, the Infanta of Portugal, soon to be his queen. He mentioned the invitation casually, his back pressed indolently against the library door, twirling the ribbons on his walking cane as he surveyed her, mentioning she would be but one of the court there to greet the Portuguese Princess. Although her father and stepmother were going, Sophie had no wish to be involved in the forthcoming wedding and lavishly planned celebrations.

'How can you marry a woman you have never met, and may prove obnoxious to you,' she inquired, putting aside a treatise on the plague she had been studying, engaging him with her direct blue stare.

'What a question from one who married an elderly man for convenience sake!' He smiled contritely as she coloured angrily for the remark stung. 'Nay sweetheart, forgive me! I know you had little choice in the matter, any more than I am in a position to turn down Catherine's dowry of 200,000 crowns and the Ports of Tangiers and Bombay! Besides, this marriage makes for a fine balance of power in Europe.' He spoke lightly, but his face betrayed his own frustration at his lack of any real choice in the matter.

'Is she beautiful,' she asked inconsequently?

'Well—small and dark and her face not so as to be unpleasing I am informed. Her portrait if true to the sitter proclaims her appearance is tolerable.' He swished his cane lightly through the air, as though he would likewise dismiss any adverse discussion of his future bride.

'Certainly looks are not the most important factor,' said Sophie practically. 'Let us hope she has a kind and gentle nature, and does not take too close an interest in the doings of certain ladies of the court.'

'Enough Sophie, my wife will have to learn to accept my private—friendships!' He strolled away, leaving Sophie to reflect that his future queen would need to show much toleration in her married life. She lowered her eyes back to her book, secretly delighted that she would possibly have many weeks or even months for quiet private study, with Charles and the court proceeding first to Portsmouth and then if she had understood him rightly, on to Hampton Court for the honeymoon.

It was just before the news that the vessel the Royal Charles had safely arrived at Portsmouth after weathering ferocious storms, bearing the Portuguese Princess to the land she would never leave, that Sophie had a visitor. She was sitting cradling her daughter in her arms, marvelling at how little Minette was growing. At eight months old she had started to crawl and was attempting to stand up, but would fall onto her small seat with gurgles of laughter. Now Sophie sang a nursery rhyme to the little one who clapped her hands in delight.

The loud knock made her raise her eyes in surprise, surely not the king? They had already spoken today in the library. Tonight she was alone with the maid, her father and his wife away at a court function. Jenny ran to open the door. She stared in awe at the richly gowned woman, hair extravagantly dressed, pearls glistening at throat, who stood there impatiently.

'This is the apartment of Lady Mereton,' demanded the visitor?

'Yes, my Lady. Shall I tell her who wishes to see her?'

'I'll do that for myself—stand aside, wench!' Her perfume wafted in before her, as Barbara Villiers, the king's foremost mistress pushed past. Sophie rose to her feet still holding her child, who bounced in her arms demanding more of the song she loved.

'Why, Lady Castlemaine, welcome! This is a—surprise,' exclaimed Sophie. 'May I offer you some refreshments, a glass of wine perhaps?'

Barbara ignored the offer and stared hard at the child in Sophie's arms. She studied the small face curiously. Yes, despite her fair colouring, there was no mistaking that this child was of the king's making. Her hands went instinctively to the fullness under her gown that bespoke the second child she would give birth to in June, also fathered by the King.

'You have a lovely daughter, Lady Mereton. How old is she?'

'Minette was born in October of last year,' she replied steadily. Barbara calculated and nodded.

'So—my Ann was also born last year, in February. I imagine Minette was conceived at around the time I was giving birth!' She looked at Sophie mockingly. 'You cared for the King's sister Mary, when she was sick unto death of the smallpox, did you not. Your daughter's face explains the form of the King's gratitude. You left the court, and according to gossip, apparently married an elderly Knight, who died months afterwards?'

'You take an inordinate interest in my affairs,' returned Sophie hotly. What gave this woman the right to interrogate her in this manner? She became aware that Jenny was listening to the exchange and gestured for her withdraw. But Jenny did not see the sign, for she was pulling a chair forward for the visitor.

'Will you not have a seat, my Lady,' she said. It was obvious to her that their visitor was heavily pregnant, seven months perhaps more. Then she saw Sophie's repeated gesture.

'Thank you, girl,' Barbara lowered herself down and Jenny hastily hurried off into the kitchen. Now that Barbara had made herself at home, Sophie realised she could not easily just show her the door as she felt like doing.

'My interest in you is merely that of one who does not easily brook a rival,' said Barbara frankly. 'The King's future queen arrives any day now, or such is the report of a vessel that has preceded her ship! Not that I think I will have much to worry about, if what I have heard of her is true!'

'What mean you?'

'It is said she is small, dark, with protruding teeth and avidly religious! Not I am glad to think such as will hold the King's interest for long, merely his duty!' She shrugged casually, 'But what of you? It is said that the King is frequently closeted with you in the library—alone!' Her eyes travelled thoughtfully over Sophie's loveliness, her slender figure and chestnut hair and startlingly blue eyes. But the girl did not paint her face or place fashionable patches to emphasise the fineness of her complexion, and her hair was plainly tied back with a ribbon, not dressed in curls and ringlets. There was nothing in Sophie that she recognised as being attractive to such a connoisseur of women as Charles Stuart.

'The King has kindly allowed me to study his books on medicine. I wish to become a physician, but know this is a supposedly forbidden territory for women! He humours me in my love of learning, it is no more than this!' Her voice held a note of utter sincerity and Barbara stared at her in astonishment.

'But your child—it is obvious who fathered her!'

'Minette is the acknowledged daughter of my late husband, Sir Gareth Mereton!' replied Sophie firmly, but bright colour flooded her cheeks. Barbara nodded.

'Of course she is! Just as my Ann is officially my husband's child, for now at least! Now Sophie—that is your name is it not?'

'It is.'

'And mine as you doubtless know is Barbara! Let us be friends. Perhaps it may be to both our advantages one day.' She leaned forward and offered her hand. Sophie took it hesitantly and then smiled.

'Yes—friends then,' she said.

'I must go. But will call on you another day and bring my daughter Ann. Our babes should play together.' She rose awkwardly. 'You accompany the court to Portsmouth to greet the Infanta Catherine?

'Not so. I intend to use the time to study. Goodbye, Barbara!'

Her visitor disappeared with a rustle of expensive silk, her perfume lingering long after she had gone. Sophie frowned and sighed. It was obvious through her offer of friendship, that Barbara, Lady Castlemaine had decided that Sophie offered no challenge to her own position as court favourite. But what would happen to this beautiful, voluptuous, self seeking woman, when Catherine of Braganza became Queen.

Minette tugged at her bodice for attention and Sophie's thoughts returned to this small person on whom she now directed all of her love. The next few days flew by. Her father and his wife Madeleine tried unsuccessfully to persuade Sophie to accompany the King and court to Portsmouth, there to greet their future queen.

'You still insist on burying your head in those medical books and ancient charts? What do you think to achieve by this, child?' asked Lord James Hawksley in exasperation. 'You are young, beautiful—have been endowed with a good fortune by the late Gareth. Surely now would be the right time for you to seek another husband, this time one of your own choice?'

'Father, I shall never marry again, have no need to. As an independent woman, I make my own choices in life, nor wish this freedom curtailed at the whim of a husband!' As he stared into Sophie's determined blue eyes, Hawksley shrugged helplessly.

'Madeleine, can you not persuade her?' But his wife shook her head.

'She has a mind of her own, dear husband.' Madeleine leaned forward and kissed her. 'Sophie, I admire your strength of purpose,' she said quietly, but her husband persisted.

'Daughter, surely you can see how happy Madeleine and I are in our marriage. It could be the same for you,' exclaimed Hawksley in utter frustration, then bowing to the inevitable reached for his small grand-daughter in Jenny's arms and kissed her, as the couple took their farewells.

Whitehall was strangely quiet now that the majority of its courtiers had departed for the coast. But it gave Sophie time to reflect on her future. Happy as she was to share her parents' accommodation, she decided that it was time to find apartments of her own. Chancellor Hyde's daughter Ann, wife of the Duke of York, had become a good friend to Sophie. Ann may not have been a raving beauty, but had a fine mind and was one of the few people who had shown an interest in Sophie's desire to study medicine.

A few weeks ago she had offered Sophie a small house bordering the river, at a low rent. She had instructed the girl should be given the key, saying that she could move in at any time she chose. Sophie had hesitated to accept the offer. Perhaps she had not really wanted to leave her father's protection, even though life was so radically different now with the advent of her beautiful stepmother filling he father's vision.

She fell in love with the small house as soon as she opened the door and explored its empty rooms. She must buy furniture of her own now, and carpets for the floors, even the kitchen would need equipping. But with its fine views across the river and small garden where she could plant herbs, Sophie realised it was perfect.

Two weeks later, she moved Jenny and little Minette into the new house. Although of necessity she had to be careful with her small store of money, Sophie felt real excitement in furnishing her first independent home. The reception room now boasted comfortable chairs in dark blue velvet, long gold curtains of an Indian weave framed the view of the river and a large rug in shades of deep blue, gold and crimson covered most of the dark oak floorboards.

Another smaller room was to serve as her study. Here bookshelves now held her grandfather's medical books and others of her own choice. She had hung one of his anatomy charts on the wall, and jars of dried herbs were stored in a corner unit. A scrubbed pine table would serve as a desk to begin with and already it was littered with notes recently made in the King's library.

There were two bedrooms on the first floor, one next to her own chamber to be used as Minette's nursery, whilst up yet another flight of stairs, two attic bedrooms provided accommodation for Jenny and for Daniel, a young boy she had engaged to do any heavy jobs about the place—carrying in buckets of coal, scrubbing floors and attending to any shopping needed. She also engaged a daily cook, a Mrs Crabtree who lived nearby.

It was the first time she had ever had complete privacy and was glad she had made decision to take sole charge of her own life and that of her small daughter. Today she looked down on the turbulent brown flow of the Thames, gay with barges and small craft and regretfully closed the casement. However beautiful the river was to observe, the stench from its waters could be overpowering when the weather was warm as today. Surely something ought to be done about London's famous river. For all of the city's effluence was emptied into its tide. No fish ever broke surface as in the clear sparkling country streams, but children waded in its mud, searching for any small treasure cast up on its noisome shore. Could the Thames perhaps be responsible for some of the sickness experienced in the city?

She sighed and turned away, wishing there was someone she could discuss her thoughts on the cause of sickness with, but also knew that so far she was only scratching at knowledge deliberately left unexplored by men who preferred to follow the treatises of the ancients of Greece and Rome.

It was in late August that Sophie with Jenny at her side stared down on the great confluence of craft surrounding the royal barge being rowed up the Thames, as Catherine of Braganza, now England's Queen was brought into her capital by her husband, after their honeymoon at Hampton Court. Musicians played on flute and lyre in their accompanying barges, as the mighty flotilla passed by, all in adoration of the small, dark haired woman, who looked slightly ill at ease as she sat glancing shoreward.

At least Catherine would be treated with care and courtesy if not with fidelity by Charles, thought Sophie and wished happiness to the young twenty five year old woman, who had left her native Portugal and arrived last May to wed a man she had never previously met. Perhaps one day, women would not have to marry at the wish of others, nor to be treated as pawns!

The following day her father wearing a fine new brown velvet suit and wide brimmed hat arrived with Madeleine, also looking very fine in a loose gown of amber taffeta, both of them exclaiming in delight to see little Minette standing up, holding onto a chair and attempting a few steps as she saw them.

'Sophie darling, she is just amazing! Not even a year old and starting to walk!' Her father kissed Sophie and scooped his little grand-daughter up into his arms. He examined her small piquant face curiously. Her colouring was Sophie's but her features bespoke her royal father. He handed her to Madeleine, as he smiled at Sophie. 'She will have a playmate next year.' Then as Sophie glanced at him inquiringly, 'Madeleine is pregnant!'

She looked at him in shock. She had never considered the possibility that her stepmother might bear a child. And yet after all, Madeleine was only about thirty and so still of childbearing age. She recognised as she stared across at her, that small mound beneath the full taffeta skirt.

'When,' she inquired stiffly?

'In early December,' smiled Madeleine.

'Then, I am soon to have a brother or a sister,' said Sophie quietly. 'Congratulations to you both!' She tried to mean it, but felt a sudden unreasoning pang of jealousy, that she would no longer to be her father's only child. It vanished almost as suddenly as it came. No. She would be glad for her father—and of course, for Madeleine. It was as though Madeleine had read her thoughts, for as he handed Minette back to her and squeezed her arm lightly, she spoke.

'Nothing will ever break that special bond between you and your father,' she said softly. 'Be happy for us, Cherie!' And Sophie nodded, shamefacedly.

The year sped by. There was much gossip about the Queen's anger and frustration to find that the woman her ambassador had informed her was the King's mistress, had been appointed by Charles as a lady of her bedchamber. When Sophie heard of it, she felt much sympathy for the young woman who had arrived in an unknown country and attempted to adapt to its very different customs and dress.

Catherine had discarded her native farthingale and conformed to those more feminine gowns disported by the ladies at court and charmed most of the courtiers by her pretty broken English. But for a girl who had received a strict religious upbringing and was a devout Catholic, to have to accept as her personal attendant her husband's voluptuous mistress, who had borne him as gossip suggested two children thus far, this was just too much!

But Catherine's storm of tears availed her nothing and eventually on the surface at least, she appeared to accept Barbara. There were other ways to attract Charles caring and sympathy and tantrums went unheeded, unless displayed by Barbara.

The day came when Sophie was presented to the Queen by Ann Duchess of York. Still wearing the unrelieved black of mourning for the late Gareth Mereton nevertheless Sophie attracted Catherine's attention with her unpainted beauty and indefinable quality of quiet assurance.

'I have heard you spoken of Lady Sophie, as having an unusual interest in medicine,' said Catherine curiously. 'You are a widow I believe with a small daughter?' Her dark brown eyes examined Sophie calmly, for she had also heard it rumoured that this was yet another woman who had proved attractive to her husband.

'Sadly my late husband, Sir Gareth Mereton died last Christmas, when our carriage overturned in a severe snowstorm as we were returning from church,' replied Sophie soberly. Catherine's face relaxed at the mention of church. Perhaps the gossips that made suggestive remarks about the lovely young widow were mistaken.

'Sophie spends most of her time studying great, dry tomes in the royal library,' smiled Catherine's sister-in-law. 'Medicine is an unusual topic to be of interest to one of our sex—yet I do not understand why, apart from it being considered so from ancient custom! What say you, Catherine?' The queen smiled thoughtfully as her fingers played with the silver lace of her gown.

'We women are taught from our earliest years to respect men and that we are of lesser worth than they, yet perhaps in our hearts we suspect that we are their match in most matters apart from physical strength. Yet it is necessary I think to allow the male sex to enjoy belief in their superiority, for otherwise they might prove to be less of men!'

Ann nodded with a smile of delight, and glanced to see Sophie's reaction.

'Majesty, that remark was quite profound,' breathed Sophie in surprise. Obviously Charles Portuguese wife, for all her reclusive upbringing, had a fine mind able to dissect that which passed for truth, but was not. Then before she could say more Charles strolled over to them, his brother James at his side. They casually acknowledged Sophie's presence, Charles giving her a slight wink, as they started to speak to their wives of the latest addition to the fleet. Sophie curtsied and attempted to slip away, but Ann placed a restraining hand on her arm

'Are you happy in your new home, Sophie?'

'Yes—and I am most grateful to you for your help in finding it for me. If there is ever anything I can do in return?' queried Sophie.

'Who knows, perhaps one day there may be,' replied the duchess lightly and turned back to the royal group, where the King was voicing like many in his kingdom his growing dislike of the Dutch, which would culminate eventually in outright war.

It was in late September that her father announced that he had decided to move back to the country, where Madeleine might have quiet in the last months of her pregnancy and to give birth at Hawksley Manor. He looked hopefully at Sophie.

'Perhaps you might wish to return to Oaklands at this time?'

'But it will surely hold memories of the terrible time when Gareth died! I want Christmas to be a special for Minette, different in every way to that of last year!' But even as she spoke, Sophie began to reflect that in all these months, she had given little more than a passing thought to Martha, whose love and care had sheltered her from her stepfather's violent excesses over her early years and who had taken over the running of Oaklands without question when asked, although she might have started a whole new life of her own. Did she not owe it to Martha, to return for a time at least to Oaklands—and to visit The Willows once more, with all its wonderful memories of her grandfather and to see Beth Giles again?

'Sweetheart, we will make it a very different Christmas, this I promise you,' returned her father. 'I know that Madeleine would love to have you with her, when her time comes!' To his relief, she nodded assent that yes, she would return.

Martha was surprised and overjoyed to see the carriage arrive. She watched from a window and saw Jenny handing the sleeping child with a mass of dark curls to Sophie. She was back—Sophie was actually back! She called out to the servants that Lady Mereton had returned, to prepare food, air beds and then ran through the great hall to the massive door and stood on the steps, almost overcome with delight.

'Oh, Sophie—you should have sent word! But oh how happy I am to see you! And Minette—how adorable, I would hardly have known her she is grown so! May I hold her?' She opened her arms for the baby who was beginning to stir then holding her close, kissed the small pink cheeks in delight as Minette opened those bright blue eyes, so like her mothers. Sophie slipped her own arms about Martha, as together they progressed through the hall to the study where a warm fire was burning for September mists lent an early chill to the house.

'I was almost afraid to come back,' confided Sophie later, when Minette now fed and content had been put to bed. 'I had so many unhappy memories of this place, constrained here by the convention of an unwanted marriage, for despite Gareth's kindness I always felt a prisoner here!

'He was a good man though,' replied Martha gently. 'And surely the fact that you now have a secure home for yourself and little Minette is some small compensation for those few months you were at his side?'

Sophie nodded. 'You are right I suppose. Now how are you, dearest Mama? Have you been terribly lonely since I left?'

'Not altogether lonely,' said Martha with a slight blush. 'The Rev David Markham has taken to visiting me. You remember him do you not, Sophie?'

'David Markham—he who took grandfather's funeral, and Gareth's,' she asked, with sudden mental vision of the vicar, with his broad kindly face, silver hair and wise grey eyes. Sophie stared at Martha in surprise, saw the warm colour flood her features and suddenly guessed the cause. 'You mean he has been visiting you for other than spiritual comfort, Mama?'

'We love each other, child. He has asked me to be his wife. But how can I accept when I have the responsibility of Oaklands?' she blurted out. Sophie looked at her in dismay.

'Do you love him, Mama?' Her blue eyes searched Martha's face and read the answer in her eyes as well as her lips.

'Yes, I love him. Know him for a kind and wonderful man and were circumstances different, then I would be honoured to become his wife!' she replied simply.

'Then marry him you shall! I will take over the running of Oaklands from this time on!' Having decided so, Sophie realised that this visit instead of meaning a temporary absence from court and that all important library, would now entail total commitment to this old house and estate. Her heart sank. But seeing the joy on Martha's face, she forced a smile.

Martha and David were married two months later, the wedding taking place at his own lovely old Anglican church and officiated by a visiting clergyman. Lord James Hawksley and Madeleine, now noticeably pregnant were present at the ceremony, as were Beth Giles and many from the village of Stokely including Thomas Appleby and his sons Harry and

Richard, Paul Masters, and Daniel Dawlish and of course a compliment of servants from Oaklands.

The old manor house seemed strangely empty now that Martha had departed to take up residence in her new home in the vicarage. As she settled into her new routine, Sophie tried to quell the rebellious thoughts that assailed her. Was this to be the way life would be from now on? She quickly learned how to accept her new responsibilities though, as it dawned on her that running a place of this size took both mixture of patience and ingenuity, making decisions that affected the members of staff dependant on Oaklands for their home and upkeep.

She realised what difference Martha had wrought in the place during her own absence at Whitehall. All was polished and clean, new curtains hung, the heavy furniture rearranged, chairs and sofas bearing embroidered cushions and certainly the staff went about their tasks cheerfully. But still to its mistress, Oaklands presented a slightly grim presence, as though it held trace still of the fighting that had once taken place under the Commonwealth, previous damage to walls apparent despite more recent repair. Today she was in the courtyard, speaking with the bailiff who had charge of the farmlands, when a horseman came into sight riding towards the house with obvious urgency. Sophie recognised him as one of her father's men.

'Wait Samuel—I must see what this messenger wants!' She hurried to the door, as the man bounded up the steps.

'Lady Mereton!' He swung around as she called to him. 'Your father has sent me. Lady Madeleine has had a fall and gone into labour. You are needed, my Lady!' He fixed anxious eyes on the girl as he blurted out the news.

'How bad a fall, Roberts?' she cried anxiously.

'Caught her foot in her skirts and fell the length of the stairs, my lady. She is badly hurt.'

'Go round to the stables and have my horse saddled, Roberts! I will ride back with you—but I must just gather up some medicines first.' She flew to her study and grabbed the leather bag that contained an assortment of bandages and unguents and remedies that she kept by her for dealing with any hurt or sick amongst her employees. Then she ran to Jenny who was playing with Minette in the nursery and gave swift instructions for her small daughter's care.

She rode astride, the cold December wind jerking the hood of her thick woollen cape from her head, as with Roberts beside her she covered the short distance between Oaklands and Hawksley Manor. She flung the reins to a waiting groom and rushed up the front steps of the house that had once fleetingly been her home. The massive front door was opened to her before she could knock and her flying feet took her up the wide staircase, where her father stood anxiously on the landing, face torn with anguish.

'Thank God you have come, Sophie,' he said simply.

'How is she,' Sophie demanded with no preamble, for it was no time for pleasantries.

'I worry she has damaged her spine—for she can hardly move. Worse, she is in labour! I fear for her life, Sophie!' his eyes spoke his anguish.

'Have you sent for the doctor?'

'Of course—he was not at home!' he replied grimly. 'My darling, I only hope you can help my poor Madeleine!'

She followed him not into the couples own bedchamber, but to a nearer adjoining room where Madeleine had been laid. It was useless now to suggest that his wife should not have been moved until her hurts had been assessed, for with no doctor available what help had there been but to make the injured woman as comfortable as possible.

Her eyes were closed and she was moaning in pain. Sophie stared towards her stepmother appalled, then stepped across the room and bent over Madeleine saw trace of bloody foam on her lips.

'Madeleine, my dear—it's Sophie. Can you hear me?' At the sound of her voice, the patient opened her eyes and stared up beseechingly into Sophie's face. She attempted to speak, but her voice was more than merest whisper that Sophie could barely catch. But she rallied slightly. The voice became firmer.

'Sophie. Please help me—if you can. I have a terrible pain in my back and chest....'and she coughed.

'Can you move your legs?'

'It hurts too much—but a little,' was the forced, laboured whisper.

'Then thank God your back is not broken,' Sophie breathed. Then bending lower she gently examined the woman's rib cage—felt the broken ribs move slightly to her touch and guessed that one of those broken rib ends had possibly penetrated a lung, knowledge of such happening remembered from books she had studied. The distressed breathing told its own tale of the lung filling with blood. Sophie knew that she had not the experience to deal with what was a surgical emergency.

'Save my child,' the woman whispered now. Sophie had never delivered a child, nor seen any give birth other than herself. She knew she had to act quickly. She had uncovered Madeleine's abdomen and saw the hardening of strong contractions.

'Father, have hot water brought—clean towels, a knife!'

'At once,' he cried and shouted an order

'Also I need to wash my hands—need a clean apron,' added Sophie.

'Listen Father, when Minette was born I had a very good midwife, a

Mistress Annie Saunders who has a cottage at Oaklands. You must send for her immediately! I will do what I can, but.....'

Almost two hours dragged by, with Madeleine growing steadily weaker, whilst her body desperately endeavoured to bring new life into the world. But the contractions were weaker. But with her last strength the mother was striving to give birth to her child. Now as the top of the small head presented, the door opened and the elderly midwife they had been anxiously waiting for so long, came in and hurried over to the bed. She motioned Sophie to one side, as her wise old hands examined Madeleine.

'She has almost lost consciousness,' murmured Sophie. 'Her ribs are broken—lung penetrated I fear!'

'We will have to use forceps if we are to save the child,' muttered the midwife. The patient uttered a slight moan as the stretched vaginal opening was slightly cut and the forceps gently applied to the baby's head.

'A boy, lady—you have a fine son!' cried the midwife exultantly. But the news fell on deaf ears. Madeleine's spirit had passed even as the child she craved uttered its first wavering cry. Sophie uttered a gasp of horror as she realised what had happened. She placed confirming fingers on the white throat. No pulse to be found. She stared down in shocked disbelief, then gently closed the lovely dark sightless eyes and turned away from the bed, tears coursing down her cheeks. How to tell her unfortunate father that his beloved wife was dead? That twice in life he had lost a wife to the vagaries of childbirth? But Sophie did not have to tell him, James Hawksley had been standing at the door during those last fraught minutes.

They stared at each other wordlessly. Then the midwife stepped forward. She had washed the birth stains from the child and held him naked towards the man who had fathered him.

'I am so sorry, my Lord—truly sorry. Your lady was a fighter. She used what little strength was left to her, to deliver your son. Here, take him. He will need you—and this sweet lady too, I think!' she gestured towards Sophie. Hawksley stared at the mewing infant from stony eyes that softened at last as the cries penetrated his brain.

'Give him to me then,' he choked and held out his hands. Sophie stepped towards him holding a shawl as between them they wrapped the motherless infant in its softness.

'My Lord, should I now do those last services required for your lady,' asked the midwife?

'No—wait. I would say my farewell,' said James Hawksley brokenly. He bent, the child still in his arms and placed a kiss on Madeleine's still face, his tears splashing down on her brow. At last he straightened and held the baby towards Sophie.

'Will you take care of your brother, my dear,' he asked quietly? You could perhaps take him to Oaklands for now. We will need a wet nurse.'

'My grand-daughter would be pleased to help you there, sir!' put in the midwife, 'She is nursing a four month's son of her own?'

Hawksley nodded distractedly. He wanted no part of this alien small creature whose very being had destroyed the wife he so dearly loved. Had she not been heavy with her pregnancy, he reasoned, she would not have tripped and fallen down those stairs. He wanted to be alone with his grief, a grief that even his beloved daughter could not share.

'Where does your grand-daughter live, Mistress Saunders?' inquired Sophie.

'Why, with me—her man died of a fever. Their cottage was needed for the next worker—so she stays with me!' the old woman stared at Sophie. 'Lottie's a good girl,' she said softly. Sophie came to a decision, for her father was in no state to give advice.

'Lottie shall bring her child to live at Oaklands and be wet nurse to....?' She looked at her father. 'What name shall your son have?' she asked quietly.

'You name him,' was all he said.

'Wet nurse then to—Henry James Hawksley,' she asserted. The journey home was by carriage, as Sophie decided to take old Mistress Saunders back to her cottage and meet her grand-daughter Lottie. The young woman who curtsied to Sophie was fresh faced, with intelligent hazel eyes and frizzy brown hair under a white cap. She listened intently to what her grand- mother now told her looking with instant sympathy at the tiny baby who was burrowing his face in Sophie's bosom, seeking the milk she was unable to give him and uttering the urgent cries of the newborn. Sophie took to Lottie immediately and held the baby towards her.

'His name is Henry,' she said.

And so it was, that Lottie and her baby son Paul took up residence at Oaklands, a new nursery equipped for little Henry and Paul next to that of little Minette, who was fascinated by the new arrivals.

Little Henry Hawksley accepted Lottie as the mother he had never known and she gave him a share of her love equal to that she showed in abundance to four months Paul. The baby started to thrive almost immediately, and gave promise of being a handsome child, with Madeleine's dark eyes and his father's dark hair and strong features.

Lottie had indeed been an excellent choice as wet nurse and Sophie thought that she would retain her in her service once her duties of wet nurse should no longer be required. True she had Jenny to care for Minette and she could possibly have coped with Henry as well—but one day, little Henry would have to be returned to his father when his grief had subsided that was. At that time little Henry would need the continuing assurance of Lottie's presence.

Jenny also took a liking to Lottie, indeed it was hard not to do so, for the young woman exuded a sense of calm and fortitude and recognising their growing friendship, Sophie decided that she could safely leave Minette and the babies with the girls, while she attended to matters of the estate, squeezing in time for studying more of her medical books whenever possible.

It was the 24th of December, Christmas Eve and Sophie was in a quandary. Madeleine had passed away almost three weeks ago now and Sophie was wearing continuing mourning not only for Gareth the anniversary of whose death fell tomorrow on Christmas day, but for her stepmother. When she had returned to Oaklands, she had planned that despite her official mourning she would decorate the house to delight little Minette. But what to do now that her father was mourning Madeleine's death?

She came to a decision. She ordered greenery cut and the hall and drawing rooms and nurseries festively decorated, adding scarlet ribbons amongst the fir boughs and holly and ivy. She had already put aside small presents for the house staff and chosen a small embroidered purse as gift for Lottie and a new gown for Jenny. A tall vase of winter jasmine was placed beneath Gareth's portrait in the hall.

The staff responded gratefully to Sophie's attempt to fill the house with the joy and peace of the little Christ Child whose birth they would be celebrating. Last year's festivities had been woefully cut short by the shock of Gareth's death—and with recent news of Lady Hawksley's death in childbirth following injuries sustained in her fall, all had assumed that this would be another gloomy Christmas and New Year. She called them together in the great hall.

They nodded understandingly as Sophie explained that it was as important to celebrate new life, a reference to Minette and little Henry, as show sorrow for the departed, who would be at peace in Heaven. She thanked them all for their efforts in decorating Oaklands and for their support of her through difficult times, and offered their gifts which were received with delight. A strong bond was forming between Sophie and all who sustained Oaklands through their uncomplaining efforts.

It was Christmas morning. Unlike the previous year, there was no snow as yet although crisply cold, with trees and lawns glittering with haw frost in the thin sunlight. Sophie decided to drive to the church, where Martha's husband would be taking the service. Perhaps her father would attend?

She had made several attempts to see him following Madeleine's death, but whenever she arrived at the Manor house, it was to be told that her father had shut himself up in his study and refused to see anyone, apart from the man who brought him his meals. She had hammered on that locked door, pleaded with him to let her in—at least to speak with her. But only silence attended her efforts and deeply worried she had turned disconsolately away.

It was three weeks since Madeleine's death. Surely now however deep his grief, being the strong determined and assured man that he was, Lord James Hawksley should be coming to terms with what sadly was a common occurrence, a mother's death in childbirth?

Perhaps one day, when men learned more of the complexities of the human body, then such unnecessary deaths would cease to occur. Again it all turned back on the fact that human beings were still woefully ignorant of the workings of the body. This must change, but would only do so when men opened their minds to new knowledge and discarded outdated medical dogma.

She sighed as she seated herself in the carriage. It had been long repaired after the terrible accident that had robbed her elderly husband of his life exactly a year ago. The wheels crackled over icy puddles, but it was an easy drive. Her thoughts as she glanced at Ned the driver were a confusion of memories of Gareth's death—of Madeleine's and the birth of her tiny brother Henry. Why had she named him so, but of course she realised, in memory of the King's favourite youngest brother who had died only months before his sister Mary of Orange!

The service started and Sophie took her place next to Martha, who squeezed her hand in pleasure.

'Is my father here?'

'No,' whispered Martha, 'David visited the Manor several times and tried to speak with him, but to no avail!' Martha's face was sad. 'Poor man, his grief is terrible they say.'

'I am going to drive over there after the service—demand to see him!' whispered Sophie.

'How is the baby?'

'Little Henry is a fine child and...' She stopped perforce, for David Markham now stood before the altar, hands raised in blessing to the congregation as the service began. The old much loved carols and hymns in praise of the Saviour's birth released the tension coiling inside her, for Sophie had a feeling that it was more than grief that had caused her father to shut off as he had.

She left the church with new serenity, smiling at those many villagers who glanced at the black clad young widow with sympathy. True her late husband had been far on in years, but a shock for a young girl to be widowed and left with a baby daughter—and now if gossip was right, also caring for the baby born to her Father only three short weeks past, his own beautiful French wife dying in childbirth. And so they called words of sympathy now, as she climbed into her carriage. She drove off to Hawksley Manor.

Chapter Eleven

As Sophie descended from the carriage, a man shouted a greeting and waved as he hurried towards her. It was Thomas Appleby his red hair ruffled by a freakish wind that had arisen. Her father had mentioned that his decision in leaving the estate under Appleby's management when away in London was an inspired one, for under Thomas all ran smoothly and he was widely respected by the workers.

'Thomas—it's good to see you,' and she extended her hand, which he took and bowed over.

'And what relief to see you, my Lady!' he cried. 'Thank God you have come. I do be that worried over your father.' His bluff open face was worried. He hated to worry Sophie for whom he had a tender spot, but needs must.

'He's still not seeing anyone?'

'Refuses to! We wondered whether we should send for a doctor. If only your dear grandfather were still alive.' His face expressed his anxiety.

'I have tried to speak with him several times before, but now I shall insist on seeing him,' she declared as she marched up the steps.

The housekeeper directed her to the study. Apparently he alternated between this and his bedroom. She knocked at door.

'Father—it's Sophie! We need to talk, and I shall not leave this door until you open it and speak with me!' Her words were met with the silence that had attended her previous visits. She stared at the heavy door in exasperation, then taking off her shoe she commenced to beat upon the door with relentless blows. It seemed to work, for she heard him utter an oath, then the door was flung open and her father stood before her, his face haggard, unshaven, his eyes bloodshot, a forbidding scowl knitting his dark brows—his dress in disarray. .

'I do not wish to see anyone—not even you, Sophie! Go home!' and he made to close the door again. But she was too quick for him and forced her way past before he could prevent her. She plumped down determinedly on an armchair, hands folded serenely in her lap. He glanced across at her in frustration then slowly came to sit opposite.

'Why are you here, Sophie?' His voice was emotionless, his dark eyes dull. What had happened to him? Where was that bright courage and cavalier charm he normally wore like a cloak about him, his usual amazing vitality? She stared uncertainly.

'Perhaps if you are not pleased to see me father—then at least you may be interested to hear news of your little son!' Her voice was low and expressed the hurt she was feeling.

'Why should I wish to hear about a child whose birth cost me his mother's life?' he ground out. But the words he threw seemed but a shield, a formula devised to contain his pain. Then he uttered a deep groan and put his hands up to his face. 'Oh, Sophie child—I lie! Her death was down to me, not to the infant torn from between her thighs as she lay dying.'

'What do you mean, Father?' She stared at him in confusion.

'Sophie—I mean that we quarrelled near the top of the stairs! She wanted me to promise to return to the court a bare few weeks after the birth and to make our home there! I love this place, or did. I tried to reason with her.' He paused and passed a weary hand over his brow

'Most of my early life was spent with the Civil War raging, one battle after another, attended by constant danger—then as wanderer in exile on the Continent. Yes, there was the eventual joy of Charles restoration but then recognising the artificiality of the court, I developed a deep hunger for a place I could call home, a longing in fact to return here, to this house of my fathers.' He was silent for several moments and she waited for him to continue. What exactly had happened that fatal day?

'So there we stood outside our bedroom. She was upset that I would not agree to return permanently to court. She—pulled away from me—we were holding hands you see. I tightened my grip, not wanting her to rush off in anger. Pregnant women's emotions are said to be volatile. I wanted to soothe her. But she twisted her hand from mine and ran towards the top of the stairs, turned to shout back at me—and lost her balance. She fell! I will never forget the sight of the woman I loved, hurtling down those stairs.' There were tears in his voice.

'But this was no fault of yours, Father!' she reached forward and gently took his hands. 'You had no wish to hurt Madeleine. Everyone knows how much you adored her! It was her rash movement that caused the tragedy!' Sophie spoke urgently. Now that she knew what caused his excess of pain, at least she could now attempt to assuage it. He merely shook his head sorrowfully.

'Sophie, when I heard of your own dear mother's death, I sorrowed for many years. Then came the joy of meeting you, realising that I had a beautiful and talented daughter so very like to your mother. Certainly at no time did I think I would ever love again or remarry!'

He raised his head now and looked full at her, trying to convey his depth of feeling. 'When Madeleine with whom I had been slightly acquainted in France came into my life—it was magic. The last year was so full of love and happiness. Now it has been taken from me and by my own obstinate desire to remain here at Hawksley Manor. I should have been more understanding, put her desires before my own!'

'Father, married couples rarely agree on everything in their lives, or so I am told. But it is customary for the woman to accede to her husband's wishes if they are for their joint good.'

'But was this for Madeleine's good or merely my own?' He shook his head. 'No good now to go back over such matters.' He rose to his feet and opened his arms to her, and she felt him trembling as he held her.

'Grief is a terrible thing, Sophie. You travel through a deep valley of despair where no one can reach you—unless you let them. I have moments of lucidity, when I know that this pain will lessen given time, even as grief for your own dear mother's death lessened. But will I ever get the vision of Madeleine falling to what was to prove her death, from my mind—my soul? I think not.'

'It may take a year—even two for you to completely let go of this hurt, Father. But it will go. Prayer helps I think. It did when my grandfather died and so that now I just remember all the happiness we shared together, the wisdom he imparted.'

'I have not been able to pray!'

'Is this because you unreasonably consider yourself responsible for Madeleine's death? You were not! Father, I think you need to see a priest of your religion—a Catholic. Yes, I know that they are still banned. Yet I remember that special secret chamber you showed me, the priest's hole. I will not inquire into how you will manage to contact a priest, but know that if you wish it then you will!' Her blue gaze held his bloodshot eyes in pity and determination that he should find healing.

'Your little son needs you!' she said gently, 'Henry James Hawksley needs to know a father's love!' The words seemed to penetrate the miasma of grief that beset him. He let her go and stared at her.

'Henry—you named him Henry?'

'Yes. A fine name and once belonged to the King's late brother of Gloucester,' she replied quietly. 'He greatly resembles you, father. His wet nurse Lottie is showing him every care and devotion—but he needs to know you, to feel his father's love and protection. I suggest that in a few weeks time, Lottie with baby Henry and her own little son Paul come to stay with you here at the manor house!' He looked as though he would refuse out of hand, but seeing the steely determination in her eyes he nodded slowly.

'It shall be as you advise,' he said softly. 'Thank God you came today Sophie, for I was feeling like leaving this earth myself with nothing to live for any more.'

'That is a selfish thought and one you will never explore again!' she almost shouted. 'You have a son now—Madeleine's son and you owe it to her memory to care for the child! Yes, and you also have a daughter in case you have forgotten. Have you no love left for me?' There was shock in her eyes.

At that he broke down in tears and folded her close to him as her words brought a flush of shame to his cheeks.

'Go home now, Sophie. When you return tomorrow, we will make plans for the future.' And with that she had to be satisfied, but knew the crisis had passed.

Over a year had passed and in it little Henry Hawksley had become a lively child with a happy temperament, already taking his first steps. He still lived with Sophie, for his father although frequently visiting Oaklands had decided it would be better for his son to have the company of little Minette until he was older. James Hawksley now wore his grief lightly, outwardly at least. Neither Sophie nor her father had revisited London in the meanwhile. But rumours reached them of a grumbling unrest with the Dutch, whose slight superiority in trade in the East was undermining Britain's own.

It could come to war! But war always bled a country's finances, resulting in the need for ever higher taxes and the hope was that temperance in these matters would prevail.

Sophie still delved into those few books she possessed, once her grandfather's, as she pondered on the suggested treatment of the various ills that beset mankind. Her grandfather's own closely written notes suggested alternatives to those instructions handed down over the centuries, explaining how in certain cases his experimental treatments had brought relief from many ailments.

She also considered the notes left by Jessie Thorne, advising the efficacy of certain herbs that her grandfather had also used. She knew that Jessie had been regarded as a witch by some of the superstitious villagers, although they had secretly visited her cottage when need arose. But Jessie had been no witch, merely a wise woman, living alone and with a deep knowledge of medicine. Now she was long dead—murdered by Harrison's men, her cottage burned to the ground, but her memory was still green in Sophie's thoughts.

Why do men always fear that which they do not know, rather than by attempting to study and so understand it? She found her thoughts returning to the King's library, those fascinating books which she had regretfully been forced to leave behind, when accompanying her father and his late wife back to the country. A new longing arose within her to go back to Westminster. After all, she had her own small house there, overlooking the Thames. She walked to the window and looked out. Bright sunshine was flooding across the lawns and early spring flowers were swaying in the breeze. It would be spring in London too! She remembered the fine parks there, gallants riding beneath the trees, others playing Pall Mall—and the tall, elegant, sardonic King sauntering with his courtiers.

'Jenny, will you start to pack Minette's clothes. We are going to London!'

'Oh my lady—how exciting!' and her eyes sparkled at the prospect. Then she hesitated. 'But what about little Henry? Will you be taking him too, or will he perhaps stay behind with Lord Hawksley?' They both turned and stared at the little boy who was building a tower of bricks and chortling with laughter when he knocked them over. As for Minette she was prancing around the room on her hobby horse.

'I suppose they will miss the freedom of this place,' said Sophie slowly, as she realised how her decision was to affect the lives of others. What would her father decide to do for instance? Accompany her, or remain with his memories at Hawksley Manor. And yes, what about little Henry? She had come to love her small brother almost as dearly as she did Minette.

The staff would run this house efficiently while she was away, no fears on that score. Martha would doubtless visit from time to time to supervise their efforts, and they all loved Martha.

'Henry—well, I think I will have to discuss his future with my father,' she said decisively.

James Hawksley listened in dismay as Sophie made her intentions plain to him. 'But my darling, you have done wonders with Mereton Hall. Why would you wish to leave it?'

'I just need to get away for awhile. You love the countryside, father. Well so do I, but I have a house in London that I have had little time to enjoy. You must remember that it was because you wanted to return here with....' she bit off the sentence.

'With Madeleine, you would say?' he replied steadily. 'It is alright, Sophie. We can speak of her. Perhaps a spell in town would do me good as well. Even now, when I stare at the staircase here...!'

'Then you will come too?' she asked. He nodded affirmation and she kissed him. And so it was settled and plans made. Although baby Henry's wet nurse Lottie had remained to care for her small charge when he was weaned leaving Jenny free to devote all her time to Minette, it was whispered that the young widow had an admirer, Jack Lynden, the bluff faced bailiff. Now as Sophie discussed the date of their leaving for London with Lottie, the girl showed signs of distress.

'But my lady, London is so far away from Jack!' she blurted.

'Jack?' queried Sophie in surprise as a red face Lottie explained that they were planning to wed. He was fond of her small son Paul and they would become a family.

'Of course you must remain behind then,' said Sophie. 'I will speak with the housekeeper to see that you are given other employment here at Oaklands. I hope you will be very happy, Lottie!' The girl smiled her relief and withdrew.

Jenny when asked readily agreed to look after both small children and so it was settled. It was June before they finally set off in James Hawksley's carriage. The weather was fine, the fields bright with buttercups and clover and pale dog roses starred the hedges, England looking at its loveliest. Sophie had a moment's doubt as she stared from the carriage window and her father sitting beside her glanced inquiringly as though reading her thoughts. But she tossed her head, chin held at a determined tilt.

When they stopped at coaching inns for refreshment, the talk amongst those at bar and tables was of their dislike of the 'Hollanders' as the Dutch were commonly called. War! It seemed it was the word on many lips— people wanted war officially declared. Their navy would sort out those who dared to interfere with England's rightful trade!

A few days later, now settled back in her small rented house overlooking the swirling, brown Thames, Sophie paused and glanced around her triumphantly. All was clean and shining once again. She had paid Mrs Clegg who had been her daily cook to look after the place while she had been away for the almost two years spent at Oaklands and the woman had kept the dust down but little else. But now it had become a home again and one that she hoped would provide a happy environment for little Minette and Henry.

Her father had rented an apartment of his own within the confines of Whitehall, for Sophie's house did not afford the space for him to join her there. Today he arrived and nodded approvingly at this transformation, for the house had appeared tired and unloved when they had first returned. He swung his small son up into his arms.

'Henry, have you a kiss for your father?' and the toddler squealed with delight as Hawksley swung him around. Then Minette pulled at his coat, asking to be lifted too.

'Sophie, the King is aware of your return. We are invited to a ball at the palace tonight. He also wishes to see Minette in the next few days!'

'A ball—tonight? What shall I wear,' she gasped.

'What about that blue gown you wore last Christmas?' he suggested, adding, 'I imagine those whom you formerly knew at court will be surprised to see you out of mourning black at last!' He looked towards Jenny trying to restrain the two excited children. 'Jenny, would you take them back to the nursery, please.' He waited until the door was shut and beckoned Sophie over to the table. He opened the neck of a soft leather pouch and poured the contents in shining heap on the dark surface.

'Father,' cried Sophie in surprise, 'What jewels are these?' She touched them with an exploring finger, and then she knew, recognised a pearl and ruby collar Madeleine had delighted in. 'They are Madeleine's!' she cried.

'And now are yours, my darling! She would have wished it so, for she was very fond of you,' he said softly. 'These are her own family jewels which she inherited, but some gifted to her by Henrietta Anne—Madame, as all are now calling the King's sister.'

Sophie looked down at the glittering gems doubtfully. She remembered her own slightly aggressive and rebellious thoughts about Madeleine when her father had married the beautiful French woman. Was it correct then for her to wear her late step mother's jewellery? Then the practical side of her nature took over and she smiled gratefully at her father.

'Father, I will wear these with love and pride,' she whispered.

The once familiar combination of heavy perfumes, perspiration and candle wax greeted her nostrils, as Sophie entered the elegant reception room where the court were assembled in whispering groups, women fanning themselves for the night was hot and humid. The King had just walked into the room just before her, his wife on his arm and he smiled as he led the Infanta to an ornate gilt chair next to his own, watching as she sank down, her pale pink gown billowing about her slim ankles.

Two years after their marriage, Catherine now held herself with the same dignity but greater assurance, coming to terms with the realisation that to retain her husband's affections she must perforce accept with good a grace as she could muster those ladies of the court with whom he chose to consort. A surface friendliness now existed between Catherine and Barbara, despite the Queens's frustration that on a regular basis, the voluptuous favourite was able to give Charles those children, she his wife so deeply desired to bear. He had already left her side tonight and was bowing to his latest favourite Frances Stewart whom rumour had it, was denying him her person.

As Catherine looked lightly around now, her eyes fell on the slim figure in deep blue, entering on the arm of a distinguished looking man, whose hair was streaked with silver, she stared at the couple inquiringly.

'I seem to know that lady,' she whispered to her sister-in-law Ann, Duchess of York. Ann followed her gaze curiously

'Why, it is Lady Sophie Mereton, with her father, Lord James Hawksley. Remember we heard of his wife Madeleine's sad death about eighteen months ago?'

Catherine nodded and watched the couple, noticing that Hawksley had entered into conversation with portly Lord Hyde. She beckoned to Sophie who approached and curtsied, as Catherine's thoughtful gaze swept over her,

'We are pleased to see you returned to court, Lady Mereton. Do you plan to make further study of those medical tomes that so absorbed you here before?' She smiled pleasantly as she asked the question.

'Majesty,' Sophie murmured, 'I am hopeful that the King may allow me access to his library once more.' She looked at Catherine hopefully.

'I am sure of it! But tell me, how is your father managing after his wife's tragic death? We heard of it here with sorrow.' There was real compassion in the Queens's eyes as she spoke.

'A fall down a flight of stairs when she was near her term,' replied Sophie. 'But at least my father now has a fine little son to remember Madeleine by!' she added soberly.

'A son, I had not heard,' interposed Ann, 'and who is caring for the child then? Has he been left in the country with his nurse?'

'Not so. I am caring for little Henry together with my own small daughter Minette! We live in that house overlooking the river that you were kind enough to make available to me,' she volunteered. Ann nodded approvingly, as did the Queen

'I should like to see these little ones. You may bring them to me,' said Catherine. 'I love children—so much wish...?' and sadly she bit off what she would say. They continued to chat together until Sophie swung around as she heard her name called.

'So, my little physician is returned,' came that well remembered deep voice and Sophie found the King smiling down at her. 'Let us see if you remember how to dance!' He signalled to the musicians who were playing on the low stage at the far end of the reception hall. 'Strike up,' he cried. He turned a conciliatory smile on Catherine, before taking Sophie's hand and leading her out before the court. He bowed and she curtsied as they commenced a spirited jig, her full blue skirts swirling about her ankles and her cheeks flushed before his inquiring gaze, then at his gesture, others joined them on the floor. When the music ended, both were laughing and breathless.

'May I have your permission to study in your library again,' she asked?

'You may, Sophie. Is this the only reason you returned to my court,' he asked deflated and he stared down into face looking at her quizzically, almost disbelievingly, seeing her smiling delight at his affirmation. It was then that Sophie saw her father's eyes upon her and knew he would not be pleased to see her close to the man who had fathered her child. Charles followed her gaze and Sophie sighed as he led her across to James Hawksley.

'Hawksley, it is good to see you again,' said the King heartily. 'I heard about Madeleine and my heart goes out to you. But there is a child I understand?' Warming to the genuine kindness in the King's voice, the man forced a smile. After all, Charles had been his friend at whose side he had fought and then accompanied him in exile, their friendship spanning many years. That the King had taken advantage of his beloved daughter Sophie was deplorable, but then life goes on and now Sophie was a woman of independent means.

'Yes, I have a fine son. Sophie has been caring for little Henry quite wonderfully, together with her daughter Minette,' and he gave Charles a direct stare.

'Mea culpa, James!' said Charles quietly. 'I cannot say that I regret Minette's birth though, she is a lovely child of whom I am proud to be a father!' He reached out his hand and Hawksley bore that hand to his lips. Then the King turned away to seek the company of Frances Stewart.

Sophie returned to the King's library with suppressed excitement. She was determined to copy out important sections of those fascinating medical books that particularly intrigued her. She did not know whether she should ask permission to do so and would thrust her notes in the capacious pockets of her cape in case she was observed. But very few gave her more than a fleeting glance. She had shown no particular interest in the King on her return and as for Charles, all his energies were at present divided between preparations for war with Holland and his unsuccessful suit to the lovely Mistress Stewart.

Always when she returned home tired from much studying, the children would cry out in delight to see her, reaching small arms up to be lifted. She delighted to feel the softness of their cheeks against hers and would feel a pang of near guilt that she was depriving them of the comfort of her presence, but assuring herself that Jenny was a treasure, her wonderfully caring manner endearing her to little Minette and James. But watching them respond to Jenny, she wondered whether the girl was replacing her in their affections. Yet, it would not be for too long. Eventually she would return to Oaklands she supposed.

The year sped by, with the country now considering itself on a war footing with Holland, although peoples enthusiasm for conflict was somewhat dampened by new demands for higher taxes. Yet still it was thought that time had come to give the Hollanders a bloody nose! None doubted that ultimate victory was assured—but still Charles hesitated, allowing exchange of a few sea skirmishes, but holding back from outright war despite persuasion from his brother James and Admirals of the fleet.

It was Christmas again. Sophie's small house was hung with evergreens and Mrs Clegg was busy preparing special delicacies for the children, who loved to invade her kitchen, where all of those interesting smells enticed. It was now that Sophie had slightly wistful thoughts of Oaklands and the ancient splendour of the great hall, the spaciousness of lovely old house, the crackling wood fires, the views across the lawns to nearby vista of forest and rolling countryside all of which she had so despised when first she had seen her new home, the reason only because it was not Hawksley Manor.

As she gave their small presents to the excited children, she began to ask herself whether she should return to the country next spring. She glanced down at them fondly. Minette's cheeks were pink with pleasure, her blue eyes shining, as she held up her new doll dressed as a lady of fashion.

'Thank you, mother,' she said in her clear high voice. 'I shall call her Princess, because she looks very fine!' She glanced across at Henry, who was chortling with delight as he pushed his new wooden horse and carriage along the floor. 'Look—look at Princess, Henry!'

But the little boy merely gave a quick disparaging glance at the doll and returned to his play completely absorbed. Then suddenly he raised his head and looked up at Sophie.

'Is my father coming to see us today,' he asked? She looked at him lovingly and bent to stroke his dark curls. Even at two years of age, he greatly resembled James Hawksley. It was strange to think that Henry was Minette's uncle, whilst her little daughter was over a year older that the boy.

'I am sure your father will come,' she said softly, but inwardly she was unsure, for disturbing rumours had come to her ears, regarding her father's recent activities at court. It was said that he was involved with a set of men who gambled heavily and for a man whose income was slender despite his estate, this was worrying indeed. His visits had become infrequent and Sophie had detected a brittle, uneasy edge to his conversation with her.

Lord James Hawksley did not attend church that morning with others of the court. Sophie has been sure he would be there and returned home with spirits dampened. Was he ill perhaps? She decided to call at his lodgings at Whitehall.

She knocked at the door of his apartment, but there was no answer. She knocked again and thought she heard a curse from inside. The door was not locked. She walked in. He was sitting at the table, an empty bottle of brandy at his elbow, his face puffy and eyes over bright.

'Father!'

'What are you doing here, girl,' he grunted, voice slurred, aggressive.

'Why, I have come to give you my Christmas greetings,' she replied steadily. 'The children are asking for you!'

'Christmas! Christmas—what kind of a Christmas is this, when I will probably have to sell the manor to pay my debts!' He glared at her as if the fault was hers. She stared at him appalled.

'What have you done, father?'

'I've enjoyed a little excitement with friends, gambled—and lost!' he exclaimed with false heartiness. 'That is the long and short of it, Sophie!' He stared at her waiting for recriminations and outrage. But she merely looked at him with a kind of pity. And as he looked into those compassionate blue eyes, his mood of bravado crumbled. 'What have I done, fool that I am!' His voice now held trace of maudlin self pity.

'How much do you owe,' she asked crisply?

'Too much!'

'Just tell me?'

'Almost a thousand pounds,' he faltered and as he came out with the large amount, Sophie's face blenched in shock. 'I have to pay this sum in a week's time or else I lose Hawksley Manor, my son's inheritance!' The act of bringing himself to admit the fact of impending financial disaster brought him to his senses. He rose unsteadily to his feet and hurried from the room. She heard the sound of retching and knew his stomach had thrown up the excess of brandy. When he re-entered the room, his hair was wet, a towel around his neck. But he looked sober.

'Child—what have I done, to you—to all of us?'

'That which we have to attend to and speedily, it would seem. Father, you are to come home with me! Just bring a change of linen. You shall have the attic bedroom and it will serve for now. Come!' At the note of authority in his daughter's voice, James Hawksley nodded miserably and packed a few items of clothing.

Sophie left him playing awkwardly with the children. She went into her chamber and unlocked the small chest in which she kept her few treasures. She would sell Madeleine's jewellery. She knew it was extremely valuable, but not what it was actually worth. She hailed a carriage and asked to be taken to the shop of a Jewish goldsmith much used by the court.

The man pondered over the quality of the jewels she offered for his appraisal, with his shrewd dark eyes.

'May I ask the source of these jewels, Lady?' he asked politely.

'They belonged to my stepmother, who died two years ago. They were given to me by my father. I now need to raise a substantial sum. I know that some of these were passed down in Madeleine's family, others given her by Henrietta Anne, the Princess Royal! She was once her lady in waiting.' He stared at her and nodded thoughtfully.

'Do you wish to sell all,' he asked at length?

'Well, I need to realise at least a thousand pounds!'

'The pearl and ruby collar, the emerald ring and brooch of rose diamonds---for these I will pay one thousand pounds. Another five hundred pounds for the sapphires! The other pieces are of comparatively little value.'

'I accept,' she replied softly, eyes registering her relief. She gathered up the few jewels he had rejected. Perhaps it was good that she was able to retain some small remembrance of Madeleine.

'What is the name of the man to whom you owe the thousand pounds, father?' she asked on her return. He was sitting by the fire, little Henry on his lap and stared up at Sophie with dejection in his eyes.

'What does his name matter?'

'I wish to know it!'

'Sir Jordan Loxley! He holds my note for the money—and on my default will soon possess Hawksley Manor. How do I explain this to my son when he is old enough to understand?' There was genuine remorse in his voice.

'I am going out again,' was all she replied. He nodded and continued to stroke the child's hair, nor did he raise his head as he heard the door close.

Christmas festivities were in full swing when Sophie arrived at the court, with all present dressed in their finest and a sense of jollity abounding. She inquired of an usher for Sir Jordan Loxley and was directed to an alcove where she found the man in intimate conversation with a hard faced, fair haired woman, who looked up at Sophie in annoyance. Sophie ignored her and spoke directly to her companion.

'I believe you know my father, sir. I am come from Lord James Hawksley to settle his gambling debt with you!' The words came out clearly and several standing nearby turned and glanced at her. As for Loxley, he stared at her bemused and pushed his woman friend away as he straightened up, his eyes considering her curiously.

'Why, it is Lady Mereton is it not? How delightful of you to make yourself known to me. Come let us find a quieter spot to discuss your father's situation, and perhaps how you might care to remedy it!' His eyes slid over her suggestively, hard green eyes, she noticed, a thin down turned mouth and double chin.

'I would prefer that our business is conducted here and now, sir! If you will be so kind as to hand over my father's note of hand for sum incurred, then I will immediately pay the thousand pounds in question to you to you, preferably before witnesses! I will also require a receipt!' Her blue eyes were flashing as she spoke with a decisiveness he was unused to encountering in the women he consorted with. He smiled awkwardly now, looking around uncomfortably, realising that a crowd were gathering about them—amongst them the King. It was said that this girl was one who had appealed to the royal taste and Loxley wanted no friction with his monarch. He must get her away from the court.

'I do not know that I have your father's bill with me,' he began loftily. 'Perhaps if you were to accompany me to my lodgings we might accomplish all in some privacy.' Again his eyes swept over her, mentally undressing her.

'I suggest that you now examine the contents of your pocket book sir,' came a sudden harsh voice and Loxley realised that the King had indeed been close enough to have overheard the conversation.

'But of course, Sire. Ah—yes. It seems that I have indeed got the note with me.' He glared angrily. He had already looked on Hawksley Manor and its fine lands as his own. He held the paper towards Sophie, but it was Charles who bent forward and took it from the man's hand. He glanced at it scornfully and handed it to Sophie.

'This is what you want I believe, Lady Mereton?'

'Thank you, Charles!' she said in a low voice as her eyes examined the scrap of paper that had almost deprived little James Hawksley of his future home. She handed her purse with the thousand pounds to Loxley.

'Perhaps you would examine the contents, see that the sum in question is correct?' She looked on as he poured the money onto an ornate, walnut table nearby and counted it under many watchful eyes. He nodded. It was correct.

'Shame Hawksley had to send his daughter with it but hey, it is good to have so lovely a messenger! Perhaps we may meet again soon lady, in a happier situation!' Then at a gesture of dismissal from the king, he walked nonchalantly away, inwardly fuming that Hawksley had managed to pay his debt. No doubt the fool would risk another session in the future though, at a time when he would again be too drunk to notice the weighted dice!

'Charles stared after the man. 'How did your father come to gamble such a sum,' he asked slowly. 'And how did you manage to realise enough gold to repay it?'

'My father gave me Madeleine's jewels,' was all she said shortly and he nodded.

'It is to be hoped that he will never again gamble using the home he so dearly loves as collateral!' He smiled down at her and Sophie lifted his hand to her lips. He patted her shoulder. Just let Loxley try to ensnare Hawksley again into his crooked gambling schemes, thought the monarch.

'Thank you,' she said quietly and left the gathering with many throwing measuring glances after her.

'What is this,' cried James Hawksley in amazement, as his eyes scanned the paper she offered him, and the receipt bearing Loxley's signature.

'It is your release from your debt to that obnoxious Loxley fellow! He now has his money—the King was witness, so there will be no further dispute!'

'But how....?'

'I will tell you later,' for Jenny was tending to Henry. It was not for her ears. That night, when the children were in bed and they were alone together, James Hawksley took his daughter's hand and stared at her gravely.

'I promise you that never again will I gamble with our family's future,' he said and she knew that he meant it. 'I should have had more sense than to have associated with Loxley and his friends. The man has an evil reputation, has brought several good men to financial ruin, and it is said broken the hearts of at least two women. What a fool I have been, and now you are once again without jewels to grace your lovely throat child. Ah, what would Madeleine have said, if she knew what had happened!' and he sighed.

'Once the weather improves I think we should return to the country,' said Sophie decisively and he nodded approval.

'Yes child, I think you're right. It is time now to put aside the pain of Madeleine's death, and the manner of it. I will never forget her. But when I held little Henry on my knee this afternoon, I realised where my priorities must lie. Hawksley Manor is his home, yours also Sophie, for Oaklands will one day pass to your daughter.'

It was true. She nodded thoughtfully. One day Minette would inherit Oaklands and Henry would make Hawksley Manor his own. But she actually had a home of her own, The Willows—her late grandfather's house and willed to her. Yes it was much smaller, not as imposing as either of the two manor houses, but it was a place where she had received much kindness from that wonderful old doctor, John Wheatley. One day she would make it her permanent home! But she sensed that much had to happen beforehand.

They did not immediately return to the country after all, for the King offered a paid position to his friend Hawksley as a gentleman of the bedchamber. Hawksley hesitated at first but then accepted, leaving Sophie to reflect that at least she could now continue to study in the King's library.

Chapter Twelve

It was spring 1665 and flowers were once more blooming in London's gardens, splashes of white, gold and purple gladdening the eyes, and trees beginning to break into fine new leaf. Sophie and her father were walking in St James Park together with four year old Minette, little Henry toddling behind in the care of the devoted Jenny.

'On a morning such as this, I could wish myself back in the country,' declared Hawksley to his daughter. His eyes expressed his longing. Did this mean he was finally over Madeleine's death? She stared at him, thoughts racing.

'Then if you feel that way, I believe you should return there, father!'

'Would you accompany me, Sophie?'

'Not right away, but in a few months time perhaps, once I'm satisfied that I've gleaned all possible information on the history of medicine to be found in the King's library!' She smiled at him encouragingly.

He sighed, 'I had hoped.....'

'Look father, how would it be if you were to go in advance, taking the children with you and Jenny? Just do it! Explain to Charles, who will quite understand your need to revisit your estate. As for me, I will be perfectly alright here and join you in the autumn?'

'But the children would miss you, my darling!' He shook his head, but his face betrayed his desire to take the course she offered. Two days later, Sophie held little Minette to her in a fond embrace, pressed the child's soft cheek against her own, then kissed little Henry. Blinking back sudden tears, she handed them up into the carriage. Her father smiled down at her—then she waved and watched as all whom she loved disappeared along the busy narrow street. Above her the sun beat down, its heat unusual so early in the year.

She tried to tell herself that the country air would be good for the children and this of course was true, as well as the greater freedom they would experience. It would also give opportunity for her father to take up the reins of his estate once more, and hopefully have a care of Oaklands as well as his own beloved manor.

It soon became public knowledge that Lord James Hawksley had taken temporary leave of absence from his position about the King to visit his estate.

'Do you plan to join James and the children soon, sweetheart?' inquired the King, as he entered the library silently and came to stand beside Sophie.

'I know I should. I love Minette so dearly, and almost feel as though Henry is my own! But it will do my father good to take responsibility for the children for a while, he will not have time to brood with them around!' and she smiled. He placed a hand on her shoulder.

'Perhaps you and I may spend an hour or two in sweet dalliance once again,' he whispered softly, 'When you decide to take time for your monarch from these dry tomes!' His dark eyes swept over her and she caught her breath.

'I understand that as always you have no apparent shortage of ladies to fill your bed, Charles!' she riposted lightly.

'But alas, no legitimate children to fill my arms!' and his voice expressed frustration that it was so. 'Not but that I love every one of my children, will always have a care of them—and their mothers,' he declared.

'You think of the succession?'

'Of course! At this present time, my brother James remains my natural successor. But he is an avowed Catholic, the people may not accept such!'

'But Catherine may yet conceive,' she said comfortingly. He nodded but shrugged his disbelief. Then lifting her hand to his lips with gallant gesture, he disappeared as casually as he had come.

Sir Jordon Loxley also heard that Hawksley had left court, and Sophie now living alone. He considered the information. That little baggage should be taught her place, he thought. She it was who had provided the means for Hawksley to pay his debt, and in doing so deprived Loxley of the fine manor and lands he had already considered his own! That his use of weighted dice had given him advantage over a man deep in his cups was of no concern—indeed more fool Hawksley he sneeringly thought.

But now at last, Sophie would pay for his discomfiture before the King. He straightened his lace cravat and brushed a few crumbs from his black velvet suit, pushed his chair back from the table and rose. There was a knock at the door and he called to his servant Patsy to open it.

'It's a man from the docks, sir!'

'Ah, show him in!' and he brightened. He had an arrangement with one of the ship masters, to illegally get his hands on a few choice items captured from time to time from Dutch merchant ships. All should of course go to the crown, be assigned to the exchequer. But if none knew, then he and the captain involved could happily accumulate these illegal funds.

'Well Jenkins—what news for me?' he asked flicking a speck of dust from his blue velvet coat. He stared at the shifty faced fellow in his faded jacket and frayed trousers.

'Captain asks that you visit the docks tonight sir, have a carriage ready to bear away certain items.' The seaman looked at him respectfully. He knew this man was engaged in wrongful dealings with the captain, but that was not his affair and he always benefitted from keeping his mouth shut.

'I will be there Jenkins. Now sit down man. There's a certain other matter in which I need your assistance and for which I am prepared to reward you substantially.' The plan took shape in his mind as he spoke.

'What sort of matter, sir?'

'To put it concisely, I wish to have a certain woman forcibly taken to a house I own in Drury Lane. You may have to engage another man to assist you in this. He like you will be well paid.' He looked at Jenkins. 'Well? Will you do it?'

'I don't rightly know, sir! Sounds rather like kidnapping to me and if this woman is one of the quality, then it could be a hanging matter!'

'I promise you your name shall be kept out of this. The lady in question will I am sure not wish to make public her stay at the house in question!' He grinned, savouring the delights to come. And so it was agreed, the plan to be carried out the following night.

Sophie was totally unprepared for the attack made on her as she returned to her house above the river. It was dusk as she made to open her door. Then it happened. A heavy cloak was thrown over her head and shoulders and tied about her waist, preventing sight of her attackers. Instinctively she brought her knee up and heard a cry of pain. Then a vicious blow to her stomach caused her to collapse retching to the ground. Her assailants stared uneasily around. An old man was staring at them along the darkening street. He shook his stick and shouted threateningly, calling for help.

'Make haste! Into the carriage with her!'

'You shouldn't have hit her like that! Loxley wants the goods delivered to him in good shape!'

'It quietened her down though! He will still be able to have his pleasure with her,' snorted her other captor. 'Still, I'll be glad when we have safely delivered the wench. You are sure she's the right one, Jenkins?'

'Think I would make a mistake when there is money involved? Come on Pelham let's drive to that address Loxley gave us in Drury Lane, nor waste any more time! He is in an excellent mood with his illegal purchase of goods from the Master of the Penguin, all those silks, spices and jewellery taken off the Dutch ship they seized, and this of the girl should delight him further.' There was a pause and the sound of a groan.

'Hey—what's wrong with you?'

'I feel sick.'

'You probably drank too much ale last night, so serve you right!'

Sophie had stopped struggling. She was listening intently to the men's conversation, Loxley? The man who had tried to ruin her father, he was behind this indignity?

The carriage stopped and the men manhandled her up some steps and into a house, a door slammed. They threw her roughly onto a sofa. Then the rope holding the cloak partially smothering her was released. She pretended to unconsciousness as for the first time she saw the men's faces from under her lashes.

'Looks like the wench has fainted!'

'So what? We've done our part in this. Here—what's the matter with you Bob?'

Jenkins stared uneasily at his companion, whose face was flushed a brick red, his brow perspiring and whose breath was fetid when he collapsed into his friends arms, vainly attempting to speak. 'Hell, you don't look too good. I'm off. You stay here with the woman until you feel better. Don't forget to lock the door after you when you leave. I'll just tie her wrists before I go—there!' He made for the door, leaving his companion groaning where he had slipped down onto the floor.

Once out of the house, Jenkins returned to the carriage and shook his head as he brought his whip down on the horse. Bob Pelham had looked really sick. Supposing Loxley found the man still there when he visited the woman brought there for his pleasure. Bah! At least the job was done and the money he had been promised soon his to enjoy. But as he drove the carriage away, he realised that he too felt very unwell.........very hot, head burning. He slipped from his driving seat on the front of the small battered carriage. His head struck the cobble stones, stunning him, as the horse ambled on towards its stables.

All was quiet. Sophie dared to open her eyes. She thought at first she was now alone, until she became aware of the man lying on the floor. He started to moan. She rose and raised her wrists in front of her. The rope was cutting into her skin. She looked desperately around.

She was in a sparsely furnished room, with a couch and a chair and a low table bearing a bottle of wine and glasses, a bowl of fruit and a knife! She stared down at the man groaning on the floor and walked past him. She set the knife between her knees and rubbed the cord binding her wrists across it, biting her lips as the blade drew blood. But at last she was free. She straightened. Now to find the door. But she paused as she glanced across at her former assailant now struck down by what? What illness had produced this sudden collapse?

Her every instinct was to escape from that house and to raise the alarm. She could only imagine the King's wrath, when he heard what had been done at Loxley's instigation. But as she stared at the desperately ill man lying before her, she dropped to her knees before him.

'What is your name?'

'Bob Pelham,' he replied in an almost whisper.

'How long have you been feeling unwell, Bob?' At first he didn't reply but continued to groan and pointed down to his groin.

'I've been feeling rotten for two days now—and there's a pain like fire down below—and under my arms.' His voice came pantingly and he vomited and she saw there was blood in the vomit. And as she stared at him, Sophie realised what ailed the man, and if she were right then this man might die—and possibly, indeed almost inevitably she also would die. The man was almost certainly suffering from Plague!

She had read of all the symptoms of the feared disease and knew that there was little one could do for sufferers, who normally died within a few days. No one knew for certain how it spread, but that people in close contact with a victim inevitably succumbed also.

There had been rumours of a fresh outbreak of the disease at St Giles in the Fields, but there again some few cases seemed to surface yearly. She had heard of an epidemic in 1625 when over sixty thousand reportedly died and another with less mortality in 1636. All this and much more she had discovered in her studies, together with the fact that when cases of plague were recognised, then the house in which the victim lived had to be boarded up for a month until all residents in that house had either died or improbably recovered.

But she could be wrong about the man, may have misread his symptoms. She stared down at him. Surely she had no reason to stay with him, should make good her escape from this place, call the authorities to deal with him.

First she had to be sure of her diagnosis. He was panting now with faint struggling breaths and seemed to be unconscious. She bent and unbuttoned his shirt, pulled it off his shoulders and saw the plague swelling, the bubo in his armpit and the red circular blotches on his chest. There was no doubt that this was plague! For an agonising few moments Sophie looked down on the man who had kidnapped her and brought her here for Loxley's pleasure. Why should she feel that she had any duty of care to him?

Then slowly she straightened. She knew there was little she could do for the man, but how would any reputable physician behave in these circumstances? Surely any who aspired to be part of the profession had a duty to care for all who were sick without heed to their own safety. She was no real physician she thought, but would try to act as though she were.

She placed a cushion under his head, found a clean towel from which she ripped a small square, wrung it out in a bowl of water and applied it to his burning forehead. She tried to get a few drops of water past his lips. Hours passed. Suddenly the man stirred, started to sneeze violently—and expired! She could hardly believe he was dead, that the virulent disease could so quickly reap a life. There was nothing to keep her here now—except the knowledge that she might carry the infection with her, spread it in a way which none understood, but was all too obvious.

She sat on the sofa and stared at the corpse. The death would have to be reported to the authorities and the body removed. Hours sped by and the night watch passed under the window.

She opened it and called out to the man. 'There is a corpse within this house. The man died of plague!'

'Are you sure, Mistress?'

'I am. The body needs to be removed!'

'I will arrange for the dead-cart to come. As for you Mistress, are there any others in the house there with you apart from your husband? You know of course that the house will now have to be boarded up, notification of the plague upon its door!' The man stared up at the lovely face at the window. Shame that one so fair would probably soon be sick of the plague.

'The man in question was not my husband. His name is Pelham. He and another fellow called Jenkins kidnapped me, and brought me here on the instructions of Viscount Loxley. My name is Lady Sophie Mereton. I need you to get this information to the King!'

As he listened to her urgent tones and recognised from her speech and bearing that she was one of the aristocracy, he stared up in indecision.

'If I let you get away and it's discovered, then I will be imprisoned—or worse!'

'I do not ask this—only that you get the facts I have made you aware of to the King!' She stared at him urgently. He did not reply and walked on. Later a cart trundled along the night time street. Sophie opened the door and stared at the cart which already bore two corpses. The fellow driving it called to her, 'Bring out your dead!'

'You will have to come in and get him.' She had no intention of struggling to lift Pelham to the door. Hearing the authority in her tones, he swore and entered, dragging the corpse down to the cart, its head banging on the many stone steps. Then another man came and she heard the sound of hammering.

'You can order food brought to you if you have the money,' called this individual. 'Someone will call by in the morning'

If she had the money—suddenly Sophie gasped and felt in the pocket of her gown. She gave a sigh of relief, for it contained her purse and luckily it was heavy! What now? She looked at the bottle of wine and felt calmer after she had taken a glassful. She decided to explore the house. Above stairs she found two bedrooms, one furnished with a large bed covered with a crimson satin quilt. Explicit paintings on the walls gave impression of the use Loxley found for this chamber. The other room was more simply furnished, possibly to house a servant. This would have to do. The bed was hard, unyielding. She did not undress, just lay there thoughts whirling through her head until at last she slept in spite of herself.

The watchman in the meanwhile debated with himself as to whether he should really try to get Sophie's message to the King? He shook his head. Let some other do it. He wanted no truck with the mighty ones of this world, for it brought only trouble! No doubt the young woman would soon be dead, an end to the problem. As it happened, another man had been found that night lying on the cobbles in Drury Lane, and almost certainly suffering from plague, a seaman by his appearance. He was taken to the pest house.

That night Loxley waited in vain for Jenkins to call with the good news that the Mereton woman was in that house in Drury Lane and at his disposal. What had happened? At last in frustration he called for his carriage, was driven to his property in Drury Lane and stared out of the carriage window in shock for it was barricaded, the plague notice affixed. Was it really the right house, he may have mistaken it in the dark—but it was and deeply troubled he ordered his driver to turn the carriage about.

Lady Mereton had disappeared from court and none knew her whereabouts. Two days went by. Loxley shook his head in frustration. He had received no word from Jenkins, who like the woman he was supposed to have abducted had also disappeared. It was all very puzzling. But his head ached and he thought he must be going down with flu.

A messenger from the court visited Sophie's little house. He received no answer to his knock in the King's name. But an elderly man slowly approached the uniformed officer. He had seen a young woman kidnapped a few nights back by two ruffians. No, he could not identify them—it had been almost dark.

A hard faced woman knocked with a stick at the lower window of the Drury Lane house where she had been told a woman was boarded up and who might need provisions—maybe nursing later. Sophie looked out.

'I hear you may want food. Do you have any money, dearie,' asked the woman.

'I have a little,' replied Sophie. She tossed a few coins down from the window. The woman nodded satisfaction. She lifted up a basket on a wooden pole with a notch at the top. Sophie reached into the basket and withdrew bread, cheese and smoked fish and a bottle of ale.

'Will you be wanting more tomorrow?'

'I will—and thank you, mistress!'

'Are you alone there?'

'I am,' replied Sophie and the woman stared and then walked on, pocketing the coins.

Three days had passed and when she wakened, Sophie realised that her head was aching. She glanced into the gilded wall mirror in the reception room, and cried out as she noticed some red blotches on her throat. She pulled her bodice open. Rose coloured blotches were also apparent on her body and she recognised the signs of fast increasing fever. There was no doubt as to the diagnosis. She was suffering from bubonic plague. As the day progressed she found strange aches in groin and armpits. Almost clinically she recognised the buboes, betokening approaching death within a few days or less in most cases.

'But I am not going to die,' she cried out fiercely, choking back tears. 'I have my little Minette to care for and there's baby Henry!' Then she fell on her knees bowed her head and prayed—prayed that she might survive the plague so that she might help others.

She heard the familiar daily knock on her window, and the plague nurse who also delivered food stood there. Sophie made herself smile down at the woman. These plague nurses were reputed to enter houses of plague victims and steal whatever they could find, even hastening the deaths of the unfortunates.

'You are still well?'

'I am well. Have you some food for me? Here, some more money,' and she threw down a few coins as usual. She made herself behave naturally as the food basket was lifted to the window, as she nodded her thanks. She almost collapsed on the floor once the woman had gone.

During the night the bubo in her right groin had grown huge, a tense purple mass that throbbed fire. She tried to recollect all she had read about possible treatment of bubonic plague, mostly fanciful cures which she knew instinctively would be useless. Then realising how fast the disease was progressing through her body, she seized the knife she had used to cut through the cords that had bound her wrists four days ago. Her grandfather had instructed her always to cleanse a knife with fire before use in surgery. She found some kindling in the grate—some sticks. She watched the flames curling up and seized a saucepan and poured a little water from a dwindling supply she had found in a jug in the bedroom.

The water began to steam. Her head was throbbing unmercifully now. She ripped a portion of her lace petticoat. Then she seized the knife, held it in the flames, and reclining in a low chair she thrust the knife into the bubo. She almost fainted with the excruciating pain. She dipped the length of lace into the steaming water, waited a moment and then applied it to the bleeding, suppurating mass in her groin. As she did so, she found her senses slipping away and she slid to the floor.

In the morning she came to. Her head still ached abominably, but she realised her fever had broken. She made herself stare down at the wound in her groin. It had started to form a scab. The buboes under her armpits were smaller in size and no longer ached as much. Was it possible that she had beaten the plague?

She knew herself to be incredibly weak still. Somehow she managed to down a few mouthfuls of ale. Food was out of the question as she still felt nauseous. Then she heard the daily knock at the window. She could hardly make herself move over to it. But she did and tossed a few coins down.

'You still well then,' called the woman in surprise.

'So it would seem,' called back Sophie. She went through the routine of lifting out the food from the basket and managed a weak smile as the woman disappeared. Sophie walked slowly through to the bedroom and collapsed on the bed. She slept for twelve hours and woke about ten in the evening. She lit an oil lamp. She knew she felt stronger. Her fingers explored the buboes. They were softer, fast disappearing and the rose coloured spots on her body fading. She fell on her knees and whispered a heartfelt prayer of thanks to Almighty God for her healing.

Another ten days passed during which Sophie felt her strength slowly returning. She could still hardly believe it that she had actually survived the plague, 'black death' as it was sometimes called.

'I have to get away from this house,' she whispered to herself. She knew that the door had been nailed up, a red cross denoting the plague painted there for all to see. A watchman always patrolled the streets, checking that none escaped from their boarded up homes. How long she was supposed to be immured here she did not know. Normally as in that last major epidemic of 1625, whole families were boarded into a house where the first plague victim had been diagnosed, the intention being that since all would inevitably die, then at least the disease could be contained from spreading in this way.

But she was alone and had beaten the disease. The official who supplied her with food still came, and had decided that the beautiful young woman who always paid her well was unlikely to sicken now. But people in several other houses in Drury Lane and other adjacent streets were falling ill of the plague, which was spreading across the city at a ferocious rate. At night Sophie could hear the trundling noise of the dead cart stopping nearby, the sound of screams and weeping.

Then one morning Sophie realised that the money in her purse was dwindling. What would happen when she no longer had the means to pay for her daily food—starve perhaps? That night she peered out of the back window. It looked out on a small yard, bordered by an alleyway beyond. Sophie ripped the curtains into strips, made a rope which she attached to a leg of the heavy table. She landed soundlessly in the rubbish filled yard, opened the gate onto the alleyway and grimaced as several large rats scattered before her.

Once in the street she waited her chance to get past the watchman. She would find it difficult to remember the return journey to her own home, passing many houses with the dreaded red cross on the doors and the words 'God deliver us'. She had made her way along back streets to the river, asked a boatman to row her the short distance, paid him the last of her money and ascended the steps that brought her within a few yards of her house. Her key was still in her purse—she opened the door and collapsed on the sitting room couch.

When after two days the nurse who delivered food to Sophie found no answer to her repeated knocking, she informed the watchman. He stared at her reflectively. 'Perhaps you had better go within and see if the woman has succumbed to the plague and died. It takes some very fast you know.'

'Then you must have the door opened up. Not going to hurt my hands on those nails!' She stared at him hands on hips. They both entered the house and quickly established that Sophie was not lying sick or dead but had in fact vanished. 'You must report her to the authorities,' said the woman officiously.

'Better not. She gave me her name and a message to the King. I didn't do anything about it. I don't want to stir up a hornet's nest! Nor will you make any mention of this if you wish to retain your position as nurse and plague seeker!' He glared at her authoritatively She nodded acceptance. There were countless other cases to deal with as the plague s inexorably advanced and money to be made from the victims and their relatives.

Sophie stood at her door waved and called to Jack Foster, a young boy who had often run messages for her in the past. She gave him money to buy food and asked that he did not mention she was back home to any nearby, saying that she did not want visitors. The lad smiled understandingly. Most people avoided others these days for fear of the sickness.

It was a swelteringly hot May, with hardly a cloud in the sky. But there was little sense of joy in weather that would normally have brought content after a long winter. The sound of the dead carts now came to be heard in the daytime, not merely during the night, people dying in increasingly large numbers. And none knew whence the plague came. Some blamed dogs and cats and a few weeks later a great many animals would be slaughtered by order, nor did any realise that it was fleas infesting the rat population that were spreading the plague virus.

Those at the court began to be alarmed. No one had succumbed to the disease in Whitehall yet, but visits that the wealthy made to their men of business in the city were curtailed as the disease was now rife there, as indeed it was at the docks, whence this present outbreak had undoubtedly come. Many of the captured Dutch vessels had been plying their trade in Africa and India, countries where the plague was endemic.

At last at the beginning of June, Sophie decided the time had come to return to the court. Physically she had completely recovered from the plague, even the scar in her groin paling to insignificance. Her hair had regained its full lustre and her blue eyes were steady with purpose as she regarded herself thoughtfully in her full length bedroom mirror. She was wearing a gown of her favourite sapphire blue, the golden pomander swinging at her waist and her mother's locket about her neck.

'I do not look amiss for a woman who has born a child, been widowed and recovered from the plague, she thought whimsically. But her thoughts were anything but peaceful as she set out in a hired carriage for Whitehall. At the height of her sickness she had cried out to God for healing—that she in turn might help others. All she had done so far was to concentrate on getting well again and making plans to return to the King's library.

She stepped lightly into the hired carriage and within ten minutes was at the palace, negotiating its many corridors, crossing reception rooms as she made her way towards the library, smiling at those who recognised her and called a casual greeting. One of these was Anne, Duchess of York.

'Lady Mereton—Sophie, where have you been these last few weeks? We feared some mishap had overtaken you!' She smiled at Sophie.

'A long story! I was kidnapped on the orders of Viscount Loxley. Luckily I managed to escape, eventually!' She gave a wry smile.

Ann looked at her incredulously. 'Loxley—he dared to behave so? Can that be why none have seen him at court these last few weeks?' her face was shocked. She took Sophie's arm. 'My dear, the King must hear of this! I will speak with him!'

Chapter Thirteen

The King was indeed shocked to hear the story. He had been disturbed to learn that Sophie, mother of one of his children had disappeared without trace, for he held the young woman in high regard, looking on her as a friend with whom he could be completely open, discussing matters of State in a way which would have been impossible with Barbara or any other of his women. He knew that Sophie had no personal desire for advancement, her relationship with him one of a special bond of friendship, her only thoughts merely a longing to enhance her knowledge of medicine. If he thought this somewhat strange in a woman, nevertheless he accepted that this was what intrigued him.

He looked at her uneasily now, for Sophie had just revealed that she had endured the plague—almost miraculously survived it. Was it possible that she still carried traces of it with her? She saw his expression and guessed the cause.

'I promise you that you are entirely safe in my company, Sire!' she said reprovingly. 'Do you think I would take risk of the health of one I esteem so dearly?' He smiled sheepishly and lifted her hand to his lips.

'There is your answer,' he said softly. 'After all Sophie, you nursed my late beloved, Sister Mary of the pox, so why should it surprise me that you have overcome the plague. I have heard that some very few do so. Here at court all carry nosegays of herbs and spices to ward off the infection, most men smoke or chew tobacco which is supposed to be most efficacious and I know the Lord Mayor is considering having all cats and dogs in London destroyed, as possibly spreading the foul disease.'

'I believe the answer may lie with certain animals, not necessarily dogs and cats, but rather rats!' Her eyes searched his face. 'They say that the plague is rife in the Eastern lands and Africa, also that it devastated Holland two years ago. Ships carry rats from these places to our docks. But how a rat may carry disease without actually administering a bite, I cannot say.' Her face was troubled.

'Certainly the plague is spreading at an alarming rate in the poorer areas and suburbs and worryingly now actually in the city—no cases so far here in Whitehall,' he acknowledged quietly, thinking that there would be but few rats in his palace, the kitchens and cellars should be checked. But there again, it might have nothing to do with vermin. The problem possibly lay in poor housing, narrow alleyways and the upper floors of buildings projecting outwards and almost meeting those opposite. He had long argued that change was needed in all this. But change needed money and parliament kept a tight hold on his purse strings. He dismissed these thoughts returning his attention on Sophie.

'Now tell me of these men who abducted you Sophie. You remember their names as Jenkins and Pelham, that they were off a ship recently docked and that Loxley had some underhand dealings with the master of the ship regarding booty captured from the Dutch? This is serious allegation indeed and one that I will thoroughly investigate.'

'The Duchess of York tells me that Loxley has not been seen at court for many weeks—do you suppose....'and her blue eyes widened?

'That he has fallen sick of the plague? I will have officers sent to his lodgings to arrest him—unless he is dead,' replied Charles grimly.

When the King's officers arrived at the residence of Viscount Loxley, none answered their knock. The door was bolted, so they went round to the back of the small, elegant dwelling. The back door yielded. They paused on the threshold, for a most noxious smell wafted towards them. There was no mistaking it. They glanced at each other and hastily shut the door and summoned an officer of the watch. 'There is one lying dead in this house,' they explained. 'It is the residence of one Viscount Loxley, and your duty to send in plague searchers to ascertain that the man Loxley is the victim and list any others found within.'

'How do you know there's a corpse in there,' demanded the officer of the watch?

'The smell my friend—phwaw!' was the curt reply.

And so it was that the King received report that Loxley was indeed dead of the plague as were his two servants. Boxes containing costly spices and jewels were found in his study. Loxley had most certainly obtained these illegally from the 'Penguin' and paid a high price for his crime with his life.

Unease spread around the court as June advanced and more red crosses were reported as seen on doors in streets not too far from Whitehall and now it was spreading fast in the city, men scared to attend their offices, the Royal Exchange almost deserted, many shops now closed, eating houses shunned. And still the temperature rose in what was the hottest summer any could remember.

July came and the plague was now ravishing thousands across London, some of the wealthier citizens and any who could afford to do so, leaving their homes behind and escaping into the country—including some already carrying the plague within their bodies, and so it spread into surrounding villages. Then a new rule was made that none could leave without a certificate of health.

'Sophie, the court is leaving London for Oxford where the air is purer,' said Charles, having tracked her down to the library. 'Pack a few of your belongings and I will send a carriage for you. We leave later today!'

His dark eyes expressed his worry at the situation. Part of him wanted to stay with his people. But should he succumb and die, where would that leave the country since he had no heir apart from his brother, with the possibility of new civil war? Parliament was also leaving and as Sophie was to discover, many of London's most prominent physicians had already departed for the safety of the country. The common people were being abandoned to their fate.

'I shall remain here,' said Sophie decisively. 'I have had the plague! Do not think people can have it twice, at least I hope not!' Her blue eyes were determined and he shook his head, knowing her too well to try to make her change her mind.

'Then may God bless you, my dear,' he said quietly and drew her to him in a quick embrace, then hurried off for there was much to be attended to.

The court had dispersed to Oxford, the exchequer to the country. To her disgust Sophie learned that most members of the College of Physicians had also fled the city, even many clergymen likewise disappearing. The citizens of London were now truly on their own, attempting to deal with an enemy relentless in its advance. More and more succumbed to the plague, the dead carts trundling through the town in daylight now, not as had previously been the case, solely during the hours of night. Corpses were merely tossed onto the carts in a tangled, unseemly mass of limbs—young, old, male and female alike. New areas of burial were set aside as most graveyards were overflowing, deep pits where people of all degree were hastily thrown and covered.

As for Sophie, she made her services available to any sick in her immediate area, knowing there was little she was able to do, apart from trying to alleviate their symptoms. The beautiful young woman was regarded by many as an angel of mercy, as she entered houses full of suffering and despair, sometimes able to do little more than place a cold compress on burning foreheads, wipe bloody vomit and cleanse away evil smelling flux of the bowels. Other houses she avoided where men and women had turned to drink, shouting bawdy songs, lewd beyond the telling.

And still the plague advanced, peaking in August. Then as autumn approached it seemed to weaken its grip—but it would not be until early 1666 that the King and his court made return to London. Gradually matters returned to approaching normal in the city, men of business bowed once more over their ledgers, some coffee houses now reopening. But the plague was still around, even though recorded deaths were thankfully dropping in number.

And Sophie was exhausted. She could not remember how many times she had fought inevitable death at a bedside and been defeated in her efforts. But at the very least, she had been able to help some few stricken human beings pass into death with the comfort of one who cared tending them, at the last.

Perhaps one day men would learn how to combat this loathsome disease, a cure found. She sensed that this would not happen during her lifetime, but prayed that one day this scourge would be obliterated.

For a month now Sophie had visited no new cases. She had thrown away all clothing she had worn and purchased new, and scrubbed her house from top to bottom. She would love to have opened the windows, but the stench from the Thames was overpoweringly offensive. Yet when the sun shone on its waters it looked idyllic, boats starting to ply their trade up and down its reaches. She knew that she longed for a breath of fresh, country air.

'You look tired, sweetheart!' The King looked down on her critically the day she returned to his newly reassembled court. She was wearing a gown of dark blue silk, the white lace at the bodice throwing up the pallor of her face, her blue eyes darkly shadowed from all she had endured. But she was the same lovely woman he remembered, who smiled at him with a challenge on her lips. 'So tell me—how has it been this many months?'

'What can I say?' her blue eyes filled with tears. 'I have fought the angel of death over the beds of countless plague victims, but heartbreakingly there appears to be no cure at this time and this fills me with sorrow! One day I believe men will have a better understanding of disease, its causes and treatment. For now all any can do is to show care and pity!'

'Sophie, you have really been nursing those sick of plague all this while?' He shook his head marvelling at her courage.

'Yes. I took decision to cease my endeavours a few weeks ago. The plague does seem to be abating now—and I am so tired!'

'Do you think that the time has come for you to return to Oaklands for a few months? You need to rest, walk in the sunshine—take our little daughter in your arms! I am wishful to see Minette again, when it is safe for her to come. Your father too must be sick with worry as to your safety!'

'I managed to get word to him that I was well, had survived the plague,' was all her quiet reply.

The carriage she had hired drew up outside Hawksley Manor, and she stepped down, glad to stretch her limbs after the jolting on rough roads. She glanced around. The gardens were bright with the flowers of spring, and fruit trees a mass of pink and white blossom. She drew a deep breath and the air was like fine wine.

As she glanced up towards the massive manor door, it suddenly swung open and her father stared, then came hurrying down the stone steps towards her.

'Sophie—child!' he cried, 'God be thanked, you are here at last!'
He swept her up into his arms as his lips sought hers. Then he loosed her and held her back from him as he examined her face, saw the shadows around her eyes, her pallor—and she had lost weight. And even as he appraised her, she was taking in her father's own appearance and delighted to see him looking so well. It was as though the years had slipped away, all signs of his overwhelming grief for Madeleine abandoned.

'Father—I have missed you!'

'Then why did you not return once you had so miraculously recovered from the plague?' He looked at her reproachfully.

'Because I had work to do back there in London, nursing those sick of the plague father—no, do not worry! I have not been in contact with any such for many weeks. I bring no sickness with me.' He shook his head at her words.

'You have been nursing plague victims! Sophie, such work is usually done by special plague nurses.' He looked at her in amazement.

Her eyes sparkled with indignation as she replied, 'Yes. And so often these are women who take advantage of their position to rob the dying and for the most part do little to alleviate their condition. Harpies I have heard them called!'

He chuckled. You may seem tired but have lost none of your old fire I see!' He slipped an arm about her waist, while calling to one of the servants who had appeared in the doorway, to carry in Sophie's belongings from the carriage.

She gave a sigh of delight as she looked around the great hall and found all as she remembered—and suddenly there came the sound of young voices and flying feet, and Minette followed closely by little Henry escaped Jenny who ran in breathless pursuit.

'Mama, you have come home,' cried Minette, holding her arms out to be lifted and Sophie gave a cry of joy to hold her beloved child close to her breast again after a year's absence. Then Henry was pulling at her skirts and his father held him up to receive kisses also. Sophie had tears in her eyes as she alternatively hugged the children, her little daughter and her baby brother, who was also calling her Mama!

They have grown so,' she exclaimed. Then she glanced across at their nurse, Jenny who was pink with pleasure to see her mistress again.

'Jenny—how can I ever thank you for their care. I can see how well they have been looked after! Later when I have unpacked I have presents for you all!'

Those presents were received with glee by the children, a new doll for Minette with blonde curls and dressed in the latest fashion, and a box of brightly painted, wooden toy soldiers for little Henry. They smothered Sophie with kisses as she bent down to them and rushed off to examine their gifts. Jenny gasped to receive material to make new skirts and blouses murmuring her thanks. Then when they were alone, Sophie presented her father with a handsome gold watch.

'A new start in time,' she said softly. He held it in the palm of his hand and nodded.

'Thank you my darling—a new start indeed! I will treasure it always! Now come to the library. I want you to explain in detail all that has been happening in your life since I drove off with the children a year ago and when you said that you would follow shortly!'

They sat long together in the library, exchanging confidences and sipping wine before the log fire, for although the sun was shining outside the interior of the old house was hard to heat, its ornate ceilings high.

'I was horrified by the reports we received here of the severity of the plague. When I learned that you had caught and amazingly survived it, for only a handful do so, I was filled with unimaginable relief—but unable to understand why you did not leave the hell hole London had become. We heard of mass graves, terrible happenings, of King and court leaving for the safety of Oxford, Parliament suspended—even men of the church and doctors fleeing the stricken city!' He gave his daughter a penetrating look and leaning forward in his chair, took her hand in his. 'So why did you stay, Sophie?' He stroked the fine boned hand he held, sensing her strength and something which set her apart. She looked back at him musingly.

'Although I am not a physician, I have some medical knowledge. It was my duty to help the sick where I was able. I know only too well the sorry lack of decent professional care for those afflicted by a disease for which as yet man has found no cure. One day I pray that this may change, feel absolutely sure that it will, but not I fear in our lifetime father.' Her blue eyes seemed to pierce the mists of the future.

'You are an extraordinary woman, Sophie!' and he kissed her. 'What are your plans for the future? Is this just a quick visit to regain your strength after all you have experienced from the horror of a death ridden city, or a desire to make a real home for yourself and Minette in the peace of the countryside?' He poured a glass of wine and watched as she sipped it reflectively.

'Father, the answer to your question is that I am not sure what the future holds for me. It was sheer delight to hold my little daughter in my arms once more and to embrace my small brother, wonderful to be back here with you. It is as though the years have rolled away. So let us say that I am resolved to take each day as it comes—and also to have a care of Oaklands, as it is mine to maintain until Minette's majority.'

'Oaklands and I mean the estate, is being well run! But as for the house, it functions along without a heart, if you know what I mean.' He stared at her meaningfully and she nodded and placed her glass on the table, almost untouched.

'Because no member of the Gareth's family lives there now, that is what you would say?' She sighed in frustration. 'I had thought to have remained here with you, father, merely making occasional visits to Oaklands to see all is well there. As for the thought of living in that rather soulless old building again? I am not sure I could do it!'

'You are tired, my darling and no wonder after your long journey. Have an early night's sleep and you will view the future with new eyes!' he shook his head thoughtfully after she had retired. Two fine old manor houses and two young children growing up and who would one day inherit them—his little Henry to be master of Hawksley Manor—and Sophie's small daughter Minette, her father the King, would take control of Oaklands. But both properties needed caring for in the meanwhile by those who currently owned them. He sighed and rose to his feet.

What would Sophie decide to do?

The following day Sophie arose early, her heart gladdened by the sound of birdsong, the blackbirds trill soon to be joined by the excited cries of the two small children who escaped from Jenny's care to rush into Sophie's room and throw themselves into her arms.

'Mama! Mama—please come and play with us!' She kissed them tenderly and allowed Jenny to lead them protesting back to the nursery. 'I will play with you later, I promise,' she called.

Her father noted that she wore a velvet riding suit, and sighed at the breeches, but knew it would avail him nothing to remonstrate on her apparel.

'I am going to ride to The Willows,' she announced. 'I want to see grandfather's house again.' She smiled up at him and he nodded.

'Then I will come with you, Sophie!' He rose to his feet.

'I ride alone today, father. Forgive me, but I need peace. We will ride together tomorrow, perhaps to visit Oaklands.' Then she was gone. He shook his head. He would prefer that at least she took a groom with her, for even these days it was not safe for a woman to ride alone through the woods, for such he imagined was her purpose. He knew how much she loved Epilson woods, the walks she had taken there in the past with John Wheatley.

194

He sent for Richard Appleby, the youngest son of his manager Paul Appleby, now approaching twenty years and a fine athletic young man.

'Sophie is preparing to ride through Epilson Woods. She wishes to be alone, but it would be safer if you were to ride at a discreet distance, in case of—well!'

Richard met his eyes thoughtfully, nodded and bowed. He felt extremely protective of the lovely young woman, remembered keenly that despite his efforts she had been kidnapped by Harrison's thugs a few years ago. Then he had only been a boy and almost lost his own life at their hands. Now it would be otherwise, he thought grimly. But no one had seen Harrison since he took his abrupt departure by night from the village, after attempting to set Hawksley Manor on fire. Why that must be almost six years ago now. There was still a warrant out for his arrest.

'I understand, my lord. I will protect her of that you may be assured—not that there should be any around to hurt her these days!' And he hurried to the stables, where he saw Sophie already mounted and waving goodbye to the groom, who grinned at her approvingly.

He followed her along the lane that led to the village and watched as she opened the gate and set her horses head across the field and towards Epilson woods, knew her love for the beauty of the place. She had not heard his horse's hooves behind her, for she was singing as she rode. Soon she was deep in the green leafiness of the woods, taking the path that led past the clearing where old Jessie's cottage once had stood. The rust of last year's bracken and new curling fronds disguised the fallen blackened walls and bluebells and wood anemones softened the approach.

Sophie closed her eyes, tried to recollect the face of the old woman whom her grandfather had respected and from whom he had bought healing herbs. In the past

'Jessie—why did it have to happen? I would so much have loved to speak with you, to inquire into the ancient wisdom that was yours!' She spoke the words aloud, nor saw the man who eased his stallion towards her, where she bent looking down on the ruined cottage. But Richard saw the stranger and approached nearer.

'A fine day, lady!' said a smooth cultured voice. 'I give you greeting!' As she heard the words Sophie sat upright on her mare. She stared at the man who closed the gap between them, halting his stallion at her side and jerking its head to obedience. She inclined her head to him and glanced at him curiously. He was fashionably dressed, a full wig of black curls framing a strong face and square chin, his eyes dark, inscrutable.

'A fine day indeed,' she replied lightly, and bending forward on her mare urged it forward with her knees. It responded immediately as she threw back a polite addition to her words. 'I wish you joy of it, sir!'

'Not so fast, fair one! At least tell me the name of one so beautiful and who stares with strangely sorrowful eyes at the burnt out dwelling of an old witch?' He urged his horse closer, reached out his hand to restrain her mare, his eyes smouldering with a look she recognised and felt sudden alarm. But even as he laid hold of her reins, Sophie heard a call and the sound of approaching hooves.

'Is this person annoying you, Lady Meredith?' Richard Appleby stared angrily at the man, his hand curling around the handle of his whip. The stranger's eyes narrowed, hardened slightly as he heard Sophie identified. Sophie noted it even as she smiled at Richard Appleby.

'Why Richard, I did not know you were riding this way. Perhaps you would accompany me to The Willows,' she said quietly. 'I believe this gentleman was about to go on his way.' The stranger looked at them indecisively, then with a dry laugh, tugged on his rein and they heard the sound of his stallion's hooves pounding before them along the forest trail.

'I am glad you came to my aid, Richard!' She smiled at him gratefully. 'I could probably have dealt with him myself, nevertheless, it was an unexpected encounter and the place lonely!'

'I'm wondering just who that fellow was,' exclaimed Richard. 'He looked vaguely familiar—yet I cannot recollect having met him before!'

'Let's forget him. Did my father suggest you follow me?'

'Why yes, Mistress Sophie—your ladyship, that is!'

'Sophie, will do. Come on, I long to see The Willows again!' Later, as she dismounted before the familiar old house that had been home to her beloved grandfather, Sophie glanced up and down the quiet street and stiffened slightly, to see the stranger from that recent woodland encounter watching her from his stallion from about fifty yards away. As he realised he was observed, he turned his horse and trotted off towards the square.

'He was watching you,' said Richard indignantly. 'Shall I follow and have words with him?' But Sophie shook her head. She was well used from her time at court to dealing with unwanted admirers, usually a severe glance was enough! She disguised her frown, as she handed the reins of her mare to Jack Dawlish who had just walked round from the stables.

'Thank you, Jack—it's good to see you again!'

'Why Mistress Sophie, what joy you have returned! Beth Giles will surely be delighted!' He beckoned Richard to accompany him round to the stables with his own mount, as Sophie started up the pathway towards the house, noting as she did so how well the garden had been tended, ablaze with flowers. The door opened before she could knock and the housekeeper stared at her from damp eyes.

'You are back, Sophie! Oh I am that glad to see you again.' There was genuine affection in Beth Giles eyes, who then bobbed a curtsey as she remembered that Sophie was a titled lady now. They sat together in the doctor's small parlour, as Sophie explained some of what had transpired in her life since last they met. Beth's face registered horror to learn that Sophie had been victim to the plague, recovered, and then spent many months caring for some of those many others stricken down by the foul and much feared disease.

'Were you not afeared to catch it a second time,' she asked shaking her head, as she saw the deep tiredness on the girl's face.

'I do not think it strikes the same person twice. But very few do survive. If only I knew some way to combat the disease, but once infected the symptoms advance swiftly, inexorably, with little to do but make the patient as comfortable as may be.' Sophie's blue eyes were sad. 'But one day, Beth, perhaps physicians will find a cure.'

'Well my dear, thank the good Lord that your young Minette and little Henry were safe here in the country! Your father, Lord Hawksley brought them over to see me a couple of times. He must be so relieved to have you safe home again.'

They chatted together companionably for some time over a glass of wine and a slice of Beth's cake, then Sophie followed Beth into the kitchen where they found Richard in conversation with Jack Dawlish. They looked up as the women came in.

'Mistress Sophie, I now know the name of the fellow who came upon you in the woods. Dawlish says his name is Gerald Lorrimer. Seems he is a gentleman of leisure, who bought the Falstaff Inn in Langley Morton that once belonged to Roger Haversham,. He purchased the house too. It was done through his lawyer and until now, none knew the name of the real owner.' He glanced at Dawlish who nodded confirmation.

Dawlish saw Sophie flinch as she heard mention of the name of the man who had terrorised both herself and her aunt for so many years, until they had sought succour from the old doctor. He remembered now how Haversham had come to The Willows on the death of Doctor Wheatley thinking to inherit it through Martha, the doctor's daughter, his estranged wife. He smiled grimly recollecting how Haversham in a fury of disappointment on learning Sophie had inherited the house, had suffered a fatal stroke.

'So this Lorrimer owns both Haversham's house and the Inn,' said Beth Giles curiously. 'If he is one of the gentry, then what possessed him to lay out good money to buy a house which he never uses and an inn in which he obviously has little interest?'

'Yes and what interest can he have in Mistress Sophie,' said Richard.

'Please, let's forget the man!' Sophie smiled and brushed the subject aside as she began to ask questions about all that had happened since her

197

last visit to The Willows. But Beth far from forgetting was determined to discover all she could of the stranger. Who was this Gerald Lorrimer, and what his interest in the Falstaff Inn, and in Sophie?

Sophie visited the doctor's garden and sat on the bench they had often shared overlooking the shady pool. She tried to recollect his face and found it was not as easy as it had been. Luckily there was that old portrait of him in his study portraying him as a young man. But still she sensed his presence here in his beloved garden and sighed as she left.

The ride home was uneventful, with Richard at her side. She mentioned the encounter in the woods to her father, who scowled as he repeated the stranger's name.

'Lorrimer? Cannot say I have ever heard of him before. What did he look like?'

Sophie merely smiled and shook her head dismissively as she declared, 'Like so many other gallants these days! Dressed in the height of fashion and wearing a full wig of dark curls framing an arrogant face. But oddly he seemed strangely familiar!'

Then the children were running towards her and she caught them up in her arms all thoughts of Gerald Lorrimer forgotten. The following morning saw her riding towards Oaklands, with Richard Appleby in attendance, nor did she seek to dissuade him. To her delight she found Martha there, on what was a regular weekly visit to ensure that all was running smoothly during Sophie's absence from her lovely old mansion house, that would one day belong to little Minette Mereton

'Mama!' The old term slipped out as Sophie opened her arms.

'Sophie—child! Oh, what joy to see you again! I was horrified to learn you had taken the plague,' and her aunt surveyed the girl from anxious eyes, noting thankfully that although pale and a little thinner, Sophie looked well and as beautiful as ever. 'The good Lord must have been watching over you that you made such amazing recovery!' she exclaimed as she kissed the girl, then slipped her arm around Sophie's waist as the two women made their way across the great hall surveyed by portraits of Mereton ancestors and into the oak lined reception room overlooking the garden.

They seated themselves on one of the velvet covered couches as the maid Ellen appeared and curtsied asking if Lady Mereton desired refreshments brought.

'Thank you Ellen. Tell cook that for now we would like a slice of her apple pie—and some cordial,' exclaimed Sophie. 'I have certainly missed Joan Pyke's cooking!' she added reflectively.

'Are you here to stay this time,' inquired Martha wistfully?

'The answer to that is I simply don't know. When I am in London, I sometimes long for the peace and beauty of the countryside, yet there is so much of excitement to be found in the capital.' She smiled at Martha ruefully.

'And the King, you left him well,' asked Martha carefully.

'Charles is as always much taken up with affairs of State, seeking an end to the unproductive Dutch wars, his anxiety over the numbers who died in the plague and feeling that the overcrowded, insanitary conditions prevailing in the city need to be changed. Then of course there are his mistresses.' She came out with the last phrase in matter of fact tones that made Martha shake her head.

'Are you still—I mean....?'

'Am I one of his mistresses? The answer to that is no. Not in the way you mean, Mama. We will always be close, share a unique friendship, as well as having a special bond in our little daughter.' She sighed.

'Do you love him, Sophie?'

'Yes, I suppose I do. But I will not share him, prefer to be his friend.'

'But, can that be enough?' She stared earnestly at the girl.

'Yes! For I have his enduring friendship, which with my deep love of medicine fulfils my life, and then there is my little daughter.' She spoke almost analytically, a brooding sadness in her eyes.

'And the King—I suppose he must be content with so many beautiful women rumoured to be willing to run into his arms?' Martha was curious. Sophie sighed and stared out of the window, before replying softly,

'He is not a happy man, I fear, although he might seem so to one who does not know him. Too much hurt occurred in his earlier life, the horror of his father's beheading, the years spent in penniless exile, and now having to face the fact that his Queen is barren. He who has fathered several children has been unable to have one by his wife Catherine.'

'Well, they have only been wed about three years, time still for her to conceive,' suggested Martha. 'Yet how difficult it must be for her not to hold a babe in her arms, when his mistresses are proof of his virility? Sophie child, it is a great hurt for a woman to be barren,' and Sophie realised Martha spoke of her own condition.

The next few days were busy ones as Sophie bent her head over records of the estates accounts, familiarised herself with changes of staff and rode along country lanes with Richard Appleby and with Jack Lynden now acting as Oakland's estate manager and who had married Lottie, the onetime wet nurse to little Henry Hawksley. Jack proudly explained improvements to the land, that it was now better drained, attention paid to hedging and ditching, a plan to alternate crops.

Yes, all was going very well at Oaklands, but as she pulled the coverlids up to her chin at night, Sophie realised that the place really meant nothing to her beyond the fact that it was her small daughter's heritage. She had wondered whether she might have made a home here for Minette and herself, but acknowledged in her heart of hearts that this would not be. Oaklands held too many memories of a time she wished to forget, when she had faced marriage to an elderly man whom she did not love, the shock of his death in the snow when the carriage overturned and her own sense of guilt that she had not been able to love a man who had behaved with all graciousness to her, given the protection of his name and secured her little daughter's future.

So if not Oaklands, then where, she pondered? Hawksley Manor beckoned with the presence of her father and small brother and where Minette could grow up in a happy family situation. But would she personally be happy even there? What was wrong with her that she longed for what, true independence perhaps? There was the London house of course, but that was not her own, merely a rented property received at the hands of Anne, Duchess of York—so not truly hers.

'But there is always The Willows,' she whispered and she fell asleep, a smile touching her lips. One day perhaps......?

Back once more at Hawksley Manor, she gradually began to unwind from the tensions of the last year. She still suffered occasional nightmares, in which plague victims writhed, contorted and cried out for help and relief from their pains. She would suddenly sit up in bed, her face bedewed with sweat, as it took a minute or two for her realise that what had afflicted her sleep was not real, but only the fantasy of dream.

June was excessively hot and Sophie was glad of the soft country breezes that stirred the trees and slowly wafted almost transparent clouds along a vivid blue sky. London's streets must be suffocatingly warm she thought. Today the children were lightly dressed and playing in the gardens under Jenny's watchful eyes. Sophie joined them for a while, but a spirit of restlessness forced her to order her mare saddled for a ride into the village. Her father did not see her go, for he was studying a favourite historical treatise in his library. Of course she should have waited for Richard Appleby and left a careless message with the groom that she was to ride through Epilson woods.

It was the first time she had ventured here on her own since that chance encounter with Gerald Lorrimer almost six weeks ago. She decided that she could not go through life worrying about her safety. That had never been her way. She paused again by the ruin of old Jessie's cottage and this time no intrusive stranger came to break her reverie. She dismounted and stood there, trying to recollect all the old woman had said to her—and there had been a warning, had there not? She tried to recollect Jessie's words. Frustratingly she found no answer in memory save these words, 'Do not let your heart rule your head!' Well, that could mean anything, could it not?

She remounted her mare and joyed to ride on through the cool leafiness of the woods, hearing the soft cooing of pigeons, the bark of a fox, the chattering of the small stream that wended its way through the undergrowth and drawing in her breath as a baby roe deer ran across her path. This place was magic to her, always would be. What did she need of mansions and fine clothes and jewels? She caught at a spray of honeysuckle that hung above her head, snapping it and twining it in her hair.

Nor was it the strange beauty of the woods alone that called to her, but knowledge that it was a store house of those healing herbs her grandfather had collected here as had old Jessie. 'This is what I truly want,' she whispered to herself. At last she knew, but what to do about it? She still had a duty of love and care for her small daughter, Minette, must guide and protect her into womanhood and this would take many long years.

She had left the welcome coolness of the woods and before long was riding along the village street towards The Willows, the afternoon sun blazing down on her head. She was just approaching the house when a shout made her look around. A man was spurring his horse towards her. She frowned. It was Gerald Lorrimer. He was closely followed by another, by his dress a servant, whom Lorrimer dismissed.

'Lady Meredith! Pray a moment of your time?' He reined in at her side, his dark eyes examining her face admiringly. She frowned and her mare sensed her unease and juddered. She patted its side reassuring.

She stared at him questioningly. Why did this man look vaguely familiar? She could certainly not recall having met him before that earlier encounter in the woods. He swept off his wide brimmed, plumed hat and fetched a deep bow from the waist. He smiled gently at her.

'I wish to convey my deepest apologies for my manner towards you at our earlier meeting, when I did not know whom I had the honour of meeting,' he said suavely.

'I accept your apology sir, but would suggest that a gentleman behaves with courtesy to all women, regardless of status. Now, if you will excuse me!' She urged her mare onwards, covering the short distance towards The Willows. To her annoyance he continued at her side.

'Then if you accept my apology, may I dare to ask permission to visit the beautiful house and surgery that previously belonged to a doctor widely respected in the district from what I am told. Indeed, many years ago he attended my mother when she was sick of a wasting fever.' He looked at her respectfully.

'She recovered,' asked Sophie, interested.

'Yes and always spoke well of the John Wheatley, the wonderful doctor who saved her life.'

'You are not from these parts, sir. So how was it that your mother was treated by my grandfather?' She looked at him uneasily, too many mysteries here.

'I was brought up in Cornwall, but my mother lived in this area before her marriage. Since I fear that I am being importunate—I will go!' He bowed again and gave a wistful smile. Sophie hesitated. What harm could it do to let the man see The Willows if it meant so much to him?

'Oh, very well then, come with me,' she said ungraciously, as to her relief Dawlish having heard voices, came round from the stables.

'This gentleman is making a brief visit, Dawlish.' She dismounted. The stableman who was also gardener and general handyman, gave Lorrimer a doubtful glance, as he took Sophie's mare.

'Best tether your horse to the gatepost then sir—if it is to be a brief visit,' he said and led the mare off. Beth Giles looked up in surprise on seeing a stranger at Sophie's side as she opened the door. Her jaw dropped as she took in Lorrimer's appearance.

'Beth dear, this is Gerald Lorrimer, who tells me that the doctor once treated his mother, and that like many another she owed her life to him. He wants to see the house, although I cannot think why. Would you be kind enough to show him the doctor's surgery?'

'Why of course, my lady,' said Beth formally. 'Follow me, sir!' Her petticoats rustled frustration as she led him into the surgery where on Sophie's instructions, all remained as the doctor had left it. The man stared around curiously as he noted the jars of herbs, anatomy charts on walls, shelves of medical books, a tray of instruments.

'It is said the doctor relied much on herbs, that he procured many from the old witch Jessie Thorne, who lived in the woods, if true, a strange relationship?' and he stared interrogatively at Beth Giles from shrewd dark eyes.

'You seem much taken up with affairs none of your business,' she replied tartly. 'If you have seen enough, then I suggest you leave, sir!'

'That is for your mistress to say, woman,' he replied harshly, but at her insistent stare left the surgery. She shut the door angrily behind him. He glanced around for Sophie and saw no sign of her. To Beth's annoyance the stranger opened the door to the small parlour and seeing it empty, tried the dining room, then strode along the passageway and stared at the open door that led into the garden. He peered out and saw Sophie seated on a bench, over a pool, her head bent in thought.

'I'm sorry, my lady,' cried Beth angrily, as the stranger made towards the seat. Sophie lifted her head in surprise as Gerald Lorrimer strode over to smile down gently, a pleasant smile on his lips.

'I come to take my farewell, Lady Mereton and to thank you for your kindness in allowing me to see the house where my mother received wondrous healing from a man said to have almost magical powers over sickness!' And he emphasised the phrase. Before she could prevent it he had taken her hand and lifted it to his lips in salute.

'My grandfather used no magic, sir, just knowledge born of many hard years of study.' She snatched back her hand indignantly.

'I have heard it said that you also have this exceptional power of healing, an unusual accomplishment in a woman, and of course much to be respected,' he said suavely.

'You seem be taking unprecedented attention to my affairs and those of my late grandfather,' she said steadily. 'I wish you good day, sir!' Her blue eyes darkened angrily. He hesitated.

'You look delightful when you are annoyed,' he breathed. 'One day soon, I hope to light a more tender light in those eyes, Sophie!' Then he turned on his heel and strode off an indignant Beth Giles in his wake.

Richard Appleby arrived just as Lorrimer was untethering his horse from the gate post. He stared at the man in outrage.

'What is your business here, sir,' he demanded brusquely.

'That is no affair of yours,' jerked Lorrimer, and leaping into the saddle galloped off along the street, leaving Richard scowling after him. He saw Beth Giles framed in the doorway of The Willows and hurried up the path towards her.

'Has there been a problem here, Beth,' he inquired anxiously?

'Not exactly a problem, but the man who just left was trying to force his attentions upon Mistress Sophie, until she sent him away with a flea in his ear! Trying to cast aspersions on the old doctor he was, and even making sly remarks about Sophie's healing powers!' Her honest face was red as she stood hands on hips staring in the direction Lorrimer had taken.

'If I had known that I would have taken my whip to him,' declared Richard, face tense with anger. Then Sophie appeared and smiled at them both affectionately.

'Now don't start worrying about that fellow,' she said decisively. 'I don't know what his true motive was in coming here and wishing to visit grandfather's surgery. Perhaps it was genuine curiosity to see a place where his mother received healing, but the story sounds thin.'

'He made a strange remark about the doctor having gone to old Jessie for his healing herbs' said Beth thoughtfully. 'How could he have known that? He referred to Jessie as a witch!'

'You should not have gone off without me,' complained Richard. 'Suppose he had come upon you in the woods as before—and you unattended?' His young face showed worry at what might have happened.

'Dear Lord,' exclaimed Beth Giles suddenly. 'I know now who he reminds me of! Can't think why I didn't realise it earlier, he is the image of Mark Harrison as a young man!'

Harrison? The man who had caused her to be kidnapped and Jessie Thorne murdered? Sophie turned pale, for she realised that this was the answer to the resemblance that had been troubling her as she strove in her mind for any occasion on which she might previously have met Lorrimer. It was his likeness to Harrison, the same square jaw and strange, hard eyes, even his arrogance.

'Was Harrison married,' she inquired quietly now as they sat taking a glass of wine in the parlour. Beth Giles shook her head.

'Not that I ever heard of! He had a sister though, named Myra. She up and married a man from somewhere in Cornwall. None in the village heard of her after that!' She shrugged.

'Cornwall? He said he grew up in Cornwall, which means that this Gerald Lorrimer is Mark Harrison's nephew! But what brings him here? And why did he buy Haversham's house and the Falstaff Inn at Langley Morton? None of it makes any sense!' Sophie's face expressed bewilderment.

Later that night she discussed the matter with her father. James Hawksley's face darkened as Sophie explained that the man who had twice tried to force himself upon her, was the nephew of Mark Harrison, the man who had for so many years dispossessed him of Hawksley Manor under Cromwell and who on realising that he was about to lose everything on the Restoration of King Charles, had then kidnapped Sophie and tried to force her into marriage, and when she escaped him had then attempted to burn down the manor house.

'So this fellow is the son of Mark Harrison's sister Myra Harrison, as she was before she married Steven Lorrimer! I don't like it, my dear. I cannot help but think the attention he is paying you presents danger!' His eyes glinted angrily. 'I have never been able to understand why the authorities were unable to track down Harrison and bring him to trial, nor have there been any reported sightings of him over these last years!'

'Is it possible he is living in Cornwall now, with his sister and brother-in-law? Yes, and if he has told his nephew Gerald Lorrimer of his hatred for you father, his anger that he had to give up Hawksley Manor, his fury against me for rejecting him, as my mother did before me—then this might give explanation for the nephew's presence in the district now.' She frowned and shook her head. 'But what can he possibly hope to achieve by forcing himself on me?'

'Was anything said when he was at The Willows that disturbed you in anyway?' He looked at his daughter keenly. Sophie knit her brows together.

'He told Beth Giles that it was known my grandfather purchased some of the healing herbs he used from Jessie Thorne—referred to her as a witch! Spoke to me of grandfather possessing magical powers, went on to express surprise that as a woman I should involve myself in healing!' As she spoke to him she saw her father's face darken, as a troubled look came into his eyes.

'Sophie child, I am going to suggest to you that you do not allow your interest in medicine to become more widely known.' He spoke solemnly.

'Why ever not?' she cried.

'Because a man such as this Lorrimer appears to be, might use it against you in some way. No! Listen to me in this, Sophie!'

'But what are you suggesting?' She stared at him bemused, for she saw from his expression, that her father was genuinely worried. 'Why should I worry what people think when the King approves?'

'Just trust me in this matter, Sophie! If Mark Harrison is at the back of it, then we take no chance of his causing you any harm! Some women, who have involved themselves in healing arts in the past, have been accused of witchcraft!'

'Witchcraft?' and Sophie looked outraged

'I would not have brought this up now,' he said gravely, 'Were it not for the fact that there has been previous mention by the villagers of the fact that in the past you have often collected various plants from the woods! People talk my dear, embroider truth until all is twisted and distorted! Seemingly the present rumours originated not here in Stokely, but in Langley Morton!' He drew in his breath. There, he had said it, had feared to hurt her by speaking of it before.

'Langley Morton—the village where I grew up,' she exclaimed in shock. 'It is outrageous! I can hardly understand it!'

'Yes, Langley Morton, where as we both now know, Lorrimer has taken up residence,' her father's face was grim. 'Now do you see why I advise caution?' She went pale, choked back a bitter retort and went to her room.

Long she sat there on the end of her bed, turning the matter over in her mind. She had returned to the countryside to find peace, after facing the terrors of the plague from that last exhausting year in London. But was the comparative peace and security of this quiet village to be disturbed by the advent of this Gerald Harrison? She could hardly believe that the man could contrive to use her love of healing against her. But her father obviously was worried that such might be the case and she knew that James Hawksley had a very level head.

Yes and what of those rumours about her?

If she remained there then she would have to curtail any attempt to help those sick or injured. Nor would she feel safe to roam the woods seeking those curative herbs her grandfather had so esteemed. Yet surely none would dare to interfere with the quiet life of a titled lady?

A week passed. Sophie spent most of it over at Oaklands, continuing to check over accounts of the estate, but also enjoying several meetings with beloved her Aunt Martha and her husband David Markham, the couple showing their joy at having her back. Today they had taken a picnic lunch to a shady spot beneath a clump of trees, in a nearby meadow, where a lazy stream wended its way between banks hazed bright with forget-me-nots and buttercups.

'Is anything troubling you, Sophie,' inquired David at last. 'You have been strangely silent.' His wise dark eyes considered the girl whom he knew his wife loved as a daughter. She was sitting pensively now staring into the clear waters of the stream, beneath which sticklebacks and minnows darted between water weeds. The stream was low in its banks, for there had been no rain for some weeks, the sun baking down relentlessly without even a small cloud n the sky.

'I am trying to make up my mind whether to remain here in the country, or to return to London,' she said at last. Martha looked at her in distress.

'But Sophie, you have only been back a very few weeks, and we had all hoped that you would stay this time. Little Minette needs you dear, and then there is your motherless young brother, Henry!' She looked at Sophie appealingly.

'I know. But something has happened to cause me to question the wisdom of remaining here.' And then she told them of Gerald Lorrimer and her father's fears. The couple stared at each other bewildered.

'James truly worries that Lorrimer might use your love of medicine against you?' Martha touched David's arm. 'Surely this is much ado about a few insignificant remarks? As for the villagers—so much idle gossip!' But David lowered his head thoughtfully.

'My dear wife—it is the man who has made those remarks whose motives we must question—Gerald Lorrimer! Remember, this young man is Mark Harrison's nephew!'

'I know—but...?'

'Harrison is a most vile individual, nor do I mean merely in his treatment of Sophie and his attempt to burn down Hawksley Manor! He had a bad reputation before that, treated tenants with extreme cruelty during his time in the village. Then look at the way he had old Jessie Thorne murdered, her cottage burned down.'

'You really think that Harrison would seek to hurt Sophie through Lorrimer in some way? Why, we do not even know if Harrison is still alive. After all, there is an order out for his arrest and nothing has been heard of him for years.' Martha spoke firmly in her sensible way.

'Mama, even if Harrison should be dead, then there is still the possibility that Lorrimer may try to revenge himself on me through a perverted sense of family loyalty,' said Sophie quietly. 'On the other hand, the whole thing could be a misunderstanding of a few ill chosen words and my father's suspicions of this detested family.'

'So what will you do?'

'Return to London, at least for a few months. You can write, let me know if Lorrimer leaves the district. After all, there is nothing for him here! Perhaps he will sell the Falstaff Inn and your old home. I can only think he purchased them to give himself a foothold in the district.' She spoke decisively, tossed a pebble into the water, watched it sink and rose to her feet. They followed suit.

'I will take Minette and Jenny with me. There is little in this world I truly fear, but the idea of being branded a witch would be more than I could face!' There, she had said it, come out with the fact that had been burning away at the back of her mind since her father had spoken with her, warned her. She would never forget old Jessie's fear of those who had branded her a witch and then so cruelly taken her life.

'Oh, Sophie—we will miss you so!'

'The King has expressed a wish to see his little daughter again. Nor will any dare to attack me when I am safe under the protection of the King!' She shook her head sadly, as she added, 'But why must people fear knowledge in a woman? Consider it evil? The minds of so many are corroded by superstition.'

'Why Sophie child, even our dear Lord was attacked by those of the religious establishment of his day over his own wondrous healings.' David raised a hand in blessing over her. 'You will come home here again. The man who has disturbed your peace will be dealt with by those who love you, and by our Father in Heaven.'

It was July before Sophie was once more in London and almost at once wished herself back in the countryside, for the heat that had been uncomfortable in the meadows and winding lanes, was unbearable here in town, where the stench rising from the yellow waters of the Thames, made it impossible to open her casement. Nor was there any slightest breeze to dispel the heat.

But here again she found that excitement she had been missing, as she resumed her position at court. The King sought her out at one of the many receptions attended by eager, self seeking courtiers, wiping his forehead as the weighty black curls of the periwig framing his sardonic face, added to the discomfort at the all pervading heat and mixed aroma of perspiration and over heavy perfumes. His eyes lighted on Sophie with delight as he beckoned her to approach.

'I have missed you, Sophie! The court is more bearable given your presence!' His heavy lidded, dark eyes caressed her and despite herself, Sophie's heart fluttered.

'It is good of you to say so, Sire!'

'You are looking well. The country air has brought roses back to your cheeks! How is our daughter—our little Minette?'

'You may see her for yourself, Charles, when you will. I have brought her back with me!'

'I will call on you tomorrow evening! And your father? Has he returned with you?' He smiled as he thought of the man who had spent those long years of exile at his side. He would always have a special regard for Lord James Hawksley!

'No. He remains at Hawksley Manor with little Henry. I would have stayed there longer myself, but seemingly there were unpleasant rumours about me and then a man appeared who made me feel distinctly uneasy. I thought it wiser to leave, to ask you for advice!' She glanced up at his face. His eyes darkened.

'We will speak of these matters in private tomorrow,' he said quietly. She nodded, curtseyed and drew back, but was aware that many eyes strayed in her direction. She had always appeared an enigma to those of the court.

Jenny flushed in awe when told that the King was expected that evening. Minette's hair was washed and polished with silk and set into ringlets and dressed in her best white dress sprigged with embroidered rosebuds, as the five year old bounced up and down with excitement.

Sophie had engaged another cook housekeeper. Her previous employee had disappeared during the time of the plague. Mrs Chandler was a buxom widow in her early forties, calm and efficient and Sophie had liked her on sight. The small house had been scrubbed and all wood waxed and polished, and flowers in a copper vase adorned the table. If it had not been for the almost suffocating heat, all would have been perfect, thought Sophie as she checked her appearance in the gilt framed, cheval mirror.

Jenny was to wait until Sophie summoned her to bring Minette.

Then he was there and his presence seemed to fill the room. He sauntered over to Sophie, raised her from her curtsey and lifted her hand to his lips.

'Greetings, sweetheart,' he said softly. 'You look very fair tonight. That shade of blue becomes you, almost matches your eyes! But why that small frown between your brows—what's amiss, Sophie?'

'Have you time to listen, to advise?' she looked at him earnestly. He took her hands to his.

'Tell me,' he said. She did so, poured out her worries over rumours spreading in her village, suggesting her medical endeavours were connected with witchcraft, then mentioned Gerald Lorrimer and his own veiled comments. He looked at her in astonishment. She really was upset he saw and his own indignation rose against those who had spread such tales against her. Sophie might be unwisely obsessed with a desire to glean ever more knowledge about medicine, but with one aim only, to bring relief to those suffering sickness. He remembered her original kindness in caring for his poor sister Mary, nobly staying at her bedside during the attack of smallpox, the illness that had tragically taken the life of the lovely Princess of Orange How many young women would have risked their own health in such way?

'Hush, sweetheart. Think no more on this! When you return to Stokely I will send men to protect you and to arrest any who should seek to harm you! You have my promise on this.' He turned her chin up, staring into her eyes.

'Say you believe me?'

'I do! It's just I remember what had happened to poor Jessie Thorne. She was simply a poor old woman, who had chosen to live alone and to help heal those who came to her for aid. She was no witch!'

'I believe you! Perhaps one day people will cease to be superstitious of those who possess knowledge beyond that encompassed by their own small minds.' He smiled down at her protectively, as he saw a trace of tears about her eyes.

He drew her close, then much closer and before she could protest, his lips caressed her own, his moustaches brushing her cheek. She felt a sudden throbbing sense of desire pervade her whole body, shocking her with its immediacy. It took all of her will power to draw back from him, but her response had conveyed itself to a man whose own passions were ever ready to catch fire.

'Your body says one thing, your mind instructs another. It is always so with you, Sophie. Why do you seek to deny us both, that which brings such closeness of body as well as spirit?' He placed his hands on her shoulders, and drawing her close again, stared into her eyes with almost magnetic gaze. She did not resist when he guided her onto the couch. His hands slid down to the laces on her bodice, exploring fingers pushed it lower, were suddenly caressing her breasts. Then his lips........! She knew she should pull back, attempted to do so—but it was too late. A small moan of desire escaped her lips.

Not since their lovemaking five years ago, had Sophie enjoyed a man's caresses. She had told herself that she had no need of such, and had intended to keep herself permanently inviolate, throwing all her desires into pursuing her love of medicine. But now her surrender was complete, as she gave in to body's desire, allowing him his way with her, joying in it. They climaxed together and she lay shaking afterwards, as he kissed her lips, her throat until she quietened. Then he raised himself on an elbow and stared down at her.

'Sophie, this has been a time we will both remember with joy, sweetheart! You have shown yourself to be completely woman, not just an analytical physician!' He helped her to straighten her gown, looking at her with genuine deep affection. 'My sweet Sophie! What are the chances that we have may have made a sibling for our little Minette?'

'Oh! I had not thought—Charles, what will I do if such is the case?' Her face expressed dismay. There would be no Gareth Mereton to father another of Charles progeny. What had she done? But surely the chances of pregnancy were remote?

'Why sweetheart, you could become my official mistress I suppose. Would this please you?' He smiled encouragingly whilst considering that he would have to placate his present tempestuous mistress, Barbara Villiers. As for Frances Stewart, she was proving impregnable, so.......

'No! Oh, no!' The reply burst out into the silence that followed.

'But surely you enjoyed our lovemaking, even as I did?' His eyes expressed sudden hurt. She reached out a hand.

'I did enjoy it, but also know it to have been a sin. You are married, Charles!'

'But sinning is such sweet pleasure,' he replied with a sigh. 'In biblical times a man might have many wives, David and Solomon for instance!'

'That was thousands of years ago!' She rose to her feet and attempted to tidy her hair, as he straightened his wig. 'We must not let Jenny suspect, well, that we have been having more than polite conversation. Besides, you want to see your little daughter, do you not?'

When Sophie rang the bell, Jenny hurried in with Minette, who gazed up in surprise at the tall, dark eyed man, so splendidly dressed, who stared down at her so affectionately.

'Do you remember me, little Minette,' he asked gently. She frowned for a moment and then gave a small smile as she recollected having seen him before.

'You are the King,' she said in her childish treble, and dropped a careful curtsey. He lifted her up into his arms and placed a kiss on her cheek.

'Yes, I am the King, child. But I am also your Papa!' Minette just shook her head at him.

'My Papa is dead,' she explained. 'His name was Gareth Mereton! I never met him, but Mama says he was a kind man.'

'So he was, my child, a kind and honourable man. But you deserve a real father, and I will try to be that to you.' He swept her up in his arms and kissed her. She smiled, liking this man who was holding her close. She reached for the medallion shining on his breast.

'It is beautiful,' she said. 'Like mother's golden pomander!' As he set her on her feet, she pointed to the pomander suspended from her mother's waist.

Charles eyes sped down to the ornament. He looked seriously at Sophie.

'Sweetheart, if ever you are in any kind of trouble in the future—send that pomander to me and I will come!' And Sophie nodded.

Chapter Fourteen

The king was observed spending much time at the side of Lady Mereton. Very often they were heard discussing the costly and disastrous war with the Dutch. Last June a four day war had demanded the lives of six thousand seamen, many ships sunk and other humiliatingly captured. Citizens demanded revenge, and at the end of July a small victory gave some consolation. But there was little money left to continue a conflict which Charles personally had not been inclined to start in the first place. But the Dutch were supplanting England's self proclaimed right to commerce in Africa and beyond—slaves, spices, gold, all returning from long sea voyages in the holds of Dutch merchant shipping.

'In the end, Louis of France and De Witt of Holland, together with ourselves will have to call a truce. I hope it may be before we suffer more losses,' he said to Sophie, as he partnered her in a dance

'Diplomacy is ever better than war,' she replied quietly. The music stopped and she curtsied to him, as his eyes strayed lazily across her bosom. She blushed, then looking up as she felt the Queen's eyes upon them. 'You should seek another partner, Sire. We have danced twice together.'

'So?' His eyes followed the almost imperceptible glance in hers. His wife, but then Catherine had become more accepting of his amours now, unlike the tantrums she had thrown in the early days of their marriage, when she had been forced to accept Barbara as a lady of the bedchamber. But he respected his Portuguese wife and despite some of his ministers suggesting a future divorce should she fail to conceive, would never give slightest credence to such notions.

'I will come to you tonight,' he whispered.

August was as hot as ever. Would the heat never abate? As Sophie lay in her monarch's arms in only her shift, she felt she would have done anything to have felt a cool breeze sweeping through the trees in far off Epsilon woods, the sound of the stream blending with birdsong. But then all such thoughts were banished as this man who was such a consummate lover, brought her to gasping climax.

'That was wonderful, sweetheart! I am only sad that we wasted so many years denying ourselves,' he said, stroking her hair and pressing a grateful kiss on her lips. She almost felt like agreeing with him, for Sophie was happy and fulfilled as never before.

'I did not wish to be thought of as just one of your women,' she confessed naively and he smiled down at her whimsically.

'That is one thing you could never be, my Sophie—for you are unique!'

'I love you, Charles, truly love you,' she murmured now. 'I know this cannot last, nothing ever does in life, but I have never been as completely happy as I am now.' He stared down into her blue eyes and read the truth there.

'That is the first time you have ever said that, Sophie—that you love me!' He was deeply touched by her whispered confession and drew her to him. He was the more startled and perplexed by what she went on to say.

'It is because I do love you with all my heart that I have decided to go back to the country. I want to remember this time, this precious time as it is now, not sullied by having to share you with those others, who will inevitably come into your life. You are not as other men, Charles! You possess a fatal attraction to all women. Nor is it merely because you are the King.'

'Now what is all this foolishness? Return to the country? You know how bored you would inevitably be there. Nor will I permit it, for you have become very dear to me!' He spoke firmly, but knew that her decision made he might have to accept it, for he would never force her to stay against her will.

Then all thoughts of their romance were put violently aside by an event that happened in the early hours of the second day of September, in Pudding Lane. The fire that started that morning in a baker's shop was not at first thought cause for concern by those nearby, as the baker and his family escaped by a window from their burning home and business. For London was subject to sporadic outbursts of small fires, the wooden tenement houses build so close together that their upper floors were almost touching across the narrow streets, invited disaster. The last appreciable fire however had been in 1632.

But this fire started to spread rapidly and the Lord Mayor was informed. His was the right to call for neighbouring buildings to be demolished, thus causing firebreaks. But he refused to give the necessary order. The King became aware that something was seriously wrong during Sunday morning, as the smell of smoke was carried towards Whitehall on the strong Easterly wind, funnelling the flames between those narrow city streets and alleyways to devour all within their path.

Charles response was immediate, as he gave orders that the Lord Mayor should have all houses in the path of the flames immediately demolished. Still this was not done and over the next few days reports came flooding in to Westminster of mass destruction of the whole city, those who could do so fleeing the conflagration by river in barges or small boats, until the wharves along the banks of the Thames became a flaming inferno as warehouses of combustible goods exploded in a firestorm, passage to the river curtailed. The small rickety horse drawn or manually drawn fire engines thus had no water supply to draw on to attack the flames and were overturned by those desperate to escape the path of the raging flames that engulfed everything within their path.

Charles and his brother James and a few of the abler courtiers worked amongst those throwing buckets of water and trying desperately to pull down buildings with iron hooks, and tried to restrain a terrified citizenry from attacking any foreigners they found as being responsible for the fire. It was a world gone mad. A city burning, burning, the smoke and choking fumes damaging people's lungs even as they sought to escape by the cities few gates, where they fought in the bottlenecks that formed there.

On Wednesday the 5th of September, the worst of the fire was under control—but it had left total ruin in its wake. Upwards of 13,000 homes destroyed, most of London's churches and even St Paul's Cathedral had succumbed to the flames. It would take a fortune to rebuild the city. A fortune neither Charles nor his ministers had access to.

Sophie smoothed a healing ointment onto Charles badly scorched face, as he fell wearily into a chair in his bedchamber. He had sent for her and she had hurried there without question, just relieved beyond measure that he had not perished in the flames he had so nobly attempted to quell. Nor would the citizens of London ever forget the bravery of their King and his brother James, as with faces black as soot and clothes soaked and torn, they had themselves enforced the demolition by gunpowder of those buildings now providing firebreaks, as gradually the fire subsided and the ferocious, relentless wind dropped.

'Let me see those hands,' she demanded quietly. The skin on the back of his long tapering fingers was badly burned, his hair scorched at the temples as were his brows also.

'Those little hands have mercy in their touch,' he sighed.

'It must have been terrible out there! Did the fire claim many lives,' she asked? He shook his head.

'Less than a score, or so it has been reported to me. Yet personally I consider that hundreds may have perished, the fire so fierce, so all consuming that any caught in its fury would have been charred beyond recognition, nor identified amongst the huge piles of blackened wreckage.

Perhaps we may never know, for who keeps a count of the common people, the poor.' His face expressed his sadness. 'It was a tragedy waiting to happen,' he added. 'Only last year I asked that some of those illegally constructed tenements, made of wood and pitch and thatch should be demolished. Nor should those many small warehouses be placed in city streets.'

'I heard that St Paul's was lost?'

'It was. But this I promise, a new St Pauls will rise from the ruins, a building raised to the eternal glory of God. I know just the man for the task—Christopher Wren!' He rarely if ever spoke of religion and Sophie had never questioned him on his belief or lack of it. Now she read a depth to his character she had not previously discerned.

'Would you care to accompany me on the morrow? I go with a small escort to Moorfields where a great company of those who have escaped with little but their lives are said to be assembled.'

The great park was crammed as far as the eye could see with shocked, despondent Londoners, some in tents, others merely sitting helplessly on the ground, hoping that someone in authority would instruct them what next to do. Babies wailed, children pulled at their parents' sides demanding food, where there was none. The old and frail lay on the ground, staring blankly up at the sky. The pall of smoke still lingered over their heads. This was misery on an immense scale.

The King addressed his people, promising to do all he could to rebuild their beloved city that it should be better constructed and in the meanwhile, he would try to have food sent to them. He also suggested that those able to should disperse into nearby towns and villages and find work. There was a slight cheer, as many remembered the King's bravery in helping to put out the flames, at risk to his own life. But for the most part, the shocked citizenry were apathetic to his words, too traumatised to take any decisive action.

And still a few sparks were carried towards them on the breeze while fragments of charred, blackened residue born of the conflagration floated many miles further on. The ferocious East wind that had driven the fire up the Thames and caused it to spread at such terrible pace producing holocaust had now dropped. But still some few fires remained to be extinguished in the city that lay devastated behind its walls.

Charles gazed with real compassion on the huge crowd. He remembered only too well, their sufferings from the plague last year and now this. Some of the more vociferous of those assembled now started to shout at him, apportioning blame to the Hollanders, whom some were already accusing of setting the fire, others blaming the French, the non conformists and above all the papists!

'This fire was caused by the will of God and none other,' the King suggested quietly. 'We should now seek His mercy as we begin our task of rebuilding the city we love.' The cries subsided and Charles left the scene, followed closely by Sophie and a few of his gentlemen, their horses picking their way carefully until clear of the demoralised refugees.

'The weather broke on Sunday, torrential rain pouring down and finally dampening any small smouldering areas that remained. Now the clear up could start. Charles was close closeted with Christopher Wren, to whom he was delegating the arrangements for rebuilding the city. But they would need money—and the Dutch wars had left the exchequer in dire straits. The King had little time for Sophie now, the task before him all consuming of time and energy.

Then Sophie began to have worries about Minette.

The little girl had developed as nasty cough since the fire, for she had inevitably inhaled some of the acrid smoke when Sophie's orders that all windows should remain closed in the house, had been ignored. Jenny had heedlessly pushed open a casement in absolute horror as she had realised the approaching danger, when the glow in the sky from beyond the bend in the river painted the heavens a terrifying vivid orange. She closed it quickly enough as both she and the housekeeper had felt a searing pain in their throats, as the smoke penetrated their lungs.

Their discomfort gradually subsided, but little Minette who had come to stand beside Jenny to peer in towards that fearsome glow in the sky, had also inhaled that scorching, putrid smoke and it had left her with an irritating cough. Sophie held her daughter in her arms, had just administered a healing mixture to soothe her small throat, when she came to a decision.

Her daughter's health was of more importance than her own deep feelings for the King. She had to leave this devastated city and return to the countryside once more. After all she had recently endured, the comparative dangers of a few mischief making villagers and the man Lorrimer, were of small account.

Charles was disappointed by her decision. He truly cared for Sophie, his little physician, valued her company as well as those special delights experienced in their lovemaking. But he was completely involved in all the work and planning that required his undivided efforts that he regretfully accepted her decision. He also loved little Minette and was troubled that his young daughter was unwell. He stood looking at them in frustration now.

'Go then, Sophie. But take great care. The roads will be full of those who have lost all their possessions in the fire, and now making their way towards whatever place they consider they may find succour.'

'I will be careful, will return one day in the future, God willing,' she said steadily, trying not to let the tears pricking behind her eyelids fall. He embraced her and then took Minette up into his arms.

'Always remember thy Papa,' he instructed—then to Sophie, 'I will send an escort with your carriage. Should you ever need help in any way, just remember to send your golden pomander!' He turned and stared at them for a brief moment, his tall, regal figure filling the doorframe, as he bowed and blew a kiss—and was gone.

Sophie realised how necessary her escort of four armed men were, as hundreds upon the road called out to them for alms as her carriage passed, or shook their fists at one of the aristocracy as the traveller appeared to be. And still the rain that had started a few days ago, poured down nonstop soaking those already shocked and dispirited. At last after the first fifty miles, the homeless procession diminished in number. Then with great relief, Sophie realised the carriage was rattling over the ruts in the country road that led to the village of Stokely and home.

'Sophie—Thank the Lord you are safe,' cried James Hawksley, as he lifted Minette from the carriage and handed her to Jenny and then took his daughter into his arms. 'They say the fire was terrible, like to that which ravaged Sodom and Gomorrah!' His eyes scanned them both, seeing the tiredness on Sophie's face, the pallor of his small grand-daughter. Then Jenny curtsied, took Minette by the hand and hurried into the house before them, out of the rain.

'The King sent these officers to have a care of me on the journey,' said Sophie. 'We can accommodate them can we not?'

'Of course. They are welcome!' He gestured towards Thomas Appleby who had come striding towards them, his eyes lighting up as he saw Sophie.

'These men need accommodation and food Tom, their beasts stabled. Order it done if you please.' His estate manager nodded, casting a smile at Sophie.

'I'll attend to it right away, my lord! Welcome back, Lady Mereton!'

'Sophie to you, Tom,' she cried happily. 'How is Richard?'

'Why that young son of mine will be quite made up to see you back again!' he said heartily, 'As will many another!'

Minette was given a bowl of soup and then tucked up in bed. She stared up at her mother in slight bewilderment, as she took in the once familiar nursery walls.

'Where is my Papa,' she asked perplexed? James Hawksley standing at Sophie's side stared down at the five year old in surprise.

'Why, your father is in heaven, child,' he volunteered softly. But Minette shook her small head.

'No. My real Papa is the King and he is not dead!'
Then she yawned, her eyes closed and she fell asleep. In the adjacent
nursery, little Henry was already curled up asleep and dreaming of the joy
of having Minette back.

Father and daughter sat long into the night discussing the fire and
possible repercussions for the country from a disaster that was like to cost
the exchequer dear, especially following on the ravages of the plague and
disastrous events of the ongoing Dutch wars. Already taxation was at a
point that was causing deep distress in the land. Then, the ongoing drought
during the summer months had prevented an all important decent harvest.

'How are you managing, Father? Financially things must be difficult?'
She looked at him sympathetically. She knew how hard he had worked to
restore Hawksley Manor and the estate to much of its former glory.

'These taxes are a setback that I will not deny.' He stroked his slightly
greying, dark hair back from his forehead. 'But Appleby and his sons have
worked unceasingly and with such good spirit. Indeed, I almost look on
them as family.'

'Especially Richard,' she volunteered, thinking of his determined
protection of her over the years.

'He is a fine young man, who incidentally has been borrowing books
from my library recently. He has a surprisingly good mind.' He looked
carefully at Sophie. 'Now tell me, child—why did Minette call the King
her Papa? I thought she was being brought up to consider herself Gareth
Mereton's daughter?'

'It was the King himself who taught her that she should call him her real
father!' She shook her head. 'Charles loves her,' she said softly. Hawksley
stared at her thoughtfully. He had noticed her colour heighten when she
spoke of the king. And as he stared at her, he guessed that her earlier
association with the monarch had now flowered into something deeper. His
eyes were troubled.

'And you—you love this most amoral of kings,' he asked probingly.

'Yes, I love Charles,' she said quietly. 'But I'm wise enough to know
that it is a love that can lead nowhere. We shared that special closeness
between man and woman in the weeks prior to the fire that devastated
London. He asked me to become his official mistress, which I realised I
could not agree to. Perhaps I was tempted.'

'Oh, Sophie, why did you bring further heartache into your life?' he
shook his head sadly. 'I blame Charles! He should not have behaved so
with you!' She reached over and placed a hand on his arm.

'There is always a moment when man or woman can draw back—and I
decided to give in to my desire for man I have loved since first I met him.
My heart is the King's for all time!' There were tears shining on her lashes.

Neither of them saw Richard Appleby enter the room. He heard those words with a stony face, before slipping quietly away, unnoticed.

The following morning dawned with thin bright sunlight. Sophie stretched and sat up in bed, looking around bemused, suddenly realising that she was back in her father's home. She slipped out of bed and stared from the window and saw the rain battered flowers of late summer flattened in their beds, great puddles in the sweeping driveway. But oh how the ground had needed that rain!

Minette's cough seemed slightly better and to be responding to her mother's medicine, although her little face grimaced as she sipped the mixture. She took an immediate delight in playing with Henry once more and Sophie left the youngsters chasing each other around the great hall, with Jenny trying to keep order.

Later Sophie walked with her father along a path between the newly waterlogged meadows. She paused as they reached a style and looked at him

'Have there been any more of those rumours about me?' she asked directly and did not need to stipulate what she meant. He hesitated uneasily.

'Please, father?'

'Very well—I'll tell you, but you must not worry. Appleby traced them to Langley Morton and the Falstaff Inn! He actually overheard a couple of men, strangers to the village, stating that it was common knowledge that as it was put—the Mereton woman was a dabbler in the black arts!' he stared at her sympathetically.

'But that is dreadful, slanderous!' She had gone pale.

'Appleby took his staff to the fellows, said he would hale them before the magistrates for spreading inflammatory lies! Seems they took to their heels then and have not been seen since!'

'So it is almost certainly Gerald Lorrimer's work!'

'I feel sure of it in my own mind, but we need to have proof if we are to charge him with it!' His face was dark with anger. 'Nor was that all, the same men had been suggesting that the drought that ruined all the villagers crops was not only your work, but that of the Catholics, mine in particular!'

'But surely no one in their right senses would give credit to such nonsense?' she stared at him appalled.

'Sophie, have you not just been telling me that those who lost their homes in the great fire of London have been blaming not only the Dutch, but the Catholics for starting it!' He placed his hands on her shoulders. 'When disasters of any sort strike, men seek in their minds for someone to blame. Persons of another nationality or different in some way! Luckily, most of the local people here in Stokely are well inclined towards our family. In Langley Morton I had thought it to be so also.'

'Father, even though you are a devout Catholic, I believe you continue to attend the Anglican Church in order to conform to the law?' She looked at him steadily. She knew it was a painful situation for him and deplored the unreasoning detestation of Catholics by the majority of the population.

'Yes, Sophie—I do attend their services, admire the Rev David Markham as a fine preacher and honourable man. But on those rare occasions when a brave priest dares to slip unobtrusively into the house by night, I confess to having joined in worship not of my own denomination and pray for understanding and forgiveness.' His face sadness and resignation.

'It is wrong that you should have to live so! I know that Charles has a kindness towards Catholics, has tried more than once to have the harsh laws relaxed—but Parliament would not let him have his way. They fear a Catholic uprising, but without just cause.' Sophie's face was sad. A drop of rain splashed down and then another and the sky opened. They sprang to their feet and hurried back to the house.

'How we could have done with this rain earlier,' Hawksley sighed, 'Still we managed to harvest some good grain despite the drought,' he added.

'I must go to Oaklands and see how all is there,' said Sophie.

'Then I insist that you ride with men to protect you—just in case of any trouble!' Nor did she refuse now as once she might carelessly have done.

'I will take Richard then and since the king's escort have not yet left for London then perhaps they might come too!'

Her escort from London were nothing loth to spend extra time away from the trauma of the still smouldering city. Their orders passed down from the King personally so they had been told, was to have a special care of the lovely young woman he esteemed. So now it would appear to be perfectly correct to ride with her the short distance to her own property of Oaklands.

'Why not leave Minette here with me,' suggested her father. 'Henry adores playing with her!' But Sophie shook her head.

'No! Mama will wish to see her again, and David—but I will bring her back in a few days time, I promise!' He watched as she set off on her favourite mare, little Minette seated on her small pony with Richard Appleby at her side, Jenny on a quiet cob and the four uniformed officers riding by twos, in front and behind. He smiled as he watched them go, would count the days until they returned. He did not notice a small group of men watching from behind the screen of trees that bordered the gates to Hawksley Manor.

The intruders swore as they saw Sophie disappearing with her armed escort, then consulted together and rode off.

A housemaid saw the riders approaching the stately old house along the wide avenue of oaks, and rushed to call Martha who was there on her weekly visit, checking that all was in order. She dropped the embroidered cushion she was plumping up and flew to the door and stood at the top of the steps to welcome her visitors, and with joy recognised Sophie.

The reunion between them was ecstatic.

'Sophie! We were all so worried when news of the great fire reached here!' cried Martha. She caught the girl in her arms and hugged her.

'It was truly awful, Mama. I have read of the great fire of Rome in the reign of Nero and think this must have been even worse!' declared Sophie.

'Did many lose their lives?'

'Very few, at least less than twenty deaths declared officially. But Charles considers a great many more perished, but were charred beyond recognition. As for the fire itself—half a mile wide and a mile and a half long, leaving total destruction in its path. Even St Pauls is no more. Scaffolding around it caught first, then its beams and the lead on its roof melted and all collapsed!'

'Why, but that is so terrible. Come, let us go in and you must rest and tell me all.' Then her eyes lighted on Minette, who was being helped from her pony by Richard, and now stood holding Jenny's hand, as she looked around her. 'I did not know that Minette could ride?' Martha's face expressed concern and pride as she embraced the little girl fondly and admiring her blue velvet riding habit and small brimmed hat with its curling plume.

'The King insisted she learn. She loves it!' she paused and smiled at her escort. 'These men brought me safe from London at the King's order—the roads are dangerous to negotiate, being full of those who lost everything in the fire and made desperate by hunger and fear.'

'Then I am sure you will wish that these officers should stay here tonight. Once they have stabled their horses, they can go through to the kitchen, where Joan Pyke will see they are well looked after!' said Martha efficiently.

'Richard will you show them round to the stables,' said Sophie. 'Ned and the other grooms will have a care for the horses.' Richard nodded and walked off leading Sophie's mare and Minette's pony and Jenny's mount.

The staff expressed delight that their mistress was back again and smiles greeted Sophie as she walked around the house with Martha at her side. Would she stay this time, they wondered?

All was as she might have guessed in perfect order, rooms welcoming, furniture polished, silver and crystal gleaming. Even the great hall, always slightly forbidding as it usually appeared to Sophie, seemed less so today, as its very familiarity invited respect.

There on the walls were those many portraits of Mereton ancestors—and she paused beneath a painting of Gareth as a young man, his first wife smiling at his side, their two young sons small, handsome replicas of their father. Now all four were dead. Gareth's wife had died many years ago, his two sons had lost their lives fighting the republican forces in the royalist cause—and Gareth, who had married her at the King's request, to give his child by Sophie, name and status, had also died, when their carriage had overturned in that violent snowstorm—why, she could hardly believe that five years had passed since then. Her thoughts drifted further back.

So much had happened in her life, since she had run from the house in Langley Morton to escape the cruelties of her stepfather Roger Haversham, Martha's first violent husband, and found sanctuary and kindness in her grandfather's lovely old house, The Willows. She thought wistfully now of Dr John Wheatley, whose love and support had meant so much, as had his patient instruction of Sophie in medical matters.

So many people had already died. Poor Jessie Thorne cruelly murdered—next her first patient, Mary of Orange from smallpox—her grandfather—then Haversham, but he was no loss—her husband Gareth Mereton—and what about those thousands who had died of the plague!

'What is it, Sophie?' Martha realised the girl was no longer walking at her side, but was staring up pensively at the painting of Gareth and his family.

'I suppose I was just thinking how brief our life really is! We are always so busy making plans, wondering which path to take, that we do not stop to realise how little our individual lives matter.'

Martha placed a hand on the girl's arm. 'But we do, each one of us matters, child! Our Father in Heaven knows every hair on our heads, and the feathers on a sparrow's breast. All we can any of us do is to show kindness to our family and friends, help others whenever we can and always to remember our dear Lord whom we worship!'

'I know you are right, Mama.' Sophie turned troubled blue eyes upon her. 'But this same God whom we worship and love as we follow the precepts of the Protestant faith, is the same God worshipped by relatives and neighbours who adhere to the earlier Catholic faith and still face persecution for holding to their beliefs. Then there are the non conformists so out of fashion since the Restoration! Why can there not be true freedom of worship?' She desperately needed answers.

'Hush, child! It is better to discuss these things when we are alone,' she nodded towards a frankly curious young maid who was dusting a shelf of small copper ornaments Gareth had once collected. And Sophie nodded and sighed. 'You should perhaps speak with David,' added Martha gently.

Sophie inclined her head without comment. She doubted whether she would find any real answers by discussion with the Rev David Markham.

Later that day, as Jenny played with Minette in the nursery, Sophie wandered with Martha across the lawns at the back of the garden, to where a trellised walkway led towards an old summerhouse, its bleached timbers set amongst shrubs and flowerbeds and shady trees.

As they walked companionably together in that direction, Richard Appleby noticed them and followed unobtrusively on the outer side of the trellised path. Lord Hawksley had instructed him to have a special care of his daughter, not that Richard needed any heeding. He sighed now as he slipped behind some bushes so that he might keep the summerhouse in sight.

He remembered Sophie's words spoken in private to her father, that she loved the King, who returned her love, and it had been a shock to hear it! He knew in the depths of his heart, that his own love for the beautiful girl who had asked him for directions to The Willows six years ago, had first been that of an adoring boy of fourteen. Now at twenty years old, in the full flush of his young manhood, she continued to fill his thoughts and nightly dreams. He knew of course, the impossibility of his love being returned. She was far above him in station.

He also knew it was wrong to attempt to overhear what she now discussed with Mistress Martha Markham, but deliberately drew closer to the open door of the summerhouse and strained his ears to listen to the women's soft voices.

'Mama, there is something I must tell you,' said Sophie now, as she leaned forward in one of the rickety wicker chairs, where they sat facing each other. 'I am with child!'

'Sophie!' Martha's voice expressed her shock. 'But how—I mean...?' her voice trailed off.

'Why, the King's of course! Charles is the father,' replied Sophie.

'And does he know of this?'

'No! For if I told him, then he would doubtless try to marry me off to another elderly courtier, as he did before!' She spoke clearly and her words pierced Richard's heart. So Minette was the King's daughter, not a child born to Gareth Mereton in his old age. The reason for Sophie's surprising choice of the elderly Knight was now manifest.

'But Sophie child, what will people say if you give birth to a child when you are not wed?' Martha's face expressed her consternation. 'Why, they will call you a harlot!'

'Charles has fathered several children already, Mama. Their mothers are treated with respect at court.' But even as she came out with the defiant words, Sophie knew they were untrue. Barbara Villiers name had become a byword for immorality, as had the names of others she knew of who had borne children to the charming, debonair King who despaired of getting a child by his barren wife.

But what could she possibly do now? She had almost shared her worry with the King, but knew what his solution would be, another unwanted marriage!

'So how far along are you,' demanded Martha, glancing across at her keenly. 'Your waistline suggests it is early days yet?'

'I have missed two courses—but my breasts are tender and I just know that I am with child.'

'Have you told your father? Does James know?' Martha was still in shock, as her mind darted desperately about for a solution to the problem.

'No. You are the only one I have taken into my confidence. But in a couple more months, then it will start to become apparent, I suppose.'

'How can you appear so calm?' Martha stared at her indignantly.

'Because panic will not supply an answer!' cried Sophie in exasperation, then she paused as she heard the sound of twigs crackling just outside the open door of the small rustic building. She sprang to her feet, ran forward and stared in outrage, to see Richard Appleby standing alongside the door and saw from his face that he had most obviously been listening.

'Richard!'

'My lady—I am sorry. Please forgive me. I wanted to ensure your safety as your father instructed,' he stuttered, his face reddening under her inquiring stare.

'Oh? And did my father suggest you should deliberately listen to my private conversation?' Her blue eyes were stormy with annoyance and embarrassment. He looked at her appealingly and blurted out words without stopping to consider the consequences of them.

'It was wrong of me! But I swear I will never reveal what I've heard!' He held his hands out pleadingly. 'But Sophie, perhaps I can be of some service to you now. We could marry, your child be brought up as my own!'

'You joke, Richard!' But as Sophie stared into his honest face, looked at him objectively for the first time and saw the obvious devotion in his eyes, she suddenly realised that he loved her. But he was just Richard, the youngest son of a yeoman farmer who had always protected and more recently quietly advised, nor one who she had ever looked on as a woman does a possible lover. It was as though her world had turned upside down.

He saw the rejection in her eyes, and shook his head regretfully.

'I apologise! Of course what I suggested is quite impossible, I realise that,' he choked out now. But even as he did so, Martha who had come to stand beside Sophie and overheard the astonishing exchange, placed a restraining hand on Sophie's arm.

'Yet may not this be an answer, Sophie? I do not think anything happens by chance! Richard is an honourable young man and your father has leased him several acres of his own. I know he is not of noble birth, but then nor was your true mother, my beloved sister....' Her voice trailed off.

'Think you that rank is any concern of mine,' snapped Sophie. 'I just do not want to marry, to be subject to a husband's whims and authority!'

'Our marriage would be in name only, my lady, to protect your own good name,' put in Richard earnestly, emboldened by Martha's interjection.

'Enough! I have heard quite, enough' exclaimed Sophie in exasperation and rushed off, walking swiftly along the trellised walkway, her long chestnut hair floating behind her in the breeze, as she made purposefully towards the house. Martha followed slowly behind, and smiled at Richard encouragingly.

'If you love her, then do not give up hope,' she instructed him.
The next few days passed without further word being spoken of what had occurred in the summerhouse. Martha knew that to bring the matter up again before Sophie was ready, would only provoke another outburst. As for Richard, he kept a respectful distance.

The guards should really be set on their way back to London now, Sophie realised, but suggested they remain another day or two and escort her back to Hawksley Manor before departing and so delighted to spend more time at ease, the men agreed.

Martha's husband the Rev. David Markham arrived to find out why his wife had not returned to the vicarage and greeted Sophie with obvious pleasure and exclaimed at how Minette had grown in the few months away in London.

Sophie told him of the fire that had devastated the capital and of her concern when Minette's throat had become badly inflamed from the smoke, the reason why she had decided to leave Whitehall.

'And was that the only reason,' he probed?

'You have been speaking with Mama! She told you that I am with child?' She came out with the question forthrightly, colouring slightly under his thoughtful gaze.

'Yes, my wife mentioned it, and that the King is responsible?'

'Charles and I are jointly responsible,' she said quietly. 'I knew when we lay together the chances were that I might conceive—but I love him!'

'But does he love you, to put you in such a situation?'

'Yes, I believe he does. But I am under no illusion that I am the only woman in his life.' She smiled broodingly. 'But we are true friends and friendship is more enduring than body's passion. I know that you will tell me that I have sinned and yet perhaps there are worse sins than truly loving, and I also understand that there may be repercussions. I am trying to think what best to do,' she exclaimed frankly.

'Marriage might be an option. Now Martha tells me young Richard Appleby made a somewhat unplanned proposal to you, my dear.' He paused as he saw her colour and her eyes flash indignation. 'Wait! He is a fine and decent man, who has known you for several years now. As a husband, he would take good care of you and Minette—and the child to come!'

'But apart from the fact that I do not love him, how would such an ill assorted match appear to neighbours? Surely as well, they might guess that a baby born at what would appear to be a seven months pregnancy was suspicious?'

'But none could dispute what both you and Richard attest to be fact!'

'So—you as a man of God, would encourage me to live a lie?' she challenged him. He returned her scornful glance firmly.

'I would suggest that you consider marriage to a young man, who knowing the situation you find yourself in, is nevertheless prepared to accept you as his wife and give you the protection of his name! Think about it at least, Sophie!' But she merely cast him a withering glance and stalked out of the room. He sighed and shook his head. She was certainly her father's daughter, strong as steel and also it would appear, as unbending.

The following morning, Sophie waved farewell to Martha and David who were returning to the vicarage. She was playing with Minette in the garden, when she heard the sound of horse's hooves and a rider swung round the curved driveway, dust flying up behind him, as he pulled hard n the reins and dismounted. She gave Minette into Jenny's charge and hurried over to see what brought the man whom she recognised as one of her father's workers, in such furious speed. Richard Appleby also saw the rider and strode towards him.

'Joel Croft, isn't it? What brings you here? Does my father have need of me?' She looked at him anxiously.

'My lady, I bring terrible news! Your father has been attacked in the grounds by masked riders, who thrust a sword into his breast and snatched little Henry up and fled with the child!' The man's face was working with grief and shock. For a split minute Sophie just stared at him in horror.

'My father—is he—dead?'

'Near to death! Thomas Appleby saw what happened and ran to help his lordship. As for the rest of the men of the estate, they have gone off in pursuit of the fiends who stole the child. It all happened so quickly! The men were mounted, wore masks!' He drew a hand across his sweating forehead.

Sophie swayed and would have collapsed with shock, had Richard not slipped an arm about her.

'Steady, Sophie—you must be strong,' he said now and at the sound of his calm voice she rallied and cried out to Jenny who had come over to see what was happening.

'Take Minette within the house! Make sure she is guarded at all times. My father has been attacked—near to death. Call the guards!' Jenny gave one appalled look at Sophie's face and snatched Minette up into her arms and ran towards the house.

Minutes later Sophie rode astride her mare, holding her small medicine chest under one arm, as she urged the animal on, knees pressing its sides. Beside her rode Richard, followed by Croft and the four London guards, faces grim. They held themselves responsible not only for the lady put in their charge, but to a degree for her relatives also. Lord Hawksley was said to be a friend of the King's!

They swept in through the gates of Hawksley Manor and now Joel Croft took the lead, galloping across the grounds to where a group of servants surrounded the body of their employer, cries of grief filling the air and making Sophie fear for the worst. She almost fell off her mare in her haste and ran the last few yards. As she did so, the sergeant of the guards, brought his horse to snorting halt and looked fiercely around

'Which way did the villains go who did this deed?' he demanded.

'Towards the village,' cried the onlookers pointing and the guards sped off furiously in the direction indicated and Richard rode with them.

'Out of the way,' shouted Sophie and fell to her knees beside James Hawksley's inert body, as Thomas Appleby lifted his head from his position at the side of the man he looked on as good friend as well as employer. He glanced pityingly at Sophie.

'I fear he has gone, my lady,' he said gently. 'I tried to staunch the blood, did all I could! The blow penetrated low in the rib cage....'

'Move back,' instructed Sophie, opening her medicine chest. She tore the remnant of her father's shirt off, removed the pad of material over the wound, and stared in horror at the white edges of the gaping wound revealed, noting that blood was still slowly welling from it.

She placed her fingers against his neck, felt the almost imperceptible pulse there. 'He lives,' she whispered. She noticed a bottle of brandy lying close by on the grass. She pointed to it. 'You gave him some of this, Tom,' she asked and he nodded.

'I thought it might revive him. Did I do wrong?'

'Pour a little on my hands—now on the wound!' There was no reaction from Hawksley, who lay deeply unconscious beneath her hands. Sophie had on occasion, stitched wounds in the past but nothing as serious as this, nor did she know of what deeper damage had occurred within the injured man's tissues. But something had to be done and she threaded a needle with fine thread and commenced closing the edges of that open wound, praying as she did so, that no infection might develop.

At last it was done. She placed a pad of soft clean linen over the wound, bandaged it in place.

'Now we move him indoors,' she said, voice shaking in reaction. She watched as careful hands eased Hawksley onto an improvised wood stretcher covered over with a cloak as they slowly carried him back towards the house. She followed behind, her thoughts now racing to the situation of her small brother—where was Henry? Had the fiends who had left her father for dead, also killed his little son? She waited until her father was carried into his bedchamber and settled in the large four poster bed before bending to check his pulse and to her relief found it to be a little stronger, although his skin still held a deathlike pallor.

'Send for Beth Giles,' she said now. 'She has nursing skills learned of my grandfather, will know how to proceed here! Take the carriage for she does not ride.' Then leaving her father breathing evenly now, although shallowly, in the care of her father's housekeeper, one of the grooms keeping armed watch at his side, she hurried off down stairs, beckoning Thomas Appleby to follow her.

'Now, tell me exactly what happened? Was my brother Henry injured when those devils snatched him?' She blinked back tears, thinking of the little boy whom she loved almost as much as Minette. Where was he now?

'Well my lady, your father was walking across the grass with young Henry, when the child threw a ball towards that cluster of trees bordering the east side of the grounds. They both set off after it. I was standing some fifty yards away, was on my way over to speak with Lord James when it happened. It was all so quick—so unexpected!'

'Just tell me, Tom!'

'Half a dozen men on horseback suddenly broke free of the trees and galloped towards your father and the child. I could not hear all that they shouted, caught only one phrase—Damned Papist! Your father was unarmed.....'

'They named him Papist?' She seized on the information, drew in her breath. Appleby nodded miserably and at her gesture continued his account.

'They surrounded him and while one snatched up young Henry, another of the fiends drove his sword into his Lordship's breast and he fell, holding his hands out desperately towards his son. I shouted, started to run towards the assassins, calling for those working in the nearby field to come to my aid, which they did immediately! The intruders saw us and hesitated, then looking down at the man bleeding on the ground, they laughed loudly, contemptuously and rode off, one holding the child before him on the saddle.'

'You say they were masked? Did nothing identify them to you—their speech, appearance?' She looked at him urgently. He frowned.

'The fellow who called your father papist spoke in accent of a gentleman! The others, well I just heard loud voices shouting and swearing, so difficult to say. I sent our men off in chase, but those who held young Henry were well mounted. That would be about an hour ago now.'

'You have done all you possibly could, Tom! Without your immediate help to him, my father would indeed lie dead, murdered!' She placed a hand on his arm as she smiled her gratitude.

'I sent Joel Croft for you—then wondered if I had done the right thing in case you might encounter those murdering swine, but I knew you would have the King's guards about you still, thought you might send them in pursuit!' He nodded his greying head approvingly. 'That sergeant took his men off like a shot didn't he, but I fear the time lapse may make it difficult to catch up with them. Some of our own lads rushed off on foot, but they would not have had a chance I fear.'

Even as he spoke, a group of workmen strode towards them, heads down.

'We did our best, Master Appleby,' said on, as they bowed on seeing Sophie. 'They had too much of a start. Some guards came upon us and instructed us to return and keep watch here. They are searching the whole of Stokely. Your son Richard is with them!' They turned to Sophie. 'We are so sorry, my lady!'

'My thanks to all of you,' called Sophie. 'Get you to the house and keep watch in case they should return, though I think it unlikely.' She followed quietly behind, Tom Appleby at her side.

'Do you have any suspicion of who might be behind this,' he asked now?

'I am wondering if this can be the work of Gerald Lorrimer!'

'Lorrimer? The man my son Richard told me had been pestering you in the woods and again insisted on visiting your grandfather's house, Sophie?' He stopped and stared at her in astonishment. 'But why, what motive would he have?'

'I believe him to be the nephew of Mark Harrison, his sister Myra's son.' She drew in her breath and forced out the next words. 'My father told me of rumours being spread, that I was involved in witchcraft, which may have been started by him!' She came out with the words almost breathlessly and saw from his expression that the words came as no shock to him.

'I heard some such wild talk in Stokely,' he said grimly, 'traced it to Langley Morton and dealt with those who spread such calumny.'

'My father told me you had taken your staff to some of them!'

'I most certainly did and threatened them with the magistrates and they took to their heels. I thought it odd that they were strangers to the district!'

'But others repeated their words,' queried Sophie?

'It was your love of medicine that set it off seemingly. Folks just love gossiping, nor trouble to think what harm their careless tongues can cause.' He smiled down at her comfortingly. 'But my lady, all around here love you dearly, for your many kindnesses and bright spirit.'

'Father said the men were staying at the Falstaff Inn, which Gerald Lorrimer now owns! What are the chances that he ordered not only the rumours but also the attempted murder of my father this day—and the kidnapping of little Henry?'

'Wish I had thought on this before those guards set off—for I think you may be right!' He smote his knee with his big hand in frustration.

'What if they are holding the child there?' her eyes expressed her agony of spirit, as she thought of the terrified little boy who had seen his father struck down before him.

'If he lives, then we will rescue him, have no fear of that!' he said soothingly and looked up as the carriage returned and Beth Giles stepped carefully down and hurried over.

'Sophie! Lord Hawksley—is he....?'

'He lives, but is gravely injured, Beth! Little Henry is kidnapped and I must try to find him. Can I rely on you to watch over my father, nurse him?'

'Need you ask, my dear? Take me to him!' They mounted the stairs together, as Sophie related more of the terrible events that had occurred. She stooped over her father now and felt his pulse. It was slightly stronger, but he was still deeply unconscious.

An hour later the guards returned, crestfallen as they explained they had searched Stokely from one end to the other and found no sign of the villains nor had any seen a small boy carried through there on a horse. They added that Richard Appleby had decided to ride further to the next village, to Langley Morton, but they had returned to check that all was well at the manor.

'Do you have any idea who might have attempted to kill his lordship,' asked the sergeant, relieved to hear that James Hawksley lived.

'I have no real evidence against him, but suspect Gerald Lorrimer the present owner of the Falstaff Inn may be behind it. His uncle, a man called Mark Harrison was given Hawksley Manor by Cromwell during the days of the Commonwealth and then kidnapped me in attempt to force me into marriage when the King restored his manor and lands to my father. Luckily I escaped!'

The guards looked at Sophie in shock.

'He also ordered the murder of a poor old woman who lived in the woods,' she continued. 'There is a warrant out for the man's arrest, but there has been no word of him for nigh on six years now. But as I say, his nephew has bought the Falstaff Inn in Langley Morton, as well as the red brick house next to the inn.'

'We consider that the child could be hidden in either of these buildings,' said Tom Appleby. 'My son Richard is aware of Lorrimer's animosity towards Lady Mereton and I fear may have ridden there alone to see if he can find young Henry!'

'Well, he would have done better to take us into his confidence,' swore the sergeant, 'Even if it was only a suspicion! Come on lads—we had better ride for Langley Morton! If only we had known much time could have been saved!' Before Sophie could remonstrate, to suggest she should ride with them, they had remounted and were off.

It was now three hours since Henry had been taken, the late September sunshine fighting through a mist that was creeping over the fields and within another hour it would be getting dark. Sophie stared from her father's bedroom window. If only he would regain consciousness—but if he did, what then would be the result if he learned his son was being held captive in a place unknown? She put her hands over her face and whispered a prayer to God, to heal her father and to keep his beloved small son safe from harm.

Chapter Fifteen

Richard Appleby tethered his horse to a railing in the courtyard and approached the open inn door, the warm smell of beer and perspiration wafting towards him. The Falstaff Inn was full. Men were exchanging raucous comments on the government's inability to bring the Dutch war to a satisfactory conclusion.

'If the King showed as much interest in the defence of his country as he does in fondling his women, then times might improve,' quoth a heavily bearded, sour faced man.

'We did better under Cromwell,' put in another. 'He knew how to defeat the Hollanders!'

'Maybe—but he was a right miserable killjoy,' snorted the third. This was Jed Brownley the local butcher, a red faced, jovial individual, who pressed his paunch against the bar and as he called for more drink. 'They say the devil came for Oliver in a night of storm!' he added defiantly.

Richard ordered a flagon of ale, and slipped quietly onto a bench at the back of the room and sat to drink, and listen unobserved.

A florid, heavily built man who appeared to be the landlord grinned amiably at the raucous crowd. He lifted his own tankard.

'Let us drink a toast then, lads! Here is to the damnation of the Dutch and all papists! Yes and to all who practice witchcraft,' the man continued. A great roar went up at his words as men greedily downed their ale.

'Well, if what I've heard be true, then there is one less papist polluting our land,' snarled a mean faced individual, wearing dusty black velvet, a pistol strapped at his side. 'They say that Lord James Hawksley has been killed this day by patriots of our country!'

There was a moment's silence. Men stared at their neighbours uneasily. It was one thing to decry all papists as good Englishmen should, but when it came to an individual as esteemed locally as was Lord Hawksley, then it behoved men to show discretion.

'What be you a talking of,' asked one old man now, frowning at the speaker. 'Who says Hawksley's dead? Who killed him then? He and his family are well liked in this district!' He rose to unsteady feet. 'You be a stranger here—as are some of you others! So who dares to speak of killing James Hawksley?' and he swept his arm around. As he spoke, men seemed to draw into two groups, the locals closing up to the elderly man who had declared his wrath—and others who seemed of a different cast drawing apart. The tension in the air was tangible.

'Calm down, lads,' called the landlord sensing trouble. 'Another toast! To all good Englishmen!'

'I want an answer to my question,' cried the elderly man, emboldened by support from his friends. 'What kind of lie is this, that Lord Hawksley is dead?' His thin straggly beard quivered his indignation. The man in black velvet glared back at him in scorn.

'Gutted like a pig in his garden, so I've heart tell!'

'Oh—and who told you that—unless you were involved in some such deed?' cried another man.

'Well, I imagine the manor will need another owner, now that Hawksley's gone!' was the mocking retort.

'Oh and should anything have happened to his lordship, then his young son Henry Hawksley would inherit, as next in line,' said another man sagely.

'Children's lives are somewhat precarious,' scoffed a tall, indolent man in an embroidered blue doublet, who wore a sword. 'They can be snuffed out like a candle flame!' He stood shoulder to shoulder with the man in black velvet, backed by half a dozen others. They were observed uneasily now by the regulars of the hostelry, as the speaker continued, 'If the Hawksley line should be at an end, then surely the next heir would be Mark Harrison who is the true owner of the manor, given to him by the late Lord Protector of blessed memory, to be followed by his own heirs!'

'What,' cried an indignant voice, as a tall muscular fellow pushed his way forward, 'Mark Harrison say you? My name is Robert Fenton and I know a thing or two about Harrison! He is wanted for murder and kidnap hereabouts and likely to swing if caught!'

'Besides which, Lady Sophie Mereton is daughter to Lord James Hawksley and heir after her brother Henry!' It was Richard who spoke up now and at the authority in his voice all turned to look at him.

'Some say she's a witch,' called an unidentified voice.

'Who dares to say so,' cried Richard? There was silence as he glared around. 'I would ask a question of these men, strangers who are so free in their attempt to interfere with affairs not their own.'

'And who are you, fellow,' exclaimed the man in black velvet, eyes narrowing.

'Richard Appleby, son of Thomas Appleby, estate manager to Lord Hawksley. Now more to the point, who are you?' attacked Richard.

'Lance Pendleton and no friend of papists and those who serve them!'

233

'That I believe! Since you announce the attempted murder of James Hawksley this day, I suggest that you and your friends are those who plunged a sword into the breast of an unarmed man and left him for dead, and stole his young son! But his Lordship survives and those who did this deed shall answer for it with their lives.' They drew back before the fury on Richard's face as he swung round and addressed the other drinkers, who were listening with mouths open to this shocking statement.

'Men—I believe little Henry Hawksley is held captive here in the Falstaff Inn, either that or in the house next door, both owned by Gerald Lorrimer, who is nephew to Mark Harrison! So, who will help me to search for the child, lest he be murdered as they attempted to murder his father?'

'Why—I'll help thee, young Appleby,' said Robert Fenton, handling the knob ended staff he carried. 'What about you others? Stand back, landlord—if a child is being held captive on these premises, then woe betide you!' At this a great murmuring arose and men surged forward and pushed into the room at the back, then descended into the cellars calling out Henry's name. But no sign was found of the child.

'On to Lorrimer's house then!' Richard started up the road, followed by a crowd of about twenty men. As for those who had spoken out about Hawksley in the inn, they seemed to have vanished. Soon led by Richard, they had pushed in through the gate set between those high yew hedges and knocked loudly on the door of red brick house, once owned by Haversham, now home to Gerald Lorrimer. A maid opened it and stared open mouthed at the crowd of angry men.

'What do you want here? The master is away from home. Now go away!'But her words availed nothing as men swept past her, as room after room was explored, but still found no sight of little Henry Hawksley.

'I have it!' cried an elderly man, chewing his lip. 'At the back of the inn there's a small outbuilding, adjoining the churchyard. It's said goods are smuggled in there at night. Worth a try lads, perhaps?' And they were off again, running and jostling. There partly hidden by a huge spreading yew tree and bordered by ancient gravestones stood the old stone building.

It was locked! Richard Appleby put his shoulder against it, as did brawny Robert Fenton. At last after several attempts it yielded so that they almost fell across the threshold. It was dark inside. Someone lit a taper. They stared in amazement. The sides were stacked high with barrels and sealed boxes.

'Why, 'tis brandy,' exclaimed a man, 'Brandy and fine wine! So Lorrimer is smuggling as it's known Roger Haversham was before him!'

'It probably explains why he purchased the Inn—saw it as a lucrative way of increasing his income,' said Richard scornfully. 'But our present business is with the child—to find Henry, and he does not appear to be here!'

'No, look Appleby, over there in the corner, under that pile of sacks, isn't that a child's foot protruding?' Fenton snatched the taper and strode over to the heap of sacks, pulled them aside. With a cry of horror Richard followed him and stooped over the small form. He lifted little Henry Hawksley gently. The villagers drew back and allowed him through the darkened doorway, into the early evening light.

Fenton pulled off his jacket, spread it on the ground as Richard laid the child down and knelt beside him. He was bound and gagged they saw, eyes shut, face deathly pale. Richard choked back a sob fearing they had come too late. He released the gag, took the knife one of the men proffered, and cut the rope securing wrists and legs. He pulled the child's shirt open and put his head to his breast. The faint heartbeat was just about discernible.

'He lives, thank God!'

'Here, let me see the little lad!' A large woman hearing the commotion had made her way with many others to join the crowd who had assembled around the Falstaff Inn and outbuilding. People fell back as Bessie Pawson advanced. She stared down at the child. 'Is he alive?'

'Just,' said Richard quietly.

'Then bring him into my house, it is but a short distance away. He needs warmth, comfort!' Richard stared at her, sensed the strength and integrity in her eyes, lifted the boy up in his arms and followed her to her house about a hundred yards along the village street.

'Lay him on the couch, sir! See, he's shivering with the cold!' She threw her shawl about the child, tucking it close as she stroked his hair back from his forehead, exclaiming at the bruising about one eye and at his swollen lip, as she started to gently sponge his face.

'I must get him to his sister as soon as possible. She is skilled in medicine. I speak of Lady Mereton. This is her brother Henry!' Richard chafed the little boy's hands, and grimaced as he saw the cuts where the cords had bitten into the young flesh.

'What—you speak of Sophie then, Martha Haversham's child? Well at least so she was supposed to be, but seems she was her sister Lucy's daughter and her father Lord Hawksley! It was I who brought Dr Wheatley to rescue his daughter Martha from her brute of her husband who almost killed her in his evil temper, and used to brutalise young Sophie, whipped her something cruel at times! Bad cess to him! Well, he's dead these last five years and no loss, say I!' The words poured out in a torrent as she poured a teaspoon of brandy from a flask and touched it between the child's lips. 'This may help!'

The little boy coughed and spluttered and opened his eyes. He stared around in obvious terror, uttering a piercing scream.

'Papa—my papa!'

'It is alright, you are safe now, little one,' cried Richard bending over him and taking his hands into his own strong grasp. 'It's Richard Appleby—you know me young Henry!' And he smiled gravely.

'Richard—some bad men hurt my father,' he blurted out fearfully. 'I think they killed him. Oh, my Papa! I want my Papa!' and he burst into a flood of frightened tears.

'Did they hurt you too, Henry?'

'They hit me when I tried to get away. Then they tied me up and threw me in a dark place and said I would die there! My chest hurts,' he said as he tried to sit up. Richard's hands gently explored the child's ribs. Hopefully there were no fractures, just bad bruising. Tears were welling up in the boys eyes and spilling down his pale cheeks.

'I want Sophie,' he said now. 'Please take me home, Richard!'

'Best you do as he asks, young sir,' said Bessie Pawson nodding her head sagely. 'But will it be safe to ride with those devils at large who did this to the little lad—and what about his Lordship? Is he badly injured, sir?'

'Dangerously wounded,' whispered Richard out of the child's hearing. 'I rode off to discover his son's whereabouts as soon as I came upon the scene. Lady Mereton is at Hawksley Manor now and if anyone can revive her father, then it will be her. I thank you for your kindness, Mistress Pawson, will see that you are rewarded for it!'

'I want no reward for doing a simple kindness. I just hope those who did this deed will be brought soon to justice,' she added scowling, hands pressed against massive hips

Several willing men who owned horses, agreed to accompany Richard through the gathering dark, along the road from Langley Morton to Stokely, among them Robert Fenton. As they were about to start out, Sophie's four guards approached at speed, mounts snorting. They pulled up, their sergeant at once recognising Richard and espied the child in his arms.

'You found him then—this is his lordship's son?'

'He is safe. We are returning him now to Hawksley Manor. Do you ride with us?' The officers looked disappointed that they had not personally been involved in the rescue. Then their sergeant brightened.

'Where are those who kidnapped him and attempted to murder his father?' he asked authoritatively, straightening his sword belt.

'Many in the village will tell you what happened, give you details. My duty now is to get the boy safe back home.' Richard's voice was firm.

''I'll stay behind with them—tell all I know to these officers,' offered one of the villagers. 'Quite a story it is too!'

At last they were off. Trees and bushes soon became black shapes, as a thin shaft of moonlight lit the road before them. Owls hooted and a fox streaked across their path as they sped onwards, mile after mile, until at last they reached Stokely and then left the small village behind and took the lane that led to Hawksley Manor. Little Henry had his head pressed against Richard's chest and was sleeping.

Sophie had heard them approach and peered anxiously from the window as the horse hooves drummed up the driveway. Had those would be murderers returned? Then she recognised Richard's face, and saw the precious burden he clasped to him as he dismounted and made towards the front steps. She flung the door open.

'He's safe, Sophie! He has been roughly used, but not badly injured. Here, take him!' He handed the child to her and saw her blue eyes fill with tears of gratitude.

'Oh, Richard, how can I ever thank you1 I feared they had killed him.'

'Your father...?'

'Alive, but the sword thrust went deep, and he will take some time to recover from the wound He regained consciousness less than an hour ago!'

'Why thank the dear Lord for his recovery. Only you could have brought him back from near death and that with God's help,' he said huskily. 'Look Sophie—Lady Mereton that is...

'Sophie is my name, Richard. Just use it from now on! These men with you?'

'They helped me to find your brother! Without their assistance I would have searched in vain. You put the boy to bed—reassure him. I will take these good friends to the kitchen, see they are well looked after and perhaps they should bed down at the house tonight? I doubt if Lorrimer's men will return, but a few extra men on duty will be a good precaution. Incidentally, your four guards are in Langley Morton, trying to discover details of the villains who wrought this deed.'

'Was Lorrimer there?'

'We saw no sign of him. His maid said he was away from home.' He nodded and left Sophie to care for the tear stained little boy just as Thomas Appleby descending the stairs from James Hawksley's bedchamber, heard voices and crossed the great hall to see his son restoring the lost child to Sophie. He caught him in his arms in a great bear hug.

'Well done, Richard! I am that proud of you!' They walked off together, followed by Richard's new found friends.

The guards returned the following morning. None of the men who had cast defamatory remarks about Lord Hawksley were to be found, despite a thorough search of the village. They had vanished! The landlord Samuel Miles though had been interrogated and threatened with jail if he did not disclose all that he knew about the contraband found in the inn's outbuilding. He refused to implicate Lorrimer in any smuggling activities, saying he knew nothing about it, was only an employee. He also denied any knowledge of the child's kidnap or the attempt on James Hawksley's life.

'I suspect he is in greater fear of those who employ him, than of the law,' ground out the sergeant. 'I gave him due warning of a flogging at the very least, if he made any further defamatory remarks about Lord Hawksley or her young ladyship!' The sergeant had heard those allegations of witchcraft made against Sophie with absolute shock.

'Now I should by rights be returning to London,' he explained to Sophie. 'I know it was at the King's own order that we were sent to protect you, my lady and feel concern at leaving you at this time. Have you any message I should bring back with me?' His grizzled eyebrows drew together as he looked down kindly at Sophie.

'Yes, I have a commission for you, sergeant!' Her hands went to her waist, detached a small object from her girdle. 'I want you to take this golden pomander, keep it safe and give it to the King!'

'To the King, my lady?' he looked at her open mouthed, as he saw that she meant it. 'Well if you say so, then you have my promise that he shall receive this!' He slipped the shining gold pomander into his pocket.

'It is most urgent you get this into his Majesty's hands as soon possible! Tell him all that has happened here and that... no wait! I'll also write a few lines for you to deliver.' She ran to her desk and penned a short message and sealed the letter. She reached for a purse she had placed ready. 'This gold is for you and your men. My grateful thanks for all you have done. Goodbye, sergeant! God bless you!'

'Minutes later, the guards were mounted and on their way back to London, their horses eating up the long miles ahead, the sergeant wondering at the commission laid on him by the lovely young woman in whom he knew the king took an interest. What meaning would the golden pomander convey to the monarch?

Sophie sighed in relief that her message was on its way to the King. The fact that the guards had been unable to discover the whereabouts of the villains who had almost killed her father and kidnapped his small son surely only meant that they were hiding in another of the nearby villages. Might they not attempt to strike again, while her father was barely holding onto life? Then her thoughts sped to her own small daughter, to Minette whom she had left at Oaklands in Jenny's charge.

'Minette! I must bring her over here where I can watch over her,' she exclaimed to Richard who had just returned from the stables after seeing the guards on their way.

'Minette? She should be safe enough at Oaklands,' he started, then sensing the fear in her voice. 'You fear an attack on her too?' He turned his troubled gaze on her. 'Do you wish me to bring her to the manor then, Sophie?'

'Yes, I do Richard! Tell Jenny to pack her clothes. Also, send word to Martha and David Markham of what has happened!'

'How is your father this morning?'

'He is in fever which I am trying to reduce. But the wound looks clean and we can only pray! Beth Giles is with him now.' Her worry was obvious, the dark shadows around her blue eyes telling of a sleepless night at her father's bedside.

'And the child?'

'Little Henry is resting. I gave him another sleeping draught, for he is very fearful still and his chest painful. What fiends those men were, to hurt a little boy!' she cried passionately.

'At least he is safe,' he said gently and she smiled slightly at him now, realising how much she owed to Richard's quick thinking in the recovery of her small brother.'

'Sophie, I will ride for Minette now. Take a few men with me in case any should try to waylay us on return. Never fear, I'll bring her safely back to you, sweetheart.' The word of affection slipped out incautiously, and to his dismay he saw her flinch as he used it. 'Listen, Sophie—you know now that I love you more than anything else on this earth. But I will never try to force myself on you in any way and seek only to serve you!' He bowed and turned away, then paused and called back quietly.

'Sophie, I heard you tell your father of your love for the King!' and as she reddened at his words, he was gone.

He was back in late afternoon, little Minette proudly riding her pony under Jenny's watchful eye, surrounded by men from the estate. The Rev. David Markham and Martha were not with them he explained, as Martha was nursing her husband of a high fever and could not leave him. Sophie heard the news with sadness, then caught her daughter up in her arms as the little girl slid down, looking adorable in her riding outfit.

'My darling! Come, let us go inside. Your grandfather is unwell and we must stay here until he is better.' She stroked the child's chestnut hair.

'Where is Henry,' asked Minette in her childish treble, ignoring the news of her grandfather.

'He has a sore head and is resting. But it will do him a lot of good to see you when he wakes up, Minette!' She glanced across at Jenny as the girl prepared to lead Minette away. 'Did Richard tell you what happened, Jenny?'

'Yes, my lady. It is all sounds so terrible. Will we be safe here in the house, if those wicked men are still on the loose?' She fixed uneasy brown eyes on Sophie. 'Was it some of those vagrants we passed on coming out of London?'

'No, Jenny, but those who plan harm to this family. But have no fear. I have sent message to the King!' Jenny relaxed at this. There was no way in which the King would allow any to harm her mistress.

On the third day, James Hawksley's fever broke, and as Sophie lifted the cold compress from his brow, his dark eyes opened and he stared uncomprehendingly around him. Minutes later he became aware of the pain from his wound and tried to reach an exploring hand to it.

'Do not touch!' said Sophie urgently. 'Father, you have been gravely wounded, but I promise you will soon recover!' For a moment he focussed on her face, trying to remember recent events and suddenly all flooded back into his mind in shocking detail.

'My son? Where is Henry—those devils took him!'

'He is safely home again. We have Richard Appleby to thank for his rescue,' and she started to fill him in with all that had so recently transpired as he stared at her in gathering horror.

'I must get up!'

'No! If that wound opens again it may fester, bring death!' He saw from her face that she did not exaggerate and nodded compliance.

'Then bring Thomas Appleby here to me!'

'I'm here, my lord,' said a firm voice. 'It seems that we have Gerald Lorrimer to thank for this outrage, although there is no real evidence to lay it on his shoulders at this time. He was away from his home three days ago, at the time when you were attacked! But I think it likely that he may be hiding somewhere nearby in the area with his cutthroats!''

'Three days ago? I have lain here for three days, say you?' Hawksley looked about him unbelievingly.

'We feared you dead, my Lord! Had it not been for your daughter's wonderful skill of healing, you would be under the ground now and that be a fact!' His honest face expressed the truth of his words. 'For 'twas meant to be a mortal wound those devils dealt you!'

'Tom is right, father! And it was Richard who rode into Langley Morton to the Falstaff Inn and discovered Henry bound and gagged thrown into a building behind the inn, where he tells me much contraband was stored!'

Little by little he began to absorb the story.

'Those guards the King sent to accompany me back from London told me they put the fear of God into the landlord of the Falstaff Inn! Richard told how he was trying to inflame those drinking there against Catholics—you in particular, and another couple of strangers according to Richard, were suggesting that should you die, then Henry might not survive either and that Mark Harrison or his heir, would then be the rightful owner of Hawksley Manor.

'So all was planned!' He fell back on his pillows, face white, the effort to concentrate too much for him yet. Sophie bent and kissed him.

'Sleep, father! All will be well—I have sent word to the King by the guards.' She signalled to those about the bed to leave the chamber. She bent over him. 'Father, there is something else which I must tell you now. I would rather not, but sooner or later you will have to find out.

'Why, what is it Sophie? You are not ill?' and he looked up at her anxiously.

'No—not ill. Pregnant! I should have waited until you were stronger to reveal this.' Her colour rose as she made the announcement.

'Charles?'

'Yes, the King!'

'Damn the man!' his eyes were angry. Then he sighed. 'So, another arranged marriage then?'

'Not so! I want no more old dotards!' she cried angrily, then bit her lip, realising how disrespectful her words were of the late Gareth Mereton.

'Then how will you manage,' he asked, trying hard to concentrate.

'I'm not sure yet. Oh, I did receive one unexpected offer of marriage though. This should amuse you, father! Richard Appleby!' she exclaimed scornfully and saw a slight smile curving his lips.

'Ah—Richard,' he said and closed his eyes and slept.

A week had passed and James Hawksley was definitely on the mend and able to leave his bed. Today he sat on a cushioned chair, fondling his small son. Henry's bruises were still apparent and his father's ire was rekindled as he examined the boy's face and ribcage. His cold anger against those who had perpetrated this hurt to an innocent child, seemed to spur his recovery. He looked up as he heard a knock and the door opened and Thomas Appleby stood there.

'Is something amiss, Tom?' He saw the anxiety on the man's bluff features and set the child aside, calling for Beth Giles to take him to the nursery. Thomas waited until the door closed behind them.

'Do you remember a fellow called Rupert Mereton—he who disputed your daughter's legal right to Oaklands on the death of her husband?'

'I most certainly do, a most insolent fellow as I recall! The court case he brought in dispute of the will was decided in Sophie's favour without question. Go on, man?' said Hawksley

'I've heard news that he is entertaining Gerald Lorrimer at his home, a property about ten miles from Oaklands called Park Lodge! From what I'm reliably told, there are a quite a few strangers in and out of the place, rough looking characters, among them one known as Lance Pendleton. Now that's the name of the villain Richard named as stirring up trouble at the Falstaff Inn—and who announced that you were dead, which he could only have known through involvement!'

'So, what do we have now? Rupert Mereton who shouted his hatred of me, and who tried to dispossess Sophie, is in close association with Gerald Lorrimer who has been seeking to blacken her name! So the attack on me and my son was obviously of their planning!' he exclaimed in rising fury. 'If I get my hands on them!' and his face darkened with anger. Thomas held up a restraining hand.

'Forewarned is forearmed,' he said quietly.

'Does Sophie know of any of this? I do not want her worried at this time when she is with child!' the words were out before he could stop them and he saw the consternation on the other man's face. 'None are to know of the matter at this time,' he said sternly, and Thomas nodded.

'We all love her and will care for her with our own lives,' he said stoutly. 'As you know my lord, there have been tales of witchcraft levelled against your daughter by those who gossip and I for one will cheerfully wring the neck of any who repeat such calumny in my hearing!'

'Just make sure she does not wander into the woods on her own again, to gather those herbs she uses.' He sighed. 'I tried to forbid her not to take too close an interest in medicine, but to no avail. Yet without her skill, I would probably lie dead now, as would many another.'

Thomas nodded. 'Sophie has a wondrous gift of healing, and most speak of her with kindness and respect. As for those who listen to Lorrimer's lies, they should have more sense that to attend to such foul vapourings! Yet men ever fear that which they do not understand.' He shook his head. 'So, have you any new orders for me, sir?'

'Just that you keep all workers continually alert!' He sank back in his chair, face showing the exhaustion he was experiencing and Thomas turned for the door, calling for Sophie.

'Your father do not look so good, my lady,' he said urgently as she ran up the stairs. 'I discussed certain matters with him that might better have waited until he was stronger.'

'Oh, Tom. I will go to him. Look, will you instruct Jenny to let Minette play on the lawn near the house, for she hates being cooped up in the house so much, especially when the sun is shining as it is today. She must stay close to her at all times!' she added anxiously. He nodded. The little maid should be safe enough under the watchful eyes of the staff.

Sophie looked at her father and saw the tiredness on his face. 'You are going back to bed,' she said firmly. Nor did he argue the point with her. When he was comfortably settled against his pillows, she checked his wound and saw how well it was healing. He took one of her hands in his.

'Now sit down, Sophie child. We must talk,' he said.

Jenny spread out a shawl on the grass, threw down some cushions and watched as Minette started to play with her miniature tea set, holding the tiny china cups up to the mouths of her favourite dolls. The late September sun shone with welcome warmth and bees still hummed in the hollyhocks and late roses. She sang some of Minette's favourite nursery rhymes with her until the little girl seemed to tire, and cuddled up to Jenny and closed her eyes.

Jenny stroked the silky head, thinking how like to Sophie the child was, and to another, and she smiled as she thought of the handsome King. So many adventures they had been through back there in London. Then tired after all the tension of recent days, Jenny's head drooped on her breast and she sank down on the cushions, still holding Minette close—and she too slept.

Half an hour sped by. Minette yawned, opened her eyes and found Jenny gently snoring. She was about to shake her arm to waken her, then thought better of it. 'I will go and find my pony,' she whispered softly. She loved the little animal dearly, knew it would be in the stables. She rose softly to her feet and walked quietly away. Jenny still slept.

No one saw the child walk round the side of the house towards the stables. Minette slipped through the gate to the paddock and crossed the stable yard and looked around, breathing in the familiar smell of horses and hay and straw. Now where was the stable-boy, Josh? She liked him. She walked slowly from stall to stall, staring up in admiration at the horses which in turn looked down on her from questioning eyes, snorting as she passed by.

'Oh there you are, Peterkin,' she cried, as at last she found the stall housing her beloved pony. She knew she should not open the stall without a groom to help her, but there did not seem to be anyone around. The pony snuffled at her hand as she patted its shining coat and rubbed its head against her, then looked longingly at the open stall door. It took a few tentative steps forward, snorting in anticipation of a run in the fields nearby.

'No—stop!' cried Minette sternly, trying to restrain the pony by catching at its long mane. But it was too late. The pony pulled away from the child, clattered across the stable yard and paddock and leapt the low gate into the field beyond and was off!

'Peterkin—come back! Bad pony,' scolded Minette, running after the vigorous little animal as fast as her young legs would carry her. But Peterkin was thundering across the meadow, neighing pleasure in this unexpected freedom with no human load to hold it back. Minette watched it disappearing into the distance with utmost dismay. Suppose the pony became lost and she was never able to ride him again?

'I will try to find him.' she muttered feeling vexed and looking around her uneasily, for she knew she would probably get a scolding from Jenny for her disobedience. She had been told never to go anywhere on her own, as there were bad people about who might hurt her. But surely she should be safe enough on grandfather's estate? After all, Jenny and her mother would be even more cross if they knew she had let the pony go!

Jenny woke to find someone shaking her shoulder. She opened her eyes and saw Richard Appleby staring down at her sternly.

'Where is Minette,' he demanded without preamble.

'Why, she was here with me, playing with her dolls......' her voice trailed off in shock as she realised that Minette had disappeared. 'Oh, Master Appleby, I'm that sorry, I must have dozed off! Minette fell asleep you see....!' But she found she was talking to herself, the young man farmer had dashed away calling for help. Jenny's face blenched as she realised that she would be solely to blame for anything that should befall the child.

Sophie heard Richard's voice as she came down the wide staircase. He had burst into the house, shouting that they should search all rooms for the missing child. Her hand flew to her throat in sudden fear, as at once servants started to rush about looking into every room and cupboard, until it became apparent that Minette was definitely not there.

'Oh Richard, where can she be? Suppose she falls into the hands of Lorrimer's bullies! She is so small still, and just remember how they treated Henry!'Her eyes were filling with tears as she tried not to panic.

'Hush, Sophie. Now just think. Where would she be most likely to go to, on her own?' he asked, placing a soothing hand on her arm.

'The swing in the orchard—or to see her pony!'

'You men search the orchard,' instructed Richard. 'Sophie, you come with me. Oh, thank God, here's my father!' he breathed as Thomas Appleby came riding up the driveway towards them and seeing the distress on their faces, halted abruptly beside them.

'What's amiss then, Richard,' he asked in his calm, strong voice, taking in Sophie's tear stained face. 'Is anything wrong with his Lordship?'

'No, but Minette's missing,' cried Sophie. 'We are just going to check the stables!' And as they blurted out the situation, Thomas Appleby swore softly, immediately turning his horse towards the stables as they followed running swiftly in his wake.

They found the stable-lad, young face distraught, looking around in obvious confusion. He looked up guiltily as the three approached.

'The young lady's pony has disappeared, Master Appleby,' he called as Thomas leapt off his horse at strode up to him.

'How did this occur,' growled Thomas angrily.

'I did but go to the privy to relieve myself and when I came back, found the pony's stall empty! I don't know who would have taken it, sir!' The boy looked shaken.

'Well where's the groom? He should have been on duty—where's Ben Fletcher?' put in Richard

'Why, he's taken his Lordship's stallion to the village blacksmith, one of its shoes was loose sir and his Lordship being abed and not needing the horse it seemed a good time to get it to Paul Masters!' The boy looked frightened. 'I'm so sorry about the pony. It cannot have gone far though.....'

'Josh—did you see my daughter, Minette here in the stables?' asked Sophie cutting into his words incisively. 'She is missing!'

'No, my lady. I saw no sign of the little maid.'

'See Sophie, down here where the mud is still damp from yesterday's rain. Are those not a child's footprints?' It was Thomas who had been examining the ground and now straightened. 'We now know for certain she was here. See, her footprints are close to the pony's tracks—but she was not riding it!'

'So the pony ran off and Minette after it,' cried Sophie. She took a deep breath, trying to remain calm. 'Get every available man to search the fields and pathways. I dread to think what may happen if she falls into the hands of Lorrimer's bullies!' She turned to the red faced stable-boy. 'Josh, saddle my mare and be quick about it!'

'No, Sophie,' cried Richard in alarm. 'You must remain at the house. Your father may need you if he takes a turn for the worse. This is man's work!' He reached out to touch her arm but she shrugged him away.

'I am mistress here—Minette my child!'

'Lady, my son is right,' added Thomas Appleby warningly, but ignoring them both, she took the mare from Joshua's hands threw herself astride and was off before they could stop her, and within minutes was seen sweeping across the fields until a screen of trees hid her from sight.

'Father, get men together to search for the child, I am going after Sophie!' called Richard springing into action. He ran for his own horse, flinging himself onto the saddle. Precious minutes had already been lost. He tore off, his face tense with anxiety for the safety of the woman he so hopelessly loved. His horse's hooves pounded over the close stubble of a harvested field and on through the sweet meadowland beyond, swiftly covering the path she had taken, glancing around in both directions as he passed the screen of trees that had cut off view of her. But of Sophie there was no sign—she had vanished!

At first little Minette Mereton's thoughts had been only of her pony, forgetting the stern warnings she had received never to venture away from the house on her own. Certainly she had been told that something bad had happened to her loved play companion, Henry. Wicked men had hurt him and tried to kill her grandfather. But those warnings had somehow sounded unreal. After all, who would want to hurt a child whose father was the King?

Her legs were beginning to ache from running and her chest hurt. She still had some breathing difficulties resultant on the smoke she had inhaled during that great and terrifying fire in London. So now she stopped, realising in sudden panic that she was quite lost—and worse, her pony had disappeared from sight. Nor did she know any longer in which direction the manor house lay.

She gazed around, seeing that she was completely surrounded by small fields, apart from the dark shape of dense woodland thrusting up against the blue sky only some fifty yards from where she stood. Her mother had brought her here once, she remembered, called the place Epilson Woods. As she stared towards it, she thought she saw movement at the edge of the trees.

'Peterkin! It's Peterkin,' she shouted in relief! If only she could catch her pony and mount it, then all would be well, for it would certainly be able to find its way back to the stable. She ran as fast as her legs would carry her, noticing in dismay that the pony seemed to have disappeared. Had it gone into the wood?

The men watching the child's laboured advance towards the trees grinned in delight. They could hardly believe their luck. Josiah Fitch, a refugee from the great fire, who had escaped London and begged and stolen his way deep into the country, had gladly agreed to help the men who plied him with drink. He had been instructed to watch on the comings and goings of all at Hawksley Manor. If discovered, they explained he had the perfect story, a penniless man who had lost all in the holocaust in the city, hoping to find work.

He had been instructed to report on the movements of a beautiful woman with long chestnut hair and a proud bearing, a Lady Mereton who they suggested was involved in witchcraft! She also had a daughter of five years in whom they were interested and who needed to be removed from the witch's influence, they told him. Witchcraft! His blood had run cold at the word. Josiah Fitch was a superstitious man. He had also been a keen supporter of the late lamented Oliver Cromwell, Lord Protector of England

and under whom it had been hoped all rank and privilege would eventually be stamped out, all men declared equal.

But Cromwell was long gone, and the son of that late king beheaded at Cromwell's orders had returned from exile, and had occupied his father's throne these last six years. And what had this yielded? A great plague that had taken the lives of thousands, a fire that had destroyed the whole of the city of London and beyond and wars with the Hollanders that had caused the death of thousands of good English seamen, their ships sunk and with little to show for it! At least Cromwell had defeated the Dutch!

He had taken refuge in the clump of trees bordering the gates to the driveway, when he noticed the child in her blue silk dress rise from beside her nurse, to run off on her own round the side of the house, where he lost sight of her. Not long afterwards, a riderless pony leapt the gate separating gardens from farmland and shot across a field in full vision of the watcher, who then saw the child's blue dress fluttering about her as she gave pursuit.

The Mereton child! This must be the young daughter of the woman his employers wanted to get their hands on, had promised good money to any who would help them in their plans. If they could secure the child, then surly the woman could be lured into a trap! He ran after the child, keeping to the hedges where the bright berries of hips and haws were starting to colour with autumns scarlet. She could run, that little one, but not as fast as one who had outrun the flames pouring down Cheapside!

Minette did not notice the man who sped parallel across the last few yards to the woods, so intent was she on catching her pony. Those who kept vigil there in the leafy depths of the forest, waiting hopefully for some news heard him crashing through the undergrowth towards them.

'Sirs—the little maid, daughter to the woman you seek—she is here— just beyond the trees! She chased after a runaway pony, none with her!' He came out with the words breathlessly, chest heaving. The cruel faced men, grouped under a roughly constructed shelter between the trees, looked at him in delight.

'You are sure it is the right child?'

'Wearing a fancy gown and with a nursemaid to care for her? No cottar's child!' he gasped knowingly.

'You have done well! What of her mother—the Mereton woman?'

'No sign that I saw. She must have stayed within the house, sirs!' They tossed him a few coins which fell onto the dampness of the forest floor and he gasped his thanks as he bent to recover them. But they ignored the man and rushed to the point where he had indicated the child could be found.

Another man overheard the conversation, had kept very still behind a towering oak, a soberly dressed man, with short silver hair, carrying a black leather bag. He recognised the name of Mereton. They spoke of the daughter of the man he was risking his life to visit. The old priest drew in a deep, thoughtful breath. He knew he would stand little chance against the six armed men who were about to wreak their cruelty on this child. He murmured a prayer for her safety and followed swiftly and carefully behind, keeping out of sight.

Meanwhile Sophie paused on a small rise, knew that Richard and his father should be coming up fast behind her. She glanced around anxiously for any sight of her child. Nothing, just well ordered fields and coming into view the outline of Epilson Wood. Then she noticed it, a slight blurring of blue crossing the field at speed towards the wood. Minette! It was Minette's blue gown she saw and with a great breath of relief, spurred her mare forward, shouting over her shoulder to the men, her voice carrying softly on the breeze.

'It's Minette—look! Near the woods!' She didn't turn to see if they had heard but urged the mare on, screaming her impatience. Saw the pony contentedly eating its fill of grass where the meadow met the trees, as the child stumbled towards it.

Then suddenly she heard a thin, high scream, saw Minette grasped by a couple of men who leapt out of the wood and pulled her out of sight. Sophie almost fainted with shock, but rallied forcing her mare ever faster, thundering over the tussocky grass. She knew she should wait for the Appleby's to catch up with her, would need their help. But her mother's heart would brook of no delay in attempt to save her child.

'Let me go! Let me go—or my Papa will kill you!'

'Your father is dead, you witch's spawn,' shouted a jeering voice.

'My Papa is the King!' and she screamed the words.

Father Benedict heard that scream and saw the little girl being roughly handled by her captors. He uttered a silent prayer and acted.

Suddenly, the priest stepped forward, holding a golden cross aloft, the rays of the sun piercing between the trees, making it blaze with brilliant light as the man holding the child loosed his hold and gave a cry of fear Feeling her shoulders released from that pincer like grip, the child turned and took flight. Blind instinct took her out of the trees to the spot where the pony was still champing grass.

Almost simultaneously Father Benedict felt himself seized and thrown to the ground, his leather bag opened and to his horror, saw chalice and host tossed underfoot.

'It's a bloody Catholic priest,' and blows descended on the man who had cost them capture of the Mereton child.

'Minette!' It was her mother's voice and the little girl uttered a cry of trembling relief. Sophie rode towards her, leapt off her mare and lifted the child bareback onto the pony and slapped its side. 'Ride back to the house Minette. Ride for your life,' she cried and the child responded, holding fast to the pony's mane as she kicked its sides and within minutes it was streaking off across the fields.

'Damn it—we've lost the brat!' came a hoarse shout of anger, as the men burst from the trees into the sunlight

'But look what we've caught in exchange!' and before she could remount, three men had grabbed Sophie and dragged her kicking and screaming between the trees. A violent blow to the head rendered her unconscious. The assailants looked down at her in satisfaction. A tall, elegant man in ruby velvet, wearing a sword, accompanied by a shorter, thickset fellow with a florid face now stepped forward. The shorter man kicked at Sophie's prostrate body with contemptuous glee.

'Yes, this is the bitch that dispossessed me of Oaklands! Doesn't look so haughty now! Shame you fellows lost the child. The estate is supposed to go to her after her mother's death!'

'Hold there a moment. What was it the brat said about the King being her father?' Josiah Fitch straightened up from tying the old priest's hands and feet, where they had beaten him to lie on the ground.

'Merely the babbling of a lying imp,' said Gerald Lorrimer, brushing a twig from his fine ruby red coat and settling his cravat.

'Yet perhaps not,' put in Rupert Mereton considering the matter. 'My cousin was old and in ill health. I was always surprised he had the necessary vigour to make the wench pregnant!'

At his words Lorrimer negligently flicked the laces at his wrists, then paused and stared down at Sophie. There had been talk of course that the girl was a favourite of the King's and for the first time he was overtaken with a sense of unease. Too much had already gone wrong with his plans. First of all her father, Lord Hawksley had survived a wound that should have killed him, and his young heir rescued by that fellow Appleby who had dared to interfere with him in the past.

Whatever they did now, must be kept in complete secret that no man could ever speak against them. Yet what point was there in killing the Mereton woman, when her father and young brother survived? He had meant the whole family to be wiped off the face of the earth, that he might put in claim to the manor and rich lands Cromwell had awarded to his uncle. Then Rupert Mereton, with whom he had become firm friends, had offered him a goodly sum to dispose of the woman who had inherited the rich estate that he had expected to be his on his cousin Gareth's death.

She was unconscious, so far had not seen him. Accordingly if they freed her at this stage, would not be able to identify him as one of her captors. He looked down at her lovely face in indecision, for she would definitely remember the appearance of those who had perpetrated such bodily outrage against her, and if the scum he had paid were ever arrested, they would most certainly blab of his involvement in the hope of saving their own skins. Kidnap was a hanging offence, as of course was murder! Planning was one thing, facing the possible dire consequences of such acts, quite another! If only Hawksley and his young son had been killed as planned! He saw the cruel eyes of the band of thugs looking at him expectantly, awaiting orders to dispose of Lady Sophie Mereton.

And still he hesitated. And as he hesitated, an outrageous idea entered his head. Was there not perhaps a third way?

Chapter Sixteen

Charles looked up in irritation as a uniformed gentleman at arms approached him at the precise moment when he was trying to adjust the delicate workings of an extraordinarily beautiful clock he had received from France, a gift from Madame, his beloved sister.

'Sire, forgive the intrusion, but one of the men you sent to escort Lady Meredith back to Oaklands, asked me to hand this to you. There is also a letter!' and he bowed. Charles held out his hand for the shining golden pomander which the officer proffered to him. Sophie! As he looked down at it he realised how much he missed her, his little physician. She had promised to send this to him should she ever experience difficulties or face danger! He raised anxious eyes to the officer and took the letter, breaking the seal and reading its contents in growing concern.

'Bring the fellow who delivered this here at once!' he instructed. The sergeant of guards, who had acted as escort to Sophie, stood at attention under the eyes of the King, glancing at the monarch in awe. In the past he had seen Charles in the distance, never face to face, and sensed the power in the man who confronted him from frowning dark eyes.

'I wish you to explain exactly what took place at Hawksley Manor! First of all is Lady Mereton safe?' the man swallowed nervously.

'Her ladyship was in good health when I left her, but understandably much upset by all that had happened! We did all that we could, sire!'

'How badly injured is Lord Hawksley—and what of his son, Henry?'

'Both were making good recovery when I left. I would have stayed longer, but my instructions were to return to London, and I thought I should make report of what had occurred.' He looked down uncomfortably for the King was still looking at him with ire.

'I wish for an explicit account of everything that happened—omit no detail,' growled Charles and the sergeant obeyed, finally adding,

'I heard Lord Hawksley's estate manager, Thomas Appleby discussing matters with his son Richard, both of them devoted to Lady Mereton and remember a name they mentioned of one who might be the instigator of both the attack on her father and brother and the slanderous remarks made about that lovely young woman!'

'What name, sergeant?'

'That of a Gerald Lorrimer. Seems he is a nephew of a man who held the manor under Cromwell—a Mark Harrison!' At the sound of that name, the King swore an oath. He gave the sergeant a piece of gold and called out orders to his gentleman at arms and wrote out a document of arrest.

'A troop of thirty to ride at once...........!'

That night the King turned restlessly in his bed. If any ill should befall the beloved mother of his daughter Minette, then those responsible should beware! At last he slept and even as he turned in fitful slumber, a mounted, armed troop were on their way to deal most severely with a particularly unlawful situation, in accordance with the orders of the infuriated monarch.

While Lorrimer still looked indecisively at Sophie's inert form, he heard a shout from one of his men keeping watch at the edge of the wood.

'Men approaching from the direction of the manor, riding hard. Will be here in minutes!' he called. Lorrimer snapped into action.

'Bind the woman! Quickly there, that's it—up on my horse with her!' He sprang into the saddle. Sophie was bundled up before him, to hang helplessly face downwards.

'What of the priest, Sir?' the men stared up at him, hands on their knives.

'Kill him!' shouted Rupert Mereton. One of the men pulled the priest to his feet and another put his knife to the elderly man's throat. But at that moment they heard the sound of horses crashing along through the forest path towards them. The man who held the knife hesitated. If he were seen killing the priest, although such were regarded as scum, there might be trouble for him. He fetched the venerable, old white haired man a mighty buffet around the head, and watched in satisfaction as he dropped to the ground. Then the men mounted anxiously and scattered just before Richard Appleby burst into the glade.

Minutes earlier Richard had come across the terrified small girl clutching her pony's mane as she rode bareback, her face streaked with tears. He managed to head the pony off until it slowed, stopped, flanks quivering and stroked it soothingly.

'Minette, sweetheart—are you hurt?'

'No. But those bad men—they have Mama—in the wood! Please help her Richard!' She looked at him appealingly. Sophie, then every moment counted! He turned his head saw his father heading towards him with a band of workers from the estate, all riding hard. He shouted to him that one of them should care for Minette, the others to follow him, that Sophie was in danger and was off ahead like the wind.

Thomas Appleby gave swift instruction, little Minette placed securely before Josh, the stable lad, and carried back to the manor house.

Richard already riding between the trees, and glancing around, gave a cry of concern as he looked down and saw the body of the priest, whose bruised face was turned upwards, and dismounted. He recognised Father Benedict whom he had occasionally seen visiting Hawksley Manor by night and knew the brave old priest made such visits to those few Catholic families to whom the taking of the Mass meant so much. He cut swiftly through the cords that bound hands and feet, but realised the man was deeply unconscious and unable at this time to give him any information about Sophie.

'What has happened here?' Thomas Appleby had caught up with him, and dismounted as those accompanying him halted but remained mounted. Richard pointed to the priest, whom he had gently propped up against a tree.

'This is more of Lorrimer's work I think!' he said grimly.

'See, over there,' said Thomas urgently, 'Caught on that low branch—surely that is a shred of silk torn from Sophie's gown!'

'We'll leave the priest,' cried Richard. 'We must find Sophie before they do their worst to her! But which way?'

Lorrimer had made use of the brief respite by urging his men onwards.

'This is where we separate!' called Lorrimer. 'You there, Pendleton, are to ride with us. All others ride towards Stokely. Stay in the derelict house you know of, on the outskirts of the village. Mereton and I will make for his house with the girl. Remember to keep silent and you will be well rewarded!'

'What about what you owe us already,' shouted one of them truculently?

'You will be paid in full and soon—I promise! Move now or we will all be caught!' And hearing sounds of pursuit they obeyed him, swearing as they urged their horses carefully on through the trees, as each took separate path.

But one of the men was not used to riding, had earlier almost lost his seat more than once and now did not lower his head in time as he sped under a low hanging branch.

Josiah Fitch fell to the ground only some few yards from the badly injured priest and his horse glad to be rid of such awkward rider, continued gleefully on its way. He sat there under the golden shade of a tall beech, nursing his bruised elbow and hip as Richard Appleby appeared and with a cry, leapt from his horse and seized him.

'Here—just you leave me alone, master! I'm a peace loving man,' whined Fitch in fear. He had previously seen Richard at the Falstaff Arms and knew him for one of Hawksley's men.

'Where is she,' ground out Richard?'

'What do you mean, sir?' demanded Fitch in injured tones. 'This is no way to treat one who escaped the great fire of London and now seeks refuge in the country!' He looked at Richard with great show of innocence. Then suddenly he was gasping in terror, as Richard drew his knife.

'Either you tell me here and now what has befallen Lady Sophie Mereton, or I will carve out first one and then the other of your eyes!' As he spoke, Richard held the knife inches from the man's right eye. Seeing the steely determination on his captor's face, Josiah Fitch crumbled. Bad enough to have lost his home and possessions—but how would he fare without sight of his eyes!

'Only put that knife down and I will tell you all I know,' he gasped. But Richard continued to hold the knife as before.

'Tell me—or you lose your first eye,' he said coldly, and as he spoke, Thomas Appleby and half a dozen strong estate workers surrounded Fitch. The man blurted out all in frightened, disjointed sentences.

'It was a fine gentleman wearing red velvet, Gerald Lorrimer they called him and his friend, same name as the woman they wanted—Mereton!'

'What did they want with her?'

'Said she was a witch and should be burned!' The words were out before Fitch could recall them. 'There were many said the same of her, Sir!' he explained. 'You can't blame an honest man for wanting to bring down one accused of witchcraft!'

Richard and his father exchanged glances.

'Where have they taken her?'

'Why, to Rupert Mereton's house!' The knife was lowered slightly.

'And the priest?' asked Richard relentlessly. 'What business had they with him?' Josiah Fitch dared a slight smile.

'A priest? Why all know they should be exterminated, are forbidden to spread their blasphemous teaching to good Englishmen! This one interfered when the Mereton woman's child was in our hands—through his intervention the brat escaped!' At the murderous look on Richard's face, the man quailed again. 'They said the child was influenced by her mother's witchcraft,' he babbled.

'Tie this fellow up,' snarled Richard, fingers reluctantly loosening their grip on his knife as he returned it to its sheaf. 'Let us ride to Rupert Mereton's house—and pray we arrive in time!' he turned back to Fitch. 'How many men accompany Mereton and Lorrimer?'

'Apart from Pendleton, they rode on alone with the woman, all others told to gather at the old barn on the outskirts of the village to await payment,' he said.

'Payment,' quoth Thomas Appleby. 'You may be sure all will receive that—and in full!' He looked behind him as he heard sound of other horses approaching. 'Who comes?' he cried hand on the pistol he held up warningly.

'It's Paul Masters and your son Harry and Daniel Dawlish, come to help in your search for the young mistress!' came a deep voice and the men joined them looking down inquiringly at the cringing, bound figure of Josiah Fitch and at the priest lying pale and unmoving nearby.

'The stable lad Joshua sent word to the village of what was happening,' explained Dawlish. 'Is it true that Sophie is kidnapped? We spoke with little Minette before riding here and thank God the child is safe!'

'Just let me at those who have dared to lay hands on Sophie,' boomed blacksmith Paul Masters, raising an iron bar he had brought with him, while Harry Appleby who had left his own farm immediately when alerted, merely nodded his support to his father and brother. 'Do we know where they have taken her,' he asked?

'Rupert Mereton's place, Park Lodge, some twelve miles from here! Let's go,' cried Richard urgently. 'We have wasted time enough!' He cast a swift pitying glance down at the priest. The man looked sick unto death, adding 'One of you, carry this injured man back to the manor. His hurts need attention if he is not to die!' At his words, the priest was carefully lifted onto a horse by an older man, who also collected up those precious items scattered around, the empty discarded case, the golden chalice—and the cross!

Rupert Mereton with Pendleton riding hard beside him, called impatiently over his shoulder to Lorrimer who was slightly behind, a gap opening up between the men as Lorrimer had a care that Sophie did not slip from the horse.

'Hurry up, man! We have to dispose of the bitch before those pursuing us get any closer.' He waited impatiently for Lorrimer to catch up.

'Relax Mereton! No one will have any idea who has the girl! Certainly none will suspect we are involved. As for the child, even if she blabs of what happened to her, well she caught no sight of either of us, so relax, I say!' A slight moan escaped Sophie's lips—was she regaining consciousness? He came to a quick decision.

'Just to be safe, perhaps we should not actually bring the girl into your house, Mereton. Instead, why not leave her in that disused wooden hut where you used to hang game? It's only a mile or so from the house, but better so!'

'Excellent. Well we are almost there, my friend. We merely inflame the villagers into believing she is a witch, and a burning will answer all problems! My ownership of Oaklands then assured--except for the child, but the lives of such are precarious as all know!' and he chuckled.

'Then you ride on with Pendleton, Rupert! I'll see the girl is securely tied in the game hut—I think you can trust me to attend to this!' And as he looked into Lorrimer's arrogant face and read there a cruelty to match his own, Rupert Mereton nodded agreement, and with his companion spurred on towards Park Lodge.

Sophie was indeed beginning to recover consciousness and as her senses returned opened terrified eyes to find she was slung over a horse, her body jolting painfully to the animals galloping stride. She had no idea where she was, as she could only glimpse leafy hedgerows they were traversing between—and it could have been anywhere. Now they were passing over open land until at last the horse responded to the rider's reins and came to a halt.

She closed her eyes, feigning continuing unconsciousness, aware that the rider had dismounted and was now urgently pulling her off the horse. He lifted her in his arms and threw her unceremoniously down in the corner of a darkened hut. There was no window, the only light now pouring in from the half open door. She saw hooks attached to the wooden walls and blackened knives lay on a table, the skeletal remains of a deer hung mouldering on an iron nail. That swift glance between barely opened lids revealed the function this hut had offered in the past. But where was it? Where was she—and what could she expect at the hands of the man who towered over her supine body, looking down at her with brooding insolence.

Suddenly he bent low over her and pressed a brandy flask to her lips. She coughed and spluttered as he forced the fiery spirit into her mouth.

'That's better! Pray won't you sit up lady?' She recognised the mocking tones as she opened angry blue eyes and stared at him, and as she did so noticed a livid scar across his forehead. Words of old Jessie Thorne spoken in prophecy flashed into her mind.

'You will hang for this, Gerald Lorrimer!' she snapped.

'You think so? Perhaps if any knew of my involvement in this little game, but none do. Now my friend Rupert Mereton has it in mind that you are a witch. Indeed many in the district repeat the tale—and we all know the fate of witches, to be burned or drowned! Mereton favours burning!'

'You wouldn't dare! I am under the protection of the King himself!'

'Even if such were the case, then he is far away,' he sneered. 'Mereton plans to inflame the villagers into an impromptu burning, with all men involved so none to bear individual responsibility for your death!' He rested his hand against the wooden wall of the hut. 'This place should burn easily, would you not say—prove a suitable fiery exodus for you, lady!'

'I am with child,' she said icily. 'Like my daughter, the babe is of the King's making and will be acknowledged by him. None may kill a pregnant woman, a babe not be sacrificed with the mother!' He swore an oath as he looked at her beautiful determined face.

'But none know of your pregnancy I think,' he replied slowly, his brain seizing hopefully on this.

'Oh indeed they do! My father knows and several others, people of good repute who will testify to the truth.' She tried to loosen the bonds that held her. 'Why not let me go now. Perhaps your name can be kept out of this?'

'Let you go? Under no circumstances, except perhaps, one.'

'Oh, and that is?' she fixed him with a cool stare.

'Why—marriage! Become my wife and you will then be under my protection. Sadly Rupert Mereton will not inherit Oaklands, but I will enjoy it and all its revenues through you, my dear.' He looked at her triumphantly. 'Should any ill befall your father and brother in the years to come, then as next in line you will inherit Hawksley Manor—and all will pass to me!'

'I would sooner die than marry you! So get that idea right out of your head!' she spat at him angrily, while vainly searching in her head for a plan to circumvent the evil that lay in store for her.

He bared his teeth in semblance of a smile, 'You say that now in anger. A night's reflection in the cold and dark may help you to wiser decision.' and straightening up he made for the door, slamming it shut behind him, plunging Sophie into darkness.

'Come back,' she cried, but desisted as she heard the sound of horse's hooves pounding into the distance. Now what? The bonds that bound her wrists and ankles were cutting cruelly into her flesh and her head was thumping from the blow she had received, but she knew she must try to keep calm at all costs.

'He did not lock the door,' she whispered the words aloud. 'He slammed it but did not lock it!' But how could she get out of the hut while held in these bonds? She started to roll—roll over and over until one shoulder was touching the door. She turned her body and brought up her knees and pushed violently against its timber—and at last it gave and creaked open and she saw the late afternoon light. She pressed her back up against the doorframe and struggled to finally stand erect.

Now what? She had to get away from the hut, but must first dispense with these cords that restricted movement. Suddenly she remembered the knives she had glimpsed lying on the hut table. Pushing the door wide open to provide light to its interior, she re-entered by a series of small jumps, almost losing her balance as she reached the table.

She managed to pick up one of the smaller knives with her bound hands, pushed its hilt between her knees and sawed frantically at the tight cord. She winced as it gave way, cutting her wrist in the process, but she was free! Then seizing the knife firmly, bent and cut through the cord binding her ankles. She tucked the knife into the purse at her girdle, sighing relief.

She was out of the hut, and slammed its door shut behind her and glanced desperately around, wondering which way would lead back towards the manor. She realised that she had no idea where she was. In the distance she saw a substantial house rearing against the skyline. Could this be Rupert Mereton's home, Park House? Was this where Lorrimer had headed when he had left her? If so she must take the opposite direction—and fast! She thought frantically of what little she knew of Park House, only that it stood some ten miles from her own Oaklands and further still from Hawksley Manor—and housed many desperate characters in Rupert Mereton's employ.

The hut stood in a marshy field bordering a pond. She noticed a tall hedge bordering the field on the far left and guessed it hid a lane, and that the lane probably led towards Oaklands. She ran across the squelchy ground until she reached the hedge, pushed her way through it, scratching herself on brambles and scrambled down the steep bank. She found that there was indeed a lane there. It should lead her to Oaklands, but if they discovered her disappearance before morning, then this is where they would look for her. She must take great care. Listen for any sound of approaching riders!

Sophie started to walk briskly along, glancing around apprehensively as she went. Then whispering a prayer, she started to run, faster, faster, her heard pounding. How long would it take to cover ten miles? Suddenly she heard the thud of approaching hooves and forced herself up the bank and back through the hedge, just as the riders thundered past. It did not occur to her until they had disappeared, that they might be friends searching for her—but surely it was more likely that they were more of Lorrimer's men. She continued to run, this time in the field above the lane, keeping close to the hedge.

Richard Appleby together with his father and brother headed his enraged band of men from the manor together with villagers, as they tore along the lane towards Park House. Within minutes of unknowingly skirting the girl they sought, they were clattering into the courtyard of the old Tudor building, where they dismounted and rushed up the imposing stone steps to the pillared entrance. Richard thundered on the massive oak door. A servant opened it and looked uncomfortably at the scowling features of those who demanded entrance.

'I will see if my master is at home,' the man began nervously, but was brushed contemptuously aside by Richard, who beckoned the others to follow him into the opulent hall of Rupert Mereton's residence. They had an instant impression of ostentatious wealth, rich turkey rugs on the floor, paintings in heavy gilt frames, ornate mirrors and expensive looking ornaments displayed in cabinets and on shelves. The man owning all this had obviously denied himself none of this world's luxuries—no doubt this was why he was eager to obtain Oaklands and its revenues to replenish his overstretched purse, thought Richard.

'What disturbance is this,' cried a strident voice and Rupert Mereton came heavily down the wide, staircase to meet them. 'What intruders are these who disturb my peace?'

'We will disturb more than your peace, Rupert Mereton, should you not at once release Lady Sophie Mereton to us,' said Richard icily. 'Do not seek to deny that you have her! Your fellow Josiah Fitch has obliged us with many details that will put you in the dock, fellow!'

'How dare you come here making such allegation? The woman you mention is certainly not here! Search the house if you wish, after which I will have you charged with trespass and defamation of character!' His pompous cheeks quivered with assumed indignation. He gestured to another man descending the stairs behind him. 'Lorrimer, pray tell these misguided oafs that Sophie Mereton is not within these walls and that we have kept company over a game of backgammon all day!'

'Perhaps not all day, for I also beat you at cards Rupert, dear fellow,' drawled Gerald Lorrimer, his eyes narrowing as he recognised Richard Appleby. 'What do you men do here?' he asked, brushing unseen dust from his velvet coat. 'What is all this about Lady Sophie Mereton? Tell me? Perhaps I may be able to help you in your search, though most likely she has gone to meet with a lover, or perhaps to gather herbs in the forest? There have been unfortunate rumours concerning her, you know. Witchcraft!'At the word Richard leapt at him and caught him a blow on the chin that sent him flying to the floor.

'Why—now I can have you charged with assault,' Lorrimer sneered, as he rose to his feet and rubbed a trace of blood from his lip. 'A farm hand attacking a gentleman, deportation to the colonies, most like!' But ignoring Lorrimer and Mereton, Thomas Appleby beckoned the men to follow him as they spread out, searching every room and cupboard throughout that gracious house, servants pulling nervously aside before the intruders.

'Look whom we have here!' cried Richard, pointing to an individual in faded black velvet trying to sidle away out of sight. 'This is Lance Pendleton, who was spreading ill rumours in the Falstaff Inn about Lady Sophie!' He grabbed the man by the shoulders. 'Can you deny it,' he snapped?

Pendleton shrugged off the other's hands and glanced across at him disparagingly. 'Why should I seek to deny truth? I but repeated that told to me by half the village, that Sophie Mereton involves herself in witchcraft!'

Richard swore in frustration that he repeated such calumny. But he would deal with Pendleton later. For now all that mattered was to discover where they had stowed the woman he loved. Nor was she in this house. Even the attics and cellars had been searched. So where was she?

He took his eyes off Mereton, who took opportunity to whisper a command to Pendleton, who looked startled and started to demur. Then as Mereton whispered a certain sum into the man's ear, cupidity got the upper hand. Pendleton made for the kitchen which had already been thoroughly searched, thrust kindling and flint and steel into a cloth bag and managed to slip out of the pantry door and round to the stable yard.

With the general melee of explosive conversation around the front of the house, none noticed the man who silently led his horse through the garden and orchard, and when a suitable distance from the house, mounted and rode off through the darkening evening fields. It took very little time to arrive at the old game but. Pendleton remained on his horse for a few minutes, before coming to final decision, when he dismounted and approached the door. There was no sound within. Perhaps the woman was still unconscious and surely it was better so.

He placed his hand on the door, about to open it out of sheer curiosity, but hearing distant shouts coming from the house hesitated—then acted. The flint sparked. The oil he had thrown on the old timbered frame of the hut ignited, within minutes flames were shooting up into the evening sky, and he turned his horse away and galloped as though pursued by the furies. He did not wish to hear the woman's screams! Witch or no witch, she had been very fair, a fine spunky wench. Well, there were many others such and without the taint of witchcraft!

He took the roundabout way back to the house, hoping that none had missed him. But those soaring flames were seen by Daniel Dawlish, who was keeping an eye on the horses snorting restlessly in the courtyard. What had caught fire—a stack perhaps? But after some days of rain, this seemed unlikely. What then? He called to Paul Masters as the blacksmith's huge frame issued out of the doorway.

'Paul, there's something on fire over there. Quite a blaze too. You know this area, have you any idea what it could be that's alight?'
Paul Masters came down the steps and stood at his friend's side.

'Yes! I think I do. My guess is that it's the old game hut used much by the Mereton family in past times. A barn nearer the house serves that purpose now it is said!' He stared at Dawlish with a growing apprehension. 'Now why should anyone seek to burn the place down? I'll call Tom Appleby!' But Dawlish was no longer listening. He had heard the noise of a horse whinnying from the side of the house and ran towards the sound.

He saw Pendleton sliding off the horse and clutching a bag, as he turned towards the stable. He called over his shoulder to Masters.

'Here, Paul—be quick!' and he leapt on Pendleton and bore him to the ground before the man could resist. Masters reacted immediately to that shout and was instantly at Dawlish side, staring down at the guilty face of the man who was attempting to roll over and cover the bag he clutched, with his thigh.

Paul Masters, his face puzzled, dragged the man away from the bag, lifted it, saw the flint and kindling and nodded.

'So, we have an incendiary here! But what point to fire an old disused hut,' and then suddenly a terrible thought entered his head. Why would anyone burn down a derelict hut—unless there was something or someone there they wished to dispose of. Surely, it could not be where.....?

'Sophie!' and his voice came out in a strangled shout. He pulled the man to his feet, the great bunched muscles of his arms bulging as he held the man off the ground and saw Pendleton bare his teeth like a cornered rat.

'Was Lady Mereton in that hut? Speak—or I will kill you here and now!' and his hands tightened their grip as his dark eyes blazed fury. Pendleton quailed before that stare. He knew men. This man was deadly serious in his intent. But if he spoke out, then he would die anyway, unless he could maintain that he had only followed orders. But in his heart he knew this to be no defence. Paul Masters lowered him to the ground and now his hands were about Pendleton's throat, choking the life out of him. He relaxed his grip for a brief moment.

'Speak—or you will never speak again!'

'It's true!' the man babbled hoarsely, incoherently. 'The wench is dead, burned—but I was given orders you see—orders!'

'By whom?

'Why by Mereton and Lorrimer!' the last was not strictly true, but what did that matter. He quailed at what he read in their eyes. Then Masters great fist moved and Pendleton crumpled to the ground.

'I'll get Tom Appleby,' cried Dawlish. 'Perhaps there is a chance that.....!' But the two men had seen Pendleton's face, knew it to be a vain hope, and yet? Richard stared at his father and brother in horror at what Dawlish spilled out, his face torn with anguish.

'Dear God,' whispered in a voice shaken with horror.

'Let's go, Richard,' said Thomas firmly to his son. 'Sophie is resourceful and who knows, she may have survived! Harry, you and these others keep Lorrimer and Mereton under guard here until we return! The magistrates will decide their fate! Until then, they remain in your charge!' Harry Appleby rushed back into the house, calling for his companions to lay hands on those guilty of such heinous crime.

Sophie had also seen those distant flames, watched in horror as they leapt high into the evening sky. She knew at once that they came from the hut where she had been incarcerated, and that no doubt the fire had been meant as her funeral pyre.

'Then at least they now believe me dead,' she murmured shakily. 'Perhaps I need no longer fear pursuit, yet what if they find no human remains in that hut once the flames die down.' And she started to run again and as she did so, it started to rain, great heavy drops that soaked her gown in minutes.

That same heavy rain was already beginning to have effect on the spectacular conflagration caused by Pendleton. The men who tore towards it, lashing their horses to faster effort, leapt down and stared in dismay at the flaming timbers now smoking in the rain. Paul Masters, who had tied his iron bar to his horse, now whirled it high against the door with all his force, once, twice. It fell inwards, exposing the burning table—but nought besides. There was no sign of a corpse! Richard pushed Masters aside and ventured in despite danger of the pulsing red walls imploding. He had to be sure.

'She is not here—not dead!' His voice choked in relief.

'Look, down there,' said his father stooping outside and staring by the light of the still blazing structure, 'See in the mud? Two different horses have been here. And here—see, a woman's footmarks leading away from the hut. In that direction I think!' He smiled at his son. 'I think she has escaped them, Richard, bless her brave young heart!'

The men who had helped to capture Sophie on Lorrimer's instructions, had been sitting uneasily in the derelict house on the outskirts of Stokely as instructed and looked at each other as two hours passed.

'What if those two fine gentlemen have played us for imbeciles,' cried one at last. 'They have the woman, now! No need to pay us therefore and we dare not speak out against them on account of the law!' He rubbed his unshaven chin, his eyes darting around his friends who sat on upturned boxes, passing a brandy bottle around. 'What say the rest of you?'

'Why Tim, I suppose you might be in the right of it,' agreed a thickset, curly haired fellow, face flushed with the spirit he had been consuming and a growing anger. 'So what in hell can we do about it? Stay here, Lorrimer said, and we would get what was owing to us---but suppose it slips his memory!'

'You are right, Erick! As for that damned cold fish Mereton, I wouldn't trust him as far as I could throw him—and that not far, great tub of lard that he is!' The third man to speak rose to his feet. 'Look friends, either we stay here until morning, or we ride for Park House and have it out with these fine gents!'

'But what of those from the manor, who were riding to save the wench?'

'No great concern there. Probably either given up the search, or still roaming the through the trees looking! We just avoid the wood, cut across the fields and into the lane.'

'But if we are seen, caught, then the child may identify us! Then there is the old priest. Did that blow you fetched him kill him, if not suppose he also recovers and speaks out?' The thin faced man with a scarred cheek who now intervened glanced around at his friends apprehensively. Tim spoke.

'Look, I say we ride now for Park House. It was the original plan wasn't it and living quarters there better than this place of mould and damp. Let's saddle the horses I say, any sign of trouble we just disperse and meet up here again!'

It was starting to get quite dark now and Sophie stumbled several times on the rough ground, as she tried to keep to the hedge. At last she decided to risk getting down onto the lane again, where she could make faster progress. She was feeling very cold, and although the rain had stopped, her wet gown clung to her uncomfortably. Just as she found an opening in the hedge and plunged down the bank into the lane, she heard the sound of shouts and froze. Men were riding towards her, one swinging a lantern as they came. Oh, let them be friends,' she prayed, for there was no time to escape. To her dismay she recognised the face of one of her earlier captors. He gave a great bellow and was off his horse and before she could turn to flee, had her in his iron tight grasp.

'Not so fast, my lady witch!' he shouted gleefully. 'Look what we have here? She must have escaped Lorrimer and Mereton. Now with her in our hands, we are in position to demand a greater sum for bringing her back to them!' He pushed his face against hers. 'How did you manage away from those fine gents—flew on your broomstick?' The smell of his foul breath and stale perspiration almost made her retch.

'If you let me go, then I will see that my father gives you a fine reward,' she offered.

'Fine reward? The gallows most like for ridding the countryside of his daughter!' snorted Erick dourly. 'Up on my horse before me, and no tricks. I have a knife against your ribs and its kiss is keen!' Then at last did Sophie experience despair. She was pushed up onto the horse by other eager hands, and then they were off splashing through deep puddles along the winding lane, and she knew she was being taken back in the direction of Park House. She wondered if she dared attempt to jump from the horse and grit her teeth in frustration, realising that at the speed they were making, she would probably suffer severe injury.

They had not gone more than a mile than they heard the sound of other horses approaching towards them and pulled up hard on their reins, as almost at once they found themselves confronted by Richard and Thomas Appleby and Paul Masters.

Richard Appleby uttered a cry of amazement and fear as he recognised Sophie seated before Erick Marsden. The man had pulled her head back forcibly by the hair, a knife at her throat, his other arm about her waist, further restraining her.

'Let us pass or the wench dies!' he cried. 'We have nothing to gain by letting her live, and you know it!' Then Richard acted. His knife rose and flew through the air deep into Marsden's right shoulder. The sudden pain caused the man to drop his own knife as he cursed futilely. Sophie finding the pressure released, slid down from the horse and ran towards Richard, dodging other hands that tried to grasp her as she fled. He leaned down from his horse, and swept Sophie up into his arms, as with a sob of relief he pressed his lips against hers, while Thomas Appleby pulled a pistol from his belt and Paul Masters brandished his iron bar.

Now the other men formed a ring about them. They were armed and dangerous. Then Thomas Appleby raised his pistol and shot one of their assailants in the thigh. The fellow dropped from his horse and screamed in pain, as big Paul Masters approached the other riders, swinging his iron bar as he came. Now more shots rang out and Thomas gave a sudden groan as a pistol ball lodged in his left arm. They were three men and a girl against eight ruffians. Richard dismounted, screaming at Sophie to 'Ride—ride!' as he sprang at one of the riders, pulled him from his horse and struck him in the neck. The man fell, did not move. Paul Masters had accounted for two more and Thomas Appleby lifted his pistol and took aim at another.

Sophie did not obey Richard's command to ride. Instead she produced the rusty knife from the purse at her belt, took aim at one of their attackers and threw it. More by chance than skill it caught him in the chest and with a strangled cry he fell forward on his horse, which took fright, and started to gallop back towards Stokely. At this, the last two ruffians turned their horses about to flee the scene.

In all this while, the troop of armed guards dispatched by the King two days since to deal with the situation at Hawksley Manor, now arrived. Their sergeant demanded word with Lord James Hawksley and was instantly shown into the sickroom where James was struggling into his coat, only recently made aware of Sophie's kidnap, and listening in horror to his trembling grand-daughter's words. Shortly afterwards, one of his servants had murmured message quietly in his ear that had further appalled him.

He turned and stared at the sergeant, his eyes distraught.

'Sergeant Bellamy—you are well arrived!'

'My Lord, I am here with a troop of thirty men to deal with those who mounted dastardly attack on you and your small son. Furthermore, the King is concerned for the welfare of your daughter, Lady Mereton!'

'Sergeant, she is taken by those who seek her life. They attempted to kidnap my grand-daughter, Minette—but she escaped them, is safe here, but has told of her mother's capture.' He buckled on his sword belt, wincing as he did so.

'Just tell me all you know, sir! And perhaps I might have word with the little girl?' The story was quickly told by the child and added to by Josh the stable lad. Minette had been attacked on the outskirts of Epilson Woods, her mother seized as she rescued her child. Half a dozen men had ridden after Sophie and not yet returned.

'Are you able to remember the faces of those who hurt you, Minette,' asked the sergeant gently. She nodded, small tear streaked face tense. She knew she would never forget them, or the miracle that had saved her.

'They had horrible faces,' she blurted out. 'I was very frightened and told them my papa who is the King would be very angry with them. They laughed. Then something wonderful happened! '

'What was that, child?'

'A golden cross appeared, shining bright as the sun—and the man was scared, and let me go!'Her blue eyes were bright with awe as she spoke. The sergeant glanced at Lord Hawksley in amazement.

'A golden cross,' he queried. 'How was this possible?'

'Possibly a trick of the sun,' declared James Hawksley smoothly. None of his staff apart from one who had born him here, were aware that a Catholic priest lay gravely injured within these walls, for a priest so found would face imprisonment at the least, possibly death under the law— severe penalties also to any sheltering him.

'So, it seems most likely those villains who have taken the lady, will have carried her to the house of this Rupert Mereton—Park House you named it sir, beyond Oaklands? I know where that is. I think my men and I should be on our way as soon as possible.'

'I will ride with you!'

'Oh no, my Lord!' the sergeant looked at him in shock. 'You are in no fit state yet, although such determination honours you. Besides, you need to be here to keep watch over your young son and Minette! What good will you prove to either of them, if your wound opens again?'

'But my daughter...!' there was anguish on the father's face.

'Leave it to my men and to me, sir! If she is alive, we will restore her to you, never fear!' He jerked a bow and hurried downstairs and Hawksley heard the noise of shouted orders and staring from his window saw the troop of uniformed officers in the courtyard, remount and speed off along the driveway.

'Pray God they may be in time,' he whispered, then bending a kiss upon Minette, turned to Beth Giles hovering respectively at the back of the room.

'Mistress Giles, I pray you take Minette to Jenny. I suggest the little one should be put to bed to restore her strength. Thanks to God, that she at least is safe. Later I must have words with Jenny, discover how the child was allowed to wander off alone to her imminent danger!'

Now only Josh remained in the room, viewing him apprehensively.

'That will be all for now, Josh! Return below and send Master Oldham to me.' Moses Oldham, one of the servants following the old religion, had seen the old priest on occasion when he had made rare night time visits to the manor. On Richard's instructions at finding the unconscious priest, he had carried Father Benedict to the manor, first placing him in a barn, then on hurried words with Lord Hawksley, moved the gravely injured man into the library, placing him on a couch, noting that there was nothing in the man's garb to make obvious his priesthood, the bag containing cross and vessels of his sacred office hidden behind a pile of logs in the wide fireplace.

'Yes, my Lord?' Moses knocked and entered and looked inquiringly at Hawksley. 'What do you wish?'

'Help me down the stairs Oldham, to the library. Then I wish to be alone with our guest. Make no mention of him to any here.'

The library door closed behind Moses Oldham, who had been instructed to station himself outside and prevent any other from entering. Hawksley looked down at the battered features of the priest in pity, his indignation at the perpetrators of such dastardly attack upon a gentle old servant of God causing choke in his throat.

'Father. Father Benedict—it's James Hawksley. Can you hear me? ' He stroked the priest's blood streaked silver hair, then taking up the dampened cloth he had brought with him, gently sponged the bruised face. At last the patient stirred and opened questioning eyes, his relief patent as he recognised James.

'Where am I?'

'At Hawksley Manor—safe! But I must move you to securer refuge than this. Do you think with my help, you can descend the stairs to the chamber you know of?' Afterwards, and Hawksley could never recall how despite his own injuries, he was able to assist the priest across the library, propping him against the wall, as he worked the secret mechanism revealing the priest's hole. Half guiding half carrying him, they descended into this small chamber lit by lamp and candle where Benedict would be safe.

Hawksley then carried the precious bag down, placing it beside the priest's bed, and gave him a glass of wine to revive him.

'Father—I must go! I will return later tonight, but first I have my daughter's safety to attend to.' Father Benedict raised a hand in blessing.

'I will pray for Sophie, my son, that the dear Lord will have her in his tender care. Go now. And a blessing on you for risking your own safety to help an old man.'

Hawksley opened the library door and beckoned Oldham, who was still keeping watch that none approached the library.

'The Father is safe now, my friend. Ask no questions, but he is secure where none will find him. So tell me, when Richard Appleby came across him how many others saw him, realised he was a priest?' He waited the answer in some trepidation.

'I would say about a dozen perhaps. But have no fear, my lord. One of the villains we caught and interrogated said that it was through the priest's efforts the little girl escaped them.'

'She said she saw a golden cross!' exclaimed Hawksley in sudden understanding. 'It was Benedict who saved her?' Oldham nodded.

'So it would appear. He must have known what risk existed to his own life when he did so, and I tell you, whatever those of your men opposed to our faith might feel about priests in general, none will ever inform about one who saved little mistress Minette!'

'Yes, I believe you are right,' agreed Hawksley. 'They are very loyal, every one! But what if the kidnappers reveal his presence when caught and questioned?'

'Who would believe them?' snorted Moses Oldham, his lined face creasing to a smile. 'It will be the gibbet for that scum!' Then his eyes became serious. 'I pray the sergeant and his men will find them before they do hurt to Lady Mereton!' Hawksley nodded. Where was she, his beloved daughter and he uttered up a prayer to heaven, as he hurried off to the great hall, to see if any had returned with news, where to his surprise he saw David Markham and Martha being admitted. They glanced at him in distress and hurried towards him, faces grave. Markham reached out his hand to Hawksley, as Martha dissolved into frightened tears.

'David, you are welcome. You too Martha.'

'James, I wanted to come to you when we heard of that dastardly attack upon you and your son's kidnap. Would have been here earlier, but I was suffering some strange fever that only abated yesterday. Martha has been nursing me for days. We came as soon as we were able. But now hear that Sophie is taken?' he fixed troubled eyes on Hawksley.

'Pray God it is not true,' cried Martha in trembling tones in her turn, her eyes showing her fear.

'Alas it is so. But many of our people as well as a troop of guards arrived from London on the King's orders, are presently searching for her.'

'And how are you, James,' asked Markham, staring keenly at his host. For Hawksley was extremely pale and his face expressed the physical pain he was enduring as well as his intense anxiety for his daughter.

'I think perhaps my wound has reopened, I have been active this day,' he replied calmly. 'Come, I will have refreshments served and tell you all I know.'

'And Minette—how is she,' asked Martha as they were led through to the drawing room opening onto the garden and offered wine and pastries by the housekeeper, who then withdrew.

'She is sleeping now. I must tell you that she also was snatched by men serving Lorrimer and Rupert Mereton, but escaped them in miraculous fashion, as her mother attempted to rescue her, and thus Sophie herself fell into their hands!' He smiled. 'At least we have Minette safe.' They burst into words of relief at the news, tempered by growing concern and anguish at Sophie's unknown fate.

'James, there is blood on your shirt,' exclaimed Martha. 'Pray let me help you!' She looked in concern at the darkening red stain.

'Beth Giles is here, a most competent nurse and if you will excuse me, I will have her tend me.' He rose and left them staring after him, deeply worried about his health.

'I know the room where Minette will be sleeping,' whispered Martha to her husband. 'I am going to see her, will not waken her though—I just want to reassure myself that all is well with the child.' And she hurried off. After a minute's indecision, he followed her.

Jenny looked up in surprise as Martha let herself into the bedroom where Minette lay in light slumber. Every few minutes a tremor passed across her small face and she turned restlessly on her pillows as Jenny raised a finger to her lips. But as though sensing the presence of one she loved, the child opened her eyes and stared at Martha from solemn eyes.

'Minette, my darling child!'

'Aunt Martha—some bad men have taken Mama and they tried to make me go with them too!' Then her blue eyes focussed on the man coming into the room behind Martha. She loved the Rev. David Markham, knew he was a man of God who taught people in church about Jesus. He would understand about the miracle of that mysterious cross! Her murmured story made the couple look at each other in amazement. Surely this tale was a fantasy, unless there had indeed been supernatural intervention in the child's fate.

Martha smoothed Minette's curls back from the piquant little face.

'You do believe me, Auntie Martha?' she asked.

'Of course I do, sweetheart. Now just you go back to sleep again. We will still be here in the house when you awake.' And they stole away, Martha hardly knowing what to believe, while David Markham had sudden thought of his own about what had happened. A golden cross—now who would have one of those in his possession apart from a Catholic priest? If he was right in this, and such a one had sought to aid the child, where was he now? Had he lost his own life in helping Minette?

'Children often have vivid dreams,' murmured Martha as they retraced their steps down the wide staircase. 'This must be the answer.'

'Perhaps,' he said comfortingly, but had other thoughts himself. Hawksley was a known Catholic, even though he attended occasional services at David's church to fulfil the law. And there had been whispers of a priest bringing communion to those few catholic families remaining in the district. He hoped that Hawksley was not putting himself in danger by aiding such a man, although he personally deplored the anti catholic stance of parliament, and considering all men should have freedom of worship.

He made a silent prayer that if a priest had indeed helped Minette, that the Lord would look after him and keep him safe. Then his thoughts returned to Sophie. Where was she now?

In his bedchamber, having suffered the efficient ministrations of Beth Giles, who had exclaimed in dismay at the sight of his newly reopened wound, but dressed it and insisted that he now rest, James Hawksley was also now making silent prayer that his beloved daughter would be found alive.

Chapter Seventeen

The moon was rising behind fitful clouds as Sergeant Bellamy galloped his men three abreast, along the narrow country lane that led to Park House, the trees swaying above their heads casting ghostly shadows before them. They knew they should be within a mile or so of their destination, when they heard the sound of horses rapidly approaching from the opposite direction.

'Halt,' cried the sergeant to his men and with a clatter of harness, they drew up their snorting mounts and paused. Two men were riding desperately towards them, another obviously wounded coming in their wake. The newcomers cried out in fear as they saw the armed force blocking the road in front of them, and tried to turn their horses around. But behind them came Richard Appleby and Paul Masters followed by Thomas Masters, one arm hanging limply at his side—and to the sergeant's amazement, there riding close behind was Lady Sophie Mereton, dirty, dishevelled but alive!

'Detain those men,' cried Richard! 'They would have murdered Lady Mereton, and there are others of their ilk at Park House.' and he gave brief outline of all that had so recently happened, referring lightly to his own efforts and that of the others.

'Thank God all is well with your ladyship,' cried the sergeant in relief. 'Don't worry about those villains who committed this outrage, I will see all are arrested and brought to justice. We are sent here by the King himself!'

'We will ride with you then,' cried Sophie.

'Not so, Lady! You will return to your father's house under safe escort. These brave friends of yours shall come with me and identify the rogues we are after!'

'No. I want to see them arrested for myself,' she cried, but Richard leaned towards her and took one of her hands into his.

'Listen Sophie, you have been incredibly brave. But now is the time to be sensible as well. Just think how worried your father and little Minette must be. Go now, dear heart,' and he lifted her hand to his lips and kissed it. As he did so for a split second, she looked back at him uncertainly, then urging her horse even closer, leaned and offered him her lips.

'I think I love you, Richard Appleby,' she whispered softly.

The sergeant detached four of his men to accompany Sophie and watched as they disappeared into the night. This part of his mission at least was successfully accomplished. Now for the perpetrators of this evil. But first he ordered one of his men to have a care of Thomas Appleby's arm. The bullet had passed right through it and the wound would need cleaning as soon as possible, but a hasty dressing was applied.

Now they were off and as they passed, Richard pointed out the smouldering ruin of the game hut, still glowing red in part, that should have been Sophie's funeral pyre. The sergeant swore.

'Onwards,' he shouted. 'Let's at the swine!'

Waiting uneasily in Park House, Dawlish and Harry Appleby and the men from the manor, had herded Mereton and Lorrimer with Pendleton and those others who served them, into one room where they held them under guard. They had not heard any news yet of Sophie's fate nor whether Paul Masters and the Appleby's were safe, and guessed that sooner or later Mereton's other thugs would inevitably arrive here and that they would probably face further fighting. Then so be it!

At the sound of those hooves thundering into the courtyard, their faces stiffened with resolve. Then a great cry went up, as Richard flung open the heavy oak door with exultant shout.

'She is safe! The King has sent men to our rescue and to deal with those thrice damned malefactors,' cried Richard, as great cry of jubilation rose up.

'Hurrah! Hurrah—and now to deal with this lot,' they shouted as the guards piled through the great hall and into the reception room where the owner of Park House awaited them with insolent face.

'Are—officers of the law,' he cried. 'You are come in good time to arrest these men who have dared to enter my house and abused me and my servants. Have them in irons, my friends!'

'And you are.....' asked the sergeant?

'Why, Rupert Mereton, owner of this property and this is my good friend Gerald Lorrimer, who has also suffered at the hands of these rascals!'

'And I am Sergeant Jack Bellamy, here in the service of the King and to arrest those who have dared to lay hands on Lady Sophie Mereton!' and he advanced on Mereton.

'And that fellow is Pendleton, he who put light to the hut in which Sophie was supposed to have burned to death,' cried Richard, pointing at the man who shook in sudden fear.

'I only did what I was told, my masters,' he began. 'They said she was a witch, should be burned and the child dealt with. I only obeyed orders, sirs!' At his words, Lorrimer turned pale. He pointed at Pendleton with accusing finger.

'I was not party to any such order to burn the woman,' he began indignantly, but Pendleton merely continued to babble, every phrase more incriminating than the last, until pausing and looking at Lorrimer, he stared and said. 'Maybe you did not order the burning, but were prepared to go through with it—even tied the woman up yourself in that hut!'

'I think I have heard enough. That will do nicely,' announced the sergeant in satisfaction. 'Many have witnessed the words of this man. Have them in chains, men and then ride we for the jail in Stokely where they shall be secured until I have further orders concerning their disposal!'

Sophie rode between her armed escorts, now totally exhausted. Her heart was full of conflicting emotions. Relief that she had avoided death in such terrifying form, anger at those who had mistreated her, combined with certain knowledge that the prayers she had uttered in her despair had been most wonderfully answered.

Then too, there had been that moment of sudden arousal as she had given Richard Appleby her kiss. But he was younger than she and her heart belonged to the King. Or did it any longer? And so she rode, becoming uncomfortably aware of a pain that gripped her abdomen—and she knew what it betokened. She was losing her child. There was still a mile to cover and she uttered a slight moan.

'Is all well with you, Lady,' asked one of the guards.

'Not really, just get me to Hawksley Manor,' she whispered. The man was married, saw the way the girl held one hand across her stomach and guessed the cause, woman's problems. They could stop, but surely it was better to get her to her father's house where there would be women to have a care of her. She gritted her teeth. At last the horses came to a halt before the pillared entrance to the manor. One of the men lifted her from the horse and carried her up the steps, knocking and calling for help from those within.

It was Martha who came to the door and gave great cry of relief as she saw Sophie in the guard's arms. Then she noticed Sophie's face contorted in pain and indicated the man should place her on a cushioned wooden settle in the hall. Having done so, Martha told him to take his companions to the kitchen for food and would speak with him later.

'Thank God you are safe, my darling! Are you injured—have those brutes hurt you?' Her worried eyes swept over the girl. But Sophie shook her head.

'I need to lie down in my bed, Mama. I think I am losing my baby,' she whispered. Before dawn broke, her fears were justified. She had indeed lost the little life she had been carrying and although the logical part of her brain suggested that perhaps it was better so, her mother's heart ached at the thought she would never hold her babe in her arms. A great sense of desolation swept over her as she fought back tears and tried to smile up at Martha who was holding a glass of cordial towards her.

'Drink a little, my darling. Then we will tidy you up, for your father wishes to see you—and I think you must go to him, for his wound has reopened and he is in fever.'

'Father—is ill?'

'All I can tell you is that he insisted that David helped him down to his library last night. What the two of them wished to do down there I have no idea. Later, much later I saw David helping James back to his room, where Beth Giles took over his care, scolding that he had been so foolish!'

'Ah—Beth is here? I will go to father, examine his wound, but Beth will have done all that is needful.' She sighed in relief. 'And Minette?'

'Longing to see you. Not quite her happy small self yet, very subdued. Thank the dear Lord that you got her safe away from those wicked men. I must tell you that she speaks of miracle of a golden cross that terrified the men and made them let her go!' Martha shook her head, while Sophie stared at her in surprise.

'Such a night we have had,' continued Martha, her comely face showing tiredness of a night without sleep. 'First the joy of your safe return and the worry of your condition. Then Richard arrived with his father and the others together with a company of the King's guards who had taken those responsible for your kidnap to Stokely jail. So many men! I had them bedded down in the barn. And now the sergeant is asking to speak to your father—and to you!'

'Tell him I am not yet ready to speak to anyone,' said Sophie, then relented. 'But I suppose I must, for without his help I might very well be dead now!' and she told of the letter and golden pomander she had dispatched to the King.

'First I want to see Minette, and then go to my father.'

It was Jenny who brought the little girl into Sophie's bedchamber. For a moment she just stared at her mother now sitting on the side of the bed in a loose gown and with a cry of pure joy, threw herself into Sophie's arms.

'Oh, Mama, my dearest Mama! They were going to hurt me—but there was a wonderful bright golden cross!'

'A golden cross, sweetheart?'

She looked at the child incredulously, but Minette just continued, 'I feared those wicked men would kill you, mother! But Richard saved you, didn't he!' Then she burst into choking sobs. 'It was my fault, because I went after my pony when he ran away!'

'The real fault was mine, my lady,' admitted Jenny shamefacedly. 'I was caring for her, and fell asleep.'

'Take her to play with little Henry. I must go to my father, Jenny. I know you will never let her out of your sight again.' And that was the only rebuke she gave. Then leaning on Martha's arm, she made her way along the landing to her father's room. It was still early, only eight in the morning, but James was out of his bed, face flushed with fever and sitting in his comfortable leather chair, where Beth Giles was tending his hurt. His face brightened in extraordinary way when Sophie appeared.

'Sophie, child! They told me you were safe returned and my prayers answered!' He held out a hand to her and she hurried to his side and kissed him, pressing her face against his. He looked at Beth.

'Mistress Giles, I would be alone with Sophie for a time. She will finish dressing this annoying wound of mine.' He smiled kindly at Beth, who inclined her head, just giving a warm smile to Sophie, as she left the room.

'Is it true that you have miscarried, Sophie dearest?'

'It is true.'

'Then I am heartily sorry. But you are very young, one day there will be other babes.'

She did not reply but examined the wound that was suppurating slightly. 'How did this come about? You were almost healed—before all this horror took place!' She opened the bag she had brought with her and extracted a bottle of amber liquid, which she gently applied to the wound, as he exclaimed at the smarting it induced. 'Now Father, you are to drink this,' she said authoritatively. He did not question the potion she offered him, but swallowed it down obediently.

'That should reduce the fever and bring relief of pain,' she said. 'Now tell me how you managed to reopen your wound?'

'To do so, I must put the life of one very dear to me in your hands, even as I did in those of David Markham last night.' He watched her face carefully.

'Father—Martha tells me that David took you down into the library last night. That when you came back you were in much pain from your wound. So what was so important that you ventured there in the dead of night?'

'We were in the priest's hole, Sophie!'

'But why—why there at such a time?'

Can you not guess? Because I am harbouring one such as that secret chamber was made to protect—a priest!' and he smiled gently. She looked at him in shock.

'A priest here—at this time?

'Richard made no mention of him to you?'

'Why—no!'

'Nor Minette of a golden cross? Father Benedict was hiding in Epilson Wood waiting for nightfall to make visit to me for he had heard I was wounded, when he suddenly saw Minette in the hands of the villains who later seized you. He raised his cross up high and stepped forward from his cover, and in shock at suddenly seeing the cross blazing where the sunlight caught it, the fellow who held Minette let her go and in her own words, she ran very fast!'

'So she saw the priest?'

'Her only memory is of that golden cross!'

'But he saved her life! What happened to this Father Benedict then? I saw no sign of him. I was knocked unconscious when they seized me on the outskirts of the wood.'

'They beat him, brutalised him. Had been about to cut his throat when they heard Richard and his father and those with them approaching towards them. They panicked and made their escape.' He paused to take breath.

'Richard saw him lying unconscious on the ground, recognised him and sent one of the men Moses Oldham carry him back here, who did so putting him in an outhouse. I told Oldham to bring him into the library, and while this good man kept watch outside the door, I managed to revive Benedict and helped him down into the safety of the priest's hole—where he still is.'

'So that is why your wound opened up again?' Tears came into her eyes. 'Oh, Father, what can I say, except that I am very proud of you, and that you could not have done other than you did for this man who saved my little daughter.'

'I know you are not of my faith, Sophie, but I can tell you that Father Benedict is a very wonderful man of God.' He tried to get up from his chair, wincing as he straightened. 'Now listen, Sophie. I had to reveal the secret of the secret chamber to David, as I feared Benedict might die, and although not a Catholic priest, I thought David Markham might bring comfort to a dying man.'

'So you trusted him, father. Well I am sure you will never regret it. I just know he will tell no-one of what he has seen, not even Martha!'

'He said as much. Now I want to go down to see Benedict again, but I know there are many of the King's guards around and must be careful.'

'Sergeant Bellamy is asking to speak with both of us!'

'Then better get it over with. But be circumspect in all that you say!' He looked at her, his dark eyes serious. He did not have to spell out the danger they would all be in, should it come to light that they were harbouring a priest. She nodded, then clutched onto the back of his chair as she felt her head swim.

'You are faint, child? You should be abed, I was forgetful of the fact that you have just miscarried—the pain.' His face was troubled, but Sophie forced a smile and kissed him reassuringly.

'We are a fine pair are we not! I think we will ask the sergeant to meet with us up here, for I consider risk of your wound reopening too grave for you to attempt the stairs!'

The Sergeant entered and bowed before Lord Hawksley and turned a glad smile on Sophie, sitting pale at his side.

'My Lord—Lady Mereton, I give you good morrow,' he said warmly. 'I am come to give you details of what is proposed to be done with those who perpetrated such outrage upon all in this family! I speak of the your wounding, my lord and the kidnap of your son Henry. Then this most recent outrage upon this lady and her small daughter. I am pleased to tell you that I am to conduct all the perpetrators to Canterbury where they can be more safely imprisoned, the jail in Stokely a poor affair, not meant for the incarceration of so many at one time!'

'There will be a trial there, Sergeant?' asked Hawksley.

'Why yes, indeed there will my lord—and if you want my opinion, the whole lot are for the gallows!' and he smiled his satisfaction.

'They are certainly deserving of it,' declared Hawksley feelingly. 'If released they might once again attempt hurt to my daughter, who is in state of exhaustion after all she has experienced.' He looked compassionately at Sophie. 'She should be resting.' he said feelingly.

'True, my lord and I will be brief! I have to return to the King who will be waiting to hear the outcome of his orders.' He paused, then looked not directly at Hawksley but somewhat above his head, as he continued, 'However, there is one point I would like to lay before your lordship, regarding a certain Catholic priest, whom the man Josiah Fitch admits they planned to kill. Seemingly the man had intervened when they had young Minette in their hands and through that intervention, the child escaped.' He paused and glanced quickly from one to the other, then away again, clearing his throat noisily.

'An incredible story, Sergeant Bellamy! All know Catholic priests are proscribed from teaching in this country, the laws against which being strict. Why then should a priest put himself at risk in such way?' Hawksley spoke in measured tones. 'A fantasy invented no doubt like the accusation of witchcraft against my daughter, for their own ends!'

'I'm inclined to agree with you, sir,' replied the sergeant carefully. 'However, this Josiah Fitch says he observed the priest put on a horse by a man from your estate, to be taken to safety at the manor. The point is, if Fitch and his villainous friends should speak of this in court, then it might sound awkward for you, my lord, as it is known that you are of a Catholic family.'

'So what is it you are implying sergeant?'

'Why only that if with your permission, my men were to search your house and outbuildings, then I could state that the man was definitely not in hiding here!'

'You insult me, sergeant!'

'Such is not my intention!' He reddened under Hawksley's stare and squared his shoulders. 'Do I have such permission?'

'As you wish. I have nothing to hide in this respect, so please make your search and be careful not to frighten the women or children!' Then Hawksley smiled. 'You have done a great service to me and my family and for that I am truly grateful!' he added graciously.

'There are no words to express that gratitude,' put in Sophie. 'You have been absolutely wonderful, Sergeant. I shall tell his majesty so when next we meet!' and he thawed under her sweet smile. 'Why do I not come with you, show you around the house. It is a rambling old place, it should help I think!' She walked towards the door, and bowing to her father, he followed her.

She found that a dozen of his men were assembled below in the great hall. They raised a cheer when they saw Sophie, and she raised a hand back in greeting. 'It would seem that there is a rumour that a Catholic priest is harboured in this house,' she announced daringly, 'And I am going to help you prove that such is not the case!' It was at that precise moment that the Rev David Markham descended the stairs and looked around inquiringly. He was wearing his clerical black gown and white bands and came forward and kissed Sophie on the cheek.

'It is good to see you looking better, but you should be resting' he said quietly. 'What is happening here?'

'I think your presence has been mistaken for that of a Catholic priest,' said Sophie innocently, as she gave him her hand. The guards looked at each other and grinned.

His appearance there also relieved the sergeant. He remembered this Anglican minister, whom he had met at Oaklands after conducting Sophie back from London. What better proof that no Catholic priest was here, than to have the minister of the village church present. He smiled relief. The brief inspection of the manor that followed was accompanied by good humoured banter from the men and indignant glances from Hawksley's staff.

The outhouses and barns were also inspected and no priest found cowering in hiding. If the sergeant had his own lingering doubts, born of Minette's tale of a mysterious golden cross, he now dismissed them. What mattered was that he would be able to diffuse any future allegations of a phantom priestly guest at Hawksley Manor that might arise in the future. He and his men were given a splendid meal before they departed to collect their dismayed prisoners from Stokely Jail and convey them to Canterbury.

Sophie stood on the front steps with Martha to watch their departure, then closed the door and sank wearily into a chair, and breathed sigh of relief.

As for the sergeant, he hummed under his breath as he rode, for Sophie had given him a note to the King, applauding both his behaviour and that of his men. There had also been a certain heavy purse.

'Now you must return to your bed, sweetheart,' instructed Martha firmly. 'Come, lean on my arm,' and she led her upstairs to her bedchamber and nothing loth, Sophie lay down and fell into troubled sleep. She slept for twenty-four hours, awakening morning of the following day to see her father smiling down at her, wearing a brown velvet mantle and moving with ease.

'Father—your wound?'

'Whatever it was you put on it, all inflammation has gone and it heals well,' he said heartily. 'Your knowledge of medicine is proving a true blessing, dear child!' he bent and kissed her. 'If you feel well enough to rise, then there is someone below who wishes to speak with you. I refer to Richard Appleby!'

She blushed under his stare and shook her head. 'I am not sure I wish to speak with Richard yet, except to thank him for his rescue of me!'

'Why, what else,' was his careful reply. 'Beth Giles is waiting without to bring in your breakfast. Perhaps later you might wish to speak not only with young Appleby, but also with his father and brother. We also owe much to blacksmith Paul Masters, Daniel Dawlish and quite a few others!'

She nodded thinking of the courage of all those he mentioned and what her fate might have been without their brave and determined rescue.

Beth fussed about her while she picked at her food, then once bathed and dressed stared into the oak framed cheval mirror, as she settled the folds of her full burgundy skirt that still felt tight at the waist.. Her blue eyes were shadowed, her face pale, and yet no wonder after all that had happened, but strangely that feeling of deep loss experienced on losing her child, seemed to have receded—in fact, she felt almost as though her miscarriage had not occurred, mental refusal to face up to the truth she thought, and sighed.

She walked slowly down the stairs at her father's side and smiled to see an expectant crowd waiting for her in the great hall. David Markham and Martha hurried forward smiling encouragement, but before she could speak, Minette broke away from Jenny's restraint and rushed into her arms, small face beaming.

'Mama! Mama—you are well again?' she demanded.

'Yes, I am indeed well, my darling,' and she kissed her. Then, as she glanced around at the faces of those who had rescued her from certain death, she poured out a message of gratitude in simple words that were both touching and powerful with meaning.

'Our whole family give thanks to God for your devotion and care,' she concluded, 'And I give note that we will be having a feast to celebrate this good outcome!' Then she went from one man to another, making personal thanks to each. Finally, she found herself facing Richard Appleby. He bowed before her and looked at her searchingly.

'Richard, there are no words to thank you,' she said simply.

'None are needed, my Lady,' he replied formally. His eyes slid down to her waist and she guessed he had heard of her miscarriage. 'My duty and love are always yours to command.'

'Where is Thomas, I do not see him here?'

'My father's wound would seem to be infected. He is in his bed and asks forgiveness for not attending this morning.' She saw the worry in his eyes.

'Why wasn't I told sooner? Take me to him, Richard!' She turned and called to Beth Giles, asking that she should bring her medical chest. Then minutes later, as people dispersed to take up their usual tasks, Sophie followed Richard to the cottage just beyond the orchard that was home to Thomas Appleby.

Sophie stared at the grossly swollen arm in dismay. It was obvious that the pistol ball had gone through above the elbow, the wounds of entrance and exit ugly, the surrounding area red and tight. At least the bone had not been shattered, but infection had set in. Thomas Appleby smiled at her, gritting his teeth as she worked on the arm.

'Tom, I have cleaned it. You must leave this dressing alone until I come again. Do not attempt to use the arm! Here, drink this. It will help you to sleep.' She lifted a glass to his lips and watched as she saw the opiate relax the pain he was in. When she was sure he was comfortable, she turned to the door. Richard held it open then accompanied her back through the orchard, carrying the small medicine chest. The light wind that had risen rustled through September's golden leaves, as they walked slowly together, each bound up in their own thoughts. At last Richard spoke.

'Sophie—I heard Mistress Markham speaking with her husband—and know that you have lost your child. I just want to say that I am desperately sorry that such is the case. I pray you will forgive my previous reckless offer of marriage to you, only made to help in the matter of the babe!' As soon as the words tumbled out, he saw the hurt on her face and could have bitten his tongue. But he knew that now there was no need whatsoever, for her to look to one of his station as future husband.

'Then if that was your sole reasoning, then let us forget the offer ever made,' she exclaimed and snatching the chest from him, hurried on towards the house, sudden tears starting to her eyes. He stared after her perplexed. He had thought she would be at ease with him, once she realised he no longer expected anything of a personal nature between them.

Martha saw Sophie arrive back in the hall calling that she was going up to her room. Then she noticed Richard enter, walking slowly with lowered head and doleful expression. She supposed they had quarrelled and whispered quietly to her husband who smiled and took Richard aside, as Martha mounted the stairs behind Sophie.

'How does Thomas Appleby,' she asked following her into her chamber.

'His wound was infected—I imagine a pistol ball carries much dirt with it, which causes the inflammation. I have done my best for him,' and she sighed. 'If only we understood exactly what causes infection?'

'So that is why you are sad, child,' she said as she seated herself next to Sophie on the bed and seeing traces of tears on the girl's face.

'What else, except as you would expect pain in the loss of my baby!' and she lowered her head with a sob. Martha placed a comforting arm about her waist sensing there was more, and decided to probe further.

'Perhaps the time was not right for the precious babe to come into this world,' she said sympathetically. 'At least now you need not worry about a rushed marriage of convenience, to Richard for instance?'

'As he him-self made clear today! Why should he think I would consider marriage to him I wonder! It's laughable! Charles Stuart is the only man in my life!'But the hurt in her voice carried its own message.

'Sophie, you have a fondness for Richard I think,' she said slowly and rose to face her. 'He is a fine and honourable young man and one who would always love and be true to you.'

'But who told me he withdrew his offer of marriage since I am no longer pregnant,' exclaimed Sophie angrily. Then Martha bent and kissed her.

'Do you not see—he thinks only of what is best for you, not what he wants! Think about it long and hard, Sophie. He would lay his life down for you, loves you dearly, and little Minette is very fond of him. But like all men he has his pride and fears rejection.'

She sat for an hour on the bed after her aunt had left her, trying to analyse her feelings and to face a future that suddenly felt very bleak. Did she really want to return to the court with all its intrigues, enjoy the occasional lovemaking of a King whose amorous glance ranged lazily to any pretty face. True she would always enjoy a special friendship with him and as mother of his child, a place in his heart, as would others though. Would it be enough? She knew the real answer was—no.

But what of the future if she decided to remain here in her father's house, or eventually return to her own home at Oaklands? Would she ever feel truly safe again, knowing that people had actually been swayed by those foul rumours of witchcraft instigated against her? Suppose such should start again? She shuddered. Then the terrors she had experienced in that game hut assailed her again. Would she ever forget Lorrimer's leering face, his ultimatum of marriage to him or the fierce embrace of flames—or the mocking shouts of his men who blocked her escape on that wet road, the thug who grabbed her and held knife to her throat? Then that nightmare road home, knowing that she was losing her child.

And now vision of Richard's face as he came to her rescue, spun before her eyes. She remembered the kiss he had placed on her hand, the expression in his eyes, her own response as she had recklessly given him her lips. And at last she realised the truth. Yes she did love this man. Not as she loved the King it was true, but with something more delicate, truer and yes, strangely exciting. But did he truly love her, for she was a few years older than he. Her thoughts continued in turmoil as she sat there, then lifted her head as a tap came at the door.

It was Richard. He stood in the doorway, looking at her, an unfathomable expression in his eyes.

'Come in,' she said shakily. He glanced towards the bed and smiled.

'It is not fitting,' he replied quietly. 'But Sophie, I would speak with you if you permit. Perhaps we might go into the library. Your father is there and awaits us.' Then he reached out a hand to her. She rose and took it. Then as though it were the most natural thing in the world found she was in his arms, his lips on hers, as suddenly they strained together. He released her, a look of wonderment in his eyes.

'Can it be true—that you have feelings for me?'

'Yes. I love you, Richard Appleby,' she said softly.

'Then Sophie, will you do me the honour of becoming my wife?' Again they were in each other's arms. He held her to him tenderly as she whispered her response and as she did so, knew how right it felt.

Hand in hand they made their way down the stairs and into the library. There they found not merely her father, but David Markham and both the older men smiled at them.

'I see that the question I would ask is not necessary,' said her father, noting her flushed face and Richard's bright eyes. 'Richard has formally asked permission to propose marriage to you Sophie. I told him the answer must come from you alone. Am I right in assuming the question has been asked—answered?'

'Yes, father! We love each other, but I need time to think of marriage. So much has happened all so traumatic!' He looked at her understandingly.

'But of course, and preparations to be made!' and he kissed her, as did David Markham in his turn.

'Now Sophie,' said Hawksley quietly, 'there is another here who would like to pray a blessing on your engagement. I speak of the man who saved Minette's life at risk to his own, of Father Benedict!' Firstly he locked the library door, then walked over to the far corner of the library to section of books in the Latin, where he placed his hand under the fourth shelf down until his fingers were in contact with the carved hawk's head that when turned, set secret hidden mechanism in motion, revealing the steps leading down to the priest's hole. Richard watched incredulously.

'You are a part of my family now, Richard,' said Hawksley sternly, 'What you see must be disclosed to no-one!' and Richard inclined his head obediently. Hawksley stood before that dark opening, lit by candlelight.

'Father Benedict,' he called. 'Can you manage to ascend the stairs unaided?' Then he leaned forward and took the hand of an elderly, silver haired man, helping him up out of his hiding place.

The priest blinked for a moment as he stepped into the light of day once more and glanced around at those staring at him, with a gentle smile.

'Why James, you must introduce me,' he said quietly. 'David I now know and feel sure that this young lady is your daughter. She is so like her lovely mother, to whom I married you so many years ago. '

'You married my parents,' exclaimed Sophie wonderingly.

'Why, yes my dear. Your mother was a beautiful and very courageous young woman, the marriage I blessed during the civil war, one of true love. I was much saddened to learn that she died soon after giving birth to you. Indeed none knew that you had survived.' He turned his eyes on Richard, questioningly. He looked familiar.

'This is Richard Appleby,' she said quietly, and Richard bowed and the priest smiled remembering that he had on occasion noticed this young man when making his dangerous night-time visits to the manor. 'We are to be married,' she continued. 'I am not of your faith Father Benedict otherwise it would have given me much pleasure for you to have officiated at our future wedding.'

'Well at least I can bless your future union,' declared the old man with a smile. He raised his hand murmuring words in the Latin tongue. Then, as Sophie and Richard suddenly knelt before him, he placed a hand on each of their heads. 'May the blessing of the Father, Son and Holy Spirit be with you now and always,' he said. They rose and looked at each other shyly. It was as though a newer, deeper bond now existed between them.

Father Benedict now listened as Hawksley explained all that had so recently happened, the careful search of the manor by the King's guards, who were lulled into lack of suspicion by David Markham's presence and the priest smiled and reached out a hand to Markham.

'Surely this is how our dear Lord would have wished us to behave,' he said quietly. 'It is true manner of our belief and customs differ, but how much more does our joint faith in the lovely Lamb of God draw us together.'

'I pray that one day all men may have the right to worship God in the way that seems right to them,' replied Markham fervently. 'Surely in heaven there will be no separate compartments for Catholic and Protestant?'

'Perhaps we should all drink a toast to that,' exclaimed Hawksley. He went to the cabinet where he kept brandy.

'To religious tolerance,' he cried and the five of them lifted their glasses. Then he turned to the priest.

'Now my dear old friend, I fear I must ask you to return to your hiding place until I can arrange safe escort for you to those who await you in Mistledene. I will bring food to you later and more candles, and new apparel to replace that torn by those fiends who attacked you.'

'Bless you, James my son,' replied Benedict. They watched as he descended into the dark mystery of his hiding place and saw the bookcase slide back into position. Then Hawksley unlocked the library door, and allowed them to file out.

'I will never forget him.' said Sophie softly to her father. 'I will always treasure the fact that the wonderful man who married you to my mother has blessed my future union with Richard.'

Two weeks sped by. Hawksley made arrangements for the priest to leave in the safety of a moonless night and now his presence in the secret place was mere memory. A message had arrived from the court that the King wished to see Sophie. Previously such a summons would have delighted her. Now she sent message back that she was unwell, would come later. In the meanwhile, her engagement to Richard was source of delight to all at the manor, especially to Thomas Appleby.

Thomas walking now with Sophie cast a thoughtful look at her. He had been told she had miscarried of the King's child, but she had a certain look about her? Should he mention it—after all, she was his future daughter-in-law.

'It might be an idea for you to speak with a midwife,' he began tentatively.

'What do you mean,' she looked at him in astonishment.

'Forgive me, lady, but for one who has lost her babe, you look as though, well......!' he struggled to go on, blushing red with confusion.

'I lost my child,' declared Sophie angrily. 'Perhaps I need to watch that I do not indulge at table, since you think me fat!' She walked swiftly away, tears smarting in her eyes. But that night as she undressed, she looked at herself in her mirror, then placed her hands over her abdomen. Surely it could not be, that was impossible. There had been no slightest mistake in that she had lost her babe—but then why....?

'Father, I wish to visit Oaklands,' she said.

'Is that wise? Hopefully all of those involved in your kidnap are now safely awaiting trial. But if you insist, then at least take Richard with you!'

'No, I will ride with David Markham and Mama—and you can send a few men to escort us.' She smiled. 'I prefer to know that Richard is watching over you and little Henry—and Minette, for I will leave her here in Jenny's care. I only intend to stay there a few days!'

Back in Oaklands it felt as though she had not been away. Martha and David had stayed overnight and then returned to the vicarage. A houseful of staff to wait on her, but she felt very alone for the first time.

She wandered into the library and sat in Gareth's favourite chair and thought of the future. Now she was Lady Mereton, but soon she would be plain Mistress Appleby. And suddenly she knew that this did not really matter. A title and all that went with it did not really lead to any particular happiness. In fact now that she was to marry Richard, all those at the manor seemed delighted at her choice. She shook her head. He was only a boy when first they met, not yet fourteen—while at sixteen and near womanhood she had regarded him as a child.

The second day she arose knowing what she must do. Before marrying Richard, she must know the truth about a womb bereft of her child, but which still felt otherwise. She would visit Mistress Annie Saunders, but first she must eat. She sat down at table and toyed with her food, then sighed and rose restlessly to her feet, her lonely breakfast almost untouched. A young maid stepped forward and curtsied, as she made to clear the table.

'It's Sarah, isn't it? Would you ask Lottie Lynden to come to me?' She walked over to the window, thinking of Lottie who had been wet nurse to her little brother Henry and had then married her bailiff Jack Lynden.

The young woman appeared and looked at Sophie with an inquiring smile and Sophie noticed that the girl was with child, Jack Lynden to be a father.

'Ah Lottie, tell me does your grandmother still live in her small cottage?'

'Why yes, my lady. She continues to be much used by mothers in the village and although troubled by arthritic knees, manages to get around.'

'I remember her service both to me when Minette was born and then when my father's small son came into the world. All was so difficult then in the tragedy of Lady Hawksley's death. I do not think I ever thanked her properly for her kindness. I intend to visit her!'

'She would be that proud to have a visit from you, my lady. I will ask Jack to accompany you to the cottage, we have all heard of the terrible events you have been through. You must take great care you know. Never go anywhere alone!' Her rosy face flushed as she spoke, wondering if she were wrong to advise Lady Mereton.

Accompanied by her bluff faced bailiff, Sophie dismounted and smiled at the man. 'Perhaps you would watch my mare and see that none disturb us when I speak in private with Mistress Saunders.'

'None shall intrude on you, I will see to that,' he replied. He watched as she approached the cottage door and knocked. Old Annie Saunders seemed untouched by the years, still a full head of soft silver hair and wise dark eyes that swept over Sophie in consideration. Women usually only came to her door for one of two things, either to confirm a pregnancy or ask help to end it, which second she had always refused to do.

'Why Lady Mereton, I wish you a good morning,' she said as she ushered Sophie into her tiny sitting room. 'How may I help you?'

'Why first of all, I would like to give you this,' said Sophie and handed the old lady a parcel which when opened revealed a beautiful black lace shawl.

'This is for me,' asked the woman wonderingly.

'A gift in recognition of all you previously did both for me and for my late mother-in-law and should have been given sooner.'

'You paid me generously at the time,' replied Mistress Saunders. 'But this shawl is the most beautiful thing I have ever owned!' She looked up at Sophie. 'So how is it with you, lady? I heard that you miscarried when those villains attacked you.'

'You know?'

'Little remains a secret in a village, my dear.' She glanced at Sophie appraisingly. The girl's waist no longer slender, fuller of breast—so how?

'Mistress Saunders, I lost my child—miscarried but strangely the signs of pregnancy have not disappeared.' She looked at the old midwife with pain filled eyes. 'Am I going mad that I still feel pregnant?'

'Perhaps not, my dear. But first of all I must ask some questions and examine you.' Some twenty minutes passed and now Sophie sat in a chair opposite the old lady looking at her in near disbelief.

'You say that I really am still pregnant? But I definitely miscarried. No mistake about that!' Her blue eyes expressed bewilderment.

'You were carrying twins, my dear. You lost one—the other survives!'

'Twins? I had never considered such possibility! And yet it makes such sense.' A smile broke across her face, and she leant forward and squeezed the other woman's hands. 'Thank you, for this most wonderful news!'

'The father will be pleased,' ventured Old Annie?'

'I am pleased,' was the reply.

She rode back to the house almost in a dream. But then as she made for the privacy of her bedchamber confusing thoughts came crowding into her head. What now of her marriage to Richard? Would he on reflection still be prepared to father a child not of his own making, a royal bastard? And as she sat on her bed brooding this most astonishing turn of events, she knew that all would be well, for Richard Appleby loved her with a deep and unselfish love, and just as suddenly she realised that she no longer had feelings for Charles Stuart, but loved Richard with a tenderness and sense of excitement that made her long to give herself to him.

It was during the afternoon that Martha came on a visit. She noticed a change in Sophie, who was sitting staring dreamily out of the window across the grounds. Why, the girl looked almost radiant.

'Sophie, I wanted to be sure you were coping well on your own. After all that happened I felt concerned for you.' Her eyes swept over Sophie, trying to understand the difference she sensed, before she bent and kissed her.

'Mama, I am very well indeed! It seems that the babe I miscarried was one of twins. I am still pregnant, must make plans for a small brother or sister to Minette!' Her blue eyes shone with happiness. Martha gave a gasp of surprise.

'What makes you think that this is so,' she asked carefully, thinking Sophie was suffering some strange delusion born of despair at her loss.

'I visited Mistress Saunders this morning. She tells me there is no doubt I am still with child, the only explanation that the babe I miscarried of was one of twins!' she took Martha's hands. 'Come, won't you say you are glad for me?'

'Why yes, it is astonishing news! Since this is so, perhaps you should make preparation for your marriage to Richard as quickly as possible, for you must be three months at least now.' Martha's mind started to explore practicalities. They sat together for an hour discussing matters. Then Martha rose to her feet. 'I must return to David and let him know he will shortly have a marriage to bless,' she said.

Sophie was escorted back to Hawksley Manor by her bailiff and two other men from the estate, all armed and alert to any disturbance. But they met with no-one along the road. Her father welcomed her back with open arms, saying his wound had almost healed and that Thomas Appleby also was about again. He listened to her news with shock.

'The wedding must take place and soon,' he said firmly.

'I will speak with Richard first, for now there is a child to be considered, I must make sure he is still of the same mind,' she replied, ''

'Trust me, he will be,' said Hawksley. 'Now I know he is of yeoman stock, but he is a fine young man whom I believe loves you dearly, and has proved his worth in your defence! Apart from that—I like him!'

Richard came to her in the library where she sat staring unseeingly at a book. He opened his arms to her and instinctively she rose and went into them, and felt his lips exploring hers as she opened her mouth to his kiss. His hand went to her back pressing her even closer sand she felt evidence of his rising passion, knew her own arousal would brook of no delay unless she drew back, and she did so, both of them gasping.

'Wait Richard! There is something I must tell you!'

'Sophie, your father has already explained that we are soon to be parents,' was all he said. 'How amazing that you still are carrying a child, despite losing its twin. Surely the little one who has survived so much will be truly blessed!'She looked into his eyes, saw the love there, the understanding and she swallowed. She raised a hand and stroked his wavy reddish hair back from his forehead.

'Thank you for those words, Richard. But I think I must tell you, that when Gerald Lorrimer had me at his mercy in that game hut and threatened to burn me alive if I did not marry him, I told him I was bearing a child to the King, hoping thus to save my life. Now he may speak of this at his trial, and already spoken of it to others. We may not be able to keep the secret of the child's origin. How would you feel if the news was made public?' She looked at him searchingly.

'Why, that the babe of our marriage, will be mine indeed, and I would challenge any to dispute it!' His eyes flashed as he spoke and she nodded, satisfied. He was about to take her back into his arms, when he paused.

'Listen Sophie, there is nothing I want more at this moment than to feel you naked in my arms, my heart over yours, so that we become truly one. But I want our marriage to mean something special. '

'You want us to wait?'

'For our wedding night, Sophie!'

'I honour you for it,' she said softly. 'But go now, otherwise I might not be strong enough to allow it!' He pressed one more lingering kiss on her lips and walked swiftly away.

The wedding arrangements were soon made, and two weeks later closely followed by an excited little Minette and Henry, Sophie walked up the aisle of Stokely church on her father's arm to stand beside Richard, who was looking handsome in a new dark green coat and breeches, with white cravat at chin, tawny hair brushed back from his forehead. He gave a gasp of delight when he saw his bride, for Sophie looked very fair in her pale cream gown sewn with seed pearls, a wreath of cream rosebuds on her flowing chestnut hair.

David Markham smiled at the couple as he gave his final blessing and Sophie looked down almost disbelievingly at a different ring on her finger. It was actually happening, this marriage which until that moment had not seemed quite real. She half glanced at Richard and their eyes met and his hand sought hers, caught her to him in a gentle kiss. They were husband and wife, the future before them.

Congratulations abounded and the couple climbed into the Hawksley carriage for return to the manor and the celebrations which would follow.

The guests had gone as had the musicians who had entertained, servants busily clearing up the remains of the wedding feast in the flower decked hall, as James Hawksley took his new son-in-law aside.

'I charge you to care for my daughter well, Richard. Never betray the faith I have put in you,' he said firmly, then pulled the younger man to him in a hearty embrace. 'Go to her now,' he said and lifted a hand in salute and blessing.

Sophie awaited her new young husband in her bedchamber. How different this wedding night would be to that she had experienced with Sir Gareth Mereton, a marriage to an elderly man and strictly in name only. She stood back from her long cheval mirror and stared dreamily at her image. She was wearing a nightgown of the finest and sheerest white silk, a gift from the King but never worn, nor did she even think of Charles as she stood there, hair loose on her shoulders, only a slight thickening at her waist revealing her approaching motherhood.

'Sophie—my darling wife!' He had entered quietly and stood looking at her in delight. Then he opened his arms and she came to him.

The sheer white nightgown lay discarded on the carpet, as Richard took his bride. And Sophie gave herself joyfully, naturally when following their love play he entered her and they strained together in an ecstasy—and it was like nothing Sophie had experienced before, this throbbing, pulsing, all consuming passion as she gasped her climax and felt his own rush of release.

They lay quietly together in Sophie's four poster bed relaxing, whispering endearments and looking wonderingly at each other in the pale light of the flickering oil lamp, as the crackling flames of logs burning in the fireplace, cast dancing shadows. Then his lips and fingers brought her to new arousal as she passionately returned his caresses—and it was nearing dawn before they finally slept.

When they came shyly to the breakfast table the following day, Lord James Hawksley looked from one radiant face to another and relaxed. All was well, his daughter was happy in this union. He had worried that perhaps it would prove just another shell of a marriage, for the sake of the unborn child. But just looking at them, he glimpsed their joy in each other, a joy such he had experienced with his wife Madeleine and breathing a relieved sigh he raised his glass 'To you my children—and to the future—may it bring great happiness!'

For two ecstatic weeks the couple grew closer together exchanging some of their deepest thoughts and setting aside any doubts as to the rightness of their marriage, for Sophie still wondered how Richard would react when the King's child would lie in her arms. But Richard made it plain that when the babe was born he would always treat it as his own and hoped that they would provide the little one with brothers and sisters.

Then two messages were delivered to Hawksley Manor. One was from the King, again requesting Sophie's presence. The other notification brought by an officer of the Canterbury court, stated that regrettably one of the malefactors awaiting trial for the attempted murder of Lord James Hawksley, his son Henry, his daughter Lady Mereton and her child Minette, had escaped custody by feigning sickness, then violently attacking the prison guard and slipping away amongst visitors to the prison. This man Gerald Lorrimer would be arrested on sight, but in the meanwhile all at the manor should be aware that this dangerous man was at large.

Sophie sat staring out of the library window her thoughts troubled, as her husband Richard and her father discussed what best to do. Careful watch to be kept over the children at all times nor must Sophie venture outside the manor without a guard. Of course Lorrimer might make no further attempt on any of their lives, but a man with nothing to lose and only the hangman's rope to look forward to, vengeful, spiteful and violent might indeed prove a threat.

At last Hawksley came to a decision. They would all make a visit to Westminster, bringing the two small children and Jenny to care for them, and taking two carriages for the journey. Sophie was in any case bidden to see Charles, who was as yet unaware of her marriage. This would give her opportunity to speak quietly with the King explaining her new situation and bringing to a close her previous involvement with him.

'You are happy to take this course, Sophie,' asked Richard and she nodded. She did indeed need to speak with Charles. She also hoped that he would meet Richard—would understand. Also there at Whitehall they would all be safe from any fresh attack by Gerald Lorrimer, who would hopefully be arrested by the authorities during their absence.

The two carriages bumped and jolted between hedgerows bright with the splashed scarlet of hips and haws and frosty curls of old man's beard, trees showing Octobers gold and coppered touch and mist drifting across close shaven fields. Pretty villages, towns and then Sophie breathed a sigh of relief as London's skyline came in sight. Wherever Lorrimer was, she would be safe here!

Richard looked around curiously, as they drove along the cobbled streets on outskirts of the city, then as they drove further on, glancing appalled at the desolation of charred, blackened buildings stretching as they were told for over a mile ahead, with beggars at every street corner—but here and there was evidence of new building, scaffolding. But now the carriages were clattering along an area of fine buildings and Sophie pointed out the palace of Whitehall, before they came to a halt in the lane leading to the small house she still held from Ann, Duchess of York.

The house smelt slightly musty and Sophie went from room to room opening windows. Now the weather was colder, the smell of the Thames was bearable but still unpleasant and Richard who had never visited the city before wrinkled his nose somewhat at smells not encountered in the countryside, whilst Jenny busily comforted the two fretful youngsters who were tired and hungry. Soon however Sophie and Jenny prepared a hasty meal glad they had brought provisions in the last small town they had passed en route. Bedrooms were decided on, Sophie and Richard on the first floor, the children and Jenny in the neighbouring room, with James Hawksley in one of the two attic bedrooms.

Mrs Chandler, Sophie's previous efficient daily cook housekeeper knocked at the door the next morning.

'I heard you were back again, my Lady,' she said. 'And I wondered if you needed my help again?' Sophie greeted her with relief. She had thought the woman might have left town after the fire like so many thousands of others. But it would seem that people were starting to return, those with money setting about rebuilding where possible, the King much involved with future planning of the new city envisaged as rising out of the ashes.

Then a message came. The King had been informed of Lady Mereton's return and would be graciously pleased to meet with her on the morrow in his library. Sophie informed the page of her acceptance and slept restlessly that night at Richard's side, considering how she would conduct herself.

His library, where they had so often met amongst the books she so loved, it was here that Sophie in a blue court gown, now tight in the waist, her chestnut hair swept high on a Spanish comb, blue eyes tense awaited her monarch. An hour slipped by and she thought he had forgotten their meeting, was perched on a stool, studying the yellowed pages of a book, in faded Latin script when she felt his gaze upon her. He stood watching her indolently, one hand resting on a bookshelf, as his gaze sped over her, his eyes pausing as he noticed that fullness at her waist. He drew in his breath.

'So you are returned to me, and if I mistake not, carrying new gift of our love? Sweetheart, why did you not send word?' He held his hands out towards her. Still she made no reply.

'Come to my heart, my dearest Sophie! How I have missed you!' To his surprise she did not come towards him but rose from her stool and inclined her head gravely. But of course, she had endured much trauma since last they met, kidnapped by those villains soon to face justice, had almost lost her life, and as he realised that of his child! No wonder she looked solemn.

'It infuriates me that you suffered such abuse by men soon to pay for it with their lives!' He walked to her and took her hands in his. She stared up at him calmly, without emotion. And as he looked down at her hands, he noticed the ring, not that of her late husband Sir Gareth Mereton.

'What ring is this, Sophie?'

'That of my husband, Richard Appleby, whose wife I became just over two weeks ago. He saved my life, Sire!'

'Richard Appleby? I do not know the name—of what degree is he?' His eyes darkened, his lips pressed close together in annoyance as he loosed her hands.

'Richard Appleby is son of a yeoman farmer Thomas Appleby who manages my father's estate. Richard rescued little Henry, and also saved my life at great risk to his own....'she began. He interrupted her.

'I can see you would be grateful to him, will see he is well rewarded— but did you have to wed the fellow?' he exploded in ire.

'We love each other,' she said gently. 'He will care for the babe I expect as his own. Please say that you understand, Charles. It was not planned, this love we have found for each other. I thought I could never care for any as I did for you. But this life at court is not for me. I have never really fitted in here you know.' Tears were gathering in her eyes and he sighed, could never resist a woman's tears, and gently drew her to him.

'Sophie, my dearest girl, what can I say but to wish you joy! Now come with me, away from this world of books, where we will discuss your future and that of Minette and the child to come.' She walked beside him along the endless corridors, many courtiers glancing curiously at them as they went, pausing in their conversations to stare at Lady Mereton and to note that she would seem to be pregnant.

He led her into his study, a place full of clocks and strange gadgets, maps and a globe and hand written documents. He held a chair for her to be seated and stared down at her.

'Now tell me all that happened since you left London following the great fire,' he said and seated himself on the side of the desk, one long booted leg swinging back and forth. And Sophie poured the complete story out, and his jaw dropped as he heard the whole terrifying saga she and her family had experienced, swearing a string of oaths as he sprang to his feet. He stared at her and shook his head, thick dark brows knitting together angrily.

'I can hardly believe such monstrous happening! I thought the sergeant I sent to your aid exaggerated in his account, but it seems he was sparing of the truth!' His face was troubled.

'He would have spoken only of what he himself saw,' replied Sophie. 'Nor can I speak highly enough of Sergeant Bellamy and his men. Had you not sent them to my rescue the outcome might still have been—difficult! But it was Richard's bravery and that of his father and friends that saved me from death.'

'And also it would seem your own good courage!' he declared feelingly. 'But what was that you said about a miscarriage, for you are obviously with child?' And he listened in silence as she explained that she had been pregnant of twins, and had lost one precious babe. Again he swore and then brightened. He had already fathered several children to his mistresses, although sadly his wife Catherine would now seem to be most definitely barren. So another child was pointer to his own virility, besides which he had much affection for his children.

'I need time to think on all these matters,' he said now quietly. 'I will send word when I will meet with your father and your husband—and look forward to holding my little Minette in my arms!'

She rose to her feet and curtsied in confirmation of the newer, more formal relationship between them.

'I will always hold memory of all that has been between us in my heart,' she said softly. He took a step towards her, but a flash in her eyes restrained him.

'If I can do anything for you at any time,' he said.

'Well—you can make sure that Lorrimer is recaptured!' and she quickly explained her present concern regarding the man.

'I did not know of his escape. I promise you he will soon be in irons,' he said and with that he held the door open for her.

A week passed and no news arrived from the palace and Hawksley spent time taking Richard to see those parts on perimeter of the city that had escaped the earlier hellish conflagration. Then one morning the sun broke through the clouds that had brought days of rain and Sophie suggested they should take the children to walk in the Green Park.

'What is it, my love,' asked Richard, for Sophie had stopped walking and was standing very still. He glanced around and saw a tall man in full black wig crowned by an extravagant feathered hat, wearing a suit of burgundy velvet trimmed with gold approaching them, flanked by an entourage of subservient courtiers.

'It is the King,' she replied. As she watched, Charles held up his hand and his companions drew obediently aside. He walked slowly over to Sophie and Richard, but before he could reach them Minette recognised him and ran into his arms. 'My Papa—my Papa,' she cried and her fashionable brimmed blue hat matching her skirts, fell to the ground releasing her tumbled ringlets as he swung her around, and she covered his face with kisses.

'You have not forgotten your father, then my Minette?' he inquired softly, his moustaches brushing her cheek.

'No Papa! I will never forget you—I love you,' she replied blue eyes widening in surprise.

'But I hear that you have a new father,' he said, glancing towards Sophie and her husband.

'Oh no, that's just Richard,' she exclaimed and suddenly he roared with laughter. He beckoned to the couple and also to James Hawksley following behind with little Henry.

'Ah, Sophie! I think it be time I was introduced to one my daughter names as only Richard! Perhaps we should do something about such situation?' His dark eyes creased with merriment.

'My husband, Richard Appleby, Sire,' said Sophie steadily, as Richard flushed and bowed before his monarch, who had also been his wife's lover.

'Majesty?' He stared back serenely. And Charles regarded him narrowly, sizing him up, noting that strong, handsome, honest face and bright hazel eyes which held his own gaze without flinching. Yes, this was a real man he decided reluctantly and would seem worthy of a woman he esteemed differently to all others, his little physician.

'So, Richard Appleby, your wife speaks highly of you and of the courage you have shown in her defence and that of her family.' He paused and beckoned to Lord James Hawksley who approached and joined the couple and bowed to the King who looked at him in quick sympathy.

'James! I was much distressed to learn of your injury and close brush with death—and the outrage done on your little son! Are you recovered now, my friend?' His eyes examined this old friend.

'Perhaps still a certain stiffness still, Sire!' He touched his breast. 'But Sophie's medical knowledge saved my life, while my son-in-law Richard rescued Henry from the clutches of the brutes that snatched him. Young Minette also suffered outrage at their hands, and as for Sophie she will have told you of all that so dreadfully befell her, that those rogues would have burned her for a witch!'

'And I understand it was you saved Sophie from those fiends?' inquired Charles, directly speaking to Richard. 'I also know that she has given herself to you in marriage—that Lady Mereton has become Mistress Appleby?'

'To my joy this is so,' replied Richard fervently.

'But not remain so, my friend!' Richard stared back at him from troubled eyes. Did the King intend to cause annulment of their marriage?

'Kneel, Richard Appleby, my good servant!' Richard did so glancing up at the King questioningly. As for Charles, he drew his sword and lightly touched the shoulders of the young man kneeling stiffly before him.' Now, Arise Sir Richard Appleby, knight!'

As Richard rose unbelievingly to his feet, he fixed incredulous eyes on the regal figure standing before him. Could it be true? He saw from the faces of those around him that it was. He took the king's hand and raised it to his lips. 'Majesty, I am your true servant for all time,' he said quietly.

'One thing I require of you, Richard!'

'Anything, Sire!'

'Have a great care of Sophie your wife—and of my daughter Minette!' It was no request, but order and Charles eyes were stern.

'I promise she will always be safe with me while I have breath in my body! As for Minette I will love and care for her as my own, as I will with the child we expect in a few months!' As Charles met the younger man's gaze, he nodded, knew that this man would not betray his word.

'One thing more, Sir Richard. You will need land. Now I know the villain Rupert Mereton has no living heir, his estate in any case forfeit to the crown for his murderous intents. Accordingly I have made arrangements you should receive title to the house known as Park House and its estate. These legal matters take some weeks to implement—but my word is proof enough for you to begin making arrangements for your new home!'

With a final smile at them and a pat on the head for little Henry Hawksley and a parting kiss for Minette, he sauntered away. And as she saw him depart, Sophie knew that he was walking out of her life—and that it no longer mattered. She was free of her past, the future beckoned.

Next week they would return to the country.

Chapter Eighteen

They had returned to Hawksley Manor and great was the excitement of all to learn of Richard's new title. His father was overjoyed and clapped him on the back, as his brother Harry added his own congratulations.

Hawksley took Thomas Appleby on one side. 'Tell me, has there been any word of the escaped felon Lorrimer?' he asked seriously.

'No, my Lord—nothing. Possibly the man may have died in a ditch or fled north, or even taken a ship for France!' Thomas grinned disparagingly. 'He would know better than to venture back here,' was all he said, but his eyes spoke their own fierce message.

'I hope you are right! There was something of the fanatic in the man!' He paused then, 'We still do not know what became of his Uncle, Sir Mark Harrison?' Thomas shook his head.

'No. He's still wanted for murder—may have died a few years back, else someone would have heard of him! Forget the pair of them, my Lord!'

'It's James to you now Thomas, after all, our children are wed and we are family.'

'Why then, James it is, sir! Now I was thinking that perhaps I would take Richard and Harry to have a look at Park House, if it's to be home for Sophie that is?' He looked at the other inquiringly. 'It's not a bad house as I remember it,' he said.

Hawksley gave an exclamation of dismay. He had thought that the young couple might stay on at the manor, and in any case, Sophie still had her own residence Oaklands, held in trust until her daughter's majority!

'Possibly Sophie may always look on that place with horror,' he suggested now. 'Just consider what memories she would always have of the house?'

'But she wasn't actually held in the house, just in that game hut!'

'Well, go and look the place over, but I suggest no hasty plans to move in,' said Hawksley firmly, and although, Thomas was still intent on riding over to view his son's new property, he nodded his understanding. None of them would ever wish to cause further upset to Sophie.

The Appleby's returned late that night, having spent most of the day examining Park House and starting to clear the debris left there resultant on the confrontational events that had taken place following Sophie's abduction. Richard shook his head, as Hawksley questioned him as to his feelings on the place.

'I had a sense of evil there,' he said quietly. 'To my mind, that house needs a thorough cleansing, floors scrubbed of blood and wine stains, walls repainted—but it's more than that, I feel we need a man of God to say prayer there. As I say, I had a sense of evil of the place, would not wish to live there as it is!' His face expressed his unease.

'Well said, Richard!' Hawksley heard him in satisfaction. 'Certainly all this can be attended to in time to come. We should in any case await the legal documentation the King will send. I know his gift is to ensure the future of Sophie's future child.' He saw Richard frown at his words.

'When our child is born, I will always see it lacks for nothing,' he said quietly. He had put strong emphasis on the word our—and Hawksley smiled.

'Well spoken, my son,' he replied.

The weeks sped by. Late October's bronze and gold replaced by wet November's steady and unrelenting downpour, the fields waterlogged. Then came severe frosts and when Christmas day dawned, they awoke to a world of sparkling white, every branch of every tree glittering ice, the grass and hedgerows shimmering under the thin bright December sunlight.

The previous week Richard and Sophie at last left Hawksley Manor, with Oaklands to be their interim home, plans for Park House still uncertain for as her father had guessed, the very thought of the place held a horror for Sophie. No matter how much work was done to cleanse and repaint it, she would always remember it as the headquarters of those who had planned to burn her alive. Richard had patiently pleaded with her to at least ride over to see it as it was now. So far she had refused.

It was planned that James Hawksley and little Henry should join them at Oaklands for Christmas dinner, together with Thomas Appleby and his son Harry, Daniel Dawlish, Paul Masters and Beth Giles, all first attending a service held in Stokely village church by the Rev David Markham. Martha had taken over the care of Oaklands during Sophie's earlier absence and Sophie had found all running smoothly now as usual under her Aunt's efficient management.

'What do you think,' asked Martha now, stepping back in satisfaction as they viewed the holly, trailing ivy and fir boughs they had been arranging.

'How beautiful the hall looks,' cried Sophie, 'I love the evergreens tied with those bows of red ribbon! It reminds me of other Christmases here.' And for a moment she remembered Gareth's joy in similar decorations the day before his death. She realised she could at last think of her elderly late husband with lingering affection, all trace of previous resentment on that arranged marriage now gone.

'Are you happy, child?' asked Martha gently.

'Wonderfully happy, Mama! The love Richard and I feel for each other is something I never thought to experience!' And she did look radiant thought Martha fondly. Who would have thought that the young boy who had idolised Sophie, when they first they had met, at the time she had fled the cruelty of Roger Haversham, would have grown into the fine, tall, handsome young man who had earned the respect of all.

'Where is Richard now?'

'He rode at daybreak to view the alterations to Park House, said he would proceed from there directly to Stokely church and that we should take the carriage.'

'Time then to go, Sophie! See here is Jenny with Minette. How lovely the child looks in that cape and bonnet! Blue suits her well, as it does you too, my love.' Minette ran to them, new French doll clutched in her arms.

'May I take her to church, Mama?' she pleaded, holding the doll towards Sophie, who smiled and agreed.

'See that you do not play with the doll in church then, but listen to the sermon attentively,' said Sophie as she bent to kiss her little daughter. So it was that the two women together with Minette and Jenny climbed into the carriage and set off for Stokely. The driver flicked the horse with his whip and its breath steamed into the cold air as they set off at a fast trot. Almost instinctively Sophie stared at the place where this same carriage had overturned on another Christmas day, bringing death to Sir Gareth Mereton. She gave brief short shudder as they left the spot behind.

The church was already full of worshippers who smiled and bowed as Sophie came in with Martha and Minette, Jenny following. Sophie stared at her empty pew. No sign of Richard yet, but her father had arrived with young Henry and others from Hawksley Manor. Candles were alight on the altar, the church decorated for this special Feast of the little Christ Child's birth, as David Markham appeared and lifted a hand in blessing.

Where was Richard? The service began, the lovely old hymns sung fervently by those who remembered only too well the banning of such during the Commonwealth. Hawksley frowned somewhat as he noted Richard's absence. He had heard that his son-in-law had ridden over to Park House—but why could he not have waited until later, when Hawksley and the others could have accompanied him?

Sophie tried not to feel frustrated at her husband's non appearance on this special first Christmas service of their marriage—men! She sighed.

David Markham was just pronouncing the final blessing, when the church door was flung noisily open and a man staggered in along the aisle, to crash down his full length as he almost reached her, his hand extended towards Sophie, and that hand was red with blood!

People screamed. Sophie rose horrified from her seat, and rushed trembling towards him, and plumped down on her knees, turning him over face uppermost.

'Richard dear heart—you're wounded!' There was no reply. She realised he had lost consciousness, hastened to remove the bloodstained brown jacket, tearing open his white lawn shirt to reveal his injury, and saw a bullet hole below his shoulder and the wound was pumping blood. Now her father was at her side, bending down to assist her. Around them people cried out in mixture of fear and sympathy, glancing uneasily towards the door, wondering if the perpetrator was outside.

'Is he dead?' called one man.

'No,' replied Hawksley, 'but will do better if we have peace to treat him!'

Then the Rev David Markham called reassuringly to his congregation as he shepherded them out of the door, where they quickly dispersed, shocked at such occurrence on occasion of the special service of praise to the new born Prince of Peace.

Sophie ripped a long strip from her white silk petticoat, tore it in half, made pad of one portion and secured it over the wound. 'We must get him to the manor, but he must be moved very carefully!' Her eyes were steady despite the anguish she felt, knowing his life was in her hands. She hardly noticed that another's hands had been guiding hers. Thomas Appleby knelt at her side, his face grim as he realised the seriousness of his son's injury.

'Let me help you.' Now Martha was there as she and her husband stood ready to assist, with two small frightened children staring down in horror.

'Martha! Take Jenny and the children to the manor. Try to comfort them,' she whispered. Somehow the men managed to get Richard into the Hawksley carriage, and Sophie sat with him with his head on her lap, one hand applying extra pressure over his wound. Behind the carriage rode Richard's father and brother, Daniel Dawlish and Paul Masters, their hearts consumed with thoughts of vengeance on whosoever had shot the young man all loved.

They had laid him on the kitchen table, where Sophie bent over him a probe held firmly in her fingers as she examined the wound. The pistol ball was lodged between his ribs, one of which was broken and she knew she must exercise great care that the broken ends did not penetrate the lung. But that small lump of lead must be removed. She glanced at Thomas, who was at her side, staring down at his son.

'It has to come out,' she said.

'Do it, lass—and God be with you,' was his tense reply. The minutes crawled by, an hour passed. Then it was finished. The bullet meant to kill Richard Appleby now lying blood covered in a saucer. Sophie positioned a dressing over the wound, bound it into position and lifted her head and smiled shakily at Thomas and her father who let out joint sigh of relief.

'I wish he would regain consciousness,' she said quietly. 'I have done all I can, now nature must do the rest,' and her voice broke on a sob.

'And God,' said another comforting voice, 'Let us leave all in His mighty hands.' So saying, David Markham led her over to a chair. He noticed that Sophie was deathly white, knew the tension she had undergone was not good for the child she carried. 'A glass of wine, Sophie, come, you need it.'

She drank a glass of fine burgundy and found that it helped. She closed her eyes for brief moment and on opening them, saw that the men were preparing to lift Richard from the table, decision having been made to take him through to the library not risk carrying him upstairs to the bedrooms. She cried out to them to take great care, and followed anxiously.

He lay unconscious for six hours, it being almost eight in the evening before he finally opened his eyes and attempted to lift his head. He looked around bewildered to find himself lying on an old leather couch in the library, and seeing Sophie smiling down into his eyes. Then the pain smote him and he groaned.

'Richard dearest—do not attempt to move.'

'What happened?'

'You were shot. We do not know how or when! But you came into the church and collapsed.' She stroked his hair soothingly. 'I will give you something for the pain, but it will make you sleepy. So do you think that first, you can tell me what happened?' He nodded and his voice was no more than whisper.

'Lorrimer,' he said. She looked down at him in shock.

'Did you say—Lorrimer?' He nodded and tried to continue in panting breaths.

'I arrived at Park House, had just opened the main door, when I saw two men staring at me—from the end of the hall.' He closed his eyes as the pain in his chest burgeoned in intensity. Then he made new attempt to speak. 'Lorrimer—swore—raised a pistol. The man beside him sneered at me, encouraged the other to shoot. It was Mark Harrison!' She tried to restrain her cry of horror, and patted his hands reassuringly.

'Well done. Now take this draught, my love, and sleep!' He drank it down, attempting a smile, love and trust shining in his eyes, and drifted into sleep. Sophie rose to her feet. She covered him with a fine wool shawl and walked away on quiet feet. Beth Giles was waiting anxiously outside the library.

'Stay with him, Beth. He regained consciousness but is sedated.' Then she went in search of her father, heard raised voices and found him with the other men in his study.

'Sophie! How does Richard? Is he awake yet?' James Hawksley rose to his feet and held a chair for her, noting the weariness on her face—and something else, expression of new shock and outrage.

'It was Lorrimer who shot him, Father! And Mark Harrison was with him, both of them in Park House when he arrived there.'

'Are you telling me that Richard mounted and rode all the way from Park House in that condition? It beggars belief he had that endurance!' Hawksley stared at her in amazement that turned to swift fury. 'I will take men there to deal with those fiends and believe me, Sophie they will wish they had never been born!'

'Father, let Thomas and the others go. I need you here with me—in case all should not go well with Richard. Nor would I feel safe with only the servants in the house.' She knew his wound was but newly healed, could not risk new trauma. And he nodded grudgingly. Thomas and Harry glanced at each other grimly. They looked at Dawlish and Paul Masters who rose to their feet with them.

'Leave those scoundrels to us, Sophie,' exclaimed Thomas. 'Very soon such foulness will no longer infect the earth!'

'Be careful, Tom! Take men from the estate with you. Those devils may have others with them,' she exclaimed, thinking of a previous time when Lorrimer had managed to engage landless men from somewhere.

'It's my guess they will be long gone,' said a quiet voice. David Markham spread his hands. 'We have yet to establish whether they attempted to follow Richard, when he mounted and rode from them with a pistol ball in his chest! If they realised he had not fallen dead at the roadside, then they might guess he would make his way to Stokely—that retribution would come swiftly. They would hardly have stayed there where the deed was done!' He paused as a low rumbling sound was heard. 'What was that?'

'Only a clap of thunder! Must be a storm threatening!' said Harry.

'Wherever they are, we will find them,' ground Thomas Appleby.

'When you do, let the law deal with them,' exclaimed Markham. It was then that a thought struck him. 'Perhaps you should check that all is well at Oaklands as you ride. It is after all on your way!'

'Oaklands? They would never dare...'began Sophie and as the words left her mouth she paled, remembering that short time back her father had actually been attacked right here in what would have appeared the safety of the manor. She pushed her chair aside and wandered nervously over to the study window, stared out into the night. And as she stared, she thought she was hallucinating, that she saw flashback of the great fire that had consumed London, for leaping flames filled the skyline, soaring upwards in fierce red and orange glow—and those flames could only be coming from Oaklands!

'Father, come here! Oaklands—tell me it is nightmare?' Her face was devoid of colour as she looked at him beseechingly. He was instantly at her side, the others pressing behind him.

'In Heaven's name, it is Oaklands! The house is on fire!' cried Hawksley in horror. 'Now indeed I must ride with you Thomas! David, you remain here to care for the women!' And before Sophie could remonstrate, men rushed out of the study and minutes later Sophie heard the sound of horses' hooves clattering into the night. For a long moment she remained at the window, watching those flames destroying her daughter's inheritance, as David placed a comforting hand on her shoulder. It was then that they saw Martha, at the door, face full of concern.

'Whatever is going on, child?' Not waiting for an answer, she turned to her husband. 'David! Have all gone mad here? As I was coming down the stairs, I saw the men rush through the hall and out into the night!'

'Mama, go to the window,' was all that Sophie whispered. And Martha did so, frowning impatiently, then gasped at what she saw!

'Oaklands?' All colour drained from her face. 'That can only be Oaklands on fire!' she sank down into a chair, staring up at them unbelievingly.

'Yes, Mama, Oaklands is on fire, and had Richard not been brought here to the manor to save his life from his wound, then we should all have been there at Oaklands this night to have celebrated Christmas! Family, friends—all!' Sophie had only just considered the true enormity of what had obviously been planned as their fate. David stared at her, taking her meaning.

'What of the servants there, all those dear people who have given their lives to Oaklands? Pray God they have escaped! If this be indeed the work of Lorrimer and Harrison then the toll of their crimes is enormous!'

'Should you not ride there husband, see if any need spiritual comfort?' she said quietly. He shook his head in frustration

'Would that I could! But James has placed all in the manor under my protection and that of the stable lads. Consider too that those who have fired Oaklands may try to assail us here!' As he spoke, Martha descended into a flood of frightened tears. He placed his arm about her. 'Hush, my dear. We must remain calm. Sophie, do we have any weapons here at the manor that may help us in case of attack?'

'Come with me,' she said and led them to a cupboard beyond the hall, where Hawksley kept small store of swords and pistols. She lifted a sword and thrust with it experimentally. 'Father taught me to fence,' she said quietly. 'I am also a good shot!' She turned to David. 'As man of the cloth I suppose you have no knowledge of such?'

'There you are wrong.' He replied and selecting a pistol, primed it and gave it to Martha. 'Hold it so when needed—should we need to defend ourselves, we must all be ready!' Then he armed himself with sword and pistol as Sophie pounced on a musket standing dusty in a corner, as she did so, Beth Giles came hurrying towards them.

'Mercy me, Sophie!' her eyes sped over them in shock. 'What is happening?'

'Oaklands is on fire and we suspect Lorrimer, that he may come here with others,' replied Sophie. 'How does Richard? You should not have left him!'

'I came to tell you that his fever has broken and his forehead feels cool to the touch! It's early to be sure, but I think he will recover, knew you would wish to hear it, my dear! It was strange I almost sensed the presence of another in the room!' She nodded reassurance to Sophie. 'Now what is this of Oaklands?'

'Go to the nearest window and see,' she waited as Beth did so and hurried back to them, her face horrified.

'Why it looks as though the whole house is on fire—terrible, terrible,' she gasped, hand placed to her throat.

'It is. But knowing Richard is recovering, makes all else seem to pale into insignificance,' replied Sophie. 'Do you know how to use a pistol, Beth?'

'No, but if you were to show me!'

And now they waited, not knowing what to expect, all peering from the ground floor windows overlooking the drive, whilst in their two small bedrooms above stairs, Minette and Henry, shocked by Richard's wounding, had fallen into troubled sleep, unaware of any fresh danger, and watched over by a nervous Jenny who had been alerted to the situation. Others of the female staff were preparing food for the men on their return, all turning fearful glances from the windows at the conflagration painting the sky scarlet.

The explosion that had rocked the Oaklands caused the central stairway to collapse and was responsible for the deaths of two of the maids and left Joan Pyke with a broken arm where a falling shelving unit in the kitchen felled her to the ground. For a moment in time there was silence—then terrified screams arose as men and women preparing for the arrival of

Sophie and her family for the long planned Christmas dinner, picked themselves up and stared in horror at the flames now sweeping towards them.

Bailiff Jack Lynden took charge. The main stairway had gone, but the narrower backstairs still stood and down this several people descended, faces blackened eyes wild with fright and joined them in the kitchen.

'Lottie, this was no accident,' Lynden murmured to his wife. 'Where is our son Paul?'

'With my grandmother—in her cottage.' faltered Lottie.

'Good, he will be safe with Mistress Annie Saunders.'

'I want to go to him!' cried the young mother. But her husband shook his head.

'Best not. I need you here to prevent further panic. And Mistress Pyke needs help with that arm of hers. Let's get water on those flames. Perhaps we can save part of the house at least!' But as he spoke there was the sound of another explosion and ceilings collapsed and smoke and dust choked those who stood trembling in shock.

'Let's get out of here,' cried Lynden then. Lifting Mistress Pyke up in his arms he started forwards. 'Come Lottie—all of you. Make haste or we die!' And running almost blindly in the direction of the outer kitchen door that led into the courtyard, the frightened occupants fled from the burning house to gather in small group outside at a safe distance, staring in almost disbelief as the lovely old Tudor building became an inferno.

Then it was that a shot rang out—and then another, as the servants realised they were being fired upon. Was there no end to this night of horror! It was Ellen, one of the maids who fell at one of those first shots and glancing down at her, Lynden realised she was dead. They would all be in like case if he didn't take action.

'Round to the stables,' he cried and staggering under the weight of Mistress Pyke, glanced to see the others followed him. There they found the horses snorting and screaming their terror at the heat and smoke, as Lynden opened their stalls and let them rush off into the night, sweeping riderless along the driveway past the group of arsonists who stood laughing and gloating at the success of their design.

The distraction seemed to work. The shots had stopped and now the bailiff swiftly led the frightened group through the orchard to a small building used to press the apple harvest into cider. They let themselves in and sat on the wooden floor in the dark, listening fearfully, the distant roar of the flames still vibrating in their ears.

Then they heard a different sound. Bailiff Lynden opened the door cautiously and ventured out, bidding the others to bolt it behind him. Yes, he was not mistaken. Those angry shouts were of men riding to their rescue, men he knew would be from Hawksley Manor, and he sighed in his relief and started to run!

He hurried through a scene that would be beautiful were it not so terrible. Trees and bushes glittering white with frost were shining in reflected red glow of the fire and now charred particles were issuing amongst the leaping flames, descending like black snow.

The arsonists stationed between the oak trees lining the drive, had also heard those approaching horse hooves and now turning their mounts scattered across the grounds and towards the fields beyond. Two other men who had watched from a distance also took swift departure, circling the burning building and taking a byway that led in the direction of Hawksley Manor.

Lord James Hawksley gave a furious shout as he saw those fleeing forms. Should he pursue or was his first duty to see if any remained alive in the inferno the gracious old house had become? He continued towards the house, beckoning the others on, the enormous heat scorching his face. As he did so he heard a shout over the roar of the flames—saw Jack Lynden running to intercept him.

'My Lord, all are safe out of the house, save two of the maids who died in the first explosion—place must have been mined! Main stairs collapsed! No time to take the bodies out.'

'Where is everyone then?'

'In the hut housing the cider press! All safe save Ellen. She's dead. They fired on us as we escaped the flames! Some with burns, the cook has a broken arm and badly bruised.'

'Then I leave all in your charge, friend. We'll deal with those fiends, send them to the flames of hell!' And with an oath he signalled to Thomas and his companions, as they tore off in the wake of their escaping prey, their faces grim. Anger lent power to them as they thundered over the frozen fields, the light from the fire making all bright as day, as they drew level with the murdering crew. Thomas gave a great cry as he raised his sword and struck at one of the men who fell dying from his horse.

Hawksley dispatched another with lethal thrust, the others were rounded up, dragged from their horses, reins made into nooses around their necks as they made back towards the manor, their captives gasping as they attempted to keep up, the alternative to die choking for breath.

In Hawksley Manor all was still, as Sophie together with David and Martha kept watch in the front of the house, while Beth Giles was performing this task at the back. Sophie had ordered lanterns lit and placed around the outside of the house so that any intruders would immediately be seen.

'What noise was that?' Sophie looked around apprehensively, for she had heard the sound of breaking glass. But where had it come from? They had seen nothing from the windows, not had there been any sort of warning from the two young stable boys set to keep watch outside.

'It sounded above our heads—the library?' guessed David Markham. That crash wakened little Henry Hawksley. He sat up in bed and let out a plaintive cry, which brought Jenny to his side. She had positioned herself on a chair in the passageway outside the children's nurseries so that she might go to either should they wake. She stooped over the child and spoke soothingly, kissing him and stroking his soft curling hair, until his lashes drooped over his eyes.

Jenny did not hear Minette get up from her bed in the neighbouring chamber and wander out along the passageway towards the library. There it was that Richard lay and Minette decided she wanted to see how he was. She had been deeply distressed by the scene in the church, where the man she loved as a second father, had stumbled in to fall unconscious and bleeding in the aisle. Mama had said he would get better, needed to be kept very quiet. And so it was that she slipped into the library on tiptoe—and froze at what she saw by the only light in the room a small oil lamp.

Two tall men were standing over Richard where he lay on the couch, staring up helplessly. One of them applied match to a baton dipped in tar, and then brandished his flaming torch, while the other pointed a pistol to the wounded man's head. As the child watched horrified she heard them speak.

'Seems my previous bullet did not do its work! Now I will finish the job!' And was about to pull the trigger when the other stopped him, grinning evilly.

'The noise of the shot will alert any in the house to our presence. This we do not want. Let us fire the library, and make our escape! This was my house. Knowing the layout and how well all would burn here was why I took decision we should enter by this room. The ivy cladding the outer walls alongside the window, good as a ladder!'

'Yes. Good thinking, but I still believe we should finish him.' But Lorrimer lowered the pistol regretfully. Harrison snorted.

'Once before I attempted to burn this place down,' he said reflectively. 'Tonight I will not fail! The books will blaze merrily, make a great bonfire to match Oaklands!' Mark Harrison pointed contemptuously down at Richard. 'Why waste a shot when the flames will do our work for us!'

'Come then, let's have the books off the shelves, make a pile!' cried Lorrimer, eyes dancing with glee, and sending the first few fine volumes crashing to the floor, as Harrison waited to fire them.

'Stop it—bad men! My Papa the King will have you in prison for this!' the child's thin young voice suddenly raised made both men pause in astonishment. Minette faced them in her white nightgown, her blue eyes blazing. And they both burst into course laughter.

'Well, what have we here? The witch's offspring! The little wench will have an appropriate end,' spluttered Lorrimer, pointing to the torch Harrison wielded, whilst Richard struggled desperately to raise himself from the couch.

'Begone from this house!' cried Minette hotly, too angry to be afraid. Lorrimer raised his hand to fell the child, when a sudden creaking noise gave him pause. To the amazement of both men, a section of the library shelving slid aside and a dark form appeared. In his hand he held a golden cross, which blazed in the light of Harrison's flaming torch. At the sight both men fell back in terror.

'Desist in the name of God!'

'What devil's work is this,' exclaimed Mark Harrison in fear.

'It is most surely the Devil's work that you are involved in! The power of the Lord stronger than any such,' boomed the voice and as Harrison quailed away he felt the torch struck from his hand, its flame stamped out. Lorrimer recovered himself first, pointed to the shadowy figure holding that cross, its light paler now it no longer reflected the torch's flame

'It's the priest—the one who deprived us of this child before, in the woods! Kill him!' he cried and raising his pistil, fired!

Father Benedict still stood there before him. Staggered it was true, but did not fall and now Lorrimer dropped the gun and turned to run in terror towards the window.

'Let's begone out of this accursed place,' he called to Harrison. It was in that moment that Richard with intense effort managed to get to his feet and bending lifted the pistol, gesturing to Minette to hide

'Stop—or I fire!' He was swaying on his feet but his hazel eyes were steady and Lorrimer read death in those eyes. He hesitated, calculated, what had he to lose, made final dash to the window. As he did so, a shot was fired, not by Richard but by a girl who stood at the door, eyes blazing. Gerald Lorrimer barely registered it was Sophie, as he collapsed and moved no more. Then David Markham sprang towards Harrison, raised his fist and dealt him a sledgehammer blow felling him to the floor, binding his hands behind his back.

Now Minette was in her mother's arms, sobbing in aftershock.

'The child was unbelievably brave,' said Richard, as Martha and Beth Giles helped him back onto the couch. 'She told them to begone, threatened them with the King!'

'Richard—your wound?'

'Painful, but it will take more than this to remove me from this world,' he grimaced. Then he looked around. 'Where is Benedict?' he asked anxiously. 'He saved Minette's life and mine. Came up out of the secret place and brandished his cross. They were terrified at first!'

'The father is here,' said a sorrowful voice. David Markham stooped over the still form of the Catholic priest who had shown such unimaginable bravery—paid for it with his life.'

'But he did not fall when shot,' cried Richard, as David undid the black gown and saw the blood stained shirt. 'Shot in the heart and did not fall!'

'Our Lord sustained him,' said David quietly. 'He stood until his work was done. Let us give thanks for his life and bright courage.' He prayed over the old priest's body and there were tears in all their eyes as he did so. Then he turned his attention back to the bound figure of the man who had jointly planned all their deaths with Lorrimer. Mark Harrison groaned now and opened his eyes, struggled ineffectually against his bonds, which held. Now he glowered up at four people he had thought to dispose of, looking uncertainly at Sophie.

'Why were you not at Oaklands,' he asked? 'We were informed Hawksley's complete family were to gather there for celebration of your popish Christmas!'

'That was cancelled when you shot my husband,' she replied coldly. 'As you see, he did not succumb.'

'It was Lorrimer fired the shot!'

'At your bidding.' It was Richard who spoke. 'He has paid for his crime! You yet to pay for yours. The reckoning will come soon.' He stared towards his wife now and saw that Sophie had started to tremble in delayed shock. She still held Minette to her, small head buried in her mother's gown, her body jerking on occasional sobs. He beckoned them to him and Sophie lifted the child, as he made space for them beside him on the couch.

'Oaklands has gone,' she whispered. 'The fire so huge it lights up the night sky. My father and yours have taken most of our men to give what help they can and deal with those who did such deed. We knew there was a chance they might turn their attentions on this place, so David and Martha, Beth and I armed ourselves in case of attack.' He kissed her wonderingly.

'I did not know you could shoot, my darling!'

'I just pulled the trigger—he was going to kill you, Richard!' She shuddered as she stared at the corpse of the man who would have deprived her of her husband. He had fallen on his back, his hair swept back from his forehead. She pointed to the scar that disfigured his temple. 'Do you remember old Jessie Thorne? She warned me of a man with a scar on his forehead and a forked tongue!' And he nodded, face darkening.

'The old wise woman! I remember her well, of her murder on the instruction of Harrison, how he had you kidnapped!' All came flooding back to him.

'Yes and how his men left you for dead!'

'I was only a lad then. But I would have killed in your defence had I been able,' and he smiled. She kissed him again, remembering all too vividly.

'Later old Jessie's cottage was burned down!' she added.

'Fire seems your favourite weapon, Harrison,' said Richard contemptuously, as the man writhed and struggled in his bonds. 'You may not realise it Sophie, but they were about to light a fire to the library, so that it might set the whole house alight!' She stared back at him in horror.

'But how did they gain access,' demanded David of Richard.

'Climbed up the ivy cladding the walls at the back of the house, broke the window and in!'

'We heard a crash—thought it came up here from the library,' said Martha, joining in at last, her face showing the strain she had been under. 'Oh Sophie, how terrible was this night's work!'

'At least even if Oaklands has gone, this place remains, and of course, Park House,' added David encouragingly, turning a frowning face as Harrison uttered a bitter laugh.

'Rupert Mereton's old house has been torched too!' and he spat, the saliva flecking his chin. 'We sorted that after young Appleby came by. We had watched him preparing a love nest for the witch! Put paid to that!' At this Richard attempted to leap off the couch, restrained by Sophie's arms.

'Do you want that wound to open—bleed to death? Be still, ignore that vermin!' and at the authority in her words, he desisted. He relaxed, sighing in frustration. It was then that they heard sound of horses in the courtyard, men's voices raised as minutes later James Hawksley burst into the library with Thomas Appleby close behind him, others still mounting the stairs.

'How is Richard,' he began as he entered, then stared in consternation to see David Markham bending over the still form of Benedict—then noting the dead face of Gerald Lorrimer and the bound form of Mark Harrison.

'What has happened here, in God's name? Sophie—Are you hurt?''

'No father. I am not. But Father Benedict was murdered trying to save Minette and Richard from these fiends.' She tried to speak further, but found she could not continue and David took up the story, quietly explaining all as the other men now entered and crowded around Richard's couch—and stared down with utmost hatred at Mark Harrison.

'Sophie—you should have shot this one too,' cried Thomas Appleby feelingly. 'Yet why deprive the hangman of a job. Have him in the barn together with the rest of his dastardly crew. Check his bonds hold tight and that of the others.' He glanced around at Hawksley. 'That's if such suits you, my Lord—er James!' James Hawksley nodded grimly, hand caressing the hilt of his sword and looking down at Harrison, who spat up in his direction, face a mask of evil.

'It will serve right well. Tomorrow we will have them in a cart, drive them to the magistrates for charging, and then when a suitable guard is prepared, on to the jail at Canterbury, from whence Lorrimer made his escape.' He paused, adding, 'the jailors there may have disastrously let one prisoner go free, but in exchange will now have a few more!'

He drew in a breath of relief that this man who had caused so much hurt to his family was captured, his fate now irrevocably sealed and watched as his men carried out the dead form of Lorrimer and roughly pulled Harrison to his feet and dragged him away. Then he looked down on the beloved face of the old priest who had risked his own life time and again to bring spiritual comfort to Hawksley and the other catholic families in the area.

'I did not know that Father Benedict was here again,' ventured Sophie, glancing up at her father. He smiled and lifted the old man's body up in his arms and placed him on a chair, gently closing his eyes.

'Richard let him in last night, and we helped him into the secret place. He wanted to give us all a blessing at Christmas. I was going to tell you after church this morning, but then Richard arrived, his wounding sending all else out of mind.' Hawksley's dark eyes were filled with tears as he stooped and now picked up the golden cross that had saved his little grand-daughter's life. 'We will place this in the secret place,' he said.

'Do you wish that I should make arrangements for a quiet burial,' asked David Markham? 'Perhaps it should be done this night, a place I know of in the churchyard.'

'But buried in grounds of a church not his own?' ventured Hawksley.

'A church that just over a hundred years ago would have been Catholic, as would all others in the kingdom!' replied David. 'I enjoyed some interesting conversations with Benedict. We both agreed that we worship the one true God and Christ His Son as our Saviour and prayed together that one day by the power of the Holy Spirit, all men might sink their religious differences in the healing love of that same Triune God.'

'That was well said,' replied James Hawksley wonderingly, 'and may that time come soon!'

'We'll help you with Father Benedict,' said Thomas. 'Best we attend to all now, while the world sleeps.' And at his direction, the priest was reverently lifted and taken away.

Then one by one people filtered out of the library, Martha carrying a tearful Minette, leaving only Richard and Sophie.

'How does your wound, my dearest,' she asked?

'Strangely all pain seems to have gone. While Beth Giles was watching over me, I saw the panel slide open and Benedict appeared behind her back. Unseen by Beth, he raised a hand in blessing, lips murmuring in prayer and then quietly withdrew. It was then that I realised the pain had left me. I still have a great weakness—but no pain!'

She stared at him in almost disbelief and bending over him carefully exposed his wound. It was healing, had the appearance of a wound some week old. And she gave a sudden choking cry.

'This healing could not have been achieved by any normal means!' She stared at him, her blue eyes wide with wonder. 'Richard, I have prayed to God in the past, but have never really been sure of His existence. Now I will never doubt again—never! All praise to His name!' And he cradled her head against him, as their lips met.

'Tomorrow we start a new life together,' he said slowly. 'Sophie, I spent much time over at Park House trying to turn it into a gracious home for you—our own home, my darling. But it wasn't to be. If I'd any sense I would have realised that Park House was accursed. No matter how fine I made it, the very stones held evil.'

'Well now it's gone, as has Oaklands! But Richard I know what we will do. My very own property left to me by my grandfather. I mean The Willows, where we first met, this shall be our home—a place of happiness!'

Chapter Nineteen

April's breath was stirring the pink tipped buds on apple trees gently swaying in the late John Wheatley's garden, and tiny fish broke surface in the small pond overhung with graceful willow, and here on her favourite bench sat Sophie this bright sunny morning, her husband's arm about her waist. And Richard looked down fondly at the tiny boy child she nursed, conceived of another, but most surely his son. Little Benedict Appleby had been born three weeks ago, his birth easier than that of Sophie's first child.

It had been Richard's idea to name the baby after the brave priest who had given his life to protect this baby's sister, Minette. Though neither of the couple were of his Catholic faith, they both knew how much they owed to the dear old man who had shown such amazing courage in his care of those members of his flock whom he secretly visited—and who had unflinchingly suffered death to protect Minette and Richard.

'He has your blue eyes, my darling,' said Richard. 'With that dark hair of his and determined small chin, he is going to be a fine looking man in the fullness of time.' And his finger explored the dark curls which Sophie had said were inherited from her father—but both knew were in fact inheritance from his royal progenitor.

Scant six weeks ago they had left Hawksley Manor to move into The Willows, Sophie deciding that she wanted her child to be born in that well remembered bedroom she had once occupied in her grandfather's house. And so it had been. Now Richard shared that room overlooking the garden, their babe sleeping in a cradle at their side. Minette was in the doctor's old room, Jenny sleeping in Martha's former bedroom, and a fourth bedroom would be used by baby Benedict in a few months time, Beth Giles continuing in her accommodation downstairs.

Back in December during days following the trauma of that night of fire, there had been much discussion as to what should be done with the shell of Oaklands, and also of Park House, though none were too concerned over the latter. Oaklands was Minette's inheritance under her mother's guardianship until she reached maturity. What best to do with the blackened ruin it had become?

It was Hawksley who made the suggestion. The place should be raised to the ground, a new house built, not on the same scale for it would be too costly, but a fine residence for Minette to use in years to come. The work would give employment to those men who had lost their living when Oaklands burned. As for Park House, Richard decided not to rebuild but to sell the land now officially his, and with the money raised, buy a few acres adjoining the manor, next to those already on lease to him by his father-in-law. Former bailiff Jack Lynden would work for Hawksley as assistant to Thomas Appleby, while the remaining displaced servants found positions elsewhere.

Now in the security of The Willows, Richard and Sophie resolved to bring up their family in peace, and hopefully in the future, there would be other babes born this time with Richard's frank hazel eyes, so forming even closer bond between them.

Those who had sought to bring death to Lord James Hawksley and his family had paid the ultimate price for their villainy, and their remains left hanging in chains as salutary lesson to any others who should seek to copy their crimes. It was said that Mark Harrison had died with a curse on his lips before the rope silenced him forever, with Rupert Mereton screaming in terror before ever his noose tightened.

It was one rather damp day in June that a small carriage drew up outside The Willows and a woman in the sombre black of mourning stepped out and walked slowly up the path to the house and knocked hesitantly on the door. Beth Giles opened it to her and glanced at the stranger inquiringly.

'I believe this is the residence of Lady Mereton,' began the visitor diffidently. The housekeeper looked at her shrewdly.

'Lady Mereton as was—now Lady Sophie Appleby! And who might you be, lady?' Beth sensed something strange about the woman.

'That I prefer to make known to your mistress myself,' was the quiet and dignified answer, and slightly baffled Beth Giles beckoned her into the small parlour and went in search of Sophie, whom she found in her late grandfather's study, head bent over a handwritten treatise on fever. Sophie listened in surprise and immediately made her way to the parlour, where the woman in black sat head bowed, before the window. On seeing Sophie she rose and inclined her head.

'I believe you wish to see me? Have we met before,' explored Sophie, for the woman's face was veiled in fine black lace, draped from her high crowned hat.

'No. We have not met before. When you learn my name you may not wish to speak with me, but I do crave your patience. I need to express my sorrow over all that befell you at my son's hands. My name is Myra Lorrimer, sister to Mark Harrison and mother of Gerald Lorrimer.'

On hearing those accursed names Sophie's face went white with shock, but she rallied and stared speechlessly at the woman who now lifted her veil, revealing a once beautiful face, now gaunt and lined from years of stress.

'Pray sit down. You seem tired. Perhaps a glass of wine,' proffered Sophie, taking a deep breath and walking to the old oak cabinet in the corner of the room, she poured a glass of Madeira for her visitor.

The woman sipped it gratefully. It gave them both a moment's respite to assess each other.

'Just tell me,' said Sophie at last. 'What is it that brought you here, Mistress Lorrimer?'

The woman spread her hands and sighed. Where in fact should she start? At last she broke the silence and began.

'I was Mark Harrison's sister. As a child I was always fearful of my brother, who had a cruel streak, which in our early years showed itself in the way he would lash his pony and kick my pet dog and once I caught him viciously beating a young stable lad. He treated me with scorn. Our mother had died when I was five years old. After her death our father began to drink heavily and became a gambler, was heavy handed in his treatment of me!' Sophie noted the flinching in the woman's eyes as she spoke.

'I also received cruel treatment from my foster father when I was a girl. I feel for you,' she said quietly. Now please—go on.'

'When on my sixteenth birthday I received an offer of marriage from Steven Lorrimer, I accepted as way of removing myself from the family home, and went to live on my husband's estate near Falmouth. The civil war was now raging, my brother Mark a close friend of Cromwell, who gifted Hawksley Manor to him. My husband Steven, a quiet man, did not involve himself in the fighting. We had one child, a son—Gerald!' She sighed as she saw the look of horror on Sophie's face as she pronounced the name.

'Gerald was completely unlike his father. He seemed possessed of a similar cruel streak to that of his uncle Mark. I tried so hard to guide him in decent behaviour, but he went his own way. When the King regained the throne of his fathers, Mark lost the manor to its rightful owner, your father Lord James Hawksley.'

'The King restored the manor to my father in gratitude for his loyalty in both the war and during Charles long exile. But please continue.'

'I knew nothing of the circumstances that brought all this about, only that my brother arrived at Falmouth one night of storm, and demanded that we shelter him. He said that he was wanted by the authorities and that it could either mean a long prison sentence for him, or even a hanging matter. We foolishly took him in. A few days later, my husband Steven was found dead supposedly of a heart attack. But his eyes betrayed a terror—of what we never found out. Now Mark began to take over the running of our estate, with Gerald hanging on his every word, drinking in his evil. Then to my relief, my son Gerald disappeared and months later Mark did so also.'

She paused now and tears were gathering in her eyes.

'A girl who had been employed as parlour maid at your estate of Oaklands, came to me for employment. It was from her lips that I learned of my son's death, of his despicable treatment of you, that Oaklands had been burned at his instigation and that of my brother. Of how between them they had tried to murder your entire family. Instead of sorrow, there was deep relief that I would never have to see either of them again. I'm sorry if that sounds terrible—but it's true!'' Her tears were falling now and Sophie handed her a lace kerchief.

'It must have taken great courage to have sought me out. Your name is Myra, is it not? Perhaps our having met this way may bring closure to all we have both endured at the hands of cruel men.' She paused reflectively. 'If it will help, I will explain more of these matters, fill in the missing pieces, tell for instance about a man called Rupert Mereton who was friend to both of them and as cruel.' and as she did so, felt relief in the knowledge that this man also had been hanged, would wreak no more evil.

They sat together for over an hour. Beth, full of curiosity, brought refreshments, but was unable to fathom out who the mystery visitor was. Nor could the driver of the rented carriage enlighten her when she brought him a glass of ale. It was all a mystery.

Before Myra Lorrimer left the house, Sophie showed her into the nursery, where baby Benedict lay cooing in his cradle, then led her to the garden where the rain having stopped, Minette was playing with a new spaniel puppy, bursting into peals of laughter as the little animal chased her around the pond, while Jenny kept a close eye on proceedings.

'Sophie, if I may call you by name, you have turned a continuous nightmare into a wondrous memory of forgiveness and love,' said Myra as she took her leave. She reached out a hand, half expecting it to be refused. Instead, Sophie took her into her arms.

'Thank you for coming, Myra. My good wishes go with you for the future.' She watched as the black clad figure returned to the battered old carriage, which trundled away along the street. What an extraordinary meeting, she thought.

Later that night, when Richard returned from a day's work on the land, she told him of her visitor.

'So you actually spoke with her?'

'Why not, Richard? She was not involved in any wrong doing. Was herself abused first by her father and brother—and then by her own son!' She shook her head. I will always feel nothing but sympathy for Myra

Lorrimer,' she stated quietly. He looked at her, realising what a very special woman he had married, and fondly embraced her.

A year later the grounds belonging to Park House had been sold and now Richard purchased land adjoining that of Hawksley Manor and walked with noticeable spring to his step. As for little Benedict, he was starting to toddle about to the delight of Minette. He was a sturdy child, with a happy temperament and an engaging chuckle. But sometimes, Sophie had glimpsed a slight sadness in his gaze and it reminded her of a certain expression she had on occasion surprised on his royal father's face.

Charles—she hardly thought of him these days, thought Sophie, as she wandered through Epilson woods, gathering healing herbs in a basket. A new physician had moved into the village, a man named Denzil Romney and it transpired that when a student he had studied medicine with her grandfather years ago. When he learned of her interest, indeed deep knowledge of the healing properties of plants, he had called on her and they had now become good friends, who had decided they would help each other where they could for the common weal.

It was so good to be treated with respect for her knowledge by this man, not to be discriminated against on account of her sex. But Sophie secretly acknowledged that there was no likelihood of a change in these matters during her lifetime, perhaps not for a few centuries ahead. So she was compiling her own carefully written notes, detailing properties of those plants she used, together with safe dosages of the same. One day these could be passed on to others.

One fine autumn's day, her father arrived at The Willows.

'Sophie, a letter from the King! We are invited to Whitehall. He wishes all three of us to come—and to bring the children!'

'What can he want?' Sophie experienced conflicting emotions, excitement at the prospect of once again meeting the man she had adored for so many years, until all such feelings were surpassed by her love for Richard Appleby. This mixed with a reluctance to reencounter the artificiality of the court. Then with normal feminine instinct, her thoughts turned to what she would wear!

Richard was less than enthusiastic at the news and Sophie wondered whether he held an inherent dislike of the King for all that had passed between the monarch and Sophie in previous years.

'No doubt he wishes to see our son.' he said quietly.

'He delights in all children' replied Sophie lightly. 'I believe their innocence distracts him from the cares of ruling a country beset with the difficulties of bringing understanding to a previously divided people. It cannot be an easy task' Her blue eyes were sad and Richard bent and kissed her, his initial dismay at the summons fading as his lips experienced the response in hers. He had no slightest doubt that Sophie wholeheartedly returned his love, wanted no outside influence to disturb their happiness.

'When do we plan to leave then,' he asked? And Sophie smiled and knew all was well.

It was hard to believe she was back in the capital that was only now beginning to recover from the ravages of the plague which had decimated its population, followed by the exodus occasioned by the Great Fire, that two whole years had sped by since that nightmare of flames.

The journey had been uneventful, people they spoke to at the coaching inns along the way, decrying the Dutch and expressing dissatisfaction with the government. The jubilation of the first few years of the restoration seemed to have evaporated. They also heard rumours that since the Queen appeared barren, the King's foremost bastard, James Duke of Richmond might be legitimised.

The children had been restless on the journey along those rutted roads and Sophie drew a sigh of relief when after two days of travelling, they arrived back at her small rented house on the Thames. News of their arrival had reached the King and but no invitation was issued to them and Sophie began to wonder why this should be. Then a week later, on a day when Richard and James Hawksley had gone to savour the delights of a coffee house and when Sophie was playing with the three children, Jenny came rushing into the parlour, her face flushed and excited.

'Oh, my Lady—He's here!'Nor did she need to state the name of the visitor. The tall, elegant figure filled the doorway, his dark eyes smiling as they lighted on Sophie with the three children at her knee. There was a moment's silence as the children stared at him. Then Minette gave a joyous squeal and rushed into his arms1

'My Papa—my Papa!' she cried and it was as though she had seen him but yesterday. He swung her up in his arms, delighting in her kisses.

'Hast grown, little one,' he said admiringly. 'I can see that you will soon be one of the most beautiful ladies of my court!'

'Well, I am seven,' she replied. 'I am learning Latin and Greek—and French. And I am studying medicine!' He listened amazed as she chattered on, as his eyes sped to the toddler holding Sophie's hand and looking up at him with solemn curious eyes.

'And who is this,' he asked Sophie, as she rose from a curtsey, wishing she were wearing her best gown, nor realising that she had never looked lovelier than now, surrounded by the three children.

'His name is Benedict,' she replied. He nodded and stooping took the child up into his arms and his dark eyes showed his emotion in holding his son. Had only this child been born to Catherine! He handed him back to Sophie almost reluctantly and sighed.

'Your father sent me word of what had happened last year, mentioned a brave man of God who had died to protect Minette. Our son is named for him?'

'Richard and I decided so in tribute to a very gallant gentleman,' she replied quietly. 'As you will have heard, Benedict was a Catholic priest, a wonderful Christian and possessed of a remarkable courage.'

He nodded soberly and turned to Henry, who was pulling at his coat and looking up inquiringly as he remembered this fine gentleman.

'Now you must be young Henry Hawksley,' he mused and embraced the little boy. 'James must be proud of his son!' he said to Sophie. 'Where are your father and Richard, sweetheart?

'At a coffee house. They will be mortified not to have been here,' she replied.

'It is no matter. I did in fact wish a few words in private with you, Sophie. Perhaps Jenny could take these young rascals to their nursery for a while?' He seated himself on the couch beckoning to Sophie to join him and she sensed he had no idea of amour on his mind.

As they sat sipping a fine French wine together, Charles unburdened himself to one whom he knew he could implicitly trust. First though he demanded the whole story of the events surrounding the burning down of Oaklands and Park House, of Richard's wounding and of the intended arson at Hawksley Manor. And as the full horror fell from her lips, he took her hand in his and stared at her speechlessly.

'So it was you who shot the villain Lorrimer? Sophie—I wish I might have seen this!' He looked down at that purposeful little hand in almost disbelief. This was yet another facet of her character he had uncovered.

'He was about to shoot Richard?' she replied logically. He stared at her then burst into a gale of laughter.

'Well Sophie, you merely deprived the hangman of a job!'

'It was all a nightmare—horrible,' she said. 'For weeks I found sleep difficult, would dream of cruel faces fleering around me.'

'By contrast my problems seem to be of a lesser mould,' he said slowly. 'Tell me?'

'Well, those of my courtiers who dislike my brother James, have been suggesting that I divorce my wife Catherine as being barren and take another wife. James favours the Catholic faith. They wish me to provide a Protestant successor.' The long bitter lines on either side of his mouth seemed to deepen as he spoke.

'I heard that Chancellor Hyde—Lord Clarendon, your brother's father-in-law was dismissed the court in disgrace?' And as she gently probed, Charles looked away irritably.

'He was getting old, could not get on with other of my immediate circle, Arlington and Buckingham—always playing the schoolmaster to me. He has gone to live in France!' His voice warned not to pursue the matter.

'And what of Catherine, then,' she dared. 'I heard rumours from travellers along the road, that your son by Lucy Walters might be legitimised and so succeed you?'

'Senseless rumours then! I love the boy, but the Stuart succession has to be correctly ensured.' He shook his head. 'Your children, Barbara's and those of others show that the fault is not mine. But Catherine is my wife and we have a deep affection for each other. I could never hurt her through divorce.' And so they spoke for an hour or more, each unburdening themselves to the other in the confidence of an unusual friendship. At last he rose to his feet.

'Sophie, I meant to return this to you when last we met, have treasured it as reminder of my beloved young physician and confidante, who has mothered two fine children by me—and remains my trusted friend!' And he withdrew the golden pomander from his pocket. 'When you wear it now, may it remind you of one who will always feel love and respect for you!' and he took her into his arms, but it was the comfortable embrace of friendship. He turned towards the door.

'I will send invitation for James and Richard to wait upon me,' he said and was gone-and the room seemed suddenly terribly empty.

Richard told her of their own meeting with the King, of how he had questioned them both about Father Benedict.

'He seemed unusually interested in the priest, he said slowly. 'He said to your father, that he personally deplores the antagonism of his subjects towards their Catholic neighbours, but is unable to pass any laws to remedy the situation. He even seemed to indicate his own deep respect for the Catholic faith and afterwards had private conversation with your father which James has not shared with me.'

'He loves the children—has sent present to all three of them,' cried Sophie as they looked towards the youngsters at their play.

'He has gifted additional land to us to be handed on to our son Benedict!' He stared curiously at Sophie. 'He also spoke very warmly of you. I know now that whatever happened in the past between you has no bearing on our love—our marriage, Sophie!'

'He returned this to me—my golden pomander,' she said softly.
That night as they made love in that small bedroom, its window closed against the noisome Thames, she murmured something into Richard's ear that drew from him exclamation of sheerest delight!

'Are you sure, Sophie?'

'Quite sure! But it is early days. You will have to wait until March of next year before you hold our new son or daughter in your arms!' And Richard rained kisses on her face, his joy complete. Tomorrow they would all start on the long road back to the countryside and whatever the future might hold. Before they left, Sophie gave up the rental of that small house on the Thames. She had no wish to return to London. But in the years ahead, she would sometimes smile and absently fondle the golden pomander at her waist.

It is recorded that just before Charles 2nd died in 1685, after enduring much pain at the enthusiastic but ignorant hands of his doctors, a Father Huddleston was brought privately to his bedchamber, where the King stated he wished to die a Catholic, made confession and joyfully received the sacrament. He was succeeded by his brother James, who lost the crown after five short years. In 1745 a handsome young descendant of the exiled family of Stuart made vain attempt to regain the throne of his fathers. He was known as Bonnie Prince Charlie—but might have become Charles 3rd.

Made in the USA
Charleston, SC
11 December 2013